THE WORKS OF LIANG YUCHUN

梁遇春 著译全集

3
第三卷

李力夫 商昌宝 主编

海峡出版发行集团 | 福建教育出版社

本 卷 总 目

Some Best English Essays
小品文选 ··· 1
Some Best English Essays
小品文续选 ··· 323

Some Best English Essays

小 品 文 选

(英汉对照)

梁遇春 译注

"自修英文丛刊"之一,上海北新书局,1930年2月付排,1930年4月初版

CONTENTS
目　次

序 ··· 7

Richard Steele
On Conjugal Happiness
伉俪幸福 ··· 12

Joseph Addison
On Practical Jokes
恶作剧 ··· 28

Samuel Johnson
On Sorrow
悲哀 ·· 42

Oliver Goldsmith
Happiness in a Great Measure Dependent on Constitution
快乐多半是靠着性质 ······································ 58

Charles Lamb
A Bachelor's Complaint of the Behaviour of Married People

一个单身汉对于结了婚的人们的行为的怨言 ············· 72

William Hazlitt
On the Fear of Death

死的恐惧 ··· 100

Leigh Hunt
In Prison

在监狱中 ··· 142

John Brown
Her Last Half-Crown

她最后的一块银币 ································· 150

A. G. Gardiner
A Fellow Traveller

一个旅伴 ··· 160

John Galsworthy
Evolution

进化 ·· 172

E. V. Lucus
London Mysterious

神秘的伦敦 ······································· 188

Hilaire Belloc
On a Hermit Whom I Knew

我所知道的一位隐士 ······························· 194

G. K. Chesterton
On Running After One's Hat

追赶自己的帽子 ················· 214

George W. E. Russell
The Scholar

学者 ······················· 228

John Middleton Murry
Fact and Fiction

事实与小说 ··················· 246

Roger Wray
Autumn

秋 ························ 258

Robert Lynd
Trains

火车 ······················· 268

E. Temple Thurston
Ship's Logs

船木 ······················· 286

A. A. Milne
The Chase

追蝴蝶 ····················· 296

Holbrook Jackson
The Spirit of the Dance

跳舞的精神 ··················· 306

序

自从有小品文以来,就有许多小品文的定义,当然没有一个是完完全全对的,所以我也不去把几十部破书翻来翻去,一条一条抄下。大概说起来,小品文是用轻松的文笔,随随便便地来谈人生,因为好像只是茶余酒后,炉旁床侧的随便谈话,并没有俨然地排出冠冕堂皇的神气,所以这些漫话絮语很能够分明地将作者的性格烘托出来,小品文的妙处也全在于我们能够从一个具有美妙的性格的作者眼睛里去看一看人生。许多批评家拿抒情诗同小品文相比,这的确是一对很可喜的孪生兄弟,不过小品文是更洒脱,更胡闹些罢!小品文家信手拈来,信笔写去,好似是漫不经心的,可是他们自己奇特的性格会把这些零碎的话儿镕成一气,使他们所写的篇篇小品文都仿佛是在那里对着我们拈花微笑。

小品文同定期出版物几乎可说是相依为命的。虽然小品文的开山老祖 Montaigne 是一个人住在圆塔里静静地写出无数对于人生微妙的观察，去消遣他的宦海余生，积成了一厚册才拿来发表，但是小品文的发达是同定期出版物的盛行做正比例的。这自然是因为定期出版物篇幅有限，最宜于刊登短隽的小品文字，而小品文的冲淡闲逸也最合于定期出版物读者的口味，因为他们多半是看倦了长而无味的正经书，才来拿定期出版物松散一下。所以在这集里，我忽略了奸巧利诈的 Bacon，恬静自安的遗老 Izaak Walton，古怪的 Sir Thomas Browne 同老实的 Abraham Cowley，虽然他们都是小品文的开国元勋，却从 Steele 起手，因为大家都承认 Steele 的 *Tatler* 是英国最先的定期出版物。中国近代的文坛岂不也是这样吗？有了《晨报副刊》，有了《语丝》，才有周作人先生的小品文字，鲁迅先生的杂感。我只希望中国将来的小品文也能有他们那么美妙，在世界小品文里面能够有一种带着中国情调的小品文，这也许是我这样不顾鲁拙，谮译这部小品文的一些动机罢！

　　现在要把这二十位作家约略地说几句。在这二十位里，四位是属于十八世纪的，四位是属于十九世纪的，其它那十二位作家现在都还健在。Steele 豪爽英迈，天生一片侠心肠，所以他的作品是一往情深，恳挚无比的。他不会什么修辞巧技，只任他的热情自然流露在字里行间，他的性格表现得万分清楚，他的文章所以是那么可爱也全因为他自己是个可喜的浪子。他的朋友 Addison 却跟他很不同了。Addison 温文尔雅，他自己说他生平没有接连着说三句话过，他的沉默，可想而知，他的小品文也是默默地将人生拿来仔细解剖，轻轻地把所得的结果放在读者面前。约翰生不是小品文名家，但是他有几篇小品文充满了智慧同怜悯，《悲哀》这篇就是一个好例子。Goldsmith 和 Steele 很相似，不过是更糊涂一点。他的《世界公民》(*The Citizen of the World*) 是一部我百读不厌的书。他的小品文不单是洋溢着真情同仁爱，并且是珠圆玉润的文章。Washington Irving 就是个私淑他的文人，还只学到他的一些好处，就已经是那么令人见爱了。以上四位都是属于十八世纪的，十九世纪的小品文多半是比十八世纪的要长得多，每篇常常占十几二十页。Charles Lamb 是这时代里的最出色的小品文家，有人说他是英国最大的小品文家，不佞也是这样想。他的 *Essays of Elia* 是诙谐百出的作品，没有一个人读着不会发笑，不止是发笑，同时又会觉得他忽然从个崭新的立脚点去看人生，深深地感到人生的乐趣。William Hazlitt 是个最深刻不过的作家，但是他又能那么平易地说出来，难怪后来的作家像 Henley, Stevenson 对他总是望洋兴叹，以为不可复得。他写有好几本小品文集 (*Sketches and Essays*; *Table-Talk*; *Plain Speakers*; *Winterslow*; etc.) 同许多批评文字 (*Spirit of the Age*; *Lectures on the English Poets*; *Lectures on English Comic Authors*; *Characters of Shakespeare's Plays*; etc.)，他又是英国文学史坐头把椅的批评家。Leigh Hunt 是整天笑哈哈的快乐人儿，确然他一生里有许多不幸的事情，他的人生态度在他这篇《在监狱里》很可看出。他的下牢是因为他在报纸上攻击当时皇太子。他著有一部很有趣的"自传"。

John Brown 是个苏格兰医生,有一回霍乱盛行,别的医生早已逃之夭夭了,他却舍不得病人,始终是在病城中服务。他是个心肠最好的人,最会说牵情的话,他的杰作是一部散文集 *Horae Subsecivae*。他自己喜欢狗,谈起狗来娓娓不倦,他那篇 *Rab and His Friends* 是谈狗的无上佳文,可惜太长了,不能收在这本集里。近代的小品文又趋向于短篇了,大概每篇总过不了十页。含蓄可说是近代小品文的共同色彩,甚么话都只说一半出来,其余的意味让读者自己去体会。Chesterton 的风格是刁钻古怪,最爱翻斤斗,说似非而是的话的,无精打采〔采〕的人们念念他很可以振作精神。Belloc 是以清新为主,他最善于描写穷乡僻处的风景,他同 Chesterton 一样都是大胖子,万想不到这么臃肿的人会写出那么清瘦的作品。Lucus 是研究 Charles Lamb 的专家,他自己的文笔也是学 Charles Lamb 的,不过却看不出模仿的痕迹。Lynd 的小品文是非常结实的,里面的思想一个一个紧紧地衔接着,却又是那么不费力气样子,难怪有人将他同 Hazlitt 相比。Gardiner 的文字伶俐生姿,他在欧战时候写有许多小品文,来排遣心中的烦闷,《一个旅伴》也是在那时候写的。以上五位差不多是专写小品文的,自然也有其它的作品。此外 Galsworthy 是英国当代五大小说家之一,有时也写些小品文,出版有二三部小品文集子(*The Inn of Tranquillity*;*Castles in Spain*),他的笔轻松得好像是不着纸面的,含蓄是他的最大特色。Murry 是英国文坛宿将,一个有数的批评家,他极赞美俄国近代文学,对于 Dostoyevsky 尤为倾心。他的名著 *The Problem* *of Style*是一部极难读而极有价值的书。这篇《事实与小说》是从他的小品集 *Pencilings* 里选出来的。其它几位比较不重要些，下次再谈罢！

去年此日，正将去年春天所译的十篇英国小品文注好，交开明书店的老板去，当时满想写一篇三万字的序文，详论小品文的性质同各代作家，人事草草，结果是只写出一千多字的短序文。今年开始译这部小品文集时候，又动了这个念头，还想了不少意思，打了许多腹稿，然而结果又仅仅是这么几句零碎的话。对着自己实在有点难为情，真是"人生何事说心期"！

十八年八月十三日于福州

封面画是 W. S. Gilbert 的滑稽诗选里的插画，我觉得那种嘻嘻哈哈的跳舞好像小品文家的行文，并且那首诗是以人生之谜为题材的，同小品文的内容又刚相合，所以把它剪下，印在封面上。

Richard Steele

On Conjugal Happiness

My brother[1] Tranquillus being gone out of town for some days, my sister Jenny sent me word she would come and dine with me, and therefore desired me to have no other company. I took care accordingly, and was not a little pleased to see her enter the room with a decent and matron-like behaviour, which I thought very much became her. I saw she had a great deal to say to me, and easily discovered in her eyes, and the air of her countenance, that she had abundance of satisfaction in her heart, which she longed to communicate. However, I was resolved to let her break into her discourse her own way, and reduced her to a thousand little devices and intimations to

---

1 妹丈本来是叫做 brother-in-law，但是讲得亲密点或者简单点的时候，也就叫做 brother 了。

伉俪幸福

我的妹夫脱兰启拉斯离开了伦敦，要好几天才能回来，我的妹妹真妮遣人传话，说她想来望我，和我同餐，所以最好是没有别人在座。我就照着她的话办去，看她端庄地，俨然一家的主妇样子走进房来，我心里的确非常喜欢，我想这种态度于她是很合宜的。我一看就晓得她有好多话要对我说，从她的眼睛同脸上的神情，我很容易猜出她心中是十分满意，正欲说给我听。但是，我已经下了决心，要让她自己讲出那一套话，因此她不得不用千般小计同暗示，希冀我会向她提起她的丈夫。

bring me to the mention of her husband. But, finding I was resolved not to name him, she began of her own accord¹. "My husband," said she, "gives his humble service to you," to which I only answered, "I hope he is well;" and, without waiting for a reply, fell into² other subjects. She at last was out of all patience³, and said, with a smile and manner that I thought had more beauty and spirit⁴ than I had ever observed before in her, "I did not think, brother, you had been so ill-natured. You have seen, ever since I came in, that I had a mind to⁵ talk of my husband, and you will not be so kind as to give me an occasion." — "I did not know," said I, "but it might be a disagreeable subject to you. You do not take me for so old-fashioned a fellow as to think of entertaining a young lady with the discourse of her husband. I know nothing is more acceptable than to speak of one who is to be so, but to speak of one who is so! Indeed, Jenny, I am a better bred man than you think me." She showed a little dislike at my raillery; and, by her bridling up⁶, I perceived she expected to be treated hereafter not as Jenny Distaff, but Mrs.

---

1 of one's own accord: voluntarily 自愿，甘心。
2 to fall into: to begin the discussion of 开始谈话，开始讨论。
3 out of all patience: thoroughly dissatisfied 不能容忍。
4 spirit: energy or ardor 豪爽，热情。
5 to have a mind to: to be inclined or disposed to 意欲，愿，拟。

一看到我是决意不说到他的名字，她只好自己先说出来。"我丈夫，"她说，"问您的好。"我仅淡淡地答道，"我希望他也很好；"不等她的回话，立刻又谈到别的题目上去了。最后她真生气了，微笑着，含嗔带恼样子，我从来没有看见她有这样可喜的风姿同豪爽的气概，她对我说："我真没有想到，哥哥，你的性情是这么乖僻。我一进了门，你就知道我是一心一意打算来同你谈论我的丈夫，你却偏不肯给我一个机会，这也未免太狠心了。""我不知道，"我说，"也许你讨厌这个题目。你总不至于以为我是一个陈腐古板的老头子，款待一位年青姑娘时候，会用她的丈夫来做谈话题目。我晓得她所最喜欢听的是谈论她的未婚夫，但他变成了她的丈夫我们去谈论呵，[就要讨没趣了！]真的！真妮，我并不像你所想的那样子不懂礼节。"听着我这几句调侃，她稍稍有些不悦神气；从她这种昂头自许，愤愤不平里，我看出她期望人们此后不再看她是真妮·的斯塔夫

---

6 to bridle up: to express resentment by holding up the head and drawing in the chin 昂首缩头以表示愤恨。

Tranquillus. I was very well pleased with this change in her humour¹; and, upon talking with her on several subjects, I could not but² fancy that I saw a great deal³ of her husband's way and manner in her remarks, her phrases, the tone of her voice, and the very⁴ air of her countenance. This gave me an unspeakable satisfaction, not only because I had found her a husband from whom she could learn many things that were laudable, but also because I looked upon her imitation of him as an infallible sign that she entirely loved him. This is an observation that I never knew fail, though I do not remember that any other has made it. The natural shyness of her sex hindered her from telling me the greatness of her own passion; but I easily collected it from the representation she gave me of his. "I have every thing," says she, "in Tranquillus, that I can wish for; and enjoy in him, what indeed you have told me were to be met with in a good husband, the fondness of a lover, the tenderness of a parent, and the intimacy of a friend." It transported⁵ me to see her eyes swimming in tears of affection⁶ when she spoke. "And is there not, dear sister," said I, "more pleasure in the possession of such a man, than in all

---

1 humour: mood or state of mind 心境，癖〔脾〕气。
2 can not but: can not avoid or must 不得不，不禁。
3 a great deal: a large amount 大部分。
4 very: mere 就是。
5 to transport: to fill with ecstasy 狂喜。

姑娘，却是以脱兰启拉斯太太之礼待她。她这种新心境我也很喜欢；跟她闲谈几件事情，我免不了觉得她丈夫的癖〔脾〕性同态度很显明地现在她的论断里，她的辞句里，她的声调里，甚至于她脸上的表情里。这使我感到不可言喻的快乐，不单是因为我替她所找的丈夫能够教她这许多值得赞美的举动，并且因为她这样模仿他我认为是她整个心儿爱他的最好表征。这种推测我未曾看见有不应验过，虽然我记不起有谁说过这个意思。女性天生的害羞使她不便向我明说她自己的爱情是多么热烈；但是当她描摹他的性格给我听时候，我很容易窥出她的真情。"我所能希望的好处，"她说，"脱兰启拉斯真是完全具有；你先前告诉我一个良好的丈夫会给他的妻子以爱人的惓恋，父母的慈爱同朋友的亲密，这些快乐我全能够由他那里得到。"我不禁狂欢，看她说的时候双眼满溢着挚爱的泪。"好妹妹，"我说，"得到这样一个人是不是比在跳舞会里，集会里，穿着妖娆的衣

---

6 swimming in tears of affection: being flooded with tears of affection 泛滥着挚爱之泪。

the little impertinencies of balls, assemblies, and equipage, which it cost me so much pains to make you contemn?" She answered smiling, "Tranquillus has made me a sincere convert in a few weeks, though I am afraid you could not have done it in your whole life. To tell you truly, I have only one fear hanging upon[1] me, which is apt to give me trouble in the midst of all my satisfactions: I am afraid, you must know, that I shall not always make the same amiable appearance in his eye that I do[2] at present. You know, brother Bickerstaff, that you have the reputation of a conjurer; and, if you have any one secret in your art to make your sister always beautiful, I should be happier than if I were mistress of all the worlds you have shown me in a starry night. — " "Jenny," said I, "without having recourse to[3] magic, I shall give you one plain rule, that will not fail of making you always amiable to a man who has so great a passion for you, and is of so equal and reasonable a temper as Tranquilius. Endeavour to please, and you must please; be always in the same disposition as you are when you ask for this secret, and you may take my words[4], you will never want it. An inviolable fidelity, good humour, and complacency of temper, out-live all the charms of a fine face,

---

1 to hang upon: to hover around 环绕，徘徊。
2 do 下省去一 make 字。
3 to have recourse to: to resort to 依赖。
4 to take one's words: to believe one 相信，信之。

服做出小小的胡闹快乐得多？我从前却费了天大的劲才劝服你看轻那些东西。"她微笑地答道，"脱兰启拉斯在几个星期里说得我痛悔前非，变成另外一个人，虽然我恐怕你就是劝了一生，也做不到这样地步。老实地告诉你，我现在只有一个恐惧徘徊在我心里，常常当我在万分满意之中，使我顿然感到烦恼：你一定知道，我怕的是在他眼里我不能够永久保存像目前这么可喜的模样。你知道，毕克司达夫哥哥，你有魔术家之名；若使你能够传给你妹妹一种驻颜的秘术，我的快乐真是胜过于我做了大千世界的主人，就是你在星夜里指给我看的——""真妮，"我说，"用不着向魔术求助，我要教你一个简单的法则，绝对能够担保你在像脱兰启拉斯那样钟爱你的性情又温和又合理的男人眼里始终是一个可喜的人儿。努力于取得他的欢心，你就一定会得到他的欢心；永久保存着你现在求这种秘术时候的心情，我敢包你绝对不会有需要这种秘术的机会。一种不可侵犯的贞节，欣欢的心境同温和的性情在标致庞儿的各种娇媚引力失去之后，仍然能够继续存在，并且会使她的爱人看不出她容颜的

and make the decays of it invisible."

We discoursed very long upon this head, which was equally agreeable to us both; for, I must confess, as I tenderly love her, I take as much pleasure in giving her instructions for her welfare, as she herself does in receiving them. I proceeded, therefore, to inculcate these sentiments, by relating a very particular[1] passage that happened within my own knowledge.

There were several of us making merry[2] at a friend's house in a country village, when the sexton of the parish church entered the room in a sort of[3] surprise, and told us, that as he was digging a grave in the chancel, a little blow of his pick-axe opened a decayed coffin, in which there were several written papers. Our curiosity was immediately raised, so that we went to the place where the sexton had been at work, and found a great concourse of people about the grave. Among the rest, there was an old woman, who told us, the person buried there was a lady whose name I do not think fit to mention, though there is nothing in the story but what tends very much to her honour. This lady lived several years an exemplary pattern of conjugal love, and, dying soon after her husband, who every way[4]

---

1 particular: peculiar 希奇，奇怪。
2 to make merry: to feast 宴饮。
3 in a sort of: more or less completely 几分，似乎。
4 every way: completely 完全。

渐渐衰老。"

关于这点我们谈了好久，我俩同样地喜欢讨论这个问题；我要承认，因为我很深切地爱她，所以当我为着她的好，去教导她的时候，我觉得非常快乐，她自己接受这些教训时也是同样地快乐。因此我就将这类意思恳切地开导给她听，告诉她我自己偶然晓得的一段奇怪事情的经过。

有一回，我们几个人正在乡村的一位朋友家里宴饮，教区里礼拜堂的下级职员稍有些惊愕神气走进房来，告诉我们，当他在圣坛旁边掘墓时候，他的鹤嘴锄轻轻一击，却打开了一口朽烂的棺材，里面有几张写着字的旧纸。我们的好奇心立刻动起来，就走到这位下级职员刚才工作的地方，看见一大群人围着墓旁。内中有一位老妇人告诉我们埋在里面的是一位贵妇，至于她的名字，我觉得不便提起，虽然这段故事没有一点不是增加她的荣耀的。这位贵妇过了几年伉俪之爱的模范生活，她丈夫去世后没有多久她也跟着死去，她的丈夫在道德同感情两

answered[1] her character in virtue and affection, made it her deathbed request, that all the letters which she had received from him, both before and after her marriage, should be buried in the coffin with her. These, I found upon examination, were the papers before us. Several of them had suffered so much by time, that I could only pick out a few words, as "my soul! lilies! roses! dearest angel!" and the like. One of them, which was legible throughout, ran[2] thus.

"MADAM,

"If you would know the greatness of my love, consider that[3] of your own beauty. That blooming countenance, that snowy bosom, that graceful person, return every moment to my imagination; the brightness of your eyes hath hindered me from closing mine since I last saw you. You may still add to your beauties by a smile. A frown will make me the most wretched of men, as I am the most passionate of lovers."

It filled the whole company with a deep melancholy, to compare the description of the letter with the person that occasioned it, who was now reduced to a few crumbling bones, and a little mouldering heap of earth. With much ado[4] I deciphered another letter,

---

1 to answer: to correspond 符合，相配。
2 to run: to be worded 写着。
3 that 代 greatness。
4 with much ado: with much trouble 经过许多困难。

方面可以说都配得上她的性格，她弥留时要求，他所写给她的信，结婚以前同以后，全要埋在棺材里，同她在一块儿。我检查后，知道所说的信就是我们面前这些旧纸。有几封因为过了这么久的时间，变成破碎不堪，我只能东鳞西爪地瞧出几个字，像"我的灵魂！白百合！红蔷薇！最亲爱的天使！"这类的话。有一封是全篇都可以看得清楚的，内容是如下：

"小姐，

"若使你想知道我的爱情是多么热烈，请你想一想你自己是多么美丽。你那如花的庞儿，雪般的酥胸同婷婷的身材，无时无刻不是回绕在我的想像里；你那双眸的光明阻碍我不能关闭我的眼睛，自从前次同你会面时起。你还能够用嫣然一笑来增加你的美丽。你一皱眉就会使我变成世界里最可怜的人，因为我是世上最热烈的情人。"

拿信里所描状的话同本人现在的情形一比较，大家都觉得悲来填胸，因为现在只剩得几块将变成齑粉的残骨同一小堆快要崩解的尘土了。费了很大的劲，我又读出另一封信，开头是：

which began with, "My dear, dear wife." This gave me a curiosity to see how the style of one written in marriage differed from one written in courtship. To my surprise, I found the fondness rather augmented than lessened, though the panegyric turned upon[1] a different accomplishment. The words were as follow:

"Before this short absence from you, I did not know that I loved you so much as I really do; though, at the same time, I thought I loved you as much as possible. I am under great apprehension, lest you should have any uneasiness whilst I am defrauded of my share in it, and cannot think of tasting any pleasures that you do not partake with me. Pray, my dear, be careful of your health, if for no other reason, but because you know I could not outlive you. It is natural in absence to make professions of an inviolable constancy; but towards so much merit, it is scarce a virtue, especially when it is but a bare return to that of which you have given me such continued proofs ever since our first acquaintance. I am, &c."

It happened that the daughter of these two excellent persons was by[2] when I was reading this letter. At the sight of the coffin, in which was the body of her mother, near that of her father, she

---

1 to turn upon: to direct upon 以之向……，转向。
2 by: near at hand 近旁。

"我亲爱的，亲爱的妻子。"这触起我的好奇心，想去看一看结婚后所写的同求婚时写的文字有什么不同。我真是非常惊愕，看到惓恋之意却到〔倒〕增加好多，并没有减少，虽然所赞美的是另一种的好处。信里的话是如下：

"在我们这次小别之前，我真不知道我实在是这么爱你；虽然那时我也以为我是尽了爱的力量爱你。我现在非常恐惧，只怕你会有什么麻烦，我却失丢了分忧的机会，我自己也不想有什么赏心乐事，当你不能和我共享的时候。我求你，我亲爱的，好好保养自己的身体，若使不为别的，那么就为着你知道倘然你有什么不测，我是不能独生的。人们当离居时候，常常会说我心匪石，梦寐不忘这类的话，但是对于像你这样值得怀念的人，我的忠实几乎不能算是一个难能可贵的美德，尤其是这不过报答你待我的种种诚恳，自从我们初次认识以来，你是不断地常常给我你挚爱我的证据。——你的……"

当我念这封信时候，刚好这对贤良夫妇的女儿站在旁边。一看到这口棺材，里面躺着她的母亲，放在她父亲的遗体邻近，

melted[1] into a flood of tears. As I had heard a great character of her virtue, and observed in her this instance of filial piety, I could not resist my natural inclination of giving advice to young people, and therefore addressed myself to her. "Young lady," said I, "you see how short is the possession of that beauty, in which nature has been so liberal[2] to you. You find the melancholy sight before you is a contradiction to the first letter that you heard on that subject; whereas, you may observe, the second letter, which celebrates your mother's constancy, is itself, being found in this place, an argument of it. But, Madam, I ought to caution you, not to think the bodies that lie before you your father and your mother. Know, their constancy is rewarded by a nobler union than by this mingling of their ashes, in a state where there is no danger or possibility of a second separation."

---

1 to melt: to soften 化为。
2 liberal: generous 慷慨。

她简直化作一个泪人儿。我曾经听过人们说她的德性非常好，现在又看到她是这么纯孝，我摆不脱我的老癖〔脾〕性，总爱教导年青人们，所以我就对她说出一番话。"年青的小姐，"我说，"你看自然很慷慨地给你的那类美姿容的据有期间是多么短促的。你晓得你眼前这个悲伤的景象同你刚才所听的关于这件事的第一封信的话是完全冲突的；但是你可以说赞美你母亲的节操的第二封信居然能在这里发现，到〔倒〕可以证明你母亲的贞洁诚挚。不过，小姐，我应当告诉你，不要想躺在你面前的尸体是你的双亲。你要知道，他们真挚的爱情得到了酬报，他们实现有比这种同穴更尊贵的结合，他们处在极乐的世界里，不会有第二次离别的危险同可能的。"

Joseph Addison

On Practical Jokes

I shall communicate to my reader the following letter for the entertainment of this day.

"Sir,

"You know very well that our nation is more famous for that sort of men who are called 'whims' and 'humourists'[1], than any other country in the world; for which reason it is observed that our English comedy excels that of all other nations in the novelty and variety of its characters.

"Among those innumerable sets of whims which our country produces, there are none whom I have regarded with more curiosity than those who have invented any particular kind of diversion for

---

1 humourist 此字在十八世纪多作举动滑稽的人物解,现在却是指言语诙谐的人们了。

恶 作 剧

我要将下面这封信刊登出来，做读者今天的消遣材料。

"先生，

"你很知道我们是世界里最负盛名的产生所谓'怪人物'同'滑稽家'的国家，所以人们说英国喜剧里人物的新奇同复杂是无论那一国的喜剧也赶不上的。

"我们国家所产生的数不尽的种种怪人物里面，我看起来最觉得奇怪有趣的是那班异想天开，弄出很特别的把戏，替自己或他们的朋友们寻开心的人们。我的信要单述一种怪人物，他

the entertainment of themselves or their friends. My letter shall single out[1] those who take delight in sorting[2] a company that has something of burlesque and ridicule in its appearance. I shall make myself understood[3] by the following example. One of the wits of the last age, who was a man of a good estate, thought he never laid out[4] his money better than in a jest. As he was one year at the Bath[5], observing that in the great confluence of fine people there were several among them with long chins, a part of the visage by which he himself was very much distinguished, he invited to dinner half a score of these remarkable persons who had their mouths in the middle of their faces. They had no sooner placed themselves about the table, but[6] they began to stare upon one another, not being able to imagine what had brought them together. Our English proverb says,

'Tis merry in the hall

When beards wag all.

It proved so in the assembly I am now speaking of, who, seeing so many peaks of faces agitated with eating, drinking, and discourse, and observing all the chins that were present meeting together very

---

  1　to single out: to choose out for attention 选出来令人注意。
  2　sorting: picking out as of one sort 搜罗同类的。
  3　to make one's self understood: to be apprehended in meaning 使己所说者为人了解。
  4　to lay out: to spend 消费。

们最喜欢召集一班具有同样特点的客人，使人们看着会觉得滑稽可笑。我要用下面这个例子使大家来明了我的意思。前代有一位滑稽家拥有很厚的财产，他却以为开玩笑花的钱是用得最值得的。有一年他住在巴斯，看到那一大群的时髦人们里面有好几个是长下颏的，他自己脸上的这一部分也是很出色的，他就宴请十位这种出色的人物，他们的嘴都生在他们脸孔中间。他们一坐在桌旁，立刻开始彼此睇视，想不出他们怎么会聚在一堂。我们英国的俗谚说过：

　　满堂都是胡子

　　大家一定笑哈哈。

我现在所说的这群人也是一样的，他们看见当饮食谈话的时候有这么多脸孔的尖锐下颏老是摇动着，又看到在会这许多的下颏常常在桌的中央相碰，每人都了解了内中的滑稽意味，大家

---

　　5 英国Somersetshire的都会，那里有极好的温泉，是十八世纪里英国时髦人们聚集的地方。

　　6 no sooner...but：as soon as 即刻，旋即。

often over the centre of the table, every one grew sensible of the jest, and came into¹ it² with so much good humour, that they lived in strict friendship and alliance from that day forward.

"The same gentleman some time after packed together³ a set of oglers, as he called them, consisting of such as had an unlucky east in their eyes. His diversion on this occasion was to see the cross bows, mistaken signs, and wrong connivances⁴ that passed amidst so many broken and refracted rays of sight.

"The third feast which this merry gentleman exhibited was to the stammerers, whom he got together in a sufficient body⁵ to fill his table. He had ordered one of his servants, who was placed behind a screen, to write down their table talk⁶, which was very easy to be done without the help of short-hand. It appears by the notes which were taken, that though their conversation never fell, there were not above twenty words spoken during the first course; that upon serving up the second, one of the company was a quarter of an hour in telling them that the ducklings and asparagus were very good; and that another took up⁷ the same time in declaring himself of the same

---

1 to come into: to join with or take part in 加入。

2 it 指 jest。

3 to pack together: to crowd together 聚集在一起。

4 connivance: assenting or polite acquiescences, made at the wrong time, or to the wrong person 不得其时或者不得其人的目许，这是十八世纪时候的

非常高兴，从那天起他们变成很好的朋友，有什么事彼此也帮忙得很周到。

"这位先生后来他又聚集一班他所谓送秋波的人们，就是那班带有不幸的斜视眼的人们。他这次的开心是在观看这许多破碎曲折视线里的一切射眼箭，误会的表示同不经意的目许。

"这位哈哈笑先生的第三次大宴会是请口吃的人们，他集有够坐满一桌的人们。他先叫他的一个仆人坐在布幕后面，将他们酒桌上的谈话记下，这是很容易可以办到的，用不着速记的帮助。由所记下来的看起，虽然他们的谈话没有停歇，食第一道菜时候他们还说不到二十字；等二道菜捧上时候，有一位在座的整整费了一刻钟工夫，只说小鸭同龙须菜都很好；还有一位化了同样久的时间宣布他也是这样子想的。可是这次开玩笑

用法，现在是作 pretence of being unawares，tacit permission to offend 佯作不知，默许人们做坏事解了。

5 body：aggregate of persons 人的总数。
6 table talk：familiar conversation, as that round a table during and after meal 当吃饭或吃饭过后围着桌子的很随便之谈话。
7 to take up：to occupy 占据，使用。

opinion. This jest did not, however, go off so well[1] as the former; for one of the guests, being a brave man, and fuller of resentment than he knew how to express, went out of the room, and sent the facetious inviter a challenge in writing, which, though it was afterwards dropped by the interposition of friends, put a stop to these ludicrous entertainments.

"Now, Sir, I dare say you will agree with me, that as there is no moral in these jests, they ought to be discouraged, and looked upon rather as pieces of unluckiness than wit. However, as it is natural for one man to refine upon the thought of another, and impossible for any single person, how great soever his parts[2] may be, to invent an art, and bring it to its utmost perfection, — I shall here give you an account of an honest gentleman of my acquaintance, who, upon hearing the character of the wit above-mentioned, has himself assumed it, and endeavoured to convert it to the benefit of mankind. He invited half a dozen of his friends one day to dinner, who were each of them famous for inserting several redundant phrases in their discourse, as 'd'ye hear me[3],' 'd'ye see[4],' 'that is,' 'and so, Sir.' Each of the guests making frequent use of his particular elegance,

---

1 to go off so well: to succeed 进行非常顺利。
2 parts: ability 技能，天资，作这种解释时，常用复数。
3 d'ye hear me: do you hear me 你听见我的话没有。

的结果没有前回那么好；因为有一位客人是个勇士，一肚子的愤怒不知道怎地发泄好，走出房子，送来一张写的挑战书给这位诙谐主人，虽然经过朋友们的从中斡旋，这个决斗也就取消了，但是他也因此停止了这类好笑的宴会。

"先生，我敢说你一定会赞成我的意思，以为这类开玩笑既然没有寓了什么深意，是应当阻止的，认做这全是不幸的举动，并不能算为诙谐。但是我们会自然而然地将别人所想出的东西渐渐地修改好，并且单单一个人，不管他有多大本领，总不能够既发明出一种艺术，又使它达到尽美尽善的地步——我现在要告诉你我所认识的一位忠厚绅士，他听到前面所说的那种滑稽，自己也来干一下，却努力于使它变做有益于人类的东西。有一天他宴请六七位朋友来，谁也知道他们个个都喜欢在讲话时用几句特别的赘语，像'你听到我的话没有''你知道吗''这就是说''所以，先生'。每个客人常常用他特有的这些雅

---

4 d'ye see: do you see 你知道吗。

appeared so ridiculous to his neighbour, that he could not but[1] reflect upon himself as appearing equally ridiculous to the rest of the company: by this means[2], before they had sat long together, every one talking with the greatest circumspection, and carefully avoiding his favourite expletive, the conversation was cleared of its redundancies, and had a greater quantity of sense, though less of sound in it.

"The same well-meaning gentleman took occasion, at another time, to bring together such of his friends as were addicted to a foolish habitual custom of swearing. In order to shew[3] them the absurdity of the practice, he had recourse to the invention above-mentioned, having placed an amanuensis in a private part of the room. After the second bottle, when men open their minds without reserve, my honest friend began to take notice of the many sonorous but unnecessary words that had passed in his house since their sitting down at table, and how much good conversation they had lost by giving way[4] to such superfluous phrases. 'What a tax,' says he, 'would they have raised for the poor, had we put the laws in execution upon one another.' Every one of them took this gentle reproof in good part[5]. Upon which he told them that, knowing their conversation

---

1 can not but: can not for bear 不禁，难免。
2 means 作"手段"解，作这种解释时，常用复数，但是却当做是居单数。
3 这是 show 的古写。
4 to give way: to allow opportunity to 与以机会。

句,坐在旁边的人看来自然觉得很可笑的,于是这位邻座人会想到自己,觉得自己在别人眼里一定也是同样的可笑:这么一来,他们没有坐多久,每个人都是万分谨慎地谈话,小心避免他们心爱的冗字,他们的谈话因此丢去了多余的词句,包含有更多的意思,虽然没有那么多的声音。

"这位好心的绅士后来他得便又聚集另外一班朋友,他们是耽〔耽〕溺于咒诅这个坏习惯的。为的是要指出给他们看这种习惯的荒谬,他就使用前面所说那个妙法,在房子里看不见的地方安置一个书记生。喝完了两瓶酒,人们不拘地说出心里的话时候,我这位忠厚朋友看出他们坐下酒桌后在他家里说出好许多响亮震耳的费〔废〕话,他们失丢了不少有意思的谈话,全因为他们要乱说这类用不着说的词句。'他们一定可以集了一大笔的款给穷人们,'他说,'若使我们实行一种法律,彼此互相监督,说一句咒诅就要罚款。'他们都是没有生气地接受这句

---

5 in good part:without offence 没有生气。

would have no secrets in it, he had ordered it to be taken down[1] in writing, and, for the humour's sake, would read it to them, if they pleased. There were ten sheets of it, which might have been reduced to two, had there not been those abominable interpolations I have before mentioned. Upon the reading of it in cold blood[2], it looked rather like a conference of fiends than of men. In short, every one trembled at himself upon hearing calmly what he had pronounced amidst the heat and inadvertency of discourse.

"I shall only mention another occasion wherein he made use of the same invention to cure a different kind of men, who are the pests of all polite conversation, and murder time as much as either of the two former, though they do it more innocently; I mean that dull generation of story-tellers. My friend got together about half a dozen of his acquaintance who were infected with this strange malady. The first day, one of them sitting down entered upon the siege of Namur[3], which lasted till four o'clock, their time of parting. The second day a North Briton[4] took possession of the discourse, which it was impossible to get out of his hands so long as the company staid together. The third day was engrossed after the same manner by a story of the

---

1 to be taken down: to be recorded 记录下。
2 in cold blood: without excitement 冷静地。
3 Namur 是比利时的一省，接近法国。
4 North Briton: Scotsman.

温和的谴责。他跟着就告诉他们，因为他知道他们的谈论不会有什么秘密，所以他叫人记下，为着好玩起见，要将写下的念出，若使他们愿意。一共有十张，折实起来只有两张，设使没有我前面所说的那种可恶的插话。冷静地念出来，那仿佛是魔鬼聚会的谈话，不像是出自人的口里。总而言之，每人恬静地听到他在谈话的兴高彩〔采〕烈，毫不留意时候所说的咒诅，个个都战栗起来。

"我只要再说他的另一次宴会，他用同样的妙策去医好别一类的人们，他们是文雅谈话的烦累，他们的白费时间是不下于前面所说的两种人，虽然他们是比较天真些；我指那班爱说故事的无聊人们。我朋友找到六七个相识的人，他们全染有这个奇病。第一天，他们里面一位一坐下来就说到那慕尔的被围，一直讲到下午四点钟止，那是他们离别的时候。第二天，所有的谈论全给关于苏格兰人的故事所占有，简直没有法子使他停止，当他们还坐着谈天时候。第三天也是同样地费在一篇同样

same length. They at last began to reflect upon this barbarous way of treating one another, and by this means awakened out of that lethargy with which each of them had been seized for several years.

"As you have somewhere declared that extraordinary and uncommon characters of mankind are the game which you delight in, and as I look upon you to be the greatest sportsman, or, if you please, the Nimrod[1] among this species of writers, I thought this discovery would not be unacceptable to you.

"I am, Sir, & c."

---

1 宁录"为世上英雄之首。他在耶和华面前是个英勇的猎户"(见《圣经·创世记》)。

长的故事的叙述里。他们最后想到这种互相对待未免太野蛮了，因此他们从这类昏睡里醒来，他们患这个毛病已经有好几年了。

"因为你在某一篇文章里曾经说过人们古怪奇特的性格是你所最喜欢的野味，我又觉得在这类观察人情的作家里你是最伟大的猎夫或者可说是一位宁录，若使你肯让我这样称呼你，所以我想这封信里所说的新发见你一定是很愿意听的。

"先生，我是你的……"

Samuel Johnson

On Sorrow

Of the passions with which the mind of man is agitated, it may be observed, that they naturally hasten towards their own extinction, by inciting and quickening the attainment of their objects. Thus fear urges our flight, and desire animates our progress; and if there are some which perhaps may be indulged till they outgrow the good appropriated to their satisfaction, as it is frequently observed of avarice and ambition, yet their immediate tendency is to some means of happiness really existing, and generally within the prospect. The miser always imagines that there is a certain sum that will fill his heart to the brim[1]; and every ambitious man, like King

---

1　to fill one's heart to the brim: to make one quite satisfied 令人完全满意,心满意足。

悲　哀

关于扰乱人心的种种热情,我们可以说,它们是自然而然地急趋于自己消灭之途,因为它们鼓励同加快它们目的的实现。比如恐惧催促我们的逃走,希望激发我们的向前;若使有几种热情或者因为受了我们的放纵,弄得失丢了它们达到目的时候所该有的好处,贪婪同野心就常常是这样子,然而它们目前的志向还是想得到幸福的工具,那幸福又是真真存在的,大概是可以望得见的。守财奴总是以为有个数目能够使他心满意足;

Pyrrhus[1], has an acquisition in his thoughts that is to terminate his labours, after which he shall pass the rest of his life in ease or gaiety in repose or devotion.

Sorrow is perhaps the only affection of the breast that can be excepted from this general remark, and it therefore deserves the particular attention of those who have assumed the arduous province of preserving the balance of the mental constitution. The other passions are diseases indeed, but they necessarily direct us to their proper cure. A man at once feels the pain, and knows the medicine, to which he is carried with greater haste as the evil which requires it is more excruciating, and cures himself by unerring instinct, as the wounded stags of Crete[2] are related by Aeolian[3] to have recourse to vulnerary herbs. But for sorrow there is no remedy provided by nature; it is often occasioned by accidents irreparable, and dwells upon[4] objects that have lost or changed their existence; it requires what it cannot hope, that the laws of the universe should be repealed; that the dead should return, or the past should be recalled.

Sorrow is not that regret for negligence or error which may

---

1 皮洛士是希腊的伊庇鲁斯 Epicurus 国王，又是亚历山大的亲戚，他早年就有征服意大利同西西里的计划，以为若使能够达到这个目的，他是不会再有别的野心了。他在公元前二八〇年侵犯意大利。打了二回胜仗，在公元前二七五年在贝尼温陀（Beneventum）被罗马人打败了。

2 Crete 是地中海里隶属于希腊的一个岛。

每个野心家,像皮洛士王一样,心里有个最想占有的东西,得到这个东西,他的劳苦就告终止,此后他的余生要在舒服或者作乐,休息或者虔信里过去。

悲哀或者是胸中的惟一情感,不能够应用这几句概括的话,所以值得那班想干保持心境的平衡这个艰难工作的人们的特别注意。其它的热情的确也是种毛病,但是它们必然地使我们得到适当的医治。人会立刻感到苦痛,知道应当用的是什么药,他会更快地去找这个药,因为〔所以〕需要这药的病是这么苦楚的,因此,靠着那永不会错的本能,会将自己医好,好像伊恩力亚人所说,克里特岛上受伤的鹿会自己去找治创的野草。但是关于悲哀,却没有什么天生的治疗,因为悲哀的产生常是由于无法补救的意外事情,它又使人们注意着那已经不在的,或者是情形已变的东西。它绝没有希望能够得到它所需要的,它需要自然律会取消去,死者可以复生或者既往可以追回。

悲哀不是对于失检或者错误的惋惜,那倒可以鼓舞我们将

---

3 Aeolian 是古希腊三大民族之一。
4 to dwell upon: to keep one's attention fixed upon 非常注意,聚精会神。

animate us to future care or activity, or that repentance of crimes for which, however irrevocable, our Creator has promised to accept it as an atonement; the pain which arises from these causes has very salutary effects, and is every hour extenuating itself by the reparation of those miscarriages that produce it. Sorrow is properly that state of the mind in which our desires are fixed upon the past, without looking forward to the future, an incessant wish that something were otherwise than it has been, a tormenting and harassing want of some enjoyment or possession which we have lost, and which no endeavours can possibly regain. Into such anguish many have sunk upon some sudden diminution of their fortune, an unexpected blast of their reputation, or the loss of children or of friends. They have suffered all sensibility of pleasure to be destroyed by a single blow, have given up[1] for ever[2] the hopes of substituting any other object in the room of[3] that which they lament, resigned their lives to gloom and despondency, and worn themselves out in unavailing misery.

Yet so much is this passion the natural consequence of tenderness and endearment, that, however painful and however useless, it is justly reproachful not to feel it on some occasions; and so widely and constantly has it always prevailed, that the laws of some nations,

---

1 to give up: to part with 抛弃。
2 for ever: to the end of life 永世,永远。
3 in the room of: instead of 代替。

来的小心或者动作,也不是对于罪恶的痛悔,不管那罪恶是如何无可挽回的,我们的"创造主"却答应肯将这种痛悔当做赎罪;从这几种的缘因所引起的苦痛还有很大培养精神的效力,并且靠着认清祸根而痛改前非,我们能够时时刻刻减轻这个苦痛。悲哀却是一种特别心境,那时我们的欲望全放在过去上面,没有望〔往〕前向将来去着想,不断地希望有些事情从前会不是那么样子,对于我们已经失丢,无法再能得到的几种欢愉或者所有物,怀有一个急迫难忍的需要。许多人沉到这类惨痛里,因为他们的财产忽然减少好多,或者他们的名誉意外地遭瘟,或者是丧失了子女或者朋友。他们受此一个打击,就让自己一切对于快乐的感觉全归于毁灭,终其身再也不想去找别个对象,来做替身,填补这个遗憾,甘心渡〔度〕个苦闷愁郁的生涯,销磨自己于无益的自苦里面。

但是这个情感的确是深情挚爱的自然结果,所以不管它是多么苦痛的,多么无用的,在相当的情境之下,若使我们没有感到悲哀,那又是该受责骂的;悲哀的势力又老是那么广大,那么持久,所以有些国家的法律,和有些国家的习俗对于因为

and the customs of others, have limited a time for the external appearances of grief caused by the dissolution of close alliances, and the breach of domestic union.

It seems determined, by the general suffrage of mankind, that sorrow is to a certain point laudable, as the offspring of love, or at least pardonable, as the effect of weakness; but that it ought not to be suffered to increase by indulgence, but must give way[1], after a stated[2] time, to social duties, and the common avocations of life. It is at first unavoidable, and therefore must be allowed, whether with or without our choice; it may afterwards be admitted as a decent and affectionate testimony of kindness and esteem; something will be extorted by nature, and something may be given to the world. But all beyond the bursts of passion or the forms of solemnity, is not only useless, but culpable; for we have no right to sacrifice, to the vain longings of affection, that time which Providence allows us for the task of our station.

Yet it too often happens that sorrow, thus lawfully entering, gains such a firm possession of the mind, that it is not afterwards to be ejected; the mournful ideas, first violently impressed, and afterwards willingly received, so much engross the attention, as to

---

1 to give way: to give place 让与,退让。
2 stated: fixed 固定。

亲密人们的死亡同一家骨肉的永诀所产生的悲哀的露泄于外的时期，有一定的限制。

大多数人们好像都以为悲哀在相当程度之内是值得赞美的，因为它是胚胎于爱的，或者最少也是可以原谅的，因为它是人类弱点的结果；但是我们不应当放纵它，让它滋长，要在一定的时期之后，勉强从事于社会上的义务同人生日常的职务。起先原是无法避免的，所以我们只好让它去，无论我们是愿意不愿意；后来也可以看它是我们对于逝者的敬爱的一种适当亲切的证据；既是天生有情，当然免不了受了感触，并且我们的哀戚，还可以使世人看出逝者的价值。但是在悲情爆发同严肃仪式之外的悲哀，那不只是无用的，而且是有罪的，因为我们没有权利将上帝派给我们用来做分内的事的时间，牺牲在无益的渴望里面。

然而这样规规矩矩地开头的悲哀太常弄得坚固地霸占着我们的心，以后简直没有法子把它驱逐出去；那群惨然的观念开头是蛮横地印到心上，后来是愿意地吸收进去，垄断了我们全部的注意力，因此压下一切的思想，遮暗欣欢的心情，搅乱推

predominate in every thought, to darken gaiety, and perplex ratiocination. An habitual sadness seizes upon the soul, and the faculties are chained to a single object, which can never be contemplated but with hopeless uneasiness.

From this state of dejection it is very difficult to rise to cheerfulness and alacrity, and therefore many who have laid down[1] rules of intellectual health think preservatives easier than remedies, and teach us not to trust ourselves with favourite enjoyments, not to indulge the luxury of fondness, but to keep our minds always suspended in such indifference, that we may change the objects about us without inconvenience or emotion.

An exact compliance with this rule might, perhaps, contribute to tranquillity, but surely it would never produce happiness. He that regards none so much as to be afraid of losing them, must live for ever without the gentle pleasures of sympathy and confidence; he must feel no melting fondness, no warmth of benevolence, nor any of those honest[2] joys which nature annexes to the power of pleasing. And as no man can justly claim more tenderness than he pays, he must forfeit his share in that officious and watchful kindness which love only can dictate, and those lenient endearments by which love only can soften life. He may justly be overlooked and neglected by

---

1 to lay down: to establish or formulate definitely 建立（规则），规定。
2 honest: fairly earned 应得的酬报。

想的能力。一个变成习惯的悲哀捉着灵魂,所有的感官全范围在一个对象里面,这对象没有一回想到时,不是引起绝望的痛心。

从这样沉闷的心情里是很不容易升到欣欢喜乐的境界,所以许多厘定精神健康的法则的人们都以为预防剂是比疗病物容易奏效得多,教我们不要心倾于喜欢的享乐,也不可尽兴地去钟爱人们,却是要使我们的心老是超然地悬在冷淡的境界里,那么我们四围的对象尽可变迁,我们却不会感到不便,或者有甚牵情。

一字不差地守着这条法则或者可以帮助我们得到恬静,但是绝不能够产生幸福。他既是对于谁都没有关切到怕失丢了他们,这样的人一生里也尝不到受人们的同情和信任的快乐;他一定是感不到柔情的爱恋同慈悲的热心,有些人有本领使人们高兴,跟着自己也得到应当得到的快乐,这种乐趣他也是没有份儿的。因为没有人配索取比他所给别人的更多的情谊,所以他该丧失他本来应得的人们对他的小心翼翼的殷勤好意,那是只有爱才能向人要来的,同宽恕仁慈的恳挚情感,靠着它爱才能减轻人生的苦痛。他是该受心中有更多的热血的人们的忽视

such as have more warmth in their heart; for who would be the friend of him, whom, with whatever assiduity he may be courted, and with whatever services obliged, his principles will not suffer to make equal returns, and who, when you have exhausted all the instances of good will, can only be prevailed on not to be an enemy?

An attempt to preserve life in a state of neutrality and indifference, is unreasonable and vain. If by excluding joy we could shut out[1] grief, the scheme would deserve very serious attention; but since, however we may debar ourselves from happiness, misery will find its way[2] at many inlets, and the assaults of pain will force our regard, though we may withhold it from the invitations of pleasure, we may surely endeavour to raise life above the middle point of apathy at one time, since it will necessarily sink below it at another.

But though it cannot be reasonable not to gain happiness for fear of losing it, yet it must be confessed, that in proportion to the pleasure of possession, will be for some time our sorrow for the loss; it is therefore the province[3] of the moralist to inquire whether such pains may not quickly give way to mitigation. Some have thought that the most certain way to clear the heart from its embarrassment is

---

1 to shut out: to exclude 拒而不纳。
2 to find one's way: to succeed in reaching 得达。
3 province: one's concern 分内的事务。

同怠慢；因为谁肯做他的朋友，若使不管你怎地专心地去求得他的好感，替他干了多少事情，他的主张却不让他同样地来报答你，并且当凡是好意所能做的事情，你全干完了时候，你充其量只能使他不做你的仇敌？

想保持生活在冷淡中立的状况里是一种悖理无谓的举动。若使单单将欢乐赶出，我们就能把悲哀摈之户外，那么这个计划是值得很严重的注意；但是既然，不管我们怎样不准自己享受幸福，祸患还是找得出许多的进口，虽然我们可以不受快乐的引诱，免丢因此而起的苦痛，苦痛的来袭还是会迫得我们不能不注意，我们有时真该努力将生活提高到麻木无情这个水平线之上，因为它既是无论如何有时总会沉到悲哀的深渊里去。

但是固然因为怕失丢幸福而不去求幸福是很不合于道理的，可是我们一定要承认，得时的快乐是多大，将来失时，我们的悲哀也是成正比例的；所以这是道德家分内的事，去研究我们可以不可以将悲哀很快地减轻消灭下去。有人以为将心中烦闷一扫而空的最靠得住的办法是用强力将它拖到欢乐场中去。有

to drag it by force into scenes of merriment. Others imagine, that such a transition is too violent, and recommend rather to soothe it into tranquillity, by making it acquainted with miseries more dreadful and afflictive, and diverting to the calamities of others the regards which we are inclined to fix too closely upon our own misfortunes.

It may be doubted whether either of those remedies will be sufficiently powerful. The efficacy of mirth it is not always easy to try, and the indulgence of melancholy may be suspected to be one of those medicines, which will destroy, if it happens not to cure.

The safe and general antidote against sorrow is employment. It is commonly observed, that among soldiers and seamen, though there is much kindness, their is little grief; they see their friend fall without any of that lamentation which is indulged in security and idleness, because they have no leisure to spare from the care of themselves; and whoever shall keep his thoughts equally busy, will find himself equally unaffected with irretrievable losses.

Time is observed generally to wear out[1] sorrow, and its effects might doubtless be accelerated by quickening the succession and enlarging the variety of objects.

"'Tis long ere time can mitigate your grief;

---

1 to wear out: to erase or efface 抹去，销去。

人却觉得这种转移是太猛烈了,倒是主张先把心慰藉到安宁的境地里,用的法子是使它看到别人的更可怕更可悲的苦痛,将我们那很容易紧紧地钉〔盯〕着自己的乖运的注意力,移到别人的苦难上面去。

这是很可以怀疑的,到底这些药方里有没有一个是够有力量的。快乐这个医法并不是老是容易尝试的,至于耽纵于悲哀,恐怕这是属于那一类药,设使偶然不能医好,是反会致死命的。

作事可说是驱逐悲哀的又安全又普通的解毒剂。我们常常看见,在兵士同水手里面,虽他们也是很慈爱的,却只有很少的悲忧;他们看见他们的朋友中弹死了,并没有像在安逸懒惰里的人们那样恣情哀毁,因为他们已经是自顾不暇了。谁能够使自己的思虑同样地忙碌,他对于无法挽回的丧失会同样地无动于衷。

人们常常说时间可以磨掉悲哀,这种效力的速率绝对可以增加,若使事情的递迁能够加快,事务的范围又能扩大,更形出变化多端。

"你还得等了许久,时间才能够减轻你的悲哀;

To wisdom fly, she quickly brings relief.

F. Lewis. "

Sorrow is a kind of rust of the soul, which every new idea contributes in its passage to scour away. It is the putrefaction of stagnant life, and is remedied by exercise and motion.

飞到智慧那里去罢,她很快就可以给你安慰。

鲁逸思"

悲哀是心灵上的一种铁锈,每个新念头经过心中时,都可以帮助磨去一些。它是停滞的生活所生的腐朽,只有劳作同活动才是最好的医法。

Oliver Goldsmith

Happiness in a Great Measure[1] Dependent on Constitution

When I reflect on the unambitious retirement in which I passed the earlier part of my life in the country, I cannot avoid feeling some pain in thinking that those happy days are never to return. In that retreat all nature seemed capable of affording pleasure; I then made no refinements on happinese, but could be pleased with the most awkward efforts of rustic mirth; thought cross purposes the highest stretch of human wit, and questions and commands the most rational amusement for spending the evening. Happy could so charming an illusion still continue! I find age and knowledge only contribute to sour our dispositions. My present enjoyments may be more refined,

---

1 in a great measure: largely 大半,大分。

快乐多半是靠着性质

当我回忆到我年青时候在乡下里所过的无野心的幽隐生涯，我免不了感到些悲哀，想起那种快乐的日子是不可复得了。在那个僻静的地方，一切自然的东西好像都能够产生快乐；那时我对于享乐并不讲究，粗俗游戏的笨拙举动也能使我开心；我那时以为互相猜哑谜是人类诙谐的极度，拿问题同命令来相难是消夜的最合理游戏。那是多么有幸福呵！若使这么美妙的幻觉能够还是继续存在着。我看出老年同智识只是使我们的癖〔脾〕气更见乖戾。我现在的享乐也许是更讲究些，但是它们的

but they are infinitely less pleasing. The pleasure Garrick[1] gives can no way compare to that I have received from a country way, who imitated a Quaker's[2] sermon. The music of Mattei[3] is dissonance to what I felt when our old dairymaid sung me into tears with *Johnny Armstrong's Last Good Night* or *The Cruelty of Barbara Allen*[4].

Writers of every age have endeavoured to show that pleasure is in us, and not in the objects offered for our amusement. If the soul be happily disposed, everything becomes a subject of entertainment, and distress will almost want a name. Every occurrence passes in review like the figures of a procession: some may be awkward, others ill dressed; but none but[5] a fool is for this enraged with the master of the ceremonies.

I remember to have once seen a slave in a fortification in Flanders[6], who appeared no way[7] touched[8] with his situation. He was

---

1 Garrick, David（1716—1779），他是约翰生的学生，十八世纪里最有名的戏子，他自己又会编剧。

2 Quaker是教友派的信徒，此派意大利人George Fox在一六五〇年所创立，自称做"Society of Friend"。因为他们提到上帝时候，常常全身战栗，自认为受到了灵感，所以别人讥笑他们，说他们是quaker，就是"战栗的人"的意思。他们说教时用了很多有力的姿势。

3 Mattei是十八世纪一个音乐家。

4 这是英国两首民歌的题目。

5 but: except除开，除去。

6 Flanders是欧洲从前一块独立区域，现在分属法比两国。

可乐程度比从前的乐事是差了万万倍了。加立克所给我的快乐绝不能同我从前看到一位模仿教友派信徒的说教的乡间滑稽家时所得的快乐相比。马泰的音乐可说是不悦耳的声音，一比到我从前所感到的，当我们的榨取牛奶的老姑娘唱着《约呢·阿姆斯特郎最后的告别》或者《巴巴剌·阿伦的残忍》，唱得叫我流下泪来。

每代的作家都曾努力指示给我们看，快乐是在我们的心里，并不是从我们的娱乐品得来的。若使我们的精神是很快乐的，任一东西都变做可乐的事情，世上差不多没有愁苦这个字了。每件事情从我们眼里经过好像是一个赛会里的人物：有些或者是很难看的，还有些也许是穿得不整齐；但是除开了傻子没有人会因此同这仪式的总管生气。

我记得曾经在法兰德斯堡垒里遇到一个奴隶，他简直不像感觉到他自己的地位。他的四肢被人们残害了，他的躯体变成

7　no way：not at all 并不。
8　to be touched：to be affected 受感动。

maimed, deformed, and chained; obliged to toil from the appearance of day till nightfall, and condemned to this for life; yet, with all these circumstances of apparent wretchedness, he sung, would have danced, but that he wanted a leg, and appeared the merriest, happiest man of all the garrison. What a practical philosopher was here! A happy constitution supplied philosophy, and though seemingly destitute of wisdom, he was really wise. No reading or study had contributed to disenchant the fairyland around him. Everything furnished him with an opportunity of mirth; and though some thought him from his insensibility a fool, he was such an idiot as philosophers might wish in vain[1] to imitate.

They who, like him, can place themselves on that side of the world in which everything appears in a ridiculous or pleasing light[2], will find something in every occurrence to excite their good humour. The most calamitous events, either to themselves or others, can bring no new affliction; the whole world is to them a theatre, on which comedies only are acted. All the bustle of heroism or the rants of ambition serve only to heighten the absurdity of the scene, and make the humour more poignant. They feel, in short[3], as little anguish at their own distress, or the complaints of others, as the

---

1 in vain: without effect 无效。
2 light 此处作"看法"解。
3 in short: briefly 一言以蔽之,总之。

畸形，还给铁链锁住；他被迫从黎明工作到黄昏，并且是判定了终身是这样干着；可是，虽然有这么多显明的苦痛情况，他却唱着调儿，若使他不是缺了一个腿，一定会跳舞，看起来真是全要塞里最高兴，最快乐的人。这是多么伟大的一个实行哲学家！一个快乐的性质给他的达观的思想，虽然好像是一点智慧也没有，他却是个真有智慧的人。没有什么学识同研究来点破他四围的仙境。每件物事都给他一个发噱的机会；虽然有人从他这样不感到苦痛推想他是个傻子，然而他这种傻子或者是哲学家所想模仿而模仿不来的。

有些人们像他这样能够将自己放在种特别的境界，在那里一切物事都化为可笑的，有趣的，这种人们从每一个事件里都能找出怡情悦意的地方。最不幸的事体，自己的或者别人的，不能带来什么新的悲哀；由他们看来，全世界是一座戏院，在那里专演着喜剧。一切豪勇英武的慌忙或者野心勃勃的狂言不过用来增加剧中的荒谬意味，使里面诙谐更添锋芒。总之，他们对于自己的困难，或者别人的苦情，没有什么伤心，好似代

undertaker, though dressed in black, feels sorrow at a funeral.

Of all the men I ever read of, the famous Cardinal de Retz[1] possessed this happiness of temper in the highest degree. As he was a man of gallantry, and despised all that wore the pedantic appearance of philosophy, wherever pleasure was to be sold, he was generally foremost to raise the auction[2]. Being an universal admirer of the fair sex[3], when he found one lady cruel, he generally fell in love with[4] another, from whom he expected a more favourable reception; if she too rejected his addresses, he never thought of retiring into deserts, or pining in hopeless distress. He persuaded himself, that instead of loving the lady, he only fancied he had loved her, and so all was well again. When Fortune[5] wore her angriest look, when he at last fell into the power of his most deadly enemy, Cardinal Mazarin[6], and was confined a close prisoner in the Castle of Valenciennes, he never attempted to support his distress by wisdom or philosophy, for he pretended to neither. He langhed at himself and his persecutor, and

---

1 Cardinal de Retz（1614—1679）是Montmirail地方的人，进教会后，很快就飞黄腾达起来，变做很热心的政党中人，专同Mazarin作对。

2 拍卖时由叫卖人提出一件东西，买主们互相争加价钱，到叫卖人答应为止。所以叫做to raise the auction提高实价。

3 fair sex：the female sex女流，妇女。

4 to fall in love with：钟情。

5 此处将"命运"拿来人格化，这是十八世纪文人所最喜欢弄的把戏。

人经理葬事的人,虽然也是穿着黑的衣服,在埋葬时没有什么悲哀。

我在书里所曾碰到的人物里,有名的累兹主教具有最高度的这种欣欢的性情。他既是个倜傥风流的男子,看轻一切挂起道学的酸腐脸孔,所以无论那里有欢娱出卖,他常是最肯出价的。他是女性的一个普遍赞美者,当他发现一位姑娘太忍心了,他常常就爱上了另一个,他期望从她可以得到一个更好的待遇;若使她也拒绝了他的殷勤,他绝不会想起退隐到沙漠去,或者在绝望的苦痛里憔悴着。他劝自己不要想自己现在是爱着那姑娘,只当做他从前曾爱过那姑娘就是了,这么一来什么事也没有了。当"命运"戴上她最愤怒的脸孔时候,当他最后落在他最凶恶的敌人,马萨林主教手里,变做严重禁锢的囚犯,关在瓦兰遑尼斯堡时候,他也绝没有想用智慧或者哲学来支持他的苦痛,因为他并不自命自己有智慧或者哲学。他笑他自己同磨

---

6 Jules Mazarin(1602—1661),他是路易十四朝的宰相,有好几年简直是法国的实际君王。

seemed infinitely pleased at his new situation. In this mansion of distress, though secluded from his friends, though denied all the amusements and even the conveniences of life, teased every hour by the impertinence of wretches who were employed to guard him, he still retained his good humour, laughed at all their little spite, and carried the jest so far as to be revenged, by writing the life of his jailer.

All that the wisdom of the proud can teach is to be stubborn or sullen under misfortunes. The Cardinal's example will instruct us to be merry in circumstances of the highest affliction. It matters not whether our good humour be construed by others into insensibility, or even idiotism; it is happiness to ourselves, and none but a fool would measure his satisfaction by what the world thinks of it.

Dick Wildgoose[1] was one of the happiest silly fellows I ever knew. He was of the number[2] of those good-natured creatures that are said to do no harm to any but themselves. Whenever Dick fell into any misery, he usually called it seeing life. If his head was broken by a chairman, or his pocket picked by a sharper, he comforted himself by imitating the Hibernian[3] dialect of the one, or the more

---

1 wildgoose 此字译意是"野鹅",英国人以为鹅是傻的东西,这位先生又是野性难驯的,所以这个名字实在有意义的。
2 number: company 群。
3 Hibernian: Hish.

难他的人，好像万分喜欢他这个新环境。在这个苦痛的房屋里，虽然同他的朋友隔绝了，虽然剥夺人生的一切娱乐同甚至于衣食住的利便，时时被那班雇来看守他的坏蛋的无礼所戏弄，他仍然保存着他的好脾气，笑他们一切无谓的怨毒，开玩笑到写出他的狱卒的传，来当作报复。

骄傲的人们的智慧所能教我们的是在不幸事体之下倔强着或者默默地愠怒着。这个主教的例子却教我们在最苦痛的境遇里欣欢着。我们的好脾气，别人会不会认为是感觉迟钝，或者甚至于白痴，这全是不碍事的；对于我们这总是快乐，除开了傻子没有人会用世人的意见来量自己满意的多少。

狄克·魏尔德戈斯是我所知道的一个最快乐的傻家伙。他是属于那类性情温和的人们，据说他们没有害谁，只是害了自己。每回狄克堕到什么悲哀的时候，他总是说这是"见世面"。若使他的头被一个轿夫摔破了，或者他的袋子给扒手光顾了，他就去学轿夫的爱尔兰土话或者扒手的更时髦的口吻，借此来

fashionable cant of the other. Nothing came amiss[1] to Dick. His inattention to money matters had incensed his father to such a degree, that all the intercession of friends in his favour was fruitless. The old gentleman was on his deathbed. The whole family, and Dick among the number, gathered round him. "I leave my second son Andrew," said the expiring miser, "my whole estate, and desire him to be frugal." Andrew, in a sorrowful tone, as is usual on these occasions, "prayed Heaven to prolong his life and health to enjoy it himself." "I recommend Simon, my third son, to the care of his elder brother, and leave him beside four thousand pounds." "Ah! Father," cried Simon (in great affliction to be sure), "may Heaven give you life and health to enjoy it yourself!" At last, turning to poor Dick, "as for you, you have always been a sad dog[2], you'll never come to good, you'll never be rich, I'll leave you a shilling to buy a halter." "Ah! father," cries Dick, without any emotion, "may Heaven give you life and health to enjoy it yourself!" This was all the trouble the loss of fortune gave this thoughtless imprudent creature. However, the tenderness of an uncle recompensed the neglect of a father; and Dick is not only excessively good-humoured, but competently rich.

---

1 to come amiss: to be unwelcome 不受欢迎。
2 a sad dog: a merry fellow or a gay man 寻快乐的人，终日嬉笑的人。

安慰自己。由狄克看来，天下里的事情是没有错的。他银钱事体的不当心激怒了他的父亲，以致朋友们替他的从中斡旋都是无结果的。老绅士是在弥留的时候，全家人，狄克也在内，全围着他四旁。"我给我的第二儿子安德鲁，"临死的守财虏〔奴〕说道，"我的全部财产，希望他知道勤俭。"安德鲁用悲哀的声音，在这种时候就例是这样子，"祈祷上天延长老人的寿命同健康，使他自己能够享受这个。""我将西门，我第三个儿子，托他的哥哥照呼，此外还给他四千金镑。""唉！父亲，"西门喊道（绝对是很沉痛地），"愿上天给你寿命同健康，使你自己能够享受这个！"最后，转过向可怜的狄克，"至于你，你一向是一个整天嘻嘻哈哈的人，你是永不会变好的，你是永不会发财的，我给一先令做买吊绳用。""唉！父亲，"狄克喊道，没有露出什么哀情，"愿上天给你寿命同健康，使你自己能够享受这个！"除开说这句话外，财产的失掉对于这位无忧无虑的粗忽家伙简单〔直〕是没有影响。可是，一位叔父的软心肠补偿了父亲的冷淡；狄克因此不单是脾气极好，并且也都还富有。

The world, in short, may cry out at a bankrupt who appears at a ball; at an author who laughs at the public which pronounces him a dunce; at a general who smiles at the reproach of the vulgar, or the lady who keeps her good humour in spite of[1] scandal; but such is the wisest behaviour they can possibly assume; it is certainly a better way to oppose calamity by dissipation, than to take up the arms of reason or resolution to oppose it: by the first method we forget our miseries, by the last we only canceal them from others; by struggling with misfortunes we are sure to receive some wounds in the conflict. The only methed to come off[2] victorious is by running away.

---

1 in spite of: notwithstanding 虽然。
2 to come off: to emerge from action 终成。

总之，世界尽可以讥诮一个出现在跳舞场里的破产者，一个把说他是个蠢货的公众付之一笑的文学家，一个对着庸俗的责难微笑的将军或者一个不管人们怎样造谣，始终保持着她的好脾气的太太；但是这些是他俩所能做到的聪明办法，用消散来抵制灾难绝对是比拿着理性或者决心的武器来抵制灾难高明得多了：用第一个法子我们忘记了我们的苦楚，用下一个法子我们只是将苦楚隐藏起来，使别人看不见；并且同不幸去奋斗我们在冲突时一定会受些创伤。竞争得胜的惟一好法却是逃走。

Charles Lamb

A Bachelor's Complaint of the Behaviour of Married People

As a single man, I have spent a good deal[1] of my time in noting down the infirmities of Married People, to console myself for those superior pleasures which they tell me I have lost by remaining as I am.

I cannot say that the quarrels of men and their wives ever made any great impression upon me, or had much tendency to strengthen me in those antisocial resolutions which I took up long ago upon more substantial considerations.[2] What oftenest offends me at the

---

1 a good deal: a large quantity 好多。

2 兰姆在二十一岁时候，比他长十岁的姊姊玛利·兰姆一天忽然发狂起来，拿桌上的餐刀要刺一女仆，当她母亲来劝止时候，她母亲却被误杀了。玛利此后每年中常有一两月发狂。其余的时候又是很好，所以兰姆不

一个单身汉对于结了婚的人们的行为的怨言

我是一个单身汉,一向费了好多时间,去记下"结了婚的人们"的缺点,借此来安慰自己。因为他们告诉我,我始终过现在这种生活,是失丢了许多高尚的快乐。

我不能说人们同他们妻子的吵嘴曾经给我什么很深的印象,或者怎样地更坚固我这类与社会组织相冲突的主意,这类主意我是早就打定的,却是为着一个更结实的理由。走到结了婚的

忍把她关在疯人院里,情愿自己一生不娶亲,一心一意地去招呼她,因为他知道自己一结婚,对于他的姊姊就不能那么尽心了。

houses of married persons where I visit, is an error of quite a different description; — it is, that they are too loving.

Not too loving neither: that does not explain my meaning. Besides, why should that offend me? The very act of separating themselves from she rest of the world,to have the fuller enjoyment of each other's society, implies that they prefer one another to all the world.

But what I complain of is, that they carry[1] this preference so undisguisedly, they perk it up[2] in the faces of[3] us single people so shamelessly, you cannot be in their company a moment without being made to feel, by some indirect hint or open avowal, that you are not the object of this preference. Now there are some things which give no offence, while implied or taken for granted[4] merely; but expressed, there is much offense in them. If a man were to accost the first homely-featured or plain-dressed young woman of his acquintance, and tell her bluntly that she was not handsome or rich enough for him, and he could not marry her, he would deserve to be kicked for his ill manners; yet no less is implied in the fact, that having access and opportunity of putting the question to[5] her, he has never

---

1 to carry: to display 夸示。
2 to perk it up: to obtrude it 排场。
3 in the face of: in the presence of 当面。
4 to take for granted: to assume as true 姑以为然。
5 to put the question to: to ask in marriage 求婚。

人们的家里,最常使我生气的是一种和这个大不相同的错误——他们太相爱了。

也不是太相爱了:这句话不能够说清我的意思。并且,我何必因此生气呢?他俩为着要更亲密地彼此相伴,把自己两个同世上别人分开,单单这种举动早已含有他俩彼此偏爱胜过世上一切人的意思。

可是我所不满意的是他们那样不隐藏地现出他们的偏爱,他们那样无耻地在我们单身汉面前排场,你只须同他们一起一会儿,他们绝对要使你觉到,用些间接的讽示或者分明的直言,"你"不是这个偏爱的对象。有些事情当暗暗地含在意内或者仅仅姑以为然时,并不会开罪于人;可是一说出来,那就存有不少的侮辱意思了。若使一个人跑去招呼他最初认识的长得不漂亮或者穿得不讲究的年青姑娘,蠢钝地对她说她的容貌或者财产配不上他,这种人真该挨踢,因为他太无礼了;可是这个意思也同样包含在这件事实里面,当他有向她求婚的路子同机会,

yet thought fit to do it. The young woman understands this as clearly as if it were put into words; but no reasonable young woman would think of making this the ground¹ of a quarrel. Just as little right have a married couple to tell me by speeches, and looks that are scarce less plain than speeches, that I am not the happy man — the lady's choice. It is enough that I know I am not; I do not want this perpetual reminding.

The display of superior knowledge or riches may be made sufficiently mortifying; but these admit of a palliative. The knowledge which is brought out to insult me, may accidentally improve me; and in the rich man's houses and pictures — his parks and gardens — I have a temporary usufruct² at least. But the display of married happiness has none of these palliatives; it is throughout pure, unrecompensed, unqualified insult.

Marriage by its best title³ is a monopoly, and not of the least invidious sort⁴. It is the cunning of most possessors of any exclusive privilege to keep their advantage as much out of sight as possible,

---

1 ground: reason 理由。

2 usufruct: right of enjoyment 对于他人财产的暂享权。

3 by its best title: even according to its strongest claim 就是照它的最强的理由说去。

4 not of the least invidious sort: one of the most invidious kind 最招忌的一种。

却始终没有想向她求婚。这位年青姑娘也会很明白地知道了这个意思，可是没有个明理的年青姑娘会想拿这个来做吵嘴的理由。同样地一对结了婚的人们没有什么权利，配用话或者同说出的话差不多是一样地分明的脸孔来告诉我，我不是那种有幸福的人——姑娘所中意的人。我自知我不是那种的人，这已经是很够了；我不爱受这样继续不断的提醒。

炫学同夸富可以弄得使别人很难堪，但是它们还能够有点好处。特意搬出来做侮辱我用的学问或者偶然会增长我知识；在富人的屋里，在许多古画中间——在他的猎苑同花园里——我最少有暂时享用的权利。但是结婚幸福的夸示却连这些聊以减轻苦痛的好处都没有；那是种十分道地，没有补偿，没有限制的侮辱。

结婚，就是从最好的方面去着想，也只是一种独占，而且是一种最易招忌的独占。一般得到什么独享的权利的人们常有一条狡计，他们尽力地使人们看不到他们所占的便宜，这么一

that their less favoured neighbours, seeing little of the benefit, may the less be disposed to question the right. But these married monopolists thrust the most obnoxious part of their patent[1] into our faces.

Nothing is to me more distasteful than that entire complacency and satisfaction which beam in the countenances of a new-married couple — in that of the lady particularly: it tells you, that her lot is disposed of in this world; that you can have no hopes of her. It is true, I have none; nor wishes either, perhaps; but this is one of those truths which ought, as I said before, to be taken for granted, not expressed.

The excessive airs[2] which those people give themselves, founded on the ignorance of us unmarried people, would be more offensive if they were less irrational. We will allow them to understand the mysteries belonging to their own craft better than we who have not had the happiness to be made free of the company[3]; but their arrogance is not content within these limits. If a single person presume to offer his opinion in their presence, though upon the most indifferent subject, he is immediately silenced as an incompetent person. Nay, a young married lady of my acquaintance, who, the best of the

---

1 patent: sole right or privilege 专利。
2 airs: affected manners 装出来的神气, 作此解释时, 常居复数。
3 to be made free of the company: to be admitted to the rights and privileges 得享权利。

来那班运气赶不到他们的人们既是不大看出他们所得到的好处，或者会因此不大想去争这个权利。但是这群婚姻上的独占者却反将他们的独享权的最可憎的部分强放在我们面前。

天下里我所最讨厌的是新婚夫妇脸上射出的十分自得同满意，——尤其是在姑娘方面：那是等于告诉你，她在世界上已经得个归宿，"你"不能够再对于她有什么希望了。的确，我是没有希望的；也许我并不希望。但是这是属于那类事实，应当像我前面所说的，认为大家知道的，不该明说出来。

这班人们常拿出顶骄傲的神气，以为我们没有结过婚的人们对于许多事情是没有经验的，若使这种神气不是那样子不合理的，却会叫我更感到不快。我们肯承认他们对于本行的神秘，是比没有福气享受那权利的我们更懂得透彻；可是他们不甘于拘束在这个范围里面。若使一个单身汉敢在他们面前说出自己的意见，虽然是关于最不相干的题目，他们会立刻止住他的口，以为是个没有说话资格的人。不，我认得有一个结了婚的年青

jest¹ was, had not changed her condition² above a fortnight before, in a question on which I had the misfortune to differ from her, respecting the properest mode of breeding oysters for the London market, had the assurance to ask, with a sneer, how such an old Bachelor as I could pretend to know anything about such matters.

But what I have spoken of hitherto is nothing to the airs which these creatures give themselves when they come, as they generally do, to³ have children. When I consider how little of a rarity children are — that every street and blind alley⁴ swarms with them — that the poorest people commonly have them in most abundance — that there are few marriages that are not blest with at least one of these bargains — how often they turn out⁵ ill and defeat the fond⁶ hopes of their parents, taking to⁷ vicious courses, which end in poverty, disgrace the gallows, &c. — I cannot for my life⁸ tell what cause for pride there can possibly be in having them. If they were young phoenixes indeed, that were born but one in a year, there might be a pretext. But when they are so common —

---

1 the best of the jest: the most ridiculous point 最可发噱的地方。
2 to change one's condition: to get married 结婚。
3 to come to: once to begin to 开始有。
4 blind alley: a passage which has no outlet 死胡同。
5 to turn out: to be proved to be 结果是。
6 fond: foolish 傻的。

姑娘，最可笑的是她出嫁还不到两星期，当讨论一个问题时候，我不幸同她的意见相反，那是关于销卖给伦敦住民的蚝要怎样培养才是最适当的，她居然冷笑一声问我，像我这样一个老单身汉怎配说也懂得些这类的事情。

  我前面所讲的可说是算不得什么，若使拿来同这班东西后来的气焰一比较，当他们开始生了小孩子时候，他们多半是会有小孩子的。我一想到小孩子是多么普通的东西——每条街同死胡同里总是有一大群的小孩——最穷的人们在这方面常常是最富有的——结婚了而得不到这种宝贝的人们是多么少数的——多么常见，这班小孩子长大时候变坏了，使他们父母的一场痴望终于落空，走上罪恶的路，结果是穷困，丢脸，上绞架等等——我实在说不出，就是要我的命，也是说不出生了小孩会有什么值得骄傲的地方。若使小孩子真真是雏凤，世界上一年只生一个，那还可以有个借口。但是当他们是这么普通——

---

7 to take to：to be inclined to 倾向于。
8 for one's life：for the purpose of saving one's life 为着救我自己的性命。

I do not advert to the insolent merit which they assume with their husbands on these occasions. Let them look to that. But why we, who are not their natural-born subjects, should be expected to bring out spices, myrrh, and incense — our tribute and homage of admiration, — I do not see.

"Like as the arrows in the hand of the giant, even so are the young children." So says the excellent office[1] in our Prayer-book appointed for the churching[2] of women. "Happy is the man that hath his quiver full of them." So say I; but then don't let him discharge his quiver upon us that are weaponless; — let them be arrows, but not to gall and stick us. I have generally observed that these arrows are double-headed: they have two forks, to be sure to hit with one or the other. As for instance, when you come into a house which is full of children, if you happen to take no notice of them (you are thinking of something else, perhaps, and turn a deaf ear to[3] their innocent caresses), you are set down[4] as untractable, morose, a hater of children. On the other hand, if you find them more than usually engaging — if you are taken with[5] their pretty manners, and

---

1　office：form of prayer 祈祷文。

2　to church：to perform a church service in thanking for safe delivery 产后到教堂去，行感谢礼。

3　to turn a deaf ear to：to ignore 不理会。

4　to be set down：to be registered 断定。

5　to be taken with：to like 喜欢。

我并不是说到生了小孩子后,她们对于丈夫的居功。这件事让他们自己去管。但是为什么不是她们的天生奴隶的"我们"也该献上香料,没药同乳香——我们的贡物同表示我们赞美的敬礼,——我真是莫名其妙。

"少年时所生的儿女,好像勇士手中的箭。"我们"诗篇"里指定给女人产后感谢式时候用的优美的祈祷文是这样说。"箭袋充满的人便是有福。"我也是这样说;但是可不要让他将满袋的箭朝着没有武器的我们发射;——就让他们化做一束的箭罢,可是不要来擦伤我们,刺杀我们。我常常看出这类箭是带有两个箭镞的:它们有两个铁叉,这个打不准时,那个一定会打准。比如,当你走到一个住满了小孩子的家庭,若使你刚好没有去采〔睬〕他们(你或者心里想着别种事情,不去理他们天真的拥抱),他们就断定你是个顽梗的,怪癖〔脾〕气的,小孩子的厌恶者。反过来说,若使你觉得他们是特别有趣的——若使你爱上了他们可喜的态度,认真地来同他们一起乱跳乱闹,他们

set about[1] in earnest to romp and play with them, some pretext or other is sure to be found for sending them out of the room: they are too noisy or boisterous, or Mr. — does not like children. With one or other of these forks the arrow is sure to hit you.

I could forgive their jealousy, and dispense with toying with their brats, if it gives them pain; but I think it unreasonable to be called upon[2] to love them, where I see no occasion, — to love a whole family, perhaps eight, nine, or ten, indiscriminately — to love all the pretty dears, because children are so engaging.

I know there is a proverb, "love me, love my dog;" that is not always so very practicable, particularly if the dog be set upon[3] you to tease you or snap at you in sport[4]. But a dog or a lesser thing, — any inanimate substance, as a keepsake, a watch, or a ring, a tree, or the place where we last parted when my friend went away upon a long absence, I can make shift[5] to love, because I love him, and anything that reminds me of him; provided it be in its nature indifferent, and apt to receive whatever hue fancy can give it. But children have

---

1 to set about: to begin 开始。
2 to be called upon: to be demanded 来要求。
3 to be set upon: to be incited 受人唆使。
4 in sport: for diversion 开玩笑。
5 to make shift: to contrive 设法。

的父母一定要找出些理由,将他们调动出房外:故意说他们嚷得太利害了,或者是喧闹得太过了,或者说——先生是不喜欢小孩子的。用这个,或者用那个铁镞,那支箭总能够打伤了你。

我能够原谅他们的猜忌,情愿不去玩弄他们的小孩子,若使他们因此感到什么痛苦;但是我想那是很无理的,要我去"爱"他们的小孩子,当我看不出有什么可爱的地方,——要我盲目地去爱全家的人,或者八个,或者九个,甚至于十个,——去爱所有顶乖的宝宝,因为小孩子是这么有趣的。

我知道有句俗谚说,"若使你爱我,请你也爱我的狗";这不是老是那么容易实行的,尤其是若使那狗受了唆使来跟你捣乱,或者咬你来开玩笑。但是一只狗,或者一件更细微的东西,——随便什么无生命的东西,像一件纪念物,一架表或者一个指环,一口树,或者当我朋友将出外要好久才能回来,我们最后握别的地方,我能够因为我爱他,而设法去爱这些东西,以及凡是会使我记起他的东西;不过这些东西本身要没有什么意义的,容易接收想像所给它的色彩才行。可是小孩子们有一个实实在

a real character and essential being of themselves: they are amiable or unamiable per se[1], I must love or hate them as I see cause for either in their qualities. A child's nature is too serious a thing to admit of its being regarded as a mere appendage to another being, and to be loved or hated accordingly: they stand with me upon their own stock[2], as much as men and women do. Oh! But you will say, sure it is an attractive age — there is something in the tender years of infancy that of itself[3] charms us. That is the very reason why I am more nice[4] about them. I know that a sweet child is the sweetest thing in nature, not even excepting the delicate creatures which bear them; but the prettier the kind of a thing is, the more desirable it is that it should be pretty of its kind. One daisy differs not much from another in glory; but a violet should look and smell the daintiest. — I was always rather squeamish in my women and children.

But this is not the worst: one must be admitted into their familiarity, at least, before they can complain of inattention. It implies visits, and some kind of intercourse. But if the husband be a man with whom you have lived on a friendly footing[5] before marriage — if

---

1 per se: by itself 本身。
2 upon one's own stock: on one's own value 靠着自己的价值。
3 of itself: in itself 本身。
4 nice: fastidious 吹毛求疵。
5 footing: one's relation to others 与人们的关系。

在的性格，他们自己有个不可磨灭的本性：他们是可爱的，还是不可爱的，全靠他们自己的价值；我爱他们或者嫌他们，一定要照着我看他们的性质内有什么可爱或者可嫌的理由。一个小孩子的性格是太重要的一件东西，绝不能够把它只看做别人的一个附属品，跟着来受我的爱憎：据我看来，小孩子却有他们自己的价值，像大人们一样。呵！你又要说，但是他们的确是正在可爱的时期——小孩子在稚年时候真有种迷住我们的魔力。不错，所以我对于他们格外苛求得利害。我知道一个甜蜜可爱的小孩子是自然界里最甜蜜可爱的东西，甚至于比他们的幽娴织〔纤〕弱的母亲还要可爱；但是一类的东西越是悦意，我们越想得到那类中间最悦意的分子。一朵雏菊在艳丽方面跟别一朵没有什么多大的分别；可是紫罗兰却该找那色香都是最精美的。——我对于所认得的女人同小孩子也总是喜欢这样子加以挑剔。

　　但是这还不是顶坏的：最少她们先要让你同她们很亲密，她们才能说你对于小孩子的冷淡。她们总还让你去拜望她们同相当的来往。可是若使那丈夫没有结婚以前一向同你是很有交

you did not come in on the wife's side — if you did not sneak into the house in her train, but were an old friend in fast[1] habits of intimacy before their courtship was so much as thought on — look about you[2] — your tenure is precarious — before a twelvemonth shall roll over your head, you shall find your old friend gradually grow cool and altered towards you, and at last seek opportunities of breaking with you. I have scarce a married friend of my acquaintance, upon whose firm faith I can rely, whose friendship did not commence after the period of his marriage. With some limitations they can endure that; but that the good man[3] should have dared to enter into a solemn league of friendship in which they were not consulted, though it happened before they knew him — before they that are now man and wife ever met — this is intolerable to them. Every long friendship, every old authentic intimacy, must be brought into their office to be new stamped with their currency, as a sovereign Prince calls in the good old money that was coined in some reign before he was born or thought of, to be new marked and minted with the stamp of his authority, before he will let it pass current[4] in the

---

1 fast: firm 坚固。
2 look about you: take care 小心。
3 good man: master of the house 这是古时候的用法，现在已经不通行了。
4 to pass current: to be generally used 通行。

情的——若使你不是从他的妻子而认得他——若使你不是偷偷地跟着她的裙裾到那家里，却是那家里的一个老朋友，素来是过从非常亲密的，那时他们的婚事简直还没有想到——可是你要当心——那个屋子的享有权你是随时有被夺的危险的——还不到一年，你就看出你的老朋友对于你渐渐冷淡了，态度也变更了，最后他就去找个机会来同你破裂。在所认识的结过婚了的朋友里，我能够信得过他们的恳挚的，几乎没有一个不是在他"结婚时期以后"我才和他生出交情的。在相当程度之下，她们能够忍受这类交情；但是若使丈夫居然敢同人结下了严重的友谊关系，而未曾向她们商量过，虽然那时她还没有认识他——他们现在是夫妇了，那时却还没有见过面——她们觉得这是不可忍耐的。每个有很久历史的友谊，每个靠得住的老交情都得拿到她们的公事房里，按着她们的制度重新盖印过，好像一个皇帝下令将前朝（那时他还没有出世，或者谁也没有想到将来会有他这个人）铸的良好的老钱要重新印过铸过，加上他的朝号，然后才让它通行世界。你们可以猜出在那些"新铸的人物"

world. You may guess what luck generally befalls such a rusty piece of metal[1] as I am in these new mintings.

Innumerable are the ways which they take to insult and worm[2] you out of their husband's confidence. Laughing at all you say with a kind of wonder, as if you were a queer kind of fellow that said good things, but an oddity, is one of the ways; — they have a particular kind of stare for the purpose; — till at last the husband, who used to defer to your judgment, and would pass over some excrescences[3] of understanding and manner for the sake of a general vein[4] of observation (not quite vulgar) which he perceived in you, begins to suspect whether you are not altogether a humorist — a fellow well enough to have consorted with in his bachelor days, but not quite so proper to be introduced to ladies. This may be called the staring way; and is that which has oftenest been put in practice against me.

Then there is the exaggerating way, or the way of irony; that is, where they find you an object of especial regard with their husband, who is not so easily to be shaken from the lasting[5] attachment founded on esteem which he has conceived towards you; by never-

---

1 such a rusty piece of metal: such an old-fashioned fellow 这么一个古老人儿。
2 to worm: to trick 愚弄。
3 excrescences: extravagances 荒诞。
4 vein: quality 性质。
5 lasting: durable 耐久。

里面像我这样一个锈色斑烂的古板家伙常常会碰到什么运气。

她们有数不尽的法子,来欺侮你同瞒骗她们的丈夫,使他对于你失丢了信任。无论你说什么,她总是装做很惊愕的样子大笑,仿佛你是个会说俏皮话的怪物,但是的确是"一个奇人";——这是一个法子;——她们有一种特别的睇视专做这个用;——她们的丈夫本来是很顺从你的主张,愿意忽视你的意见同态度上有些古怪的地方,因为他看出你通常的想头(也不十分粗俗)到〔倒〕还不错,现在却开始怀疑你到底是不是一个完完全全的滑稽家——那种人是他当单身汉时候的好伴侣,但是若使介绍给姑娘们,却有点不大好。这个可以叫做"睇视"的法子,是最常用来抵抗我的。

此处还有个"形容过实"的法子,或者可以叫做"反语"的法子;那是当她们看出你是她们丈夫所特别看重的人,知道他那种坚固的交情不是这样容易地可以动摇的,因为那是建设于他对于你的尊敬上面;于是你每回讲一句话或者做一件事,

qualified exaggerations to cry up[1] all that you say or do, till the good man, who understands well enough that it is all done in compliment to[2] him, grows weary of the debt of gratitude which is due to so much candour, and by relaxing a little on his part, and taking down a peg or two[3] in his enthusiasm, sinks at length[4] to that kindly level of moderate esteem — that "decent affection and complacent kindness" towards you where she herself can join in sympathy with him without much stretch and violence to her sincerity.

Another way (for the ways they have to accomplish so desirable a purpose are infinite) is, with a kind of innocent simplicity, continually to mistake what it was which first made their husband fond of you. If an esteem for something excellent in your moral character was that which riveted the chain which she is to break, upon any imaginary discovery of a want of poignancy in your conversation she will cry, "I thought, my dear, you described your friend Mr. — as a great wit." If, on the other hand, it was for some supposed charm in your conversation that he first grew to like you, and was content for this to overlook some trifling irregularities in your moral deportment, upon the first notice of any of these she as readily exclaims, "This, my dear, is your good Mr.—." One good lady whom

---

1 to cry up: to extol 赞美。
2 in compliment to: to gratify 使喜悦。
3 to take down a peg or two: to bring lower 弄低一点。

她们就拼命地言过于实地赞美,她们的丈夫也很明白这全是为着要悦他的意,心里自然很感激她这么慷慨的举动,等到后来他对于自己不断的感激生了厌倦,就将他的友谊放松一些,把他对于你的热情降下几度,一直堕落到对你只存一种普通的好感,只具有个适度的尊重——一种"相当的感情同皮面的厚意";这种态度她才能够跟他同情,不至于损害到她的至诚。

还有一个法子(她们达到这么可爱的目的的法子是无穷的)是假装天真无知的神气,老是故意看错她们丈夫起先所以会爱你是为了什么。若使他是为钦重你的道德,才来同你结缔她现在所要打断的关系,她会随意发现出你的说话是太不俏皮了,高声地叫道:"我记得,我亲爱的,你说你的朋友——先生是一个大滑稽家。"反过来说,若使他是因为你的谈吐好像很有些妙处,才开始来喜欢你,因此愿意宽恕你在道德方面细微的不轨,她却一看出你这些毛病,就立刻喊道:"我亲爱的,这是你所谓

---

4 at length:at last 最后。

I took the liberty of expostulating with for not showing me quite so much respect as I thought due to her husband's old friend, had the candour to confess to me that she had often heard Mr.— speak of me before marriage, and that she had conceived a great desire to be acquainted with me, but that the sight of me had very much disappointed her expectations; for from her husband's representations of me she had formed a notion that she was to see a fine, tall, officer-like looking man (I use her very words); the very reverse of which proved to be the truth. This was candid; and I had the civility not to ask her in return, how she came to hitch upon[1] standard of personal accomplishments for her husband's friends which differed so much from his own; for my friend's dimensions as near as possible approximate to mine: he standing five feet five in his shoes, in which I have the advantage of him by about half an inch; and he no more than myself exhibiting any indications of a martial character in his air or countenance.

These are some of the mortifications which I have encountered in the absurd attempt to visit at their houses. To enumerate them all would be a vain endeavour, I shall therefore just glance at the very common impropriety of which married ladies are guilty — of treating us as if we were their husbands, and vice versa[2], I mean, when they

---

1 to hitch upon: to hit upon 得到。
2 vice versa: conversely, i.e. treating their husbands as visitors 互易亦然。

道德完好的——先生。"我曾经大胆地对一位太太理论，说她待我的礼貌有差，没有把我当作她丈夫的老朋友看待，她倒是很老实地向我自认，她在没有结婚以前常听到——先生说我，她就很想同我认识，但是一见到我，却大使她失望；因为从她丈夫所说的关于我的话，她造成一个观念，以为她要看到一个漂亮的，长得很高的，有军官的仪态的男子（我用她自己的话）；而事实却刚刚是相反的。这可说是很坦白的谈话；我却有点客气，没有去报复她，问她怎么会忽然间对于她丈夫的朋友的外貌有一个同她丈夫自己的外貌这样不同的标准；因为我朋友的身材同我是再相近也没有了：他穿着鞋子时候有五尺五寸高，我却占了便宜，比他差不多高了半寸；他在态度同脸孔上是同我一样地没有现出什么英武性格的表征。

这些不过是我傻瓜地跑去拜访他们时候所挨的侮辱的几种。要想把那许多的侮辱一个一个说出，那是办不到的事，所以我现在只将结了婚的姑娘们最常患的一种失礼稍为提一下，那是待我们仿佛是她们的丈夫，待她们的丈夫又仿佛是她们的客人。

use us with familiarity, and their husbands with ceremony. Testacea, for instance, kept me the other night two or three hours beyond my usual time of supping, while she was fretting because Mr.— did not come home till the oysters were all spoiled, rather than she would be guilty of the impoliteness of touching one in his absence. This was reversing the point[1] of good manners, for ceremony is an invention to take off the uneasy feeling which we derive from knowing ourselves to be less the object of love and esteem with a fellow-creature than some other person is. It endeavours to make up[2] by superior attentions in little points, for that invidious preference which it is forced to deny in the greater. Had Testacea kept the oysters back for me, and withstood her husband's importunities to go to supper, she would have acted according to the strict rules of propriety. I know no ceremony that ladies are bound to observe to their husbands, beyond the point of a modest behaviour and decorum, therefore I must protest against the vicarious gluttony[3] of Cerasia, who at her own table sent away a dish of morellas[4], which I was applying to[5] with great good-will[6] to her husband at the other end of the table,

---

  1 the point: the essential matter 要义。
  2 to make up: to compensate 补偿。
  3 vicarious gluttony: greediness exhibited in behalf of another 替别人弄得许多食物。
  4 morellas: one kind of cherries 一种樱桃。

我是说她们对我们很随便，对她们的丈夫却很客气。比如忒斯他西亚有一天晚上使我等到比我通常晚餐时间迟两三个钟头，她在那里所焦急的却是——先生还没有还家，弄得那晚上所吃的蚝因为放了太久，全变味了，可是她总不肯对她的丈夫失礼，在他还未回家以前开宴。这是把礼貌的意义弄颠倒了，因为礼貌的产生是为着要免去一种不安的感觉，那是当我们知道自己在别一个人的眼里不如另外一个人那样可爱可敬时候所感到的。他在细微事情方面对你加倍殷勤，想用此来补偿在重要地方他那种可妒忌的偏爱却是不能给你。若使忒斯他西亚将蚝留着给我吃，拒绝了她丈夫的先行开宴的要求，那么她的举动是非常合理的。我不知道在贞娴态度同端庄举止之外，做妻子的对于她们的丈夫还要拘什么别的礼貌，所以我一定要反对塞拉西亚的为虎作伥的饕餮，她在自己家里的餐桌上，将我吃得正津津有味的一碟摩勒拉斯地方的樱桃拿去，送到坐在桌子那端的她

---

5 applying to：partaking of 享受。
6 with good-will：heartily 很带劲地。

and recommended a plate of less extraordinary gooseberries to my unwedded palate in their stead. Neither can I excuse the wanton affront of —.

But I am weary of stringing up all my married acquaintance by Roman decominations.[1] Let them amend and change their manners, or I promise to record the full-length English of their names to the terror of all such desperate offenders in future.

---

1 兰姆前面所提的几个名字都是罗马人们所用的名字。他把真名隐去,用这些假名来代。据说全是实有其人,惯会疏注名家文集的学究们都能一一举出真名字来,他们还因为所举的人不同而互相吵架,总之是一百年前的几位死鬼而已。

的丈夫面前,却换一盘没有那么神妙的洋莓给我的没有尝过结婚乐趣的味觉。我也不能原谅那种轻佻的无礼,那是一位——

可是我已厌倦于这样用罗马的古名来将我所认得的结了婚的朋友一一揭示出来。让他们自己去悔过,改换他们的态度,否则我是要把他们真名字的英文字母全写出来,使这类横行无忌的罪人将来有所忌惮。

William Hazlitt

On the Fear of Death

"And our little life is rounded with a sleep."[1]

Perhaps the best cure for the fear of death is to reflect that life has a beginning as well as[2] an end. There was a time when we were[3] not: this gives us no concern — why, then, should it trouble us that a time will come when we shall cease to be[4]? I have no wish to have been alive a hundred years ago, or in the reign of Queen Anne[5]: why

---

1 这是莎士比亚名剧 *Tempest* 里的名句，to be rounded with: to be finished with 来作结束。

2 as well as: no less than 不下于，等于。

3 to be: to exist 生存。

4 to cease to be: to die 死亡。

5 Queen Anne (1664—1714)，英国的女皇，她在位时，英国文人极盛，英国散文可说是在她朝里才成为完善的文学工具。说也奇怪，英国的

死 的 恐 惧

"我们短促的生命是以一场大睡来结束的。"

死的恐惧的最好医法或者是去想生命是有一个开头的,好像它是有个结局。有个时期我们是没有存在的:这却没有使我们有什么难过——那么,为什么我们要觉得烦恼,一想到将来有个时期,我们的生命会告了终止?我并不希望一百年前,在安女皇朝代,我就已经活在人世:为什么我要那么惋惜,心中

诗是在伊利沙伯女皇朝达到尽美尽善的境界,英国的小说是在维多利亚女皇朝才有名家辈出。诗、散文、小说三种文学都是在女皇时代大放异彩,真是仿佛女皇同文学的发达有特别的关系一样。

should I regret and lay it so much to heart[1] that I shall not be alive a hundred years hence, in the reign of I cannot tell whom?

When Bickerstaff[2] wrote his Essays I knew nothing of the subjects of them; nay, much later, and but the other day, as it were, in the beginning of the reign of George III, when Goldsmith[3], Johnson[4], Burke[5], used to meet as the Globe, when Garrick[6] was in his glory, and Reynolds[7] was over head and ears[8] with his portraits, and Sterne[9] brought out the volumes of *Tristram Shandy* year by year, it was without consulting me: I had not the slightest intimation of what was going on[10]: the debates in the House of Commons on the American War, or the firing at Bunker's Hill[11], disturbed not me: yet I thought

---

1 to lay to heart: to be deeply concerned about 戚戚于心，挂念。

2 Bickerstaff 这个名字是刻毒的 Swift 用的假名，当他写文章同一个做历书的人为难时候。后来 Steele 写小品文时，也常常自称为 Mr. Bickerstaff（《伉俪幸福》中他的妹妹就叫他作 Bickerstaff），所以这里是指 Richard Steele。

3 Goldsmith, Oliver (1728—1774), 他是十八世纪里最可爱的文人，年青时候浪迹欧洲，靠着吹箫、雄辩等杂技度日，后来回到英国行医，没有生意，只得借着卖稿混日子。他著有一本谁也晓得的长篇小说《威克斐尔牧师传》(*The Vicar of Wakefield*), 二篇长诗，几部戏剧，几百篇绝妙的小品文（我们前面也有一篇）同许多数不尽的七古八怪杂书，那是专为钱而写的，现在只剩个考古的价值了。

4 Johnson, Samuel (1709—1784), 他是十八世纪里那个出色的大胖子，他著有一部字典，写了许多批评文字（《诗人传》）同不少的小品文（《悲哀》就是他写的）。

那样哀伤,一想到一百年后,在我不晓得是谁的朝代里,我是已经去世了?

当毕克斯达夫写他的小品文字时候,我并不晓得他写的是什么题目;不,还要近代些,好像就是前天的事,在乔治第三朝代,当哥德斯密,约翰生,柏尔克常在环球酒馆相会,当加立克正极盛时期,当棱诺尔咨埋头在他的人物写真里面,当斯腾将他的《特立斯特蓝·禅底》分年出版时候,这许多事情都未曾征求过我的同意,我丝毫也不知道当时有什么事情正在进行,下议院里关于美国战争的辩论同邦刻山上的开火也没有扰乱着我的方寸:可是我那时并不觉得这样情形有什么不对——

---

5 Burke, Edmund (1729—1797),他是英国一个大演说家,他还著一部批评名著 *Sublime and Beautiful*。

6 Garrick, David,参看《快乐多半是靠着性质》p60注1。

7 Reynolds, Sir Joshua (1723—1792),英国皇家学会第一任会长,当时最有名的画家,他又是约翰生的好朋友。

8 over head and ears:thoroughly engrossed 深陷在。

9 Sterne, Laurence (1713—1768),英国一个大小说家,他的杰作 *Tristram Shandy* 是一部怪书,里面有许多猥亵话,却又含有好多极精妙的对于人性的观察。

10 to be going on:to be getting on 进行。

11 Bunker's Hill 是美国革命首先起事的地方。

this no evil — I neither ate, drank, nor was merry, yet I did not complain: I had not then looked out into this breathing world, yet I was well; and the world did quite as well without me as I did without it! Why, then, should I make all this outcry about parting with it, and being no worse off[1] than I was before? There is nothing in the recollection that at a certain time we were not come into the world that "the gorge rises at"[2] — why should we revolt at[3] the idea that we must one day go out of it? To die is only to be as we were before we were born; yet no one feels any remorse, or regret, or repugnance, in contemplating this last idea. It is rather a relief and disburthening of the mind: it seems to have been holiday-time with us then: we were not called to appear upon the stage of life, to wear robes or tatters, to laugh or cry, be hooted or applauded; we had lain perdus[4] all this while, sung, out of harm's way[5]; and had slept out our thousands of centuries without wanting to be waked up; at peace and free from care, in a long nonage, in a sleep deeper and calmer than that of infancy, wrapped in the softest and finest dust. And the worst that we

---

1 badly off: in an unfortunate or undesirable condition 在个不幸的情境里。
2 one's gorge rises at: one is sickened by 为……作呕（厌恶的意思）。
3 to revolt at: to feel disgust 嫌恶。
4 to lie perdus: to lie hidden 隐藏。
5 out of harm's way: in a secure way 安全。

我也没有吃东西，也没有喝酒，也没有拼命作乐，但是我一句怨言也没有说：那时我还没有看到这个生气勃勃的世界，但是我也是好好地过去；世界没有我，并不感到什么不方便，同我没有世界，也不感到什么不方便是一样的！那么，为什么我要做出这许多凄呼惨号，因为将同这世界离别，又回到从前的境地里去？回想起在某一时期，我们是还没有来到这世界里，并不会使我们"胸中作呕"——为什么我们会起反感，一想到将来免不了有一天我们要走出这个世界？死去只是恢复到我们出世以前的境界；可是没有人觉得什么追悔，或者惋惜，或者憎恶，当他记起他曾有个未到世界的时期。那个时期到〔倒〕是一个很好的休息，使我们的心灵可以轻松一会儿，真好像我们的放假时期：我们那时用不着走上人生的舞台，去穿红着紫或者挂一件百结衣，去大笑或者哀啼，受人们的嘲骂或者捧场；那时我们偷偷地隐居着，舒服得很，远离开人世的灾难；我们睡了万万年，还不愿意被人叫醒；平平安安地，一些忧虑也没有，渡〔度〕个悠长的幼稚时代，我们那时的酣睡是比小孩子的睡眠还要深沉，还要恬静；隐存在最温柔，最美丽的尘埃里

dread is, after a short, fretful, feverish being, after vain hopes and idle fears, to sink to final repose again, and forget the troubled dream of life! ... Ye armed men, knights templars, that sleep in the stone aisles of that old Temple church[1] , where all is silent above, and where a deeper silence reigns below (not broken by the pealing organ), are ye not contented where ye lie? Or would you come out of your long homes to go to the Holy War[2]? Or do ye complain that pain no longer visits you, that sickness has done its worst, that you have paid the last debt to nature[3] , that you hear no more of the thickening phalanx of the foe, or your lady's waning love; and that while this ball of earth rolls its eternal round, no sound shall ever pierce through to disturb your lasting repose, fixed as the marble over your tombs, breathless as the grave that holds you! And thou, oh!Thou, to whom my heart turns, and will turn while it has feeling left, who didst love in vain, and whose first was thy last sigh, wilt not thou too rest in peace (or wilt thou cry to me complaining from thy clay-cold bed) when that sad heart is no longer sad, and that sorrow is dead which thou wert only called into the world to feel!

---

1 伦敦城里一个大教堂。
2 神圣战争就是十字军战争。
3 to pay the last debt to nature: to die 死亡。

面。我们现在所怕的最坏的却是一个短促，烦恼，发狂也似的生涯之后，在许多空虚的希望同无谓的恐惧之后，又沉到最后的安息里，忘却了人生这一场恶梦！……你们这班武士，十字军骑士，睡在古老的腾普尔礼拜堂的石廊里，在那里地上的空气是静寂寂的，在那里地下却有个更深沉的静寂（隆隆的琴声也达不到地下），你们睡在那里，还会有什么不满意吗？你们还想走出你们这个老家，再去加入"神圣的战争"吗？你们会不会诉苦，说苦痛也不来拜访你了，疾病已经是无法再来和你捣乱，你也还给自然这笔最后的债了，你不会再听到敌人的密密围来，或者你心爱的姑娘情谊日淡；并且当地球走它这个永久不停的循环时候，没有什么声音会穿过地面，来扰乱你们这最后的安眠，那是同你们墓上的大理石一样地坚固，同收容你们的坟墓一样地没有气息！还有你，唉！你，我心中所念念不忘的你，只要我的心还有感觉，我总不能够忘却的你，你的爱情是白用了，你第一次的叹气也就是你最后的叹气，你是不是也安宁地长眠（或者你还会从潮湿的土床里对我哭着诉怨），当现在你那黯淡的心也不会还感着黯淡，那个悲哀，因为要你感到那么悲哀，才叫你降生人生，也是已经消灭了！

It is certain that there is nothing in the idea of a pre-existent state that excites our longing like the prospect of a posthumous existence. We are satisfied to have begun life when we did; we have no ambition to have set out[1] on our journey sooner; and feel that we have had quite enough to do to battle our way through since. We cannot say,

"The wars we well remember of King Nine,

Of old Assaracus and Inachus divine."[2]

Neither have we any wish: we are contented to read of them in story, and to stand and gaze at the vast sea of time that separates us from them. It was early days then: the world was not well-aired[3] enough for us; we have no inclination to have been up[4] and stirring. We do not consider the six thousand years of the world before we were born as so much time lost to us: we are perfectly indifferent about the matter. We do not grieve and lament that we did not happen to be in time[5] to see the grand mask and pageant of human life going on[6] in all that period; though we are mortified at being obliged to quit

---

1 to set out: to start 出发。

2 智有所不明，数有所不逮，神有所不通，这两句里的三个人名，译者是有所不能注了。

3 to be aired: to be exposed to air 曝露在空气中。

4 to have been up: to have risen up 从床上起来。

5 in time: sufficiently early 刚刚赶得上。

6 going on: proceeding 前进。

的确，前生这个观念并没有含有什么，会像死后生活的预期那样子激动起我们的希望。我们并没有什么不满，以为我们的生命开始得太迟；我们没有更早些出发的野心；我们觉得就从我们出世的时期起，一路奋斗下去，我们已经是够有事情干了。我们当然不能说，

"我们记得很清楚奈因皇的战争，

那时苍老的亚沙腊卡斯同神圣的印那卡斯也曾加入。"

我们也不希望能够说这类的话：我们愿意单在故事里碰到他们，站起来，睁着眼睛看他们同我们所相隔的，茫茫似大海的悠悠岁月。那是太早的时代：世界还没有"晒好"，不配给我们居住；我们不想那时就已起床，去外面东跑西走。我们不把我们未出世以前的六千年世界光阴算做我所失掉的：对于这件事我们是一点儿也不关心。我们并不悲悼我们不凑巧，生得太晚，看不到这个长时代里人类生活的假装跳舞同形形色色的游行；虽然我们觉得心酸，因为我不得不走开我们站的地方，当这个

our stand[1] before the rest of the procession passes.

It may be suggested in explanation of this difference, that we know from various records and traditions what happened in the time of Queen Anne, or even in the reigns of the Assyrian[2] monarchs, but that we have no means of ascertaining what is to happen hereafter but by awaiting the event, and that our eagerness and curiosity are sharpened in proportion as[3] we are in the dark about it. This is not at all[4] the case; for at that rate[5] we should be constantly wishing to make a voyage of discovery to Greenland[6] or to the Moon, neither of which we have, in general, the least desire to do. Neither, in truth[7], have we any particular solicitude to pry into the secrets of futurity, but as a pretext for prolonging our own existence. It is not so much that we care to be alive a hundred or a thousand years hence, any more than to have been alive a hundred or a thousand years ago: but the thing lies here, that we would all of us wish the present moment to last for ever. We would be as we are, and would have the world remain just as it is, to please us.

---

1 stand: chosen standing ground 选择好了的站足地方。

2 Assyrian: of Assyria 亚述是美索不达米亚平原北部的一个国家，开国于公元前七五〇年，公元六〇六年被波斯马太加堤联军所灭。

3 in proportion as: according as 按照……为比例，依……程度而变。

4 at all: wholly 完全。

5 at that rate: in that case, under these circumstance 照这样子，在这情形之下。

大赛会还没有走完之前。

这两个态度的不同,或者有人要用下面这个道理来解释,我们从各种记录同传说,能够知道安女皇朝代里,或者甚至于亚述各朝里所发生的事情,但是我们没有法子去知道将来的事情,只好等着那件事情发生,我们的切望同好奇心会愈见热烈,愈是我们对于那件事情是莫名其妙的。这种说法是完全错误的;因为如果真是这样子,那么我们一定常常想到格林兰或者月球去探险,而我们通常却绝没有想干这些事情。说句真话,我们也没有怎样挂虑廑怀地去窥探将来的神秘,那不过做个延长自己的生命的借口是了。并不是因为我们怎样有意于在一百年后或者一千年后还活在人间,好像我们并不想在一百年前或者一千年前就已出世:真真的理由却是我们大家都希望现在这个刹那能够永久地延长下去。我们爱维持我们的现状,也希望世界能够老是这样子不变,为着来讨我们的欢心。

---

6 Greenland 是北美洲以北的一个大岛。
7 in truth:really 实在,确实。

"The present eye catches the present object —"
To have and to hold while it may; and abhors, on any terms[1], to have it torn from us, and nothing left in its room. It is the pang of parting, the unloosing our grasp, the breaking asunder some strong tie, the leaving some cherished purpose unfulfilled, that creates the repugnance to go, and "makes calamity of so long life"[2], as it often is.

"Oh! thou strong heart!
There's such a covenant 'twixt the world and thee
They're loth to break!"

The love of life, then, is an habitual attachment, not an abstract principle. Simply to be does not "content man's natural desire"; We long to be in a certain time, place, and circumstance. We would much rather be now, "on this bank and shoal of time," than have our choice of any future period, than take a slice of fifty or sixty years out of the Millennium[3], for instance. This shows that our attachment is not confined either to being or to well-being; but that we have an inveterate prejudice in favour of[4] our immediate existence, such as it

---

2 这是莎翁的 *Hamlet* 剧里 Prince Hamlet 有名的独语里的一句。

3 "我又看见几个宝座，也有坐在上面的，并有审判的权柄赐给他们。我又看见那些因为给耶稣作见证，并为上帝之道被斩者的灵魂，和那没有拜过兽与兽像，也没有在额上和手上受过他印记之人的灵魂。他们都复活了。与基督一同作一千年。"见《圣经·启示录》第二十章。

4 in favour of: in support of 赞助，帮忙。

"今天的眼睛只盯着今天的东西——"

占有着,紧紧地抓住,当能够办得到的时候;不管有多好的交换条件,总不愿意被剥夺去这个东西,什么也没有剩留下来。那是同尘寰永诀,放松我们的紧握,至亲密友,一旦分离,素志未酬,赍恨没地等等的苦痛才产生出这种对于去世的厌恶,"苦难因此得到长久的寿命",我们的确常常宁愿挨着苦难活在人世。

"呵!你这个英武的心!

世界和你立下有这样一个盟约

你们真是不愿意分离呀!"

所以生命的爱惜不过是一种已成习惯的依恋,并不是一个抽象的原则。单是"活着"不能"满足人们天然的欲望";我们切望能在某时期,某地方同某环境内活着。我们更愿意活在现在,"在时间之流的这边河岸和浅滩",不大愿从将来里挑出一个时期,不大愿,比如,从"千福年"里拿出五十年或者六十年一部分。这可以证明我们的依恋并不是对于"生存"或者"良好的生活"的;却是因为我们有个根深蒂固的成见,总觉得我们

is. The mountaineer will not leave his rock, nor the savage his hut; neither are we willing to give up[1] our present mode of life, with all its advantages and disadvantages, for any other that could be substituted for it. No man would, I think, exchange his existence with any other man, however fortunate. We had as lief[2] not be, as not be ourselves. There are some persons of that reach[3] of soul that they would like to live two hundred and fifty years hence, to see to what height of empire America will have grown up in that period, or whether the English constitution will last so long. These are points beyond me. But I confess I should like to live to see the downfall of the Bourbons[4]. That is a vital question with me; and I shall like it the better, the sooner it happens!

No young man ever thinks he shall die. He may believe that others will, or assent to the doctrine that "all men are mortal" as an abstract proposition, but he is far enough from[5] bringing it home[6] to himself individually. (All men think all men mortal but themselvs. —

---

1 to give up: to relinquish 舍弃,作罢。
2 as lief: as willingly 情愿。
3 reach: range 范围。
4 Bourbons 是当时法国皇家的姓。
5 far from: not at all 决非。
6 to bring it home: to make it vividly felt 使深印于人心。

目前的生活,像现在这样子,是最值得留恋的。山居的人不愿意离开他的岩石,野蛮人不愿离开他的草屋;我们也是不愿意弃掉当下的生活方式,包含一切它的好处同坏处,去采取任一种可以代它的别个方式。没有一个人,我想,情愿将他自己的生活同别人掉换,不管那个是多么有运气的。我们宁其"不活",而不肯"失丢了自己"。有些人们志高意远,他们希望在二百五十年后还是活着,去看一看在那时候,美国会发长成个多么伟大的国家,或者英国宪法能够不能够维持到那么久。这类意思是我所不能了解的。但是我自认我希望能够活着看波旁皇朝的倾覆。对于我这是个很重要的问题,愈早发生,我会愈觉得高兴!

没有一个青年的人曾经想过他将来是会死的。他或者会相信别人是会死的,也许肯同意于"人皆有死"这个学说,只当它做个抽象的命题,但是他绝不至于亲切地拿它来应用到自己身上。("人们都以为人们都是会死的,除开了他们自己。"

Young[1]) Youth, buoyant activity, and animal spirits[2], hold absolute antipathy with old age as well as with death; nor have we, in the heyday of life, any more than in the thoughtlessness of childhood, the remotest conception how

"This sensible warm motion can become

A kneaded clod —"

nor how sanguine, florid health and vigour, shall "turn to[3] withered, weak, and grey." Or if in a moment of idle speculation we indulge in this notion of the close of life as a theory, it is amazing at what a distance it seems; what a long, leisurely interval there is between; what a contrast its slow and solemn approach affords to our present gay dreams of existence! We eye[4] the farthest verge of the horizon, and think what a way we shall have to look back upon[5], ere we arrive at our journey's end; and without our in the least suspecting it, the mists are at our feet, and the shadows of age encompass us. The two divisions of our lives have melted into each other: the extreme points close and meet with none of that romantic interval stretching out between them that we had reckoned upon[6]; and for the rich,

---

1 Young, Edward (1684—1765), 英国诗人，他的诗句有许多变成了英国的谚语。

2 animal spirits: physical health and energy 身体健康和活力。

3 to turn to: to change into 变成。

4 to eye: to watch 望着。

5 to look back upon: to contemplate the past 回想，追想。

——杨）青春，活泼同血气对于老年是绝对的厌恶，对于死也是一样的；当我们在人生的兴高彩〔采〕烈时代，我们绝不比茫然无思的稚年，会更多些模糊的观念，知道怎样

"这个灵敏温暖的动体会变做

一块搓捏过了的泥土——"

也不能够晓得鲜艳多血的健康同精力会怎样子"变为枯槁，软弱同灰色"。若使在胡思乱想时候，我们拿生命的终止这个概念，当个理论，来想着好玩，这真是奇怪，那好像是多么遥遥无期的，内中有一个多么悠长闲暇的间隔；它那种慢慢的严肃的前进给我现在这种人生的美梦一个多么大的对照！我们望着那水平面最远的边际，心里想还用不着走到人生之路的极端，掉过头来，我们已可以看见走过有多么长的路途；可是当我们一些儿还没有料到时候，云雾却已经缠着我们的脚旁，暮年的黑影也围绕四周。我们生命的两段溶混为一：两个极端相碰，中间却没有我们所预期的浪漫时代；至于人们所谓的老年时悲

---

6 to reckon upon：to plan in confident expectation of 谋划，私自希冀。

melancholy, solemn hues of age, "the sear, the yellow leaf," the deepening shadows of an autumnal evening, we only feel a dank, cold mist, encircling all objects, after the spirit of youth is fled. There is no inducement to look forward[1], and what is worse, little interest in looking back to what has become so trite and common. The pleasures of our existance have worn themselves out[2], are "gone into the wastes of time," or have turned their indifferent side to us: the pains by their repeated blows have worn us out, and have left us neither spirit nor inclination to encounter them again in retrospect. We do not want to rip up[3] old grievances, nor to renew our youth like the phoenix[4], nor to live our lives twice over. Once is enough. As the tree falls, so let it lie. Shut up the book and close the account once for all!

It has been thought by some that life is like the exploring of a passage that grows narrower and darker the farther we advance, without a possibility of ever turning back, and where we are stifled for want of breath at last. For myself, I do not complain of the greater thickness of the atmosphere as I approach the narrow house. I felt it more formerly, when the idea alone seemed to suppress a

---

1 to look forward: to look into the future 预期，盼望。
2 to wear out: to exhaust 消耗。
3 to rip up: to recall 回忆，追想。
4 凤凰老时，积薪自焚，就又变成一只年青的凤凰了，这自然是属于神话的。

庄严肃的深浓光辉，所谓"枯黄的残叶"，所谓秋天黄昏的朦胧转暗的阴影，我们却只感到潮湿的冷雾，罩围着世上一切的东西，当青春精神已经消逝了的时候。世上没有什么，能够引起我们的向前瞻望；更可悲的是回首前尘，事事都变做那么陈腐同平庸，简直是一点儿意味也没有。我们生存的快乐已是自己消磨尽了，"成为时间上的陈迹"，不能够再鼓起我们的欣欢：苦痛不断地来袭，使我们倦于人生，弄得我们没有勇气，没有心情，肯在回忆中再同它们相见。我们不欲裂开从前的心灵伤痕，不欲像凤凰那样再恢复我们的青春，也不欲重渡〔度〕过去的生涯。一生已是很够了。树既是倒下了，就让它躺着罢。断然地把帐簿阖好，帐目结清，从此后再也不弄这种麻烦了！

有人以为人生是像探察一条甬道，我们走进去越远！那甬道就变得越狭窄，越黑暗，绝没有回身退出的可能，在那里我们最后因为着空气的缺乏而闷死。我个人并不觉得空气的更见浓密，当我走近那狭窄的部分。我年青时候还更感到这个苦处，那时单单死的观念好像就能够压下成千欣欣向荣的希望，使我

thousand rising hopes, and weighed upon the pulses of the blood. (I remember once, in particular, having this feeling in reading Schiller's *Don Carlos*[1] where there is a description of death, in a degree that almost stifled me.) At present I rather feel a thinness and want of support, I stretch out my hand to some object and find none, I am too much in a world of abstraction; the naked map of life is spread out before me, and in the emptiness and desolation I see Death coming to meet me. In my youth I could not behold him for the crowd of objects and feelings, and Hope stood always between us, saying, "Never mind[2] that old fellow!" If I had lived indeed, I should not care to die. But I do not like a contract of pleasure broken off unfulfilled, a marriage with joy unconsummated, a promise of happiness rescinded. My public and private hopes have been left a ruin, or remain only to mock me. I would wish them to be re-edified. I should like to see some prospect of good to mankind, such as my life began with.[3] I should like to leave some sterling work behind me. I should like to have some friendly hand to consign me to the grave. On these conditions I am ready, if not willing, to depart. I shall then write on

---

1 Schiller, J. C. Friedrich von (1759—1805),德国大戏剧家及大诗人,*Don Carlos* 是一部诗剧。

2 never mind: pay no attention to 不足介意,不要紧。

3 Hazlitt 生时正值法国革命爆发,人人都怀着希望,以为从此以后再不会有专制的政府了。

血管里的脉搏都见消沉。(我特别记得有一回我有这种感觉,当我念着席勒尔的《卡罗斯皇子》时候,里面有一段死的描写,写得使我差不多难过得通不出气来。)现在我却觉得世界的稀薄,找不出什么,可以做人生的支柱,我伸出我的手,想去抓点东西,却什么也没有得到,我太住在抽象的世界里了;人生的赤裸裸真相排在我的跟前,在那空虚同荒凉里,我看到:"死神"的向我来临。当我年青时候,我看不见他,因为我眼中有一大群的物事同感情,"希望"又总是站在我们中间,说道:"别去睬那老头!"若使我曾经好好地活过,那么我也不会怎样地惜死。但是我不喜欢快乐的契约还没有实践,就行废除;不喜欢不美满的婚姻;不喜欢幸福的许诺顿行取消。我所有的为人为己的希望全化为焦土,或者剩下些特意来嘲笑我的现状。我真欲把它们重新建筑一番。我欲看人类有个良好的前途,像我才入世的时候那样。我欲留下有真价值的工作,做我的遗念。我欲有友谊恳挚的手送我到墓中。办得到这些条件,我是不辞死去,若使我不是十分愿意。那时我要在墓上写着——"感谢

my tomb — Grateful and Contented! But I have thought and suffered too much to be willing to have thought and suffered in vain. — In looking back, it sometimes appears to me as if I had in a manner[1] slept out my life in a dream or shadow on the side of the hill of knowledge, where I have fed on books, on thoughts, on pictures, and only heard in half-murmurs the trampling of busy feet, or the noises of the throng below. Waked out of this dim, twilight existence, and startled with the passing scene, I have felt a wish to descend to the world of realities, and join in the chase. But I fear too late, and that I had better return to my bookish chimeras and indolence once more!

It is not wonderful that the contemplation and fear of death become more familiar to us as we approach nearer to it: that life seems to ebb with the decay of blood and youthful spirits; and that as we find everything about us subject to chance and change, as our strength and beauty die, as our hopes and passions, our friends and our affections leave us, we begin by degrees[2] to feel ourselves mortal!

I have never seen death but once, and that was in an infant. It is years ago. The look was calm and placid, and the face was fair and

---

1 in a manner: somewhat; to a certain degree 稍为，略为，似乎。
2 by degrees: gradually 渐渐。

同满足！"但是我焦心忍苦得太利害了，真不愿就这样子白白地操一世的心，挨一世的苦。——回顾起来，有时我觉得好像我也可说是在智识山旁的一场梦里或者阴影里睡过了我的一生，在那里我沉溺于书中，思想中，名画中，只隐隐地听到下面匆忙脚步的践踏声同大群人们的喧哗声。从这模糊朦〔蒙〕昧的生活里醒来，震于目前的情境，我感觉到一种愿望，想走下到现实的世界里去，跟人们一起驱驰。但是我恐怕已是太迟了，还是再回到我的书痴的幻想同懒惰罢！

这并没有什么奇怪，我们是更惯于死的冥想同恐惧，当我们一步步地更走近的时候：生命好像随着热血同壮气的消沉而俱衰；当我们看见身旁的一切物事都受机缘同变化的支配，当我们的精力同韶颜终归于毁灭，当我们的希望同热情，我们的朋友同我们的恳挚离开了我们，我们也开始渐渐地觉得我们是会死的！

我从来没有看见过死，除开一回，那回是一个婴孩的死。这是好多年前的事情。形容是安详而恬静，面貌是美丽而固定。

firm. It was as if a waxen image had been laid out[1] in the coffin, and strewed with innocent flowers. It was not like death, but more like an imago of life! No breath moved the lips, no pulse stirred, no sight or sound would enter those eyes or ears more. While I looked at it, I saw no pain was there; it seemed to smile at the short pang of life which was over: but I could not bear the coffin-lid to be closed — it seemed to stifle me; and still as the nettles wave in a corner of the churchyard over his little grave, the welcome breeze helps to refresh me, and ease the tightness at my breast!

An ivory or marble image, like Chantrey's[2] monument of the two children, is contemplated with pure delight. Why do we not grieve and fret that the marble is not alive, or fancy that it has a shortness of breath? It never was alive; and it is the difficulty of making the transition from life to death, the struggle between the two in our imagination, that confounds their properties painfully together, and makes us conceive that the infant that is but just dead, still wants to breathe, to enjoy, and look about it, and is prevented by the icy hand of death, locking up its faculties and benumbing its senses; so that, if it could, it would complain of its own hard[3] state. Perhaps religious

---

1 to lay out: to stretch out and prepare for burial 殓尸。
2 Chantrey, Sir Francis (1781—1841), 英国有名的雕刻家。
3 hard: severe 艰苦。

那真像是一个放在棺材里的蜡制人形，四旁撒铺有清白的花朵。那并不像死，却更像是生的模型！不过是没有气息吹动那嘴唇，没有脉搏跳动着，没有景物同声音会再走进那眼睛同耳朵。当我看它时候，我瞧不出那里有什么苦痛，它好像是对于已过了的短促的生之苦痛微笑；但是一看到盖棺，我真是万分难过——好像会使我闷死；可是当礼拜堂墓地角上的苎麻在他的小坟上波浪地起伏时候，迎人的和风却能恢复我的精神，解松我胸里的这个郁结！

一个象牙的或者大理石的雕像，比如产特立的二孩纪念碑，我们瞻仰时，觉得有纯粹的欣欢。为什么我们不会悲伤同懊恼，为着那大理石不是活的，或者为着我们恐怕它的呼吸是很困难？这是因为那大理石是从来没有活气的；我们总以为从生到死的过渡是非常困难，我们的想像看见生同死正在那里肉搏，所以我们将生死的性质很苦楚地混在一起，因此就想才死的婴孩还是要呼吸，要享乐，要东瞧西看，却被死的冰冷的手制止住了，将一切机官锁住，把所有的感觉弄成麻木；所以若使小孩子还能说话，一定会诉出它自己现在的苦况。或者宗教的思想比任

considerations reconcile the mind to this change sooner than any others, by representing the spirit as fled to another sphere, and leaving the body behind it. So in reflecting on death generally, we mix up[1] the idea of life with it, and thus make it the ghastly monster it is. We think, how we should feel, not how the dead feel.

"Still from the tomb the voice of nature cries;

Even in our ashes live their wonted fires!"

There is an admirable passage on this subject in Tucker's[2] *Light of Nature Pursued*, which I shall transcribe, as by much[3] the best illustration I can offer of it.

"The melancholy appearance of a lifeless body, the mansion provided for it to inhabit, dark, cold, close and solitary, are shocking[4] to the imagination; but it is to the imagination only, not the understanding; for whoever consults this faculty will see at first glance[5], that there is nothing dismal in all these circumstances: if the corpse were kept wrapped up in a warm bed, with a roasting fire in the chamber, it would feel no comfortable warmth therefrom; were store of tapers lighted up as soon as day shuts in[6], it would see no

---

1 to mix up: to mix intimately; to work into a mixture with something else 混合，调和。

2 先生不知何许人也。

3 by much: by a great deal 殊。

4 shocking: striking with disgust 为憎恶而战栗。

5 at first glance: at once 立刻。

6 to shut in: to close in 迫近。

何别的东西会更快地使我们的心对于这个变更没有什么反感，因为照它们的说法，我们的魂魄是飞到别的地方去，剩着这个躯体在后。所以通常我们一想到死，我们是把它同生的观念混在一起，因此在我们现在思想里死才会变做这么狰狞的一个怪物。我们想，我们处在那种情境时会有什么感觉，并不是想死人处在那情境会有什么感觉。

"从坟墓之中，自然之声仍然是喊着；

在我们的灰烬里，他们昔日的火长存！"

关于这个题目，塔刻的《追着自然的光》里有一段值得赞美的文字，我要把它抄出，因为那可说是我所能找出的最好的说明。

"死尸的凄惨形相，预备给它住的房子的黑暗，寒冷，闭塞同孤寂，我们想起来，会不寒而栗；但是只是对于想像才这样，由理智来看就大不同了；因为无论谁一用他的理智，立刻可以看出这许多情境里并没有什么凄怆可怕的地方：若使那死尸老是好好地包着，放在温暖的床上，房里烧着烘人的炉火，它也不会因此感到适体的温暖；若使天一快黑，接着就燃起成堆的

objects to divert it; were it left at large[1] it would have no liberty, nor if surrounded with company would be cheered thereby; neither are the distorted features expressions of pain, uneasiness, or distress. This every one knows, and will readily allow upon being suggested, yet still cannot behold, nor even cast a thought upon those objects without shuddering; for knowing that a living person must suffer grievously under such appearances, they become habitually formidable to the mind, and strike a mechanical horror, which is increased by the customs of the world around us."

There is usually one pang added voluntarily and unnecessarily to the fear of death, by our affecting to compassionate the loss which others will have in us. If that were all, we might reasonably set our minds at rest[2]. The pathetic exhortation on country tombstones, "Grieve not for me, my wife and children dear," etc., is for the most part speedily followed to the letter[3]. We do not leave so great a void in society as we are inclined to imagine, partly to magnify our own importance, and partly to console ourselves by sympathy. Even in the same family the gap is not so great; the wound closes up sooner

---

1 at large: at liberty; without restraint 自由，不受拘束。
2 to set one's mind at rest: to be quite easy about the matter 对于这件事你放心罢。
3 to the letter: exactly 丝毫不差。

蜡烛，它也看不见什么东西，会觉得开心；若使让它逍遥自在，它也不能应用它的自由，若使有伴侣围绕着，也不会笑逐颜开；它脸上丑怪的形容也不是苦痛，不安或者悲痛的表现。这是谁也晓得的，只要别人一提，他很快就会承认，但是一看到，甚至于一想到这些东西，他还是免不了战栗；因为知道一个活人处在这种环境之下，一定会受极大的苦痛，这些东西在我们心里就常常变做很可怕的，给我们一种器械式的恐怖，这恐怖会见增加，一看到我们四旁的世人也都是一样地战战兢兢。"

在死的恐惧之外，我们常常有一种不必须的，自己愿意加上的苦痛，那是我们爱同情于旁人失去了我们时的悲哀。若使这是我们对于死的恐惧的惟一原因，我们真有理由，很可以放下心来。乡间墓石上所写的动情的劝告，"请别要为着我悲伤，我亲爱的妻子同子女"等等，多半很快地能够字字发生效力。我们死去，在社会上并没有剩下那么大的一个虚空，像我们自己所想的，我们所以不禁作那样想，一半是为着要扩大我们自己的重要，一半是想用别人的同情来安慰自己。就是在自己的家里，那裂口也没有那么样大；伤痕的缝口是比我们所预料的

than we should expect. Nay, our room¹ is not unfrequently thought better than our company. People walk along the streets the day after our deaths just as they did before, and the crowd is not diminished. While we were living, the world seemed in a manner to exist only for us, for our delight and amusement, because it contributed to them. But our hearts cease to beat, and it goes on² as usual, and thinks no more about us than it did in our lifetime. The million are devoid of sentiment, and care as little for you or me as if we belonged to the moon. We live the week over in the Sunday's paper, or are decently interred in some obituary at the month's end! It is not surprising that we are forgotten so soon after we quit this mortal stage; we are scarcely noticed while we are on it. It is not merely that our names are not known in China — they have hardly been heard of in the next street. We are hand and glove³ with the universe, and think the obligation is mutual. This is an evident fallacy. If this, however, does not trouble us now, it will not hereafter. A handful of dust can have no quarrel to pick⁴ with its neighbours, or complaint to

---

1 room: a place appropriated to a person 一个人所占的地方，作此解时，多半是与company这字相对。
2 to go on: to continue in a course of action 继续进行。
3 hand and glove: in intimate and friendly association 亲密，如漆如胶。
4 to pick a quarrel: to seek a quarrel without provocation 寻衅，借端生事。

要快得多。不，人们常常喜欢我们的"让位"胜过于我们的"出席"。我们死去的第二天，人们还是照常地在街上走路，数目并没有什么减少。当我们活着时候，世界好像是专为着我们而存在，为着我们的欣欢同娱乐，因为世界的确给我们许多的快乐。但是我们的心儿停着不动了，世界仍然是照常熙熙攘攘着，并没有记念着我们，对着我们还是像我们在世时候那样的冷淡。亿万万人的心是空的，没有什么情感，看你我好像是属于月球的人们，一点也不关心。在那星期里的星期日报纸上我们的名字再现一次，或者是在月底有些报纸的死亡栏上，我们规规矩矩地同世人永诀！这并没有什么可怪，我们一离开了这暂时的舞台，就这么快被人们忘记；因为我们压根儿就不大引起人们的注意，当我们还在舞台上面的时候。不单是我们的名字没有传到中国——我们的邻街就几乎没有听到我们的大名。我们自己同世界非常亲密，我们以为这种情谊是彼此共之。这是个显明的错误。可是，若使我们现在不会因此而觉得难过，将来也是同样地不会的。一掬的尘埃不能够同它的邻居寻衅吵架，

make against Providence, and might well exclaim, if it had but an understanding and a tongue, "Go thy ways, old world, swing round in blue ether, voluble to every age, you and I shall no more jostle!"

It is amazing how soon the rich and titled, and even some of those who have wielded great political power, are forgotten.

"A little rule, a little sway,

Is all the great and mighty have

Betwixt the cradle and the grave —"

And, after its short date, they hardly leave a name behind them. "A great man's memory may, at the common rate, survive him half a year." His heirs and successors take his titles, his power, and his wealth — all that made him considerable or courted by others; and he has left nothing else behind him either to delight or benefit the world. Posterity are not by any means[1] so disinterested as they are supposed to be. They give their gratitude and admiration only in return for[2] benefits conferred. They cherish the memory of those to whom they are indebted for instruction and delight; and they cherish it just in proportion to[3] the instruction and delight they are conscious they receive. The sentiment of admiration springs immediately from

---

1 by any means: at all 全然。

2 in return for: in compensation for 报答，以报之。

3 in proportion to: according to 按照，与为比例。

也不能对"造化"说出怨词,很可以大声喊道,若使它还有理智同舌头:"走你的路罢,老世界,在蓝的净天里打你的圈儿走转,对每代人去油嘴滑舌,你同我是再也不会摩着肩儿挤在一起了!"

这真是可惊的事,富贵的人们,甚至于有些握过大政权的人们,是多么快就被人忘却了。

"一会儿的称尊,一会儿的威权,

这是伟大英猛的人们所得到的

从摇篮到坟墓期中的惟一东西——"

在这个短促的期间之后,他们差不多连一个名字都不能传下。"一位大人物的身后遗名,普通算起来,可以有半年的寿命。"他的后裔同承继者取得他的爵位,他的权力同他的财富——全是这些东西才使他变做这么重要,受人奉承的人物;他却没有剩下什么别的东西,使世人感到快乐或者得到利益。后世的人绝对不像我们所以为的那样公平,不计利益。他们的谢忱同赞美是用来报答他们所受的好处。他们蒙一班人给他们教训同快乐,他们就爱去记念他们;他们觉得受有多少的教训同快乐,他们所怀抱的记念就是做个正比例。赞美的情感是直接从这个

this ground[1], and cannot be otherwise than well founded.

The effeminate clinging to life as such, as a general or abstract idea, is the effect of a highly civilised and artificial state of society. Men formerly plunged into all the vicissitudes and dangers of war, or staked their all upon a single die, or some one passion, which if they could not have gratified, life became a burden to them — now our strongest passion is to think, our chief amusement is to read new plays, new poems, new novels, and this we may do at our leisure, in perfect security, ad infinitum[2]. If we look into the old histories and romances, before the belles-lettres[3] neutralised human affairs and reduced passion to a state of mental equivocation, we find the heroes and heroines not setting their lives "at a pin's fee"[4], but rather courting opportunities of throwing them away in very wantonness of spirit. They raise their fondness for some favourite pursuit to its height, to a pitch of madness, and think no price too dear to pay for its full gratification. Everything else is dross. They go to death as to a bridal bed, and sacrifice themselves or others without remorse at the shrines of love, of honour, of religion, or any other prevailing

---

1 ground: basis; foundation 根本，基础。

2 ad infinitum: to infinity 无限。

3 belles-lettres: writings of purely literary kind 纯粹文艺作品。

4 at a pin's fee: at the value of a pin 一针的值价，这也是莎翁的句子，见 *Hamlet* 里。此外本文中还有不少妙句都是从莎翁集中镕化出来的，Hazlitt 是个研究莎翁作品的老手，他著有 *Characters of Shakespeare's Plays*。

基础上生长出来的，这样子的确是不至于滥用的。

这种柔弱无勇的吝惜生命，普通地或者抽象地，是文明太高，矫揉太过的社会状况的结果。从前人们跳到战争的一切变迁同危险里去，或者将生命付诸一掷，或者为着一个强烈的情感不惜牺牲一切，若使他们不能满足这个情感，生命对于他们就变成重累了——现在我们最强烈的情感是思维，我们最大的娱乐是读新戏剧，新诗歌，新小说，这些事我们很可以安安逸逸地做去，一些危险也没有，永久地做去。若使我们去看古史同传奇，当文艺还没有将人事染上暗澹无光的色彩，把热情化为模棱两可的心境之前，我们觉得里面的男女主角不单是"看生命连一条针都不值"，并且当放荡不羁的时候，好像是故意去找轻生的机会。他们喜欢些中意的东西就爱到极点，到了疯狂的地步，以为若使能够满足自己这个欲望，没有个代价可说是太贵的。一切别的东西全变做不值一钱的废物。他们向死走去，好像是向新婚的床，一些也不懊悔地牺牲自己或者他人，在爱情，名誉，宗教，或任一个别的得势的情感的圣龛之前。罗米

feeling. Romeo runs his "sea-sick, weary bark upon the rocks" of death the instant he finds himself deprived of his Juliet[1]; and she clasps his neck in their last agonies, and follows him to the same fatal shore. One strong idea takes possession of the mind[2] and overrules every other; and even life itself, joyless without that, becomes an object of indifference or loathing. There is at least more of imagination in such a state of things, more vigour of feeling and promptitude to act, than in our lingering, languid, protracted attachment to life for its own poor sake. It is, perhaps, also better, as well as more heroical, to strike at some daring or darling object, and if we fail in that, to take the consequences[3] manfully, than to renew the lease of a tedious, spiritless, charmless existence, merely (as Pierre says) "to lose it afterwards in some vile brawl" for some worthless object. Was there not a spirit of martyrdom as well as a spice of the reckless energy of barbarism in this bold defiance of death? Had not religion something to do with it: the implicit belief in a future life which rendered this of less value, and embodied something beyond it to the imagination; so that the rough soldier, the infatuated lover, the valorous

---

1 *Romeo and Juliet* 是莎翁的一篇戏剧，他们是一对爱人，为着种种的障碍，最终是你为着我，我为着你，伏剑而死。

2 to take possession of the mind: to occupy the mind 萦回于心中，盘踞脑海。

3 to take to the consequenes: to acquiesce in the results 甘心挨受那结果。

欧驶他的"厌于沧海的疲倦小舟，碰在死的岩石上面"，当他一晓得自己被剥夺去了他的朱丽叶；她也在他们最后的悲苦里双臂环着他的颈项，随着他到那个死亡的岸去。一个强烈的意思占住了心田，将一切别的念头完全压倒；就是生命本身，没有了它也是毫无乐趣的，变做个不足介怀或者讨厌的东西。在这种状况之下，最少也是更多想像的成分，更多感情的力量，行动的速度也会更快，比着那为了无聊生活的本身，而生的缠绵难舍的，无精打彩〔采〕的同长久的对于生命的依恋。这或者也是更好的，并且是更英雄的，去向一个勇敢的或者亲爱的对象进攻，若使失败了，就男子汉地挨受那结果，比着那重新去苟延一种烦闷的，无精神的，无趣味的生活，最后也只是（像比野所说的）"在些恶浊的争吵里失丢了生命"为着些不值得的东西的缘故。在这种对于死的勇敢挑战里，不是有一种慷慨的牺牲精神同不顾一切的蛮劲的意味吗？宗教同这个不是有些相干吗：那种对于死后的生活的坚信使现世的生活减轻了价值，在想像里呈现出个来世的境界；所以粗野的兵士，情迷的爱人，

knight, etc., could afford to throw away the present venture, and take a leap into the arms of futurity, which the modern sceptic shrinks back from, with all his boasted reason and vain philosophy, weaker than a woman! I cannot help[1] thinking so myself; but I have endeavoured to explain this point before, and will not enlarge farther on it here.

A life of action and danger moderates the dread of death. It not only gives us fortitude to bear pain, but teaches us at every step the precarious tenure on which we hold our present being. Sedentary and studious men are the most apprehensive on this score. Dr. Johnson was an instance in point. A few years seemed to him soon over, compared with those sweeping contemplations on time and infinity with which he had been used to pose himself. In the still-life[2] of a man of letters there was no obvious reason for a change. He might sit in an armchair and pour out cups of tea to all eternity. Would it had been possible for him to do so! The most rational cure after all for the inordinate fear of death is to set a just value on[3] life. If we merely wish to continue on the scene to indulge our headstrong humours and tormenting passions, we had better begone at once; and

---

1 cannot help: must 一定。

2 still-life: that kind of subject in a picture which consists of inanimate objects, as fruits, flowers, etc. 专以静物如果子、花,为画题的图画。

3 to set a value on: to appraise 估价, 估计。

勇敢的骑士等等无妨现在这么冒险一下，跳到将来的怀中，这种豪举，近代的怀疑主义者却退缩不敢一试，虽然有那么多自夸的理性同空虚的哲学，都是柔弱得一个女子之不如！对于自己我免不了也是作这样想；但是在前面我已经努力于解释这点过，现在不再来详说了。

一个活动的同危险的生活可以压住死的恐惧。那不单是给我们以忍痛的毅力，并且时时刻刻使我们知道我们在世的生命是多么不牢稳的。惯长坐的，爱念书的人们是最怕死的人们。关于这点约翰生博士就是个例子。几年的光阴由他看来好像是很快地就过去了，比着他素常对于时空的一览无余的冥想。在文人的"静物画"里没有什么显明的理由，一定有变更的必要。他很可以坐在围手椅里，一杯一杯地倒他的茶，一直到天荒地老才止。他果能够办到，那是多么好吓！医治那逾量的死的恐惧的最合理方法是对于生命定下个适当的价值。若使我们愿意继续生存在世界里，单为着去满足我们顽梗的怪癖同苦楚的热情，我们还是立刻死去好些，若使我们对于生命的顾惜是按着

if we only cherish a fondness for existence according to the good we derive from it, the pang we feel at parting with it will not be very severe!

我们从生命里所得到的好处来定，那么我们去世时候所觉的苦痛也不会非常剧烈了！

Leigh Hunt

In Prison

The doctor then proposed that I should be removed into the prison infirmary; and this proposal was granted. Infirmary had, I confess, an awkward sound, even to my ears. I fancied a room shared with other sick persons, not the best fitted for companions; but the good-natured doctor (his name was Dixon) undeceived me. The infirmary was divided into four wards, with as many small rooms attached to them. The two upper wards were occupied, but the two on the floor had never been used: and one of these, not very providently (for I had not yet learned to think of money), I turned[1] into a noble room. I papered the walls with a trellis of roses; I had the ceiling coloured with clouds and sky; the barred windows I

---

1 to turn: to transform 改做。

在监狱中

医生就提议我要搬到监狱病院去住；这个提议得到了批准。病院这个字，我自认，带有不妙的声音。甚至于在我的耳朵里。我想那是一间同别个病人共住的房子，那班人又不是最合式的伴侣；但是慈爱的医生（他的名字是狄克孙）改正了我的误解。那个病院分做四个病房，附带有同样数目的小房。楼上那两间病房已经有人住了，平地的那两间却从来没有用过：内中的一间，不大经济地（我还没有学会打算省钱），我改做成个华贵的房间。我用玫瑰花的格子纸糊着我的四壁；我将天花板画上青天同白云的颜色；铁窗，我就用百叶窗遮着；当我的书架同架

screened with Venetian¹ blinds; and when my bookcases were set up with their busts, and flowers and a pianoforte made their appearance², perhaps there was not a handsomer room on that side the water. I took a pleasure, when a stranger knocked at the door, to see him come in and stare about him. The surprise on issuing from the Borough, and passing through the avenues of a gaol, was dramatic, Charles Lamb³ declared there was no other suchroom, except in a fairy tale.

But I possessed another surprise; which was a garden. There was a little yard outside the room, railed off⁴ from another belonging to the neighbouring ward. This yard I shut in⁵ with green palings, adorned it with a trellis, bordered it with a thick bed of earth from a nursery, and even contrived to have a grass-plot. The earth I filled with flowers and young trees. There was an apple-tree, from which we managed to get a pudding the second year. As to my flowers, they were allowed to be perfect. Thomas Moore⁶, who came to see me with Lord Byron⁷, told me he had seen no such heart's-ease. I

---

    1 Venetian: of Venice 百叶窗是威尼斯地方所最先采用，所以叫做威尼斯窗。

    2 to makes its appearance: to become visible 出现。

    3 Charles Lamb 这个兰姆就是做《一个单身汉的怨言》的那个兰姆，他是 Leigh Hunt 的好友。

    4 to rail off: to separate by a railing 用栏杆分开。

    5 to shut in: to inclose 围着。

上的许多半身像排好了,鲜花同大洋琴也出现了的时候,或者在那水的此岸没有一个更美丽的房间。当来客来敲门时候,我喜欢看他走进来,向身旁愕然睇视。他走过巴洛,穿过一个狱里的许多小道,忽然看到这样的房间,那种骇异的神情真是奇妙得像做戏一样。查理斯·兰姆说世上没有第二间像这样的房子,除非是在神仙的故事里面。

但是我还有一个别的奇异东西;那是一座花园。房外本来有个小庭,同别个属于隔壁病房的小庭用栏杆隔住。这个小庭我用绿色篱笆围着,点缀上一个花架,四边铺了从个养树园里拿来的一层很厚的土,甚至于设法弄出一块草地。在土地上我栽满了花卉同小树。有一棵苹果树,在第二年我们就设法做一盘苹果布丁。至于我栽的花,谁也说它们是十全的。托马斯·摩尔和拜伦爵士同来望我,对我说他从来没有看见过这么好的

---

6 Thomas Moore(1779—1852),英国浪漫派诗人之一。
7 拜伦,他还用介绍吗?

bought the Parnaso Italiano¹ while in prison, and used often to think of a passage in it, while looking at this miniature piece of horticulture: —

"My little garden,

To me thou'rt vineyard, field and meadow, and wood."

Here I wrote and read in fine weather, sometimes under an awning. In autumn, my trellises were hung with scarlet-runners, which added to the flowery investment. I used to shut my eyes in my arm-chair, and affect to think myself hundreds of miles off.

But my triumph was in issuing forth of a morning. A wicket out of the garden led into the large one belonging to the prison. The latter was only for vegetables; but it contained a cherry-tree, which I saw twice in blossom. I parcelled out² the ground in my imagination into favourite districts. I made a point of³ dressing myself as if for a long walk; and then, putting on my gloves, and taking my book under my arm, stepped forth, requesting my wife not to wait dinner if I was too late. My eldest little boy, to whom Lamb addressed some charming verses on the occasion, was my constant companion,

---

1 这两字是意大利文，翻成英文是 Italian Parnassus，Parnassus 是希腊一个大山的名字，据说是诗神所住的地方，所以后来人们把诗集叫做 Parnassus。

2 to parcel out: to divide 分做。

3 to made a point of: to regard as important 视为重要。

紫罗兰。在监狱期间,我买有一本意大利诗集,常常想到里面的一段,当看着这个小规模的园艺:——

"我小小的花园,

对于我,你可算是葡萄园,田野,草地同森林。"

天气好的时候我在这园里写东西同读书,有时上面还挂一幅天幔。秋天里,我的花架垂着红花彩豆,更使我的花圃生色。我常常闭着眼睛坐在我的圈手椅里,假假地想自己是处身在万里之外。

但是我最得意的是早上的出游。园里的一个小门引到属于监狱的一座更大花园。这个单是做种菜用的;但是里面有一棵樱桃树,我看它开过二回的花。我在想像里将这块地分做好多心爱的区域。我很郑重地把自己穿得好像是打算做一回很长的散步;然后再戴上手套,夹一本书在腋下,开步走出,请我妻子不必等我用餐,若使我回来得太迟。我最大的小孩,兰姆那时做有几首可爱的诗赠他,是我忠实的伴侣,我们常常一起玩

and we used to play all sorts of juvenile games together. It was, probably, in dreaming of one of these games (but the words had a more touching effect on my ear) that he exclaimed one night in his sleep, "No, I'm not lost; I'm found." Neither he nor I were very strong at that time; but I have lived to see him a man of eight and forty; and wherever he is found, a generous hand and a great understanding will be found together.

许多小孩子的游戏。那或者是当他梦着一种这类的游戏（但是在我的耳朵里那些话有个更牵情的效力）他一晚上睡着时候喊道："不，我没有失丢；我被人找出了。"那时他同我的身体都不很强壮；但是我活到看他变成四十八岁的大人；无论人们在什么地方碰到他，同时会碰到慷慨的帮助同卓越的学识。

John Brown

Her Last Half-Crown

"Once I had friend — though now by all for saken;
Once I had parents — they are now in heaven.
I had a home once —"

"Worn out with anguish, sin, and cold, and hunger,
Down sunk the outcast, death had seized her senses.
There did the stranger find her in the morning —
God had released her.

Southey"[1]

---

1 Southey, Robert (1774—1843), 英国诗人及历史家, 他的不朽名著是《纳尔逊传》(*Life of Nelson*)。

她最后的一块银币

"我曾经有过朋友——虽然现在谁也厌弃我了;

我曾经有过父母——他们现在都在天堂。

我曾经有过家庭——

"苦痛,罪恶同冻饿磨坏了她的精力,

流浪者往下堕落,死神抓住她的知觉。

陌生人在早上看她躺在那里——

上帝已经释放她了。

骚狄"

Hugh Miller[1], the geologist, journalist, and man of genius, was sitting in his newspaper office late one dreary winter night. The clerks had all left, and he was preparing to go, when a quick rap came to the door. He said "Come in", and, looking towards the entrance, saw a little ragged child all wet with sleet. "Are ye[2] Hugh Miller?" "Yes." "Mary Duff wants ye." "What does she want?" "She's deein'[3]." Some misty recollection of the name made him at once set out[4], and with his well-known plaid and stick, he was soon striding after the child who trotted through the now deserted High Street, into the Canongate. By the time he got to the Old Playhouse Close, Hugh had revived his memory of Mary Duff: a lively girl who had been bred up beside him in Cromarty. The last time he had seen her was at a brother mason's[5] marriage, where Mary was "best maid", and he "best man". He seemed still to see her bright young careless face, her tidy shortgown, and her dark eyes, and to hear her

---

1 Miller, Hugh (1802—1856), 他年青时候是一个矿工, 后来投身到新闻界去。靠着他刻苦的自修, 最终成为大地质学家。他又能写很妙的散文, 他著有好几本有文学趣味的科举书, 其中以 *Old Red Sandstone* 最著名。但是, 他的确是太劳顿了, 才五十几岁他的神经就错乱了, 在爱丁堡附近自杀死去。

2 这篇文章的问答语, 全是照着苏格兰土音写的, 同普通英文不同, 现一一注之如下。ye: you.

3 deein': dying.

4 to set out: to start 出发。

休·密勒,地质学家,新闻记者,又是一个具有天才的人,在他的报馆里坐到更深,一个凄凉的冬夜里。书记们已经全离馆了,他也正打算回去,门外来有匆忙的敲门声音。他说"进来",向着门口望,看见一个衣服褴褛的小孩,遍体给雨雪淋住。"你是休·密勒吗?""是。""玛丽·达夫要你。""她要什么?""她快死了。"对于这个名字的一些模糊的记忆使他立刻出发,穿着他那套有名的格子纹呢衣,拿着他那条有名的手杖,他很快地就跟着小孩子跨着大步望〔往〕前走,那小孩子急急地穿过那时已绝人迹的亥街,走向卡侬盖提去。当他走到老戏院小巷时候,休唤起他心中关于玛丽·达夫的记忆:一个活泼的女孩,在克洛麦替地方和他一起长大。前次他遇到她时是在一位互助团同志的结婚场中,在那里玛丽是"新娘伴",他是"新郎伴"。他好像还看到她的晴朗,年青,无忧无虑的脸孔,她的洁净短衫,同她的深色眼睛;他好像还听着她的嘲笑快乐

---

5 Freemasonry互助团,是一种秘密团体,创自中古时代,以互助为目的,团员简称做mason。苏格兰的大本营是在一七三六年设立的。

bantering, merry tongue.

Down the close went the ragged little woman, and up an outside stair, Hugh keeping near her with difficulty; in the passage she held out her hand and touched him; taking it in his great palm, he felt that she wanted a thumb. Finding her way like a cat through the darkness, she opened a door, and saying, "That's her!" Vanished. By the light of a dying fire he saw lying in the corner of the large empty room something like a woman's clothes, and on drawing nearer became aware of a thin pale face and two dark eyes looking keenly but helplessly up at him. The eyes were plainly Mary Duff's, though he could recognize no other feature. She wept silently, gazing steadily at him. "Are you Mary Duff?" "It's a' that's' o' me[1], Hugh." She then tried to speak to him, something plainly of great urgency, but she couldn't; and seeing that she was very ill, and was making herself worse, he put half-a-crown into her feverish hand, and said he would call again in the morning. He could get no information about her from the neighbours: they were surly or asleep.

When he returned next morning, the little girl met him at the stair-head and said, "She's deid[2]." He went in and found that it was

---

1 It's a' that's o' me: It is all that is of me.
2 She's deid: She is dead.

的声音。

这个穿着百结衣的小姑娘跑下这条小巷,走上一个朝街的楼梯,休很困难地紧跟着她走;在弄堂里她伸出她的手,牵着他;他用大手掌拿着,觉得她缺个大姆〔拇〕指。在黑暗里她找她的路像一个猫样子,最后开一个门,说道:"那个就是她!"一溜烟就不见了。借着将熄的火光,他看见在一个广大空虚的房间的基角上,躺有个像女人衣服的东西,走近时候,才知道有一个枯瘦无血色的脸孔,同两个深色的眼睛极注意地,但是绝望地望着他。这对眼睛分明是玛丽·达夫的,虽然他认不出她的别点相貌。她静静地哭着,不转睛地盯着他。"你是玛丽·达夫吗?""我现在变成这样子了,休。"她接着鼓起劲要向他说话,分明是很要紧的话,但是她说不出来;他看她是病得很利害,这样勉强只是使她自己更痛苦,他就将一块值得二先令六辨士的银币放在她发烧的手里,说明早他会再来看她。他从邻近的人们探不出她的近况:他们不是无礼地不答,就是已经睡觉了。

当他第二早又到那里时候,小姑娘在楼梯顶遇着他,说道:"她已经死了。"他走进去,看出这句话是真的;她躺在那里,

true; there she lay, the fire out, her face placid, and the likeness to her maiden self restored. Hugh thought he would have known her now, even with those bright black eyes closed as they were, in aeternum[1].

Seeking out a neighbour, he said he would like to bury Mary Duff, and arranged for the funeral with an undertaker in the close. Little seemed to be known of the poor outcast, except that she was a 'licht[2],' or, as Solomon would have said, a "strange, woman." "Did she drink?" "Whiles[3]."

On the day of the funeral one or two residents in the close accompanied him to the Canongate Churchyard. He observed a decent-looking little old woman watching them, and following at a distance, though the day was wet and bitter[4]. After the grave was filled, and he had taken off his hat, as the men finished their business by putting on and slapping the sod, he saw this old woman remaining; she came up and courtesying, said, "Ye wad ken that lass, Sir?[5]" "Yes; I knew her when she was young." The woman then burst into tears[6], and told Hugh that she "keepit a bit shop at the close-mouth, and

---

1 in aeternum: forever.
2 licht: light, light woman 就是轻薄的女人。
3 whiles: sometimes 有时。
4 bitter: piercingly cold 酷冷。
5 Ye wad ken that lass, sir? : You would know that woman, sir?

火也灭了,她的脸貌是安详恬静的,恢复到她年青时的状态。休想他现在绝对认得出她,虽然她那对明媚的眼睛是像现在这样子闭着,永久地闭着。

找出一个邻居,他说他愿意替玛丽·达夫安葬,他同巷里一个经理葬事人商量好埋葬的手续。关于这个可怜的流浪者的身世,大家好像知道得很少,只晓得她是个"轻薄的"或者,所罗门一定要说,"奇怪的女人"。"她喝酒吗?""有时。"

埋葬那天,巷里有一两个居民随着他到卡侬盖提礼拜堂坟地去。他看见一个容貌端庄,躯体短小的老妇人注视他们,远远地跟着走,虽然那天有下雨,又是酷冷。墓填满了,他也脱下他的帽子,当人们把土放上,用手打好的时候,他看这位老妇人还滞在那里;她走前,行个屈膝礼,说道:"你想知道这个姑娘的事情吗?""是的;她年青时,我也认得她。"那妇人不禁泪流满面,对休说她自己"在巷口开一间小店,玛丽常来买东

6　to burst into tears: to cry out suddenly 忽然哭起来。

Mary dealt wi' me, and aye paid regular, and I was feared she was dead, for she had been a month owin'me half-a-crown",[1] and then with a look and voice of awe, she told him how on the night he was sent for, and immediately after he had left, she had been awakened by some one in her room; and by her bright fire — for she was a bein[2], well-to-do body — she had seen the wasted dying creature, who came forward and said, "Wasn't it half-a-crown?" "Yes." "There it is," and putting it under the bolster, vanished!

Poor Mary Duff! Her life had been a sad one since the day when she had stood side by side with Hugh at the wedding of their friends. Her father died not long after, and her mother supplanted her in the affections of the man to whom she had given her heart. The shock made home intolerable. She fled from it blighted and embittered, and after a life of shame and misery, crept into the corner of her room to die alone.

"My thoughts are not your thoughts, neither are your ways my ways, saith the Lord. For as the heavens are higher than the earth, so are my ways higher than your ways, and my thoughts than your thoughts."[3]

---

1 全句写成普通的英文时是如下： She kept a small shop at the close-mouth, and mary dealt with me, and always paid regular, and I was afraid she was dead, for she had been a month owing me half-a-crown.

西，总是准期还钱，我就怕她是死了，因为她欠我二先令六辨士已经有一个月了"，然后用严肃的脸色同声音，她告诉他在他被叫去那一夜，他一离开，她在房里就被一个人叫醒；借着她那熊熊的火光——因为她是一个过安乐小康日子的女人——她瞧到这个憔悴快死的女人走前说道："这是一块二先令六辨士的银钱吗？""是的。""我放在这里。"将钱放在枕垫底下，她就不见了！

可怜的玛丽·达夫！她的生活一向是悲哀的，自从那天在他们朋友的婚礼场中她同休并肩站着以后。她父亲死后没有多久，她母亲占有了她所倾心的男人的爱情。这个大打击使家庭变做不能居住的地方。她从家庭里跑出，带着失望同悲酸，经过了耻辱困苦的生涯，爬到她房间的角上，孤单单地死了。

"耶和华说，我的意念，非同你们的意念，我的道路，非同你们的道路。天怎样高过地，照样我的道路，高过你们的道路，我的意念，高过你们的意念。"

---

2 bein：comfortable 舒服。
3 见《圣经·以赛亚书》第五十五章。

A. G. Gardiner

A Fellow Traveller

I do not know which of us got into the carriage first. Indeed I did not know he was in the carriage at all for some time. It was the last train from London to a Midland town — a stopping train, an infinitely leisurely train, one of those trains which give you an understanding of eternity. It was tolerably full when it started, but as we stopped at the suburban stations the travellers alighted in ones and twos, and by the time we had left the outer ring of London behind I was alone — or, rather, I thought I was alone.

There is a pleasant sense of freedom about being alone in a carriage that is jolting noisily through the night. It is liberty and unrestraint in a very agreeable form. You can do anything you like. You can talk to yourself as loud as you please and no one will hear you.

一个旅伴

我不知道我们是那个先到车里。真的,有好久时候,我还简直不晓得他是在车里。那是由伦敦到密特兰里一个小镇的最后一趟火车——一种沿途停歇的火车,一种无限量地从容不迫的火车,这类火车使你了解什么叫做永劫不灭。当它出发时候,乘客也都挤满,但是我们在外郊各站都有停车,旅客就单独地或者两人作伴地接连着下去;当我们离开伦敦的远郊时候,车上只剩我一个人了——或者要说,我想车上只剩我一个人了。

独坐在一辆轰轰地颠簸着穿过黑夜的车子,会感到悦意的自由。那是一种很可喜的自由同无拘束。你爱做什么,就可以做什么。你可以随意大声地对自己说话,谁也不会听到你。你

You can have that argument out with Jones and roll him triumphantly in the dust¹ without fear of a counter-stroke². You can stand on your head and no one will see you. You can sing, or dance a two-step³, or practise a golf stroke, or play marbles on the floor without let or hindrance⁴. You can open the window or shut it without provoking a protest. You can open both windows or shut both. Indeed, you can go on opening them and shutting them as a sort of festival of freedom. You can have any corner you choose and try all of them in turn⁵. You can lie at full length⁶ on the cushions and enjoy the luxury of breaking the regulations and possibly the heart of D.O.R.A.⁷ herself. Only D.O.R.A. will not know that her heart is broken. You have escaped even D.O.R.A..

On this night I did not do any of these things. They did not happen to occur to me. What I did was much more ordinary. When the last of my fellow-passengers had gone I put down my paper, stretched my arms and my legs, stood up and looked out of the window on the calm summer night through which I was journeying, noting the pale reminiscence of day that still lingered in the northern

---

  1 to roll him in the dust: to conquer him 打胜他。
  2 counter-stroke: a stroke or blow in return 还手。
  3 two-step: a kind of round dance in march or polka time 二拍子的圆式跳舞。
  4 without let or hindrance: without any interference; freely 丝毫不受拘束，自由地。

可以同琼斯辩论那个题目，意气扬扬地将他驳倒，用不着怕他会还嘴。你可以倒栽地站着，谁也不会瞧见你。你可以唱歌，或者跳二拍子的圆式跳舞，或者练习打杓球的一种手势，或者在地板上玩石球，谁也不来干涉你。你可以打开窗子，或者关起，绝不至引起反对。你尽可以将两扇窗子全打开，或者全关起。你可以坐在你所中意的角上，可以将所有的坐位一一依次试过。你可以手足伸直躺在垫褥上面，享受破坏《地方保护法》的条例，或者碎了她自己的心的快乐。不过《地方保护法》不知道她自己的心是破碎了。你甚至于能够躲避了《地方保护法》的注意。

那个晚上，我并没有做些这类的事情。这类想头刚好没有到我心上来。我所做的是更普通得多的事情。当我最后的一个旅伴下去之后，我放下我的报纸，伸一伸我的手臂同我的双脚，站起，从窗口望着恬静的夏夜，我的车子正从那里穿过，看到尚逗遛在北天的淡淡的白昼余意；走过车子的那头，从别个窗

---

5 in turn：in due course of succession 轮到。
6 at full length：with the body fully extended 四股开展地躺着。
7 D.O.R.A.: Defense of the Realm Act.

sky; crossed the carriage and looked out of the other window; lit a cigarette, sat down and began to read again. It was then that I became aware of my fellow traveller. He came and sat on my rose... He was one of those wingy, nippy[1], intrepid insects that we call, vaguely, mosquitoes. I flicked him off my nose, and he made a tour of the compartment, investigated its three dimensions, visited each window, fluttered round the light, decided that there was nothing so interesting as that large animal in the corner, came and had a look at[2] my neck.

I flicked him off again. He skipped away, took another jaunt round the compartment, returned, and seated himself impudently on the back of my hand. It is enough. I said: magnanimity has its limits. Twice you have been warned that I am some one in particular, that my august person resents the tickling impertinences of strangers. I assume the black cap.[3] I condemn you to death. Justice domands it, and the court awards it. The counts[4] against you are many. You are a vagrant; you are a public nuisance; you are travelling without a ticket; you have no meat coupon.[5] For these and many other misdemeanours you are about to die. I struck a swift, lethal blow with my

---

1 nippy: biting 咬人的。
2 to have a look at: to look or a minute 看一下子。
3 英国法官判决死刑时候，就戴起黑帽子来，所以戴黑帽子就是宣告死刑的意思。

口里望出；点一根香烟，坐下来开始读书。到那时候，我才觉到我的旅伴。他走来，坐在我的鼻上……他是属于那种有翅的，会咬人的，勇敢的虫子，我们模模糊糊地所叫做蚊子是也。我轻轻地把他弹开我的鼻子，他在房里旅行一周，观察他的四周，拜望每个窗口，绕着灯光飞翔，决定没有一件东西有基角上那个庞大的动物那么有趣，又来看一看我的颈项。

我又轻轻地把他弹开。他盈盈跳起，又环着房子逍遥一次，飞回，大胆地自己坐在我的手背上面。这很够了，我说：大量也有相当的限度。你两回得到警告，我是位特殊的人物，以及我尊敬的身体不甘于受生人们这种搔撩的无礼。我戴上了黑帽子。我判下你的死罪。这是公理所需要，而法庭所断下的。你的罪状很多。你是个流氓；你是个为害于公众的砺〔妨〕碍；你旅行没有买票；你没有吃肉的准单。为着这些同许多其它的不法行为，你现在将受死刑。我用右手发一个迅速的，致命的

---

4 counts：particular charge in an indictment 罪状。
5 欧战时粮食缺乏，每人每星期吃肉的量是限制的，由官府发出肉券，每人按券买肉，无券就不能吃肉了。

right hand. He dodged the attack with an insolent ease that humiliated me. My personal vanity was aroused. I lunged at him with my hand, with my paper; I jumped on the seat and pursued him round the lamp; I adopted tactics of feline cunning, waiting till he had alighted, approching with a horrible stealthiness, striking with a sudden and terrible swiftness.

It was all in vain. He played with me, openly and ostentatiously, like a skilful matador finessing round an infuriated bull. It was obvious that he was enjoying himself[1], that it was for this that he had disturbed my repose. He wanted a little sport, and what sport like being chased by this huge, lumbering windmill of a creature, who tasted so good and seemed so helpless and so stupid? I began to enter into[2] the spirit of the fellow. He was no longer a mere insect. He was developing into a personality, an intelligence that challenged the possession of this compartment with me on equal terms[3]. I felt my heart warming towards him and the sense of superiority fading. How could I feel superior to a creature who was so manifestly my master in the only competition in which we had ever engaged? Why not be magnanimous again? Magnanimity and mercy were the noblest attributes of man. In the exercise of these high qualities I could

---

1 to enjoy one's self: to be joyful or happy 高兴。
2 to enter into: to sympathize with 发生同情的心。
3 on equal terms: on equal footing 处于平等的地位。

打击。他避着我的进攻，那种骄傲地一点儿也不费力的神气使我难堪。我私下自负的心情也被激起了。我用我的手，用我的纸来向他冲锋；我跳到座位上面，绕着灯儿赶他；我采取猫儿的诡计，等到他停着不飞时候，用可怕的潜行走近，忽然地骇人地飞手打下。

这也是徒然的。他是公开地分明地跟我开玩笑，像个精练的斗牛者缠着发怒的牡牛来弄手段一样。他明明是在那里寻开心，他就为着这缘故才来扰乱我的休息。他想找些游戏，那种游戏比得上被这个庞大笨拙像风车的动物这样赶着，他身上的肉又是那么可口，他又是这么不中用，这么傻瓜样子？我渐渐钻到这家伙的心里去。他已经不只是一个虫子了。他化成一个有性格的东西，一个有理性的动物，居着同等的地位，来跟我争这间房子的占有权，我觉得我的心向他动起好感，我自高的感觉也渐渐消灭。我怎样能够觉得比他高明，他在我们所曾交手过的惟一竞争里既是这么显明地胜过了我？为什么我不再慷慨起来？慷慨同慈悲是人类最高贵的德性。使用起这类高尚的

recover my prestige. At present I was a ridiculous figure, a thing for laughter and derision. By being merciful I could reassert the moral dignity of man and go back to my corner with honour. I withdraw the sentence of death, I said, returning to my seat. I cannot kill you, but I can reprieve you. I do it.

I took up my paper and he came and sat on it. Foolish fellow. I said, you have delivered yourself into my hands. I have but to give this respectable weekly organ of opinion a smack on both covers and you are a corpse, neatly sandwiched[1] between an article on "Peace Traps" and another on "The Modesty of Mr. Hughes[2]." But I shall not do it. I have reprieved you, and I will satisfy[3] you that when this large animal says a thing he mean it. Moreover, I no longer[4] desire to kill you. Through knowing you better I have come to feel — shall I say? — a sort of affection for you. I fancy that St. Francis[5] would have called you "little brother." I cannot go so far as that in Christian charity and civility. But I recognize a more distant relationship. Fortune has made us fellow-travellers on this summer night. I have interested you and you have entertained me. The obligation is

---

1 to be sandwiched: to be insorted between things that are unlike it 夹着。
2 美国前国务卿。
3 to satisfy: to convince 使相信。
4 no longer: not any more 已经不。
5 St. Francis（1182—1226），他是非常慈爱的天主教徒，据说能够向鸟儿说教。

品性，我能够恢复我的威势。现在我是个可笑的脚色，激起狂笑同嘲弄的东西。当我现出慈悲的样子，我能够重新拿出人类道德的威严，荣耀地回到我的角上去。我取消了死刑的判决，我说时就回到自己的位子。我不能够杀你，但是我能够展缓你受刑的时期。我就这样干去。

我拿起我的报纸，他飞来，就坐在上面。傻东西，我说，你自己投到我手里了。我只须将这个可尊敬的每星期出版的言论机关两面合着一打，你就是一具死尸了，清清楚楚地像面包中间的火腿一样，夹在一篇关于"和平的圈套"同另一篇关于"许斯先生的谦逊"里面。但是我不这样子干。我既宽展了你受刑的日期，我决定要使你相信，当这个庞大动物说一句话时候，他是打算践言的。并且，我也不想杀你了。因为知道你更透彻些，我渐渐觉得——我要讲出吗？——有些爱你了。我猜圣·佛兰西斯一定会叫你做"小弟弟"。在基督教徒的慈爱同礼貌方面，我不能做到他这种地方。但是我也承认一种较疏远些的关系。命运使我们在这夏夜里成为旅伴。我鼓起你的兴味，你也使我快乐。大家彼此互相感德，这全由于一个根本事实，我们

mutual and it is founded on the fundamental fact that we are fellow mortals. The miracle of life is ours in common and its mystery too. I suppose you don't know anything about your journey. I'm not sure that I know much about mine. We are really, when you come to think of it, a good deal alike — just apparitions that are[1] and then are not, coming out of the night into the lighted carriage, fluttering about the lamp for a while and going out into the night again. Perhaps...

"Going on[2] tonight, sir?" Said a voice at the window. It was a friendly porter giving me a hint that this was my station. I thanked him and said I must have been dozing. And seizing my hat and stick I went out into the cool summer night. As I closed the door of the compartment I saw my fellow-traveller fluttering round the lamp ...

---

1 to be: to exist 生存。
2 to go on: to continue a journey 继续旅行。

同是会死的东西。生命这个奇迹是我们所共有的,生命的神秘也是大家有份儿的。我猜你全不晓得你的旅程。我不敢说,我对于我的旅程知道了多少。我们真是,若使你去想一想,很相像的——都是现在活着,后来消灭了的浮生幻影,从夜里出来,飞到点着亮的车子,绕着灯飘游一会儿,又回到外面的夜里去了。或者……

"今晚还往前走吗,先生?"窗口有一个声音说着。那是一个好意的脚夫给我一个暗示,这是我下车的站了。我谢谢他,说我刚才一定是睡着了。抓着我的帽子同手杖,我走到外面的清凉的夏夜里。当我关着我那段车子的门时候,我看见我的旅伴绕着灯儿飘游……

John Galsworthy

Evolution

Coming out of the theatre, we found it utterly impossible to get a taxi-cab; and, though it was raining slightly, walked through Leicester Square in the hope of picking one up[1] as it returned down Piccadilly. Numbers of hansoms and four-wheelers passed, or stood by the curb, hailing us feebly, or not even attempting to attract our attention, but every taxi seemed to have its load. At Piccadilly Circus losing patience, we beckoned to a four-wheeler and resigned ourselves to a long, slow journey. A sou'-westerly[2] air blew through the open windows, and there was in it the scent of change, that wet scent which visit; even the hearts[3] of towns and inspires the watcher of

---

1 to pick up: to come upon, find 碰到。
2 sou'-westerly: of south-west wind 属于西南风的。
3 heart: the inmost heart 中心。

进　　化

从戏院里出来，我们是绝对没有法子找到一辆野鸡汽车：虽然下着微雨，我们还是走过勒司特方场，希望会碰到一辆回到匹喀底尼的野鸡汽车。许多二轮轻马车同四轮马车走过，或者勒着马站住，微弱地向我们兜生意，或者简直不来引我们的注意，但是每辆野鸡汽车好像都载了人了。到匹喀底尼广场时候，等得不耐烦了，我们叫一辆四轮马车，让自己去过一个长久迟慢的旅行。一阵西南风由打开的窗口吹进来，内中带有变化的气味，那种潮湿的气味，它甚至于来到城市的中心，使城市的万千动作的旁观者得到灵感，想到那个迈进不停的"大

their myriad activities with thought of the restless Force that forever cries: "On, on!" But gradually the steady patter of the horse's hoofs, the rattling of the windows, the slow thudding of the wheels, pressed on us so drowsily that when, at last, we reached home we were more than half asleep. The fare was two shillings, and, standing in the lamplight to make sure[1] the coin was a half-crown before handing it to the driver, we happened to look up. This cabman appeared to be a man of about sixty, with a long, thin face, whose chin and drooping grey moustaches seemed in permanent repose on the up-turned collar of his old blue overcoat. But the remarkable features of his face were the two furrows down his cheeks, so deep and hollow that it seemed as though that face were a collection of bones without coherent flesh, among which the eyes were sunk back so far that they had lost their lustre. He sat quite motionless, gazing at the tail of his horse. And, almost unconsciously, one added the rest of one's silver to that half-crown. He took the coins without speaking; but, as we were turning into the garden gate, we heard him say:

"Thank you; you've saved my life."

Not knowing, either of us, what to reply to such a curious speech, we closed the gate again and came back to the cab.

---

1 to make sure: to make certain 仔细看一下，使确实。

力",它永久是叫道:"前进,前进!"但是渐渐地马蹄沉闷的得得,窗子的戛戛,轮子迟慢的碎碎的各种声音引人入睡地压着我们,所以当最后我们到家时候,我们几乎已经酣睡了。车钱是两先令,当我们没有把钱交给御者以前,站在灯下看清一下那块钱是个值得两先令六辨士的银币时候,我们偶然抬起头来。这个御者看起来是六十左右年纪的人,一副长瘦的脸孔,他的下颏同向下垂的灰色胡须好像老是休息在他的老旧的蓝色外套的反领上面,但是他脸上奇特的地方是他颊上那两个凹处,那么深,那么空,仿佛好像他的脸孔是一堆骨头,没有连贯的筋肉,在这些骨头里面,一对眼睛那么深深地陷着,它们已经现不出光辉了。他丝毫不动地坐着,直着眼睛看他的马儿的尾。差不多是不知不觉地,我们把我们所有的其余银钱加上那块银币给他。他接了钱不说什么;但是当我们转进园门时,我们听他说道:

"谢谢你;你救了我的命。"

我们两人都不知道怎样去回答这么奇怪的一句话,我们又把园门关上,回来到马车旁边。

"Are things so very bad?"

"They are." replied the cabman, "it's done with[1] — is this job. We're not wanted now." And, taking up his whip, he prepared to drive away.

"How long have they been as bad as this?"

The cabman dropped his hand again, as though glad to rest it, and answered incoherently:

"Thirty-five year I've been drivin' a cab."

And, sunk again in contemplation of his horse's tail, he could only be roused by many questions to express himself, having, as it seemed, no knowledge of the habits.

"I don't blame the taxis, I don't blame nobody.[2] It's come on us, that's what it has. I left the wife this morning with nothing in the house. She was saying to me only yesterday: 'What have you brought home the last four months?' 'Put it at six shillings a week,' I said. 'No,' she said, 'seven.' Well, that's right — she enters it all down in her book."

"You are really going short of[3] food?"

---

1 it's done with: it has been put to an end 这已经被宣告死刑了。

2 下等人同不文的人们说话时常用 double negative 实在只是一个 negative 的意思，所以 I don't blame nobody 是等于 I don't blame anybody。

3 short of: insufficiently provided with 缺乏。

"你们的生意真是这么非常不好吗？"

"是的，"御者答道，"已经是完了——这种职业。我们现在是没有人要了。"拿起鞭子，他预备赶着马儿走去。

"生意这么不好已经有多久了？"

御者又放下他的手，好像喜欢休息一下他的手，文不对题地答道：

"我赶马车已经有三十五年了。"

又沉到沉思他的马尾去了，一定要问了许多话，才能引起他来说出自己的话，好像他不知道谈话这个习惯。

"我不埋怨野鸡汽车，我谁也不埋怨。厄运来到我们头上，所以我们受了厄运。今早我出来时，我妻子在家里什么也没有。她昨天才向我说：'这四个月来，你拿回来多少钱？''一个礼拜算六先令罢，'我说。'不，'她说，'七个。'不错——她把所有进款都记在她的帐簿里。"

"你们真是快绝食吧？"

The cabman smiled; and that smile between those two deep hollows was surely as strange as ever shone on a human face.

"You may say that." he said. "Well, what does it amount to?[1] Before I picked you up[2], I had one eighteen-penny fare to-day; and yesterday I took five shillings. And I've got seven bob[3] a day to pay for the cab, and that's low, too. There's many and many a proprietor that's broke and gone — every bit[4] as bad as us. They let us down as easy[5] as ever they can; you can't get blood from a stone[6], can you?" Once again he smiled. "I'm sorry for them, too, and I'm sorry for the horses, though they come out best of the three of us, I do believe."

One of us muttered something about the Public.

The cabman turned his face and stared down through the darkness.[7]

"The Public?" he said, and his voice had in it a faint surprise. "Well, they all want the taxis. It's natural. They get about[8] faster in them, and time's money. I was seven hours before I picked you up. And then you was lookin' for[9] a taxi. Them as take us because they

---

1　what does it amount to?: what does it signify? 这又有什么关系？

2　to pick up: to take a person into a vessel or vehicle 找到搭客。

3　bob: shilling 先令（英币名）。

4　every bit: every one 每个。

5　to let down easy: to mitigate a payment 减价出租。

6　to get blood from a stone: to get pity from the pitiness 从没有恻隐之心的人们去求得怜悯。

御者微笑着；在这两个深窟中间的微笑的确是人们脸上所现出最奇的表情。

"你也可以这样说。"他说道。"这又有什么呢？在我找到你们以前，今天我只挣十八个辨士；昨天我得五先令。我的车租每天都要七先令，这也是很便宜了。有许多，许多车主已经是失败破产了——他们个个都同我们一样地困难。他们尽力地放低他们车子的租费；可是你不能从没有良心的人那里得到怜悯，你能够吗？"他又微笑一下。"我也可怜他们，我还可怜马儿，虽然我们三者之中马儿还真最过得去的，我真是这样相信。"

我们里有一个人低低地说一句关于"社会"的话。

"社会？"他说，他的声音里含有轻微的惊愕。"喂，他们都要坐野鸡汽车。这是自然的。坐汽车，他们可以走快得多，时间即是金钱。我等了七点钟才找到你。那时你还是想找一辆野鸡汽车。不能够得到更好的，才来坐我们车子的人们照例是生

---

7 此句原文缺译。——编者注
8 to get about：to go from place to place 行路。
9 to look for：to seek for 觅。

can't get better, they're not in a good temper, as a rule¹. And there's a few old ladies that's frightened of the motors, but old ladies aren't never very free with² their money — can't afford to be, the most of them, I expect."

"Everybody's sorry for you; one would have thought that —"

He interrupted quietly: "Sorrow don't buy bread... I never had nobody³ ask me about things before." And, slowly, moving his long face from side to side, he added: "Besides, what could people do? They can't be expected to support you; and if they started askin' you questions they'd feel it very awkward. They know that, I suspect. Of course, there's such a lot of us; the hansoms are pretty nigh as bad off⁴ as we are. Well, we're gettin' fewer every day, that's one thing."

Not knowing whether or no to manifest sympathy with this extinction, we approached the horse. It was a horse that "stood over" a good deal at the knee, and in the darkness seemed to have innumerable ribs. And suddenly one of us said: "Many people want to see nothing but taxis on the streets, if only for the sake of the horses."

The cabman nodded.

1　as a rule: usually 照例, 通常。
2　free with: using without restraint 无拘束地使用。
3　参阅 P176 注 2。
4　bad off: in an unfortunated condition 在不幸的境遇里。

了脾气的。有些老太太怕坐汽车，但是老太太从来是用钱不很随便的——她们多半真是阔绰不起的，这我会猜出。"

"谁也是可怜你们；我们真会想——"

他冷静地打断我的话，说道："怜悯买不得面包……我从来没有人向我问过我的事情。"慢慢地，把他瘦长的脸孔摇来摇去，他又说："而且，人们会干什么呢？当然不能希望他们来赡养你们；若使他们开始问你们许多话，他们一定会觉得很难为情。他们晓得了这些，我想。自然，世上免不了有我们这班人；两辆马车的御者的境遇同我们差不多是一样地困难。喔，我们这班人却一天一天少下去了，这到〔倒〕是一件好事。"

不晓得对于这个灭绝要不要表示同情，我们走近他的马。这是一匹膝头"弯"得很利害的马，在黑暗里好像有无数的肋骨。忽然间我们之中有一个人说道："许多人在街上不愿意看到别的车子，除开了汽车，也许是单因为马车的马儿太苦了。"

御者点首一下。

"This old fellow," he said, "never carried a deal[1] of flesh. His grub don't put spirit into him nowadays; it's not up to much in quality, but he gets enough of it."

"And you don't?"

The cabman again took up his whip.

"I don't suppose," he said without emotion, "any one could ever find another job for me now. I've been at this too long. It'll be the workhouse, if it's not the other thing[2]."

And hearing us mutter that it seemed cruel, he smiled for the third time.

"Yes," he said slowly, "it's a bit hard[3] on us, because we've done nothing to deserve it. But things are like that, so far as I can see. One thing comes pushin' out another, and so you go on. I've thought about it — you get to thinkin' and worryin' about the rights o' things, sittin' up here all day. No, I don't see anything for it. It'll soon be the end of us now — can't last much longer. And I don't know that I'll be sorry to done with[4] it. It's pretty well broke my spirit."

"There was a fund got up[5]."

---

1 a deal: a great deal 很多。
2 这是指做叫花子。
3 hard: cruel 残忍，难为了。
4 to have done with: to make an end of 完结了。
5 to get up a fund: to raise money 募款。

"这个老家伙，"他说，"从来没有胖过。他的粮草现在不能给他以精神；那不是很好的粮草，但是他也有够食的。"

"你却没有？"

御者又拿起他的马鞭。

"我不想，"他不动情地说道，"现在谁能够替我找个别的工作。我干这个干得太久了。将来若使不是别的，就是到贫民院里去。"

听我们低声说这好像是太残忍了，他现出第三回的微笑。

"是的，"他慢慢地说道，"这对于我们未免是有些太苦了，因为我们没有做什么事值得这样挨苦。但是据我所知，事情总是这样。一件东西来赶去别一件，你就是这样子前进。我曾经把它想过——整天坐在这上面，你自然会去思虑，去苦想事情的道理。我看不出什么办法。我们现在也都快死了——不能再滞留多久了。我不想我会有什么悲哀，对于这种终止。这已够使我灰心了。"

"曾有一次捐款过。"

"Yes, it helped a few of us to learn the motor-drivin'; but what's the good of that to me, at my time of life? Sixty, that's my age; I'm not the only one — there's hundreds like me. We're not fit for it, that's the fact; we haven't got the nerve now. It'd want a mint of money to help us. And what you say's the truth — people want to see the end of us. They want the taxis — our day's over. I'm not complaining; you asked me about it yourself."

And for the third time he raised his whip.

"Tell me what you would have done if you had been given your fare and just sixpence over?"

The cabman stared downward, as though puzzled by that question.

"Done? Why, nothing. What could I have done?"

"But you said that it had saved your life."

"Yes, I said that," he answered slowly; "I was feelin' a bit low[1]. You can't help it sometimes; it's the thing comin' on you, and no way out of it — that's what gets over[2] you. We try not to think about it, as a rule."

And this time, with a "Thank you, kindly!" he touched his horse's flank with the whip. Like a thing aroused from sleep the forgotten

---

1 low: sad 愁。
2 to get over: to overcome 压下。

"不错，那可以帮助我们里面一些人去学开汽车；但是这同我有什么好处，在我这样的年龄。六十，这是我的岁数；不是我一个人——像我这样的人们有成百成千。我们不宜于干那事情，这是事实；我们现在没有那股精神了。还要成千成万的钱来帮助我们。你说的话是真的——人们想看到我灭绝。他们喜欢野鸡汽车——我们的日子已经过去了。我不是诉苦；这是你自己先问我的。"

他第三次举起他的马鞭。

"告诉我，你会干什么，若使你只得到你的车资同六辨士？"

御者向下睁着眼，好似被这个问题弄迷惑了。

"干什么？怎么，什么也不会干。什么我会干？"

"但是你说这救了你的命。"

"是的，我说了这句话，"他慢慢地答道，"我觉得有些愁闷。有时你是无法摆脱的；愁闷自己跑来，你是无路可避的——它就这样子压住你了。我们照例是设法不去想它。"

这回，说一句"谢谢你，深深地！"他的马鞭打着他的马

creature started and began to draw the cabman away from us. Very slowly they travelled down the road among the shadow of the trees broken by lamplight. Above us, white ships of cloud were sailing rapidly across the dark river of sky on the wind which smelled of change. And after the cab was lost to sight, that wind still brought to us the dying sound of the slow wheels.

1910.

腹。像从睡梦醒来的东西,这个被人们忘记的动物惊跳一下,开始将这御者拉离开我们。非常慢地他们走下那道路,在树影中间,有时被灯光照着。在我们上面,白的云帆在黑的天河里很快地驶过,顺着那阵含有天气变化的气味的风。看不见那马车了,风还将那迟慢的车轮的将灭的声音带到我们耳里。

E. V. Lucus

London Mysterious

To artists the fog is London's best friend. Not the black fog, but the other. For there are two distinct London fogs — the fog that chokes and blinds, and the fog that shrouds. The fog that enters into every corner of the house and coats all the metal work with a dark slime, and sets us coughing and rubbing our eyes — for that there is nothing to say. It brings with it too much dirt, too much unhealthiness, for any kind of welcome to be possible. "Hell is a city much like London", I quoted to myself in one of the last of such fogs, as I groped by the railings of the Park in the Bayswater Road. The traffic, which I could not see, was rumbling past, and every now and then[1] a man, close by[2] but invisible, would call out a word of warning,

---

1 every now and then: at frequent intervals; from time to time 常常，屡屡。
2 close by: near 接近。

神秘的伦敦

由艺术家看来,雾是伦敦最好的朋友。不是黑雾,是指别一种的雾。伦敦有两种不同的雾——壅塞气息,把世界化作黑漆一团的雾同轻轻地铺罩着的薄雾。前一种雾走到房屋的个个角上,将一切的金属东西盖上一层暗色的黏泥,弄得我们一面咳嗽,一面擦眼睛——对于这种雾是没有好话可说的。"地狱是一个很像伦敦的城",我向自己引用这句话,在前回这种的一个雾里,当我抓着贝斯窝忒路的公园栏杆望〔往〕前摸索。车子,我所不能看见的,辚辚地走过,时常有人,就在身旁,却是看不见的,喊出警告的话来,或者有人会用受惊的声音问道他到

or some one would ask in startled tones where he was. The hellishness of it consisted in being of life and yet not in it — a stranger in a muffled land. It is bad enough for ordinary wayfarers in such a fog as that; but one has only to imagine what it is to be in charge of[1] a horse and cart, to see how much worse one's lot might be.

But the other fog — the fog that veils but does not obliterate, the fog that softens but does not soil, the fog whose beautifying properties Whistler[2] may be said to have discovered — that can be a delight and a joy. Seen through this gentle mist London becomes a city of romance. All that is ugly and hard in her architecture, all that is dingy and repellent in her colour, disappears. "Poor buildings," wrote Whistler, who watched their transformation so often from his Chelsea home, "lose themselves in the dim sky, and the tall chimneys become campanili[3] and the warehouses are palaces in the night, and the whole city hangs in the heavens."

It was Dickens[4] who discovered the London of eccentricity, London as the abode of the odd and the quaint, and Stevenson[5] who

---

1 in charge of: intrusted with the care of 负看护之责。
2 Whistler, J. A. McNeill (1834—1903), 美国的画家, 文学家及诙谐家。他的画带有印象派的色彩, 尤善于描状泰晤士河的风景。
3 campanili: detached bell-towers 钟塔。
4 Dickens, Charles (1812—1870), 十九世纪英大写实小说家。
5 Stevenson, Robert Louis Balfour (1850—1894), 近代重整起浪漫派的旗鼓的英小说家, 他的《金银岛》是近代不朽的名著。

底是在那里。这种雾的凶恶处是在于将他这种有生气的东西放在无生气的环境里——在一个蒙盖住的地方里的一个生客。普通走路的人们在这样的雾里已经是够苦了；但是只要臆想到还要去招呼一匹马同一辆车是怎样的情形，立刻可以看出一个人的运气还可以更坏得许多。

可是别一种的雾——笼着东西，而没有湮没形迹的雾，使东西的轮廓化为轻圆，而没有去沾污染秽的雾，它那种美化的能力可说是被喜斯勒所发现的雾——那种雾能够变做一种悦心的东西，一种欢喜的材料。从这种温柔薄雾看去，伦敦变做一座浪漫的都城。她的建筑物里所有丑陋粗糙的地方，她的色调里所有龌龊碍眼的地方，全消失了。"可怜的房屋，"喜斯勒在文章里说过，他是那么常从他的拆尔息家里注视它们的幻变，"在模糊的天里消失了，高高的烟囱全化为钟塔，货栈是夜间的宫殿，全城却昂在天中"。

迭更司发现了畸异的伦敦，奇妙古怪所汇聚的伦敦，史蒂芬孙发现了浪漫故事的老家的伦敦。喜斯勒所发现的伦敦是个

discovered London as a home of romance. Whistler discovered London as a city of fugitive, mysterious beauty. For decades[1] the London fog had been a theme for vituperation and sarcasm: it needed this sensitive American-Parisian[2] to show us that what to the commonplace man was a foe and a matter for rage, to the artist was a friend. Every one knows about is now.

Fogs have never been quite the same to me since I was shown a huge chimney on the south side of the Thames, and was told that it belonged to the furnaces that supply London offices with electric light; and that whenever the weather seems to suggest a fog, a man is sent to the top of this chimney to look down the river and give notice of the first signs of the enemy rolling up. Then, as his news is communicated, the furnaces are re-stoked, and extra pressure is obtained that the coming darkness may be fought and the work of counting-houses not interrupted. All sentinels, all men on the look-out[3], belong to romance; and from his great height this man peering over the river shipping and the myriad roofs for a thickening of the horizon has touched even a black London fog with romance for me. I think of his straining eyes, his call of warning, those roaring fires...

---

1 decade: ten-year period 十年。
2 Whistler 生于美国，长游于巴黎，所以作者这样叫他。
3 look-out: watch 看望。

含有缥缈神秘的美的城市。几十年来，伦敦的雾老是人们咒骂讥笑的一个题目：的确需要这位神经锐敏的生于美国的巴黎人来指示给我们看普通人所认为一个仇敌同一件该发怒的事情，却是艺术家的一位朋友。现在谁也晓得这点了。

雾对于我变成为与前大不相同的东西了，自从人们指给我看泰晤士河南岸上的一个大烟囱，告诉我这是属于供给伦敦办事房以电灯的火炉；无论什么时候，天气一有点雾意，就派一个人到这烟囱的顶上，去望一望远处的河；敌人一开始有些卷来的现象，就给底下的人们一个通告。他这新闻传出之后，火炉就重新加上燃料，做出额外的压力，借此可以同来临的黑暗奋斗，账房里的工作也不至于停止。一切巡哨，一切守望的人们都是属于浪漫史的；从他这高耸天际的所在，越过河里来往的轮船同万家的屋顶，一直看到水平线边的一块浓雾，这个人甚至于使伦敦的黑雾生色，就是在我眼里也变成浪漫史里的东西了。我会想起他的竭力望远的眼睛，他的警告呼声，那群咆哮的烈火……

Hilaire Belloc

On a Hermit Whom I Knew

In a valley of the Apennines[1], a little before it was day, I went down by the side of a torrent wondering where I should find repose; for it was now some hours since I had given up all hope of discovering a place for proper human rest and for the passing of the night, but at least I hoped to light upon[2] a dry bed of sand under some overhanging rock, or possibly of pine needles beneath closely woven trees, where one might get sleep until the rising of the sun.

As I still trudged, half expectant and half careless, a man came up behind me, walking quickly as do mountain men: for throughout the world (I cannot tell why) I have noticed that the men of the

---

1 位于意大利的大山,人们叫它做意大利的背脊。
2 to light upon: to meet with; discover 碰到,发现。

我所知道的一位隐士

在亚平宁山的一个溪谷里,天快亮的时候,我缘着一个急流的边岸下山,心里纳罕在何处我会找到休憩的所在;因为现在已经有好几个钟头了,自从我抛弃了找到一块人们可以休息的地方来过夜的希望,但是最少我也希望碰到一块干燥的沙地,上面有悬岩覆着,或者也许一床平铺的干松叶,在密密地交织着的树林的底下,在那里可以睡去,一直到太阳上升时才醒来。

当我还是辛苦地望〔往〕前走,心里一半是期望,一半是漠然时候,有一个人走近我的背后,他走得很快,像一切住在山中的人们;我看出全世界里(我也说不出理由来)山居的人们

mountains walk quickly and in a sprightly manner, arching the foot, and with a light and general gait as though the hills were waves and as though they were in thought springing upon the crests of them. This is true of all mountaineers. They are but few.

This man, I say, came up behind me and asked me whether I were going towards a certain town of which he gave me the name, but as I had not so much as heard of this town I told him I knew nothing of it. I had no map, for there was no good map of that district, and a bad map is worse than none. I knew the names of no towns except the large towns on the coast. So I said to him:

"I cannot tell anything about this town, I am not making towards it. But I desire to reach the sea coast, which I know to be many hours away, and I had hoped to sleep overnight under some roof or at least in some cavern, and to start with the early morning; but here I am, at the end of the night, without repose and wondering whether I can go on."

He answered me:

"It is four hours to the sea coast, but before you reach it you will find a lane branching to the right, and if you will go up it (for it climbs the hill) you will find a hermitage. Now by the time you are there the hermit will risen."

走路都很快，有种活泼的态度，弯起脚来，用一种轻飘一致的步容，好像脚下的小山都是波浪，好像他们心里以为是踏着浪头而走。凡是山居的人们全是这样。但是真正的山居人们也是很少数。

这个人，我说，走近我的背后，问我是不是向某某镇去，他对我说出那个镇名，但是这个镇我既是从来没有听人说过，我就告诉他我是一些也不晓得的。我没有地图，因为那个区域没有好的地图，而坏的地图到〔倒〕不如没有。那里一切镇的名字我都不知道，除开海滨几个大镇。所以我就对他说：

"关于这个镇，我什么也不能说，我也不是向那里去的。我却是想走到海滨，我知道那还要好几点钟的路，我希望在夜里能够睡一觉，在有些人家里，或者最少也在有些洞窟里，等到清早，再行出发；但是现在夜也残了，我还没有得到休憩，心里暗自纳罕，我还能够继续走路不能。"

他答我道：

"到海滨还要走四个钟头的路，但是在你到了那里以前，你会看到一条拐湾〔弯〕向右的小路，若使你爬上那路（因为那路是走上山的），你会看到一所隐舍。当你走抵那里时，隐士也已起来了。"

"Will he be at his prayers?" said I.

"He says no prayers to my knowledge," said my companion lightly, "for he is not a hermit of that kind. Hermits are many and prayers are few. But you will find him bustling about, and he is a very hospitable man. Now as it so happens that the road to the sea coast bends here round along the foot of the hills, you will, in his company, perceive the port below you and the populace and the high road, and yet you will be saving a good hour in distance of time, and will have ample rest before reaching your vessel, if it is a vessel indeed that you intend to take."

When he had said these things I thanked him and gave him a bit of sausage and went along[1] my way, for as he had walked faster than me before our meeting and while I was still in the dumps, so now I walked faster than him, having received good news.

All happened just as he had described. The dawn broke behind me over the noble but sedate peaks of the Apennines; it first defined the heights against the growing colours of the sun, it next produced a general warmth and geniality in the air about me; it last displayed the downward opening of the valley, and, very far off, a plain that sloped towards the sea.

Invigorated by the new presence of the day I went forward

---

1 to go along: to go forward 前进。

"他会正在祈祷吗?"我说。

"据我所知,他没有说什么祈祷,"我的伴侣轻快地答道,"因为他不是那类的隐士。隐士有许多,祈祷文却只有几种。可是你到的时候会看他正忙着干零碎的事情,他是个待客极殷勤的人。到海滨的路现在既是刚好缘着这里的山脚,你会同他一起俯视你脚下的海港,人烟同大路,你又能够省了整整一个钟头的时间,很可以在你到船以前舒服地休息一下,若使你的目的真是上一艘船。"

他说了这些话后,我谢他一声,送他一小块腊肠,又走我的路了,因为起先我们尚未遇着,我还是很烦闷时候,他走得比我快,所以得到了好消息,我现在却比他走得快。

一路的情形刚好像他所描状的。曙光从我背后露出,罩着亚平宁山高贵而严肃的孤峰;它先把山头的形状照得清清楚楚,拿太阳的朦胧向明的丽色来烘托着,然后在我四围的空气里产生出一种普遍的暖气同融和气象;最后照耀着溪谷的向下开溪地方,同远远地一片倾斜向海的平原。

白昼的新出现增加了我的力气,我更快地前进,最后到了

more rapidly, and came at last to a place where a sculptured panel made out of marble, very clever and modern, and representing a mystery, marked the division between two ways; and I took the lane to my right as my companion of the night hours had advised me.

For perhaps a mile or a little more the lane rose continually between rough walls intercepted by high banks of thorn, with here and there[1] a vineyard, and as it rose one had between the breaches of the wall glimpses of an ever-growing sea: for, as one rose, the sea became a broader and a broader belt, and the very distant islands, which at first, had been but little clouds along the horizon, stood out[2] and became parts of the landscape, and, as it were, framed all the bay.

Then at last, when I had come to the height of the hill, to where it turned a corner and ran level along the escarpment of the cliffs that dominated the sea plain, I saw below me a considerable stretch of country, between the fall of the ground and the distant shore, and under the daylight which was now full and clear one could perceive that all this plain was packed with an intense cultivation, with houses, happiness and men.

Far off,[3] a little to the northward, lay the mass of a town; and

---

1　here and there: in one place and another; so as to be irregular scattered处处，星罗棋布。

2　to stood out: to appear in relief; be prominent 显著。

一个地方，那里有大理石做的，雕刻的一块平片，很精巧，很近代的，雕着一个神秘的东西，来指明两条路的分界；我照着我的夜间伴侣所吩咐的，顺着我的右边小路走去。

这条小路夹在崎岖的石垣中间，老是逶迤向上差不多有一里或者一里多些，路中有几个荆棘高堤挡着，沿途有葡萄园散布道傍〔旁〕，这条路既是一步步高着，人们可以从石垣的破裂处瞥见时时长大的大海，因为当我们向上走时候，海的范围渐渐地扩大，那些很远的小岛，起先不过是水平线边的几小朵云儿，现在却明显地浮凸出来，变做景色的一部分，好似是内海的镶边。

最后，我走到了山顶，那里的路一转湾〔弯〕，就同控制海面的削壁并行，我看见底下有一望相连的大块平野，居在地盘的下陷同远岸间；在现在光明的皎日之下，人们能够看出这块平原全填满了努力的耕作，填满了房屋，幸福同住民。

在远方，稍近北边点，躺有一大块市镇；伸出到地中海去，

3　far off：at a great distance 远处。

stretching out into the Mediterranean with a gesture of command and of desire were the new arms of the harbour.

To see such things filled me with a complete content. I know not whether it be the effect of long vigil, or whether it be the effect of contrast between the darkness and the light, but certainly to come out of a lonely night spent on the mountains, down with the sunlight into the civilisation of the plain, is, for any man that cares to undergo the suffering and the consolation, as good as any experience that life affords. Hardly had I so conceived the view before me when I became aware, upon my right, of a sort of cavern, or rather a little and carefully minded shrine, from which a greeting proceeded.

I turned round and saw there a man of no great age and yet of a venerable appearance. He was perhaps fifty-five years old, or possibly a little less, but he had let his grey-white hair grow longish and his beard was very ample and fine. It was he that had addressed me, He sat dressed in a long gown in a modern and rather luxurious chair at a low long table of chestnut wood, on which he had placed a few books, which I saw were in several languages and two of them not only in English, but having upon them mark of an English circulating library[1] which did business in the great town at our feet. There was also upon the table a breakfast ready of white bread and honey,

---

1 circulating library: a library from which book can be taken for use at home or elsewhere under certain restriction 流通图书馆。

带有命令同希望的姿势的，却是海港的新手臂。

看了这些东西使我心满意足。我不知道这是彻夜不眠的结果，或者是光暗相对比的结果，但是从在大山里渡〔度〕过的寂寞的夜里走出，跟太阳光一起来到平原的文化区域，这的确是人生所能给我们的无上快事，只要他肯去受那苦痛同后来的安慰。我刚在这样玩味目前的好景，就觉得在我右边有一个洞窟这类的东西，或者该说是一个精小，收拾得很干净的神龛，从那里来有一声招呼。

我转过身来，看见那里有一个人，年纪不大，可是很可敬的样子。他大约有五十五岁，或者还不到，但是他让他的灰白色头发生得很长，他的须子是很丰满，很美丽的。向我招呼的就是他。他穿一件长衫，坐在一张近代的，稍近奢华的椅子里，旁边有一张低矮的，栗木做的长桌，桌上他排了几本书，我看那是好几种文字写的，有两本不只是英文的，上面还盖有一个英国流通图书馆的图章，这图书馆是在我们脚下的大镇里办公。桌上还放有预备好了的早餐，白面包同蜂蜜，一个棕色大咖啡

a large brown coffee pot, two white cups, and some goat's milk in a bowl of silver. This meal he asked me to share.

"It is my custom," he said, "when I see a traveller coming up my mountain road to get out[1] a cup and a plate for him, or, if it is midday, a glass. At evening, however, no one ever comes."

"Why not?" said I.

"Because," he answered, "this lane goes but a few yards further round the edge of the cliff, and there it ends in a precipice; the little platform where we are is all but the end of the way. Indeed, I chose it upon that account, seeing, when I first came here, that from its height and solation it was well fitted for my retreat."

I asked him how long ago that was, and he said nearly twenty years. For all that time, he added, he had lived there, going down into the plain but once or twice in a season and having for his rare companions those who brought him food and the peasants on such days as they toiled up to work at their plots towards the summit; also, from time to time[2], a chance traveller like myself. But these, he said, made but poor companions, for they were usually such as had missed their way at the turning and arrived at that high place of his out of breath[3] and angry, I assured him that this was not my case, for

---

1 to get out: to take out 拿出。
2 from time to time: at intervals 时时。
3 out of breath: gasping, as from exertion 喘不过气来。

瓶，两个白杯子，一个银碗里盛有些羊奶，他请我同他共享这个早餐。

"这是我的习惯，"他说，"当我看到一位旅客走上我的山路，就替他预备了一个杯子同一个盘子；或者，若使是中午，一个玻璃杯子。然而在晚上，从来没有人来过。"

"为什么没有人来呢？"我说。

"因为，"他答道，"这条小路沿着石岩的边际只能再走几码，就陡断了变成一片削壁；我们所站的平台差不多是路的极端了。真的，我拣选这块地方住，就是为着这种地势，我初次来时，从它的高度同孤独看出这是最合于做我的隐所。"

我问他那是几年前的事，他说差不多有二十年了。他又说，这二十年里他老是住在那里，每季中到平原去只一两回，他稀少的伴侣是带东西上去给他的人们同有些日子里的农夫，当他们辛苦地到近山顶他们的田地内去耕作的时候；此外有时一两个像我这样的偶然旅客。但是这班人，他说，不能做我的好伴侣，因为他们常是拐错了路，迷途的人，走到他这块高地时气也喘不过来了，总是很生气。我请他相信不是我的情形，因为

a man had told me in the night how to find his hermitage and I had come of set purpose to see him. At this he smiled.

We were now seated together at table eating and talking so, when I asked him whether he had a reputation for sanctity and whether the people brought him food. He answered with a little hesitation that he had a reputation, he thought, for necromancy rather than anything else, and that upon this account it was not always easy to persuade a messenger to bring him the books in French and English which he ordered from below, though these were innocent enough, being, as a rule, novels written by women or academicians, records of travel, the classics of the Eighteenth Century, or the biographies of aged statesmen. As for food, the people of the place did indeed bring it to him, but not, as in an idyll, for courtesy; contrariwise, they demanded heavy payment, and his chief difficulty was with bread; for stale bread was intolerable to him. In the matter of[1] religion he would not say that he had none, but rather that he had several religions; only at this season of the year, when everything was fresh, pleasant and entertaining, he did not make use of any of them, but laid them all aside. As this last saying of his had no meaning for me I turned to another matter and said to him:

"In any solitude contemplation is the chief business of the soul.

---

1 in the matter of: with regard to 关于。

夜里有个人告诉我怎样去找他的隐所，我是存心来拜望他的。听着这话，他微微地一笑。

我们现在同坐在桌旁，这样子吃着谈着，我就问他有没有圣者的名望，人们有没有白送食物给他。他有点迟疑样子答道，他想他有个会巫术的名望，却没有什么别的，所以有时他不容易说动跑差将他从下面店里定的英美书籍带上给他，虽然这些书全是顶老实不过的，照例是妇人或者学士院会员写的小说，旅行家的记录，十八世纪的杰著，或者老年政治家的传记。至于食物，那里的人民的确是替他带来，但不像牧歌里所说的全出于殷勤；却是刚相反，他们要很贵的代价，他最大的困难是在于面包；因为陈腐的面包是他所最厌恶的。关于宗教这件事，他不说他没有一个宗教，却要说他有好几个；不过在这个季节，当大地上一切都是新鲜的，欣欢的同有趣的，他用不着什么宗教，把它们全搁在旁边了。因为他最后这句话于我是没有意义的，我就转到别事上头，问他道：

"在任一的幽处里，冥想总是心灵的主要事务。你说你不行

How, then, do you, who say you practise no rites, fill up your loneliness here?"

In answer to this question he became more animated, spoke with a sort of laugh in his voice, and seemed as though he were young again and as though my question had aroused a whole lifetime of good memories.

"My contemplation," he said, not without large gestures, "is this wide and prosperous plain below: the great city with its harbour and ceaseless traffic of ships, the roads, the houses building, the fields yielding every year to husbandry, the perpetual activities of men. I watch my kind and I glory in them, too far off to be disturbed by the friction of individuals, yet near enough to have a daily companionship in the spectacle of so much life. The mornings, when they are all at labour, I am inspired by their energy; in the noons and afternoons I feel a part of their patient and vigorous endurance; and when the sun broadens near the rim of the sea at evening, and all work ceases, I am filled with their repose. The lights along the harbour front in the twilight and on into the darkness remind me of them when I can no longer see their crowds and movements, and so does the music which they love to play in their recreation after the fatigues of the day, and the distant songs which they sing far into the night.

什么宗教仪式，那么在这里怎样渡你的寂寞时光呢？"

答这个问题时他变成更兴奋些，说话的声音里带一种笑声，仿佛是好像他又年青起来了，好像我的问题勾起他的充满了甜蜜的回忆的一生往事。

"我冥想的对象，"他说，很带劲地做出许多的姿势来表情，"是下面这块宽阔隆盛的平原：这个大城以及它的海港同它的不断的商船来往，这许多道路，这许多正在建筑的屋子，这许多每年耕种有收获的田地，这种永久不歇的人们活动。我观察我的同类，我以为他们也是我的荣誉；我同他们隔得太远了，不会给他们里面个人的冲突所扰乱，然而也都还相近，这么多的生命活力的景象可以做一个日日在目前的伴侣。早上，当他们都在做工时候，我从他们的努力得到灵感；在中午同下午，我也有些感觉得他们坚忍精壮的耐劳；当黄昏到了，太阳渐渐扩大走近海缘，一切的工作都停止了的时候，我的心充满了他们的安息。从薄暮一直到黑夜里，港的前面的灯光使我记起他们，当我已不能再看见他们结群同工作；此外使我念及他们的是白天工作疲倦后他们游戏时所爱弹的音乐同他们唱到深夜的远远歌声。

"I was about thirty years of age, and had seen (in a career of diplomacy) many places and men; I had a fortune quite insufficient for a life among my equals. My youth had been, therefore, anxious, humiliated, and worn when, upon a feverish and unhappy holiday taken from the capital of this State, I came by accident to the cave and platform which you see. It was one of those days in which the air exhales revelation, and I clearly saw that happiness inhabited the mountain corner. I determined to remain forever in so rare a companionship, and from that day she[1] has never abandoned me. For a little while I kept a touch with the world by purchasing those newspapers in which I was reported shot by brigands or devoured by wild beasts, but the amusement soon wearied me, and now I have forgotten the very names of my companions."

We were silent then until I said, "But some day you will die here all alone."

"And why not?" he answered calmly. "It will be a nuisance for those who find me, but I shall be indifferent altogether."

"That is blasphemy," says I.

"So says the priest of St. Anthony[2]," he immediately replied —

---

1 she 指 companionship。
2 基督教中的一个教派。

"我那时差不多有三十岁年纪（在外交家的生涯里）一〔已〕看过了好多地方同好多人；我的财产很不够我跟我同等的人们过一样的生活。所以我的青年时期是操心的，丢脸的同磨折的，当一个烦燥〔躁〕不乐的假日，我从这邦的首都里出来，偶然走到你现在所看见的这个窟洞同平台。那是一个空气会吐出天启的日子，我清澈地看出幸福是住在这山角里。我决心此后永久同这么稀罕的伴侣一起，从那天起她也绝没有弃丢过我。起先我还同世界有种接触，我去买些报纸，里面说我是被山贼枪杀了，或者说是给野兽吃了，但是这个玩意儿我很快也厌倦了，现在我连我的同伴的名字都忘记了。

我们就静默着，后来我说："但是有一天你会孤单单地死在这里。"

"这有什么不可以？"他冷静地答道。"不过遇到我的遗体的人们会觉得讨厌，但是我都已经是漠然不知了。"

"这是亵渎神圣的话。"我说。

"圣·安秃尼派的神父也是这样说。"他立刻答道——但是

but whether as a reproach, an argument, or a mere commentary I could not discover.

In a little while he advised me to go down to the plain before the heat should incommode my journey. I left him, therefore, reading a book of Jane Austen's[1], and I have never seen him since.

Of the many strange men I have met in my travels he was one of the most strange and not the least fortunate. Every word I have written about him is true.

---

1 Jane Austen（1775—1817），英国女小说家，她的小说专描写家庭里同社交上琐事，的确是隐者读的书。

这到底是一句责备的话，一句辩辞，或者仅仅是一句注解，我是没有法子知道的。

一会儿，他劝我在暑气会使我不好走路之前开始下山到平原去。所以我就离开他，当时也念一本真·奥斯腾的小说，从那回以后，我总没有再遇到他。

在我的旅行里所碰到的许多奇怪人们里面，他是最奇怪，可是也不是最不幸的一个。我所写关于他的话，每字都是真的。

G. K. Chesterton

On Running After One's Hat

I feel an almost savage envy on hearing that London has been flooded in my absence, while I am in the mere country. My own Battersea has been, I understand[1], particularly favoured as a meeting of the waters. Battersea was already, as I need hardly say, the most beautiful of human localities. Now that it has the additional splendour of great sheets of water, there must be something quite incomparable in the landscape (or waterscape) of my own romantic town. Battersea must be a vision of Venice[2]. The boat that brought the meat from the butcher's must have shot along those lanes of rippling silver with the strange smoothness of the gondola. The greengrocer who

---

1 to understand: to be informed 听说。
2 Venice 的街道全是小河，居民天天坐船来往。

追赶自己的帽子

我感觉一种差不多是野蛮人的妒忌,一听到伦敦当我离开时候,被水淹了,而我却只住在乡下里。我自己的巴特西,我听说,特别蒙恩,变做众水的汇聚处。巴特西本来已是,这几乎是用不着我说的,最美丽的居住所在。现在又加上几片大水的伟观,我自己这个浪漫的小镇的风景(或者要说水景)必定有些无可比拟的好处。巴特西绝对化做威尼斯的影子了。从屠户那里送肉来的小船一定是沿着涟漪银色的水港飞驶,带着威尼斯小艇奇妙的流利神情。运生菜到拉取米耳路角的水果一定

brought cabbages to the corner of the Latchmere Road must have leant upon the oar with the unearthly grace of the gondolier. There is nothing so perfectly poetical as an island; and when a district is flooded it becomes an archipelago.

Some consider such romantic views of flood or fire slightly lacking in reality. But really this romantic view of such inconveniences is quite as practical as the other. The true optimist who sees in such things an opportunity for enjoyment is quite as logical and much more sensible than the ordinary "Indignant Ratepayer" who sees in them an opportunity for grumbling. Real pain, as in the case of being burnt at Smithfield[1] or having a toothache, is a positive thing; it can be supported, but scarcely enjoyed. But, after all, our toothaches are the exception, and as for being burnt at Smithfield, it only happens to us at the very longest intervals. And most of the inconveniences that make men swear or women cry are really sentimental of imaginative inconveniences — things altogether of the mind. For instance, we often hear grown-up people complaining of having to hang about[2] a railway station and wait for a train. Did you ever hear a small boy complain of having to hang about a railway station and wait for a train? No; for to him to be inside a railway

---

1 从前烧异教徒的地方。

2 to hang about: to loiternear a place 游惰。

是倚着桨，现出小艇夫不沾尘土的从容姿态。没有东西会像小岛那样含有十足的诗情；当一个地方被淹着时候，它是变成一群群岛了。

有人以为对于大水或者火灾这种浪漫的见解是有点缺乏实在。但是对于这类麻烦的事体，这种浪漫的见解真是和别的同样地可以实行，一点差别也没有。在这些事情里看出开心机会的真正的乐观主义者是同在这些事情里看出说怨言的机会的一般"忿怒的纳税者"一样样地有道理，实在还比他懂事得多。真真的苦痛，像在斯密斯飞德活活地烧死，或者患了齿痛这类的事，是一件实在的东西；能够挨着，却几乎不能拿来做开心的材料。但是，究竟我们的齿痛是例外的事，至于在斯密斯飞德活活地烧死，那是隔了很久很久的时期我们才会碰到。而通常使男人咒骂，女人号淘〔啕〕的麻烦事体多半真是神经过敏，或者幻想所生的麻烦事体——全是心理的作用。比如，我们常听成年的人们诉苦要在火车站滞了许久，等着一辆火车。你可曾听过小孩子诉苦要在火车站滞了许久，等着一辆火车吗？未

station is to be inside a cavern of wonder and a palace of poetical pleasures. Because to him the red light and the green light on the signal are like a new sun and a new moon. Because to him when the wooden arm of the signal falls down suddenly, it is as if a great king had thrown down his staff¹ as a signal and started a shrieking tournament of trains. I myself am of little boys' habit in this matter. They also serve who only stand and wait for the two fifteen. Their meditations may be full of rich and fruitful things. Many of the most purple hours² of my life have been passed at Clapham Junction, which is now, I suppose, under water. I have been there in many moods so fixed and mystical that the water might well have come up to my waist before I noticed it particularly. But in the case of all such annoyances, as I have said, everything depends upon the emotional point of view. You can safely apply the test to almost every one of the things that are currently talked of as the typical nuisance of daily life.

  For instance, there is a current impression that it is unpleasant to have to run after³ one's hat. Why should it be unpleasant to the well-ordered and pious mind? Not merely because it is running, and running exhausts one. The same people run much faster in games

---

1 中古时代比武时是以皇帝的宝杖放下做开始的号令。
2 purple hours: happy hours 快乐的时候。
3 to run after: to strive to catch 追捕。

曾；因为由他看来，在火车站里面是等于在一所怪窟，或者一座满了带着诗意的快乐的宫殿里面。因为由他看来，信号牌上的红灯同绿灯是像一个新太阳同一个新月亮。因为由他看来，当信号的木臂忽然下落时侯，好像一位大王掷下他的宝杖，算个信号，开始了喊声嘈杂的火车竞技。我自己在这方面是带有小孩子的习气。那班站着，只等那二点十五分的快车的人们也可以采取这类见解。他们的默想可以充满有丰饶膏腴的东西。我生本最艳丽的时间许多是从克拉判的换车车站里得到的，我想那地方现在也是没在水里了。我在那里曾经有过许多不同的心境，个个都是那么凝神的，那么神秘的，真的，水尽可以浸到我的腰旁，我还不会明白地晓得。但是关于这类的烦扰，像我上面所说的，一切全靠着我们的情调。你可以安稳地将这个标准用到差不多一切普通所谓日常生活特有的麻烦事情上面。

比如，人们常觉得追赶自己的帽子是不快乐的事情。为什么对于规规矩矩的虔敬心灵，这是不乐的事情呢？并不单是因为跑路，同跑路使人疲累。同一的人们在斗技游戏时还跑得更

and sports. The same people run much more eagerly after an uninteresting little leather ball than they will after a nice silken hat. There is an idea that it is humiliating to run after one's hat; and when people say it is humiliating they mean that it is comic. It certainly is comic; but man is a very comic creature, and most of the things he does are comic — eating, for instance. And the most comic things of all are exactly the things that are most worth doing — such as making love. A man running after a hat is not half so ridiculous as a man running after a wife.

 Now a man could, if he felt rightly in the matter, run after his hat with the manliest ardour and the most sacred joy. He might regard himself as a jolly huntsman pursuing a wild animal, for certainly no animal could be wilder. In fact, I am inclined to believe that hat-hunting on windy days will be the sport of the upper classes in the future. There will be a meet of ladies and gentlemen on some high ground on a gusty morning. They will be told that the professional attendants have started[1] a hat in such-and-such a thicket, or whatever be the technical term. Notice that this employment will in the fullest degree combine sport with humanitarianism. The hunters would feel that they were not inflicting pain. Nay, they would feel

---

 1 to start game: to arouse some object of pursuit 把野兽从林中赶出，以便打猎。

快得多。同一的人们追赶一个无聊的小皮球比他们追赶一顶乖乖的丝帽子还带劲得多。大家以为追赶自己的帽子是丢脸的事；当人们说一件事是丢脸的，他们的意思是那是可笑的。那的确是可笑的；但是人本来就是非常可笑的动物，他所做的事情大多数是可笑的——吃东西就是一个例子。而一切中最可笑的事却刚是那最值得干的事——比如，求爱。一个人追赶一顶帽子还没有一个人追寻一个妻子的可笑的一半。

　　一个人，若使他的见解不错，能够具着最勇敢的热情同最神圣的快乐去追赶他的帽子。他可以自命为追逐野兽的一个高兴猎人，因为实在没有禽兽会比帽子再野顽。真的，我倒有些相信刮风日子时畋猎帽子会变做将来上流阶级人们的游戏。在烈风的清晨将来会有贵妇同绅士们聚集在高地上。他们会听他们说的猎场里跟人在某某林里惊动了一顶帽子，或者其它这类的专门名词。请读者们注意这种玩意儿是游戏同人道主义的结合到了十分圆满的程度。打猎的人们会觉得他们没有使别个受苦。不，他们会觉得他们是使别个受乐，一种趣味浓厚，差不

that they were inflicting pleasure, rich, almost riotous pleasure, upon the people who were looking on. When last I saw an old gentleman running after his hat in Hyde Park, I told him that a heart so benevolent as his ought to be filled with peace and thanks at the thought of how much unaffected pleasure his every gesture and bodily attitude were at that moment giving to the crowd.

The same principle can be applied to every other typical domestic worry. A gentleman trying to get a fly out of the milk or a piece of cork out of his glass of wine often imagines himself to be irritated. Let him think for a moment of the patience of anglers sitting by dark pools, and let his soul be immediately irradiated with gratification and repose. Again, I have known some people of very modern views driven by their distress to the use of theological terms to which they attached no doctrinal significance[1], merely because a drawer was jammed tight and they could not pull it out. A friend of mine was particularly afflicted in this way. Every day his drawer was jammed, and every day in consequence it was something else that rhymes to it. But I pointed out[2] to him that this sense of wrong was really subjective and relative; it rested entirely upon the assumption that the drawer could, should, and would come out easily. "But if," I said, "you picture to yourself that you are pulling against some

---

1 就是指诅咒。

多是恣情的快乐，那是旁观的人们所得到的。当前回我看见一位老绅士在亥德公园里追赶他的帽子，我告诉他，像他这么仁慈的心肠应当是充满了安乐同感谢，一想到他每个姿势，每个体态当时给群众多少纯净的快乐。

同样的原理可以应用到家庭所特有的一切其它的麻烦。一位绅士试将一个苍蝇从牛奶里拿出或者一块软木塞从酒杯里挑出时，常常以为他是受了气。让他想一会儿坐在墨黑的池旁的钓鱼人的耐心，让他的灵魂立刻被满意同静穆照耀着。我又知道几位思想极新的人们，感到麻烦时就用了神道学的字眼，他们却又没有采取教义的意味，只是因为一个屉子紧紧地嵌在桌里，他们却没有法子拔出。我有一个朋友特别患了这个毛病。每天他的屉子总是嵌紧了，因此每天他总哼出几句别的话来。但是我指出给他看这种受枉曲的感觉真是主观的，相对的；这全由于他先假定那屉子能够，应当，又是愿意很容易被人抽出。"但是若使，"我说，"你自己假设你是同有力的压迫着你的一个

---

2 to point out：to indicate clearly 分明地指示。

powerful and oppressive enemy, the struggle will become merely exciting and not exasperating. Imagine that you are tugging up a lifeboat out of the sea. Imagine that you are roping up a fellow creature out of an Alpine[1] crevass. Imagine even that you are a boy again and engaged in a tug-of-war between French and English." Shortly after saying this I left him; but I have no doubt at all that my words bore the best possible fruit. I have no doubt that every day of his life he hangs on[2] to the handle of that drawer with a flushed face and eyes bright with battle, uttering encouraging shouts to himself, and seeming to hear all round him the roar of an applauding ring.

So I do not think that it is altogether fanciful or incredible to suppose that even the floods in London may be accepted and enjoyed poetically. Nothing beyond inconvenience seems really to have been caused by them; and inconvenience, as I have said, is only one aspect, and that the most unimaginative and accidental aspect of a really romantic situation. An adventure is only an inconvenience rightly considered. An inconvenience is only an adventure wrongly considered. The water that girdled the houses and shops of London must, if anything, have only increased their previous witchery and wonder. For as the Roman Catholic priest in the story said: "Wine is

---

1 Alpine: of the Alps.
2 to hang on: to hold fast 紧抓着。

仇敌对拉，那么这奋斗只会变做很兴奋，却不会恼人。试想你正在从大海里曳出一条救生船来。试想你正在从阿尔卑斯山的深罅里用绳子救出一位同类的人。甚至于试想你又是个小孩了，两边人扮做法英两国来干一下拔河。"说了这句话我就离开他了；但是我一些也不怀疑我的话生产出最好的结果。我相信此后每天他紧握着他的屉纽，一副红铺铺的脸膛，眼睛发着战争的光辉，向自己呐喊助威，好像听到他的四围全是喝采的观客雷一般的声音。

所以我想这并不全是痴想的，或者不可信的，去假定就是伦敦的大水也可以逆来顺受，用着诗的情调来鉴赏。好像除了麻烦之外实在并没有引起什么别的坏处；麻烦，像我们前面所说的，不过是一种看法的结果，并且是对于一个真真浪漫的情境的最枯燥同偶然的看法。一件冒险事情只是个没有认错的麻烦。一件麻烦只是看错了的冒险事情。围绕着伦敦住屋店铺的大水若使有什么效力，必定只是增加了它们本有的诱惑同奇妙。故事里的罗马天主教徒说过："酒无论同什么东西在一块都是好

good with everything except water." And on a similar principle, water is good with everything except wine.

的,只除开了水。"所以根据着同样的原理,水无论同什么东西在一块都是好的,只除开了酒。

George W. E. Russell

The Scholar

Once on a time I wrote a series of "Social Silhouettes[1]." They were attempts to depict various types of men as affected by the circumstances, of their life and occupation. One type which I omitted was the Scholar; and this was because the Scholar, as distinct from the Teacher or Professor, is now so rare a character that very few readers would recognize his portrait. For by "The Scholar" I mean the man who devotes his life to the disinterested pursuit of knowledge; with no ulterior aims to serve, and with no intention of applying what he has learnt to any practical purpose. In days gone by[2], this type of character abounded, not only in universities, which were

---

1 Silhouette (Silooette'): portrait of head or figure cut from black paper or painted in solid black on white so as to show outline, usually of the side view.

学　　者

从前有一回我写了一套"社会影像"。那些文章是试去描写被他们的境遇同职业所影响的各种人们。有一种人我忽略了,那是学者;这是因为学者,异于教师或者教授的,现在变成这么罕见的人物了,恐怕没有几位读者会认出他的肖像。因为我用"学者"这个字时,我是指不计实利地献身于智识的追求的人;不是为着什么将来的目的,也不想把所学的用到实际的事情上去。在往昔的日子里,这种的人很多,不单是大学里,那

黑纸剪成的或者是用黑色涂在白地上的人面轮廓常是侧身的。

2　gone by：past 过去。

its natural home, but in all sorts of unlooked-for quarters — in country houses, in Scottish Castles, in Cathedral Closes, in rural Parsonages, in the Temple and Lincoln's Inn[1], and in the Athenaeum Club — even, sometimes, by gross dereliction of official duty, in Whitehall[2] and Somerset House[3]. The Scholar, as then understood, studied because he wished to know; and, though he might, towards the end of his life, put forth[4] a Monograph, a Tractate, or a Treatise, the object to which he devoted his days was not publication but Learning:

"This man decided not to Live but Know."

The Scholar, thus understood, has not always been appreciated as highly as he deserved. Though Browning did his best[5] for him, he has generally been the butt of rhymesters and romancists:

"Did you ever observe in the very ripe scholar

A silent contempt for all outward display?

His clothes fit him ill, from his boots to his collar.

His hair is unbrushed, or else brushed the wrong way.

With sleeves very long, overlapping his fingers,

---

1 inns of court: four legal societies admitting persons to practise at bar (Inner Temple, Middle Temple, Lincoln's Inn and Gray's Inn) 伦敦法学院。

2 Whitehall: the government offices 政府机关。

3 Somerset House: Inland-revenue offices 内地税局。

4 to put forth: to publish 出版。

5 to do one's best: to do all one can 尽力为之。

是它天然的老家,却是在一切预想不到的地方——别墅里,苏格兰堡垒里,大礼拜堂的围地内,乡下的牧师住宅里,腾普尔同林肯法学院里,阿忒尼安俱乐部里——甚至于,有时,自然把公务全疏忽了,在政府各部的衙门同内地税局里。学者,就那时候人们的解释,勤紧地读书是因为他想多知;虽然在他老年的时候,也许会发表一篇"专门论文",一本"小册子",或者一篇"短篇论文",他天天所追求的目的并不是出版这些书,却是学问本身:

"这个人决心不想'生活'只想'多知'。"

学者,作这样解释时,没有像他所应得的那样深深地得到人们的赞美。虽然勃浪宁尽力颂扬他,一般趁韵的诗人同浪漫主义者常把他拿来做笑柄:

"你曾经在那最成熟的学者身上看出

一种对于一切外炫的暗暗看轻么?

他的衣服是不称身的,从他的鞋子到他的领子。

他的头发是没有梳的,不然就是梳错了。

袖子太长,遮着他的手指,

He's spinally crooked, and wanting in grace;

And mental abstraction provokingly lingers

In every turn of his figure and face."

George Eliot[1] was downright spiteful about poor old Mr. Casaubon[2], "chewing the cud of erudite mistake about Cush and Misraim." Mrs. Ward's[3] Edward Langham was an even weaker vessel than his pupil, Robert Elsmere. Sir Walter[4] made merry over Dominie Sampson's social shortcomings and the erudition of Erasmus Holiday. The author of *The Anatomy of Melancholy*[5] — himself a Scholar, if ever there was one — drew this unflattering portrait of his order: "Hard students are commonly troubled with gowts, catarrhes, rheums, cachexia, bradypepsia, bad eyes, stone, and collick, crudities, oppilations, vertigo, winds, consumptions, and all such diseases as come by overmuch sitting; they are most part lean, dry, ill-coloured; spend their fortunes, lose their wits, and many times their lives; and all through immoderate pains and extraordinary studies."

---

1 George Eliot是十九世纪里英国的大女小说家，她本来名字是Mary Ann Evans，——这个是她的笔名。

2 他是George Eliot的长篇小说 *Middlemarch* 里面的一个人物，一个炫学的老头子。

3 Ward, Mrs. Humphry (Mary A. Arnold) (1851—)（其卒年为1920年。——编者注），她是当代老前辈的女小说家，她的杰作是 *Robert Elsmere*，下面所说二个人都是这本书里的人物。

他的脊柱弯曲,他的身体没有风姿;

那种心不在乎的神情引人发怒地现在

他的身体同脸孔的每个动作之中。"

乔治·爱略脱是非常看轻可怜的老加索绷,"玩味着关于古实同密士勿能穆这种淹博的错误"。窝德夫人的爱德华·郎干简直是比他的学生洛贝·厄尔兹密尔更无用。窝尔忒爵士拿多密尼·散普孙的不会酬应同伊拉斯莫斯·和立地的渊博来开玩笑。《愁闷的解剖》的作者——他自己总得算是一位学者,若使世上真有过一个学者——对于他的同流人们写出这个很不恭维的描摹:"勤读的学者常犯着脚风病,风邪入肺症,鼻涕膜炎,身虚,胃弱,坏眼睛,胱麻病,疝痛,不消化,紧塞症,头晕,胃气,肺痨,以及一切从坐得太久而生的疾病;他们多半是瘦,干,皮色不好;花掉了他们的财产,失丢了他们的聪明,常常失丢了他们的性命;这全由于过度的辛苦同非常的用功。"

---

4 Scott, Sir Walter(1771—1832),是英国最大的浪漫派小说家,他所写的全是历史小说,此外又写好多长诗,歌咏古英雄事迹。

5 Burton, Robert(1576—1640),是十七世纪一位大散文家,他的杰作就是这部 *The Anatomy of Melancholy*。

This string of afflictions is long enough without the addition of moral reproaches. Yet this is the hortation which a famous divine, preaching before the University of Cambridge, addressed to the Scholars of the Cam[1]:

"A man may be a diligent student, and yet 'live to himself[2].' Indeed there is in that contracted and self-contained life, even in more than one of greater expansion and variety, a peculiar risk of doing so. That daily hoarding of intellectual stores, that daily revelling in literary or scientific pursuits, is one of the strongest illustrations of a refined and elevated selfishness. Let a man who reads in youth read with a view to[3] active work in his generation; let a man who reads on still in age also write, and the charge of mere selfishness must be mitigated or withdrawn — mitigated, if the man proposes to communicate; withdrawn, if he is enabled to cosecrate."

It is evident that the preacher had a poor opinion of the Scholar, as defined above. In his eyes the young scholar was only respectable if he was studying with a view to "active work in his generation"; the older scholar, if he was preparing a book. To "communicate" meant, in the preacher's mouth, to teach, to write, in some form to

---

1 这是Cambridge的简写。
2 to live to one's self: to live selfishly 只顾自己地过活。
3 with a view to: for the purpose of 为着……的目的。

这一串疾病的名字已经是够长了，用不着再加上道德上的责备。然而一位有名的教师在剑桥大学对着剑桥的学者演讲时，却说出这样的劝告：

"一个人也许可以做个勤读的学生，然而只是'独善其身的'。真的，在那种缩小同自足的生涯里，甚至于就是内容更宽阔，更复杂点，含有一种特别使人们只为着自己而生活的危险。那种天天地积蓄智识，天天地眈〔耽〕溺在文学的或者科学的追求是一种讲究高尚的自私的最强表现之一。在年青读书的，一个人就该注目在将来对于本代的实际服务；在年老时还念书的人，就应当此外还写文章，只图己利这个罪名总要设法减轻或者取消——减轻了，若使他打算把他所知道告诉别人；取消了，若使他借此能够献身于人类。"

这是很显明的，这位说教师很瞧不起"学者"，像前面所说的学者。在他眼里，年青的学者只当他为着"将来对于本代的实际服务"而读书，才是可敬的；年老的学者便是预备着一本书那才是可敬的。在这位说教人的口里，"告诉别人"是等于教

impart; to "consecrate" meant to write definitely for high objects, and the improvement of the reader. Such notions as these, all disparaging to the career and character of the disinterested scholar, have acquired so strong a hold upon the modern world that the few people who read at all seem quite ashamed of themselves unless they can aver that they are reading for some practical object. They are teaching schoolboys or undergraduates; or they are qualifying for a Professorship; or they are going to lecture in America; or they are contributing to a History of Crete in twenty volumes; or they are busy at a new theory of Criticism which will sweep all churches and creeds into the dust-bin. But always and in all things they are practical. They learn not for learning's sake, but with a single eye[1] to performance — and emolument. A student of this type said to a younger man whom he found busy with a book on geology, "Will geology be of any use to you with your pupils next term?" "No." "Then isn't it rather a pity[2]?" Of a famous Aristotelian it was said — "Does he read Aristotle for pleasure?" "No, he edits him for profit." I myself know a Senior Classic[3] of whom his intimate friends aver that since

---

  1 single eye: concentiation of purpose on one object 注目，着意。
  2 pity: regrettable fact 可惜。
  3 Senior Classic: person placed first in classical, tripos at Cambridge when order of merit was published 剑桥大学毕业考试得到奖章的学生。

书,写文章,以及其他灌注智识的形式;"献身于人类"是等于分明地为着一些崇高的目的而著作,使读者可以得到教训。这类的意见,对于不计实利的学者的事业同性格都是加以贬词的,是做到那样坚固地管着现代人们的心,弄得极少数真真念书的人们好像是很不好意思,除非是他们能够说他们念书为着什么实际的目的。他们是正在教小孩子或者大学生;或者他们预备当个教授的资格;或者他们快到美国去演讲;或者他们是一部二十册的克里特历史的撰稿人;或者他们忙着弄出一个新的批评学说,那能将一切教会同信条全扫到垃圾箱里去。但是时时刻刻,在一切事情里他们老是讲实际的。他们求学问,不是为着学问自身的缘故,眼睛却是全看着实用——同利益。一位这类的学者对于一个正忙着念一本地质学的年纪青点的人说道:"下学期教学生时候,地质学对你会有什么用处没有?""没有。""那么这不是有点可惜吗?"关于一位有名的研究亚里士多德的学者,曾经有人问过——"他是为自己的快乐而念亚里士多德吗?""不,他是为着挣钱才去校订亚里士多德的集子。"我自己知道一位"在剑桥大学名誉卒业试验里考第一名的人",他的密

he got his fellowship[1] they have never known him open a Greek or Latin book. "He is a man of affairs, and reads his *Times*."

From students and study of this type one turns with a keen sense of refreshment to a case such as that of Walter Headlam, whose *Memoir* has just been published by his brother. He was a Scholar in the sense in which I defined the term. He read because he wanted to know more — to know all — of a subject which fascinated him. He lived his adult life in the beautiful precincts of King's Collage, Cambridge, "studying in the grand manner which he held was alone worth while. To him the acquisition of almost all available knowledge seemed necessary in order to prepare for the criticism and elucidation of his chosen authors." Yet "his tendency as an author was to defer the publication of a formal volume." In short, he laboured intensely, but with no immediate object beyond that of intellectual identification with the subjects which he loved. In a curious mood of self-censure he wrote thus to a friend whose letters he had neglected: "It isn't that I forget my friend; but the Scholar's danger of his work becoming too imperious, claiming all his time before any form of writing at any rate. This is what Wordsworth[2] meant

---

1 fellow: graduate holding stipend on condition of research 毕业生继续研究而领到薪俸者。

2 Wordsworth, William (1770—1850), 英国歌咏自然的大诗人。

友们说自从他得到他的"学友"地位以后，他们老没有看他打开过一本希腊文或者拉丁文的书。"他是个事务很忙的人，他要读他的《泰晤士日报》。"

看了这种的学者同用功，再去看窝尔忒·赫德拉谟那类的人，人们会很锐敏地感到心神爽快。窝尔忒的兄弟刚出版一部他的《言行录》。他是一个适合我所下的定义的"学者"。他念书，因为他想多知道——全知道——一个把他迷住了的问题的内容。他的成年时期是在剑桥大学内钦格学院这个美丽区域里过去，"大规模地读书，他以为只有这样才是值得的。由他看来，一切有用的智识好像差不多是都该晓得的，为的是要做批评同解释他所中意的作家的预备"。可是"著起书来，他老是迟延，不肯出一本正式的书"。总之，他非常竭力地用功，但是没有什么当前目的，只是想能够了解他所喜欢的问题的内容。在一种自责的奇怪心境之下，他写底下这几句话给他的朋友，他许多的信他好久没有回覆："并不是我忘记了我的朋友；但是一个学者他的工作是容不得怠慢的，那是太要紧了，所以无论如何要占住他的全部时间，不让他写什么别的东西。这就是威至

when, describing Cambridge in his time, he spoke of seeing 'Learning its own bondslave.' "

Yet, in spite of this complete absorption in pursuits where not one man in a hundred — even among educated people — could follow him, Walter Headlam was neither pedant nor prig. He had no affinity to the race of Dryasdust[1]. If granted a speciality in learning, one can specialize in it still further, Headlam's "special speciality" was the genius of Greek Lyrical Metres. Besides being a Scholar, he was a poet, and still more markedly a musician; and his application of musical tests to the written words of Greek Lyricists was a lantern for his steps, which made dark places seem clear and rough places plain, and enabled him, as it were, to dance and sing while he threaded his way where unilluminated Scholars had laboured and lumbered. The most brilliant classic[2] whom Cambridge has lately produced told me only the other day that he had never known what Greek Lyrics meant till Headlam sang fragments of Simonides[3] and Sappho[4], accompanying himself on the piano, and wedding the words to traditional tunes of English folklore.

---

1 Dryasdust: dull antiquary 沉闷的考古学者。
2 classic: Greek and Latin scholar, 希腊, 拉丁的学者。
3 Simonides是希腊一位诗人。
4 Sappho, 希腊一位女诗人, 她是一个实行女性同性爱的人。

威士的意思,当描写当时的剑桥大学时候,他说看见'学问变做自己的奴才'。"

然而,不管他是多么一心一意地研究专门的学问,那些东西一百人里恐怕没有一个人——就说是在智识阶级里——能够跟着他研究,窝尔忒却既不是炫学的人,也不是沾沾自喜者。他是同沉闷的考古学者那班人没有关系的。若使在已是专门智识内我们能够有更进一步的专门,那么赫德拉谟的"专门的专门"是希腊抒情诗韵律的精髓。在一位学者之外,他又是一位诗人,同一位更出色的音乐家;他用乐律来研究希腊抒情诗人的词句,这可说是照着他工作的进行的一盏明灯,把隐晦的地方化为光明,将崎岖道路变做坦途,好像他能够跳舞唱歌着,当他兜穿过别个没有得到光明的学者步履艰难地走过的地方。剑桥大学近来所产生的最出风头的古典学者前天才告诉我,他从来不懂得希腊抒情诗的真意,一直等到赫德拉谟对他唱出施蒙尼迪同莎浮的残篇,一面用钢琴和着,把诗里辞句和英国民俗的传统调子相配。

Some years ago the present Master of Trinity[1] thus excellently illustrated some of the qualifications for the Teacher's office: —

"Teachers ought to be examples to learners, in body as well as in mind and in character. They ought to be bright, and vigorous, and energetic. There ought to be an open-air look about them, the look of blue skies, and north-easters[2], and sea, and mountain, and heather, and flowers, and cricket-ground, and lawn-tennis — not the look of the study, and late hours, and the half-digested "Epoch," and the "Outlines," and the "Analysis," and the "Abstract of the Analysis," and — more ghastly still — the "Skeleton[3]."

Teaching, in the formal and technical sense, formed a very small part of Headlam's life; but, when he encountered younger people, whether boys or girls, who were eager to follow him into that Earthly Paradise of Greek culture where he was so uniquely at home[4], he delighted in the task of guiding them; and one cannot doubt that a great part of his attractiveness was due to his truly Greek love of life and form and clear skies and open air. "If I had

---

1 Henry Montagu Butler

2 north-easters: north-east wind 东北风。

3 skeleton: an outline, as of a literary work 大纲，此字的本来意思是骸骨，作者用这字是双关的，所以前才有 more ghastly，但是这怎能够译出来呢？

4 at home: familiar 相熟。

几年前,现在的三一学院院长这么美妙地说出当先生的人们的几种资格:

"先生应当是学生的榜样,在身体上好似在精神上同性格上。他们应当是活泼,强壮同有力。他们应当有新鲜空气的神情,蓝色的天,东北风,大海,大山,草原,花儿,棒球[1]场,网球戏的神情——别要带着书房,迟睡,食而不化的'时代','大纲','纲领','纲领的摘要'同——更是鬼气森森的——'概略'的神情。"

正式的同专门的教读是赫德拉谟的生涯里的极小部分;但是他会碰到亟欲跟他到希腊文化这块地上乐团,在那里他是这么无比地娴熟的,年青人们,无论男女,他都是乐于做引导他们这个工作;谁也相信,他性格的可爱的大部分原因是在他那种真真希腊式的对于人生,美形,清澈的天同户外生活的爱恋。"若使我不是一个研究希腊文学的学者,"他常常说,"我会想做

---

[1] crickt一词在本文中译者将其译作"棒球",今译"板球"。——编者注

not been a Grecian," he used to say, "I should have been a Cricket 'Pro[1].' Cricket, music, Greek poetry, and hunting are the things that I care for." A friend who shared his rides and walks at Cambridge says: "You went through the Fellows' Gardens, where he would stop to look at the double white cherry-tree, 'the whitest white in Nature.' He delighted to ride down a certain bridle-path[2] that had tall hedges on either side, thick with a tangle of wild roses. 'Heaven was a flowery meadow: the Greeks said so, and they ought to know.' He was a fearless rider to hounds, but rode, it must be admitted, erratically. On more than one occasion, when his companions took a turn to left or right, Headlam, lost in the delight of swift motion, would hold on his way like an arrow from the bow, be seen in the distance still going hard, and seen no more that day."

Walter Headlam died suddenly in his forty-third year. If this chapter had been intended for a review of his life, it might have been necessary to discuss, in an ethical or even a religious light, the best use of time and intellectual gifts; but my purpose has been quite impersonal. I have only cited a rare and recent instance of a type which the competitive rush[3] of modern life will soon have utterly abolished.

---

1 pro: a professional 以某某事为职业的专家。
2 bridle-path: road fit for riders but not vehicles 马道。
3 rush: act of violent advance; onslaught 疾驰。

棒球专家。棒球，音乐，希腊诗同打猎是我所关心的事情。"一位在剑桥大学同他一起骑马散步的朋友说："你走过'学友园'，他一定要停着去看那一双白樱树，'自然界里最白的白'。他爱驰骋过某一条马路，那里两边有高高的篱笆，错杂地丛生着野蔷薇。'天是一块多花的草地：希腊人这样，他们应该知道这些东西。'他是追着猎狗的一个大胆骑者，但是这是一定要承认的，他是无规则地跑着。不只一次，当他的伴侣向左或者向右拐湾〔弯〕时候，赫德拉谟飞跑高兴得忘情了，会一直望〔往〕前奔，像个离弦的箭，人们看他在远处还竭力跑，那天就不再看到他了。"

窝尔忒·赫德拉谟在四十三岁时忽然死去。若使这章是打算用来批评他的一生，那么一定要从道德，或者甚至于宗教方面，去讨论时间同上帝赋与的智力的最好用法；但是我的目的却是完全不涉及个人的。我只是引一个稀少的近例子，那类人快被近代生活的竞争怒潮所完全毁灭了。

John Middleton Murry

Fact and Fiction

A Correspondent, who is a doctor, has written to me to ask me why, in a recent article, I called *Don Quixote*[1] a masterpiece. "I have tried," he says, "both in the original Spanish and in English to like it, and I always fail. It seems to me wanting in true humour to jeer at the actions of the half-witted. It always arouses pity in me. Perhaps it is because I am a doctor and see so much mental aberration, that I

---

1 Cervantes（1547—1616）是西班牙最大的文学家，他的杰作就是《吉诃德先生》。这本书是述一个西班牙武士，五十多岁年纪，很穷地住在拉曼差村中。拼命念读游侠的浪漫小说，最后把头脑念糊涂了，没有事情能够满足他，一定要骑着他的老马，带〔戴〕着头盔，提着长矛，到外面去当一个游侠，冒一切的危险，来伸雪世界上数不尽的不平的事。他有一位邻居，一个又穷又傻的农夫，叫做山差邦札，骑一匹驴子，跟他当从卒去。这位武士只由他所爱的浪漫故事这面镜子里看到人生：他把小旅馆错当做魔堡，风车错当做巨人，又把村姑错当做流落异国的公主。他的豪气同勇敢始终不衰，但是他的幻觉却带来无穷的麻烦，用着保障公道同武士

事实与小说

一位同我通信的人,他是一个医生,曾经写信来问我为什么,在最近一篇文章里,我说《吉诃德先生》是一部杰作。"我曾经试从,"他说,"本来的西班牙文同英文的译本里去喜欢它,我却老是失败。由我看来,去讥笑神经错乱的人们的举动好像是缺乏了真正的幽默精神。这班人们的举动总是引起我的怜悯。或者这是因为我自己是个医生,看了太多精神错乱的病人,所

精神的名义,他插进他所碰的人们里面,凡是他以为是倚势凌人的,他都要来干涉,结果是这位吉诃德先生同他那穷从卒到处挨打,受鞭,被骗同给人们拿来做笑柄。后来靠着他村里老朋友的好意同一班爱他这种高贵的理想的人们的帮助,这医士医好了他的瞎想,给人们带回他故乡自己家里以后就"正寝"死在家里了。

cannot find pleasure in reading about such a painful subject. I think I would rather be hanged as a criminal than die semi-insane[1]."

Don Quixote, by the way,[2] did not die semi-insane. He died in his right mind, as the peaceful citizen Alonso Quixano, having made a will which disinherited his niece if she should be foolish enough to marry a man whose reading was on romances of chivalry. But that is beside the point[3]. I have to confess myself nonplussed by the doctor's letter. I do not know how to reply to it; how to reply to it, that is, in a way which will carry conviction[4] to him. I could say, I suppose, that Don Quixote's madness is not pathological but symbolical, that it represents the inveterate tendency of the human mind towards an idealisation of reality, and that although Cervantes gave this impulse an exaggerated embodiment, succeeding generations of men have discovered enough of the Quixote in themselves to make them feel that the story of the knight's discomfiture has a universal human validity.

But argument of this kind would not convince my correspondent. It demands, in order to be convincing, a certain abstraction of

---

1 semi-insane: partly-insane 半疯。

2 by the way 当我们说话时候，偶然提到一个与本题不相干的，却又是因为刚才所说的话而联想起来的事情，我们就用这三个字做引子，所以可以潘做"却说"，有时简直可以不译出来。

3 beside the point: beside the mark 题外。

4 to carry conviction: to convince 使相信。

以念着这么苦痛的一个题材,我不能感到快乐。我想我自己情愿当个罪犯,被人吊死,而不肯半疯地死去。"

然而,吉诃德先生并不是半疯地死去。他是方寸不乱地死去,做个安分和平的公民阿伦索·吉赞诺,立下一个遗嘱,里面说明要取消他的侄女的嗣业权,若使她傻到跑去嫁给一个爱读骑士传奇的男人。但是这些全是题外的话。我要自认医生这封信使我无法可办。我不知道怎样去答复它好;那是说,答复得使他会相信。我可以说,我想,吉诃德先生的疯狂不是病态的,却是象征的,那是代表人心要将现实拿来理想化的一种根深蒂固的趋势,虽然塞文狄斯把这冲动力形容过甚地具体表现出来,后代的人们看出自己心里都蕴有吉诃德先生的精神,他们因此能够感觉到这位骑士的狼狈故事是可以应用到普遍的人性的。

但是这类的理由不能够使这位和我通信的人相信。一定要能够将内中的意义同所描写的事情相当地分开,然后才能相信

the thing signified[1] from the thing depicted[2], which is more difficult for some people to make than others. And, in the case of Don Quixote, it is, we can well believe, most difficult for a doctor. To one who is accustomed to deal with[3] cases of actual mental aberration the realistic truth of Don Quixote's affliction must be more cogent than its inward meaning. He has seen too many Don Quixotes in real life; he has been too deeply impressed by the reality of their sufferings for it to be possible for him to regard them merely as a poetic symbol of a trick of the human soul. They touch him too nearly. Instead of reading about Don Quixote's actions as though they were imaginary events in some kingdom of the mind's potentiality, at every turn he is reminded of the doings of actual men whom he remembers, and to whom he has tried, perhaps in vain, to bring relief. In the language of Croce's[4] philosophy, it is impossible for him to have other than a practical attitude towards Cervantes' masterpiece; the aesthetic approach is barred to him.

Although I was at first bewildered by the doctor's letter, and imagined that I was confronted with a case of literary insensibity — we all have blind spots[5] in our faculty of literary appreciation — it

---

1 signified是形容thing字。
2 depicted是形容thing字。
3 to deal with: to treat处理。
4 Croce, Benedetto（1866— ），意大利当代大哲学家。（其卒年为

这个道理，这件事有些人比别人特别不易办到。关于《吉诃德先生》这本书，我们很可以说，医生是最不容易取这种的态度的。对于一个已惯于处理神经错乱的病人的人，吉诃德先生的苦痛的实在情形一定是比书中的深意更打动他的心。他在现实生活里看了太多的吉诃德先生；他对于他们苦痛的实在情形有很深的印象，所以他绝不能够把这许多苦痛只当做是人心的一种癖〔脾〕气的一个文学象征。它们太震动他的心了。他不能念起吉诃德先生的行动好像它们是人心的可能性的境界里的幻想事件，因为每处他总是联想起真实人们的举动，这班人是在他的记忆里面，他曾努力，也许是枉然的，将他们的苦痛减轻。用克洛拆哲学的名词，我们可以说他对于塞文狄斯的杰作只能具一种实际的态度；美术的观察法对于他是此路不通的。

虽然起先我的心被医生这封信搅乱了，以为我碰到文学欣赏上的麻木的一个例子——我们大家的文学欣赏的机关里都有

1952年。——编者注）
　　5 人们眼睛里有一点看不见东西的地方，心理学家叫做盲点。

seemed on further thought that his attitude, so far from being peculiar, was typical of a general limitation. It is, for instance, extremely difficult for those who have been in close contact with an illness and have passed through the sickening[1] alternation of hope and fear for lives which are dear to them, to hold themselves detached when they read an account of a like illness in fiction. Either they miss the agonising note of reality in the description and feel that the author is trifling with terrible things, or they recognise the note of reality and instinctively compare his experience with their own. A crowd of painful associations swarms up to confirm or confute the author's veracity. His book is not permitted to make its own impression, and he is judged, not as he should be, by the experience he creates in us, but by his fidelity to an experience which we recall.

This distortion of judgment, in various forms, is continual. The simple fact that an experience has been crucial in our lives makes it peculiarly hard for us to adopt any but a practical attitude to an artistic representation of a similar experience. Men who have fought in the war are often dissatisfied with *War and Peace*[2]. It may have been all very well when is was written, they are willing to admit, but it is

---

1 to sicken: to make one feel nausea at 令人恶心。
2 俄国大小说家托尔斯泰的杰作,中间叙述有拿坡仑的战争。

盲点——可是再想一下，好像他的态度是一点也不离奇，却反可以代表一种普通的限制。比如，这是极端困难的，要那班同一种疾病有过亲密的接触，为了他们所爱的人们的生命尝过希望和恐惧的可怕更迭的人们能够持一种超然的态度，当他们在小说里读到一段描写同样的疾病的时候。不是他们在描写里没有遇到实在情形的苦楚状况，觉得作者是将可怕的东西拿来开玩笑，就是他们从描写里认出实在的情境，自然而然地把书中人的经验拿来同他们自己的经验相比。一群酸苦的联想涌上心来，证明或者反驳作者的真实。我们不让他的书自己来给个印象，我们判断他没有照他所应当得的判断法子做去，那是按着他会给我们以什么经验，却是靠着他所说的同我们回忆里的一个经验是否符合。

　　这类判断的偏曲，各种方式的，是接连下去没有归正的。一个经验既做了我们生命中的一个大枢纽了，单是这件事就使我们对于同样经验的艺术的描写特别不容易持别种的态度，除开了一种实际的态度。曾经参加战争过的人们常常不满意《战争与和平》。写出来的确是很好，他们肯这样子承认，但是这实

not really like war. And lately I heard a young officer, who has since become a man of letters, criticise Mr. D.H.Lawrence's[1] beautiful novel, *Aaron's Rod*, because no one who had been "through the hoop" could possibly talk as a captain of the Guards talks there. For him, as for the doctor, I had no reply. It seemed almost indecent to suggest that having been "through the hoop" was rather a disqualification than a title to judge the book. But so it was. If we begin to test the elements of a work of literature by our own practical experience, we are on the wrong road, we are considering it not as art, but as science; not as the communication of an apprehension of life, but as a more or less faithful record of observed fact.

It is, moreover, the confusion between these two attitudes which is most frequently the cause of the strange popularity of worthless books. In *New Crub Street* Gissing[2] declared that the royal road[3] to success for a novelist was to deal with the very rich upper middle-class. It is, of course, only one of the roads, but it has in fact proved uncommonly successful since Gissing's time. The moderately well-to-do like to read about a condition of life which they may conceivably attain, just as elderly spinsters made the fortune of a

---

1 Lawrence 是英国当代小说家。

2 Gissing, George R. (1857—1903), 英小说家, 他的长篇小说 *New Grub Street* 是叙述英国穷苦的著作家的生涯。

3 royal road: a road without difficulties 康庄坦途。

在是不像战争。近来我听一位年青的军官，他已变做一个文人了，批评罗凌士先生的美妙小说，《亚伦的杖》，因为没有一个"经过战地的呐喊"的人会谈得像书里一位卫队长那样谈着。对于他，像对于那位医生，我是无话可答的。这差不多好像是胡闹，去说"经过战地的呐喊"反是失丢了，而不是得到，批评这书的资格。但是实在的情形倒是这样。若使我们开始用我们个人的实际经验来判断一部文学作品内中的事情，我们是走上错路了，我们是不把它当作艺术看，而当作科学看；不当作是传达对于人生的见解，却是认为是对于所观察的事实的一种大约忠实的纪录。

并且，这两种态度的混杂常常做成无价值的书所以能够奇怪地风行一时的原因。在《新格刺布街》里季星说一个小说家的成功大路是去描写很富的上中流社会。这自然只是许多路中的一个，但是实际上从季星时候以来这的确是非常成功的路。那班都还富有的人们喜欢读一种他们想得出可以达到的一种生活情形，好似老处女们使女小说家发财，她自己也是个老处女，

lady-novelist who, herself an elderly spinster, invariably represented one of their kind as the beloved of an ardent, Apolline[1] youth. The writer who can supply an imaginary satisfaction for the practical desires of a large class of people is fairly certain of financial success among that majority of readers who do not dream that the condition of entering the world of literature is to leave all practical desires behind them.

Not that the doctor and they are really comparable. It is to his honour that he cannot read of Don Quixote's adventures without pain. It proves that he has the sensitive sympathy which is necessary to his craft. A man of pure science (which a doctor is not) might be far less disturbed. But those who ask for practical satisfactions from literature and find a book unreadable unless it has a happy ending deserve no such praise. Although we cannot blame them for desiring the happiness which we all desire, we can pity them for not knowing that the delight aroused by literary beauty is of a finer and more enduring kind than the fictitious realisation of their daily hopes can ever give.

---

1 Apolline: of Apollo 希腊的太阳神，他是个美少年。

在书里总是将一个老处女写做是一个热情的，像阿波罗神的少年的爱人。一个作者能够供给一大群人们的实际的希望以一种虚幻的满足，他的发财是很靠得住的，因为有许多读者简直没有梦想到走到文学的疆土的条件是将一切实际的希望全弃丢不顾了。

这位医生和他们并不是真真可以相比的。这是他的荣誉，他不能念着吉诃德先生的冒险而不感到苦痛。这事证明他具有他的职业所需要的敏锐的同情心。一个研究纯粹科学的人（医生并不是）也许远不会这样心中难过。但是有一班人要文学给他们以实际的满足，凡是没有个好团圆的书，都觉得是读不下去的，这些人们值不得这种赞美。确然我们不能责备他们，因为他们希望得到我们所共同希望的幸福，我们却能够怜悯他们，因为不知道文学的美所引起的快乐是一种更纯净的同更耐久的，绝不是他们日常的希望的虚构的实现所能给的。

Roger Wray

Autumn

Spring is a serenade, but autumn is a nocturne. In the waning of the year, the world is full of sombre solemnity and a pathetic sense of old age. I have gleaned[1] this information by reading poems on the subject.

"The melancholy days are come, the saddest of the year,

Of wailing winds, and naked woods, and meadows brown and sere."

So begins the dirge of William Cullen Bryant[2].

"Yes, the year is growing old,

And his eye is pale and bleared."

---

1 to glean: to pick up (facts etc.) 搜集。
2 Bryant, William Cullen (1794—1878), 美国诗人。

秋

春是良夜里在恋人窗下所奏的情歌，秋却是残夜里凄迷如梦的哀调。在一年里销沉的时候，世界是充满了惨淡的严肃景象同老年的一种悲哀情调。这个智识我是从念关于这个题目的诗歌得到的。

"愁闷的日子来了，一年里最黯淡愁人的日子，

狂号的风，赤身的树同干枯的棕色草地的日子。"

威廉·卡楞·布赖安特的哀歌就这样子开头。

"是的，年头已经变老了，

他的眼睛无光而且败烂。"

This is from Longfellow[1], and the poet proceeds to compare autumn to the insane old King Lear[2]. Wordsworth speaks of the "pensive" beauty of autumn, but to Shelley[3] —

"The year

On the earth, her deathbed, in a shroud of leaves dead is lying."

And Hood's[4] admirable little poem ends:

"But here the autumn melancholy dwells,

And sighs her tearful spells,

Among the sunless shadows of the plain."

All of which is most impressive; and reading it to an accompaniment of minor music[5], rendered by wind-demons in the keyhole, it convinced me absolutely. Accordingly, when I went a long ramble through the countryside this morning I was fully prepared to observe the sad tokens of Nature's senility and decay.

But a glorious surprise met me at the outset, and changed my mood from lamentation to exultation. I passed from the dismal poetic fiction to the actual glowing fact; from mournful reverie to

---

1 Longfellow, Henry W. (1807—1882), 美国歌咏自然的大诗人。
2 莎翁悲剧 *King Lear* 里面的主要人物，他给他的女儿骗了，把王位传给她们，受到她们的坏待遇，最后气疯了。
3 Shelley, Percy B. (1792—1822), 英国浪漫派诗人。
4 Hood, Thomas (1799—1845), 英国诗人，他最善于做滑稽诗。
5 minor music: plaintive music 怨曲。

这段是在郎匪罗的诗集里,这位诗人接着把秋同疯狂的老利亚王相比。威至威士说着秋的"萧条"的美,但是由雪莱看来——

"年头

躺在大地上,她的死床,穿着枯死的叶子织成的一套寿衣。"

呼得的值得赞美的小诗结句是:

"愁闷的秋住在这儿,

嘘出她满着清泪的蛊惑,

在平原里无日光的阴影之中。"

这许多都是再动人不过的;一面读着,一面配上了凄凉的调子,那是风魔在钥匙眼里奏出来的,使我极端地相信这许多话。所以,今天早上当我到乡下去做个长时间的漫步时候,我心里完全以为会看到秋的衰老的悲哀表象。

但是一开头我就碰到一个光荣赫赫的惊愕,我的心境由哀伤而变为狂喜。我从阴郁的诗的幻境走到生气充溢的现实;从惆怅的幻想走到有力的畅饮高歌。忧郁的诗人们的一切预言像

mighty revelry. And all the predictions of the gloomy poets were scattered like the autumn leaves. For who can look at the blaze of autumn colours and declare them solemn? Who can drink deep draughts of the autumn gales and talk about senility?

Autumn is youthful, mirthful frolicsome — the child of summer's joy — and on every side there are suggestions of juvenility and mischief. While spring is a careful artist who paints each flower with delicate workmanship, autumn flings whole pots of paint about in wildest carelessness. The crimson and scarlet colours reserved for roses and tulips are splashed on the brambles till every bush is aflame, and the old creeper-covered house blushes like a sunset.

The violet paint is smeared grotesquely on the riotous foliage; daffodil and crocus dyes are emptied over limes and chestnuts. Our eyes surfeit themselves on the gorgeous feast of colours — purple, mauve, vermilion, saffron, russet, silver, copper, bronze, and old gold. The leaves are dipped and soaked in fiery hues, and the mischievous "artist" will never rest till he has used up[1] every drop. Yet Shelley gazed at the pantomime-woods and declared (amid all the pomp and pageantry) that the year was on her deathbed, and this was her shroud!

---

1 to use up: to consume the whole of 消耗去全部的。

秋叶样一地四散凋零了。谁能够看着秋色的照耀，而说他们是严肃呢？谁能深深地吸进一口秋风，而说他是老迈呢？

秋是年青，快乐，顽皮——夏的欣欢的儿子——到处都呈出青春同恶作剧的现象。春是个小心翼翼的艺术家，他微妙技巧地画出一朵朵的花，秋却是绝不经心地将许多整罐的颜料拿来飞涂乱抹。本来是留着给蔷薇同郁金香的深红同朱红颜色却泼在莓类上面，弄得每丛灌木都像着了火一样，爬藤所盖住的老屋红得似夕阳。

紫罗兰的颜色是奇异地涂在放荡的簇叶之上；水仙同番红花的色料全倾倒在白柠檬同栗木。我们的眼睛看饱了颜色的盛宴——青莲色，红紫色，朱砂色，深黄色，赤褐色，银色，紫铜色，古铜色同暗滞的黄铜色。叶子是蘸上了，浸透了如火的颜色，这位爱捣乱的，"艺术家"非等到把每滴的颜料全用完时，是不肯住手的。然而雪莱瞧着这群扮哑剧的森林，却说道，（在这么多华丽同辉煌陈列之中）年头躺在她的死床上，这些是她的寿衣！

Why do the poets feel that autumn is ancient? He romps over the earth, chasing the puppy-like gales, making them scamper over the mirrored pools, and ruffling their surface till the water-reeds hiss him away. He revels in boisterous gaiety, playing pranks like a schoolboy on the first day of his holidays. He turns on[1] the rain-taps to try the effect; he daubs a few toadstools blood-red; he switches on[2] summer sunshine for an hour and then lets loose[3] a tempest. He torments the stately trees, tears their foliage off in handfuls, rocks them backwards and forwards till they groan, and then scampers away for a brief interval leaving heavenly peace behind him. The fallen leaves are set racing down the lane. With madcap destructiveness he wastes his own handiwork, stripping the finery from the woods and forests. The bare trees sigh and shiver, but he mocks them with howls and caterwaulings. Then he sets the bracken afire and pauses to admire the October tints. Finally, with deceptive golden sunshine, he tempts the sage out of doors, suddenly drenches him, and drives him home saturated to the skin. The sage thereupon changes his raiment, and murmurs about the solemnity of the dying year and the pensive beauties of autumn!

---

1 to turn on: to set going; begin 发轫。
2 to switch on: 开电灯。
3 to let loose: to set free 与以自由。

为什么诗人们会觉得秋是带着老气呢？他在大地上喧跳着，追赶那班同小猫一样轻捷的狂风，使他奔窜过波平如镜的小池，将水面吹皱，一直等到水草发出咝声，将他逐去。他沉溺在嘈杂的乐事里面，捣乱得像个放假第一天的学童。他发下滴滴打打的一阵雨，看有什么结果没有；他就把一些菌染得血红了；他又放出整个钟头的夏天太阳来，跟着有一场的狂风暴雨。他磨折庄严的大树，一把一把地扯下它们的枝叶，把它们拿来向前向后摇动，一直等到它们呻吟出声，然后他才暂时跑去，剩下天堂也似的安静。落叶被赶得沿着小路飞奔。带着狂暴汉的破坏性，他弄坏他自己的作品，树林的华饰全行剥落。赤条条的树林嗟叹，又寒战，但是他却用怒号同猫儿叫春的声音来嘲笑它们。然后，他使羊齿红得像着火，停步来赏玩十月里的彩色。最后，假假地捧出黄金的太阳光，他引诱聪明人走出门外，忽然间把他淋住，将他赶回家里，已经是湿透到皮了。聪明人于是换了衣服，喃喃地说着将尽的年头的严肃同秋的萧条的美！

The whole spirit of autumn is frolicsome and changeful as that of an eager child. The "solemntints" are the grotesque hues of the harlequin, and the "mournful winds" are suggestive of young giants playing leapfrog over the tree-tops. The lengthening period of darkness is a reminder of the long sleep of a healthy child, and when the sun awakes each autumn morning he rubs his misty eyes and wonders what antics he will see before bed-time.

Spring is a lovely maiden; Summer a radiant bride; but Autumn is a tomboy[1] whose occasional quietness is more alarming than her noisiest escapades.

---

1 tomboy: a romping girl 顽皮的女孩。

秋的整个精神是顽皮，喜动，像个热心的小孩。所谓"严肃的颜色"是小丑的古怪彩衣，所谓"如怨如诉的悲风"却暗指着年青巨人在树顶上玩着跳背戏。黑夜的渐见悠长使人想到一个强壮的幼童的长久睡眠，每个秋天早上，当太阳醒来时候，他搓着他的朦胧睡眼，心里纳罕在睡觉以前他会碰到什么把戏。

春是一位可爱的少女；夏是一位艳丽的新娘；但是秋却是一个顽皮的女孩，她那种偶然的安静是比她最吵闹的恶作剧还要更可怕些。

Robert Lynd

Trains

It is, apparently, just a hundred years since the Stockton and Darlington Railway[1] was opened. That was the beginning of railways as we now know them, and many of us, I am sure are in doubt, as we look back, whether we should be congratulated or commiserated. From the first, the voices of the prophets were divided on the matter. Some said that railways would prove a blessing, some that they would prove a curse. Today the most that we know is that we have accepted them, and the smoke of a train as it passes into a wood is now all but[2] a part of nature in which poets and painters can take delight. Certainly, if the railway train is to be condemned, it is

---

1 这是英国第一条铁路。
2 all but: almost 几乎。

火　车

　　斯拖克敦达林敦铁路的开幕到今年的确是刚好一百年。这是我们现在的火车的开始,我敢说,当我们回顾时候,有许多人心里会怀疑,我们是值得庆贺,还是值得矜怜。从开头起,预言家对于这事的意见就不一致。有几位说铁路最终是一种幸福,有几位说铁路最终是一种灾祸。我们今天所知道的只是我们采用了铁路,同当火车穿过森林时候,它的烟现在差不多变成自然的一部分,可以供诗人和画家的欣赏。真的,若使我们要说火车的坏话,也不能拿它破坏了世界的美观来做理由。小

not on the ground[1] that it has spoiled the look of the world. Children, as soon as they are able to walk, ask to be taken where they can see a train passing. It is as though the engine were as much alive as a horse or a hen. In my own childhood I knew by name the engines that pounded by at the foot of the Wallace Park in Lisburn. Not that I could even now analyse my interest in them. But at the sound of an approaching train I was aware of a rising wave of pleasure that drowned my whole being for the moment as the great greenpainted engine bore down towards me along the shining rails and passed in thunder and vanished with the rattle of the last carriage into the distance. Children, it may be, feel in presence of a locomotive in motion something of the awe that Blake expressed in "Tiger, tiger." To them a locomotive is a beautiful and powerful creature of awful symmetry — a dangerous creature of incredible swiftness. Their world is not ruined but enriched by the multitude of such wonders. Children, no doubt, are like cats: they are interested in anything that moves. And there are few things in the civilized parts of the world that move with such majestic speed as a railway train. The motor-car can hardly displace it in the childish imagination. There is no comparable music in a motor-car, no plume of cloud by day and of fire by

---

1 on the ground: for the reason 因为。

孩子一能够走路，就要人家带他们到看得见火车经过的地方。好像机关车也是有生命的东西，同一匹马或者一只鸡一样。在我自己的稚年时期，我晓得利斯本地方的华勒斯猎苑底下轰轰地走过去的一切机关车的名字。并不是我现在还能分析我对于火车的爱好。但是那时一听到火车走近的声音，我觉得有快乐的波浪涌上心来，暂时淹没了我全部的生活，当这个庞大，油着绿色的机关车缘着发亮的栏杆，向我前进，同雷一样响地经过，带着最后车辆的刮辣声音在远处消灭了。或者小孩子在一个动着的火车头面前，感到些勃来克在"老虎，老虎"那首诗里所表现的敬畏。由他们看来，一个火车头是一个具有可怕的对称，美丽有力的动物——一个疾驰得出奇的危险动物。他们的世界并没有被这群奇怪的东西所破坏，却反增富了许多。小孩子真像猫儿：对于一切走动着的东西都感到兴味。世界上文明的地方很少东西具有火车这样伟大的速度。在小孩子的想像里，汽车几乎不能代替它的位置。汽车没有相类的音乐，白天

night as a sign of its living energy. If Ruskin[1] had foreseen how much pleasure children would get from the look and the sound and the very smell of railway trains, he would have moderated his rage against them as defilers of the countryside. For it is possible that the child enjoys the passage of an express train in much the same spirit in which Ruskin enjoyed a resounding waterfall. See a family of small children hurrying to get under a railway bridge in time for the train to go roaring over their heads, and you are forced to the conclusion that they are infant poets, rather than infant sensationalists who enjoy the din of pseudo-danger, like visitors to the Amusements Park at Wembley. Hence I think that, whatever may be said against railways, they cannot be convicted of spoiling the landscape. A landscape that is spoiled by a railway must be a very poor landscape. Houses have done infinitely more to injure the beauty of country places than railways; yet no sentimentalists has ever used this as an argument for not having houses.

On the other hand, when we come to the alleged advantages of railways, it is more difficult to praise them without qualification. Admirable as railway trains are from an aesthetic point of view, their utility is not quite so obvious. In the nineteenth century, it was gene-

---

1 Ruskin, John (1819—1900), 英国十九世纪里一个大思想家同批评家。

没有云般的羽冠,晚上没有火,可以表示内中的活力。若使纳斯钦早看出小孩子从火车的形状,声音,甚至于气味,会得到多大的快乐,他的怒气也会减轻,不至于那样子把它们当做田舍风光的沾污者。小孩子欣赏一列特别快车的经过,他的精神很可以和纳斯钦欣赏回响的瀑布时一样。看到一家小孩子赶紧跑到一架铁路桥下,刚好让火车轰轰地从他们头上走过,你是逼得不能不承认他们是稚年的诗人,不好说只是爱听假危险的嘈响的唯觉主义者,像那班到卫卜来的游艺场的人们。所以我想,无论我们对于铁路有什么责难,总不能够说他们破坏了风景。一个风景会给铁路所破坏,本来也一定是个很可怜的风景了。房屋糟塌〔蹋〕田舍美景的地方是多过铁路万万倍;但是没有易感的人们曾经用这个做理由,来反对房屋的存在。

然而当我们讲到大家所认为铁路的好处,我们却反更难于说出不加贬词的赞美话。虽然由美术方面观察,火车是很值得颂扬的,它们的功用却没有这么明显。在十九世纪里,大家常

rally thought that swift mechanical means of transport would do a great service to mankind by bringing the people of different nations within easier reach of one another. In theory, benefits of this kind ought to have resulted. But have they? Do the French love the Germans any the better because the Germans are so many hours nearer to them than they used to be? Does the Pole love the Russian more ardently because the Russians can hasten to him with the aid of swift locomotives instead of slow horses? The Great War does not encourage us to believe so. People with any acquaintance with human nature, indeed, ought to have known in advance[1] that human beings do not like each other any better as a result of living next door to each other. It is the very proximity of the Germans, indeed, that makes the French hostile to them, and they are now in practice twice as near as they were before the opening of the Stockton and Darlington Railway. The only thing that could make the French and Germans love each other as, I am sure, both nations deserve to be loved, would be the invention of a machine in all respects[2] opposite to a railway engine — a machine that would make transport so slow that Paris and Berlin would be as distant from each other in time as if they were on opposite sides of the globe. If all transport could be slowed down till no one could move faster than in a slow-motion picture on

---

1 in advance: beforehand 预先。
2 in all respects: in very particular; throughout 于各点上全然。

常以为迅速的运输机器会大有裨于人类，因为可以使各国的人民彼此更容易接近。照理论来说，结果是应当有这类的利益才是。但是，实际上有没有呢？法国人有没有更爱了德国人，因为德国人到他们那里比从前会这样子更快了几个钟头？波兰人有没有更热烈地爱了俄国人，因为俄国人能够靠着迅速的火车头的帮助赶到他那里去，用不着靠那迟慢的马儿？这次"大战"并没有鼓励我们去这样子相信。真的，稍懂得人性的人们应当先就晓得人们并不会因为做了邻居，而彼此更见和爱。真的，正因为德国住在邻近，所以法国人才那样恨他们，他们两国现在实际上是比斯拖克敦达林敦铁路开幕以前更近一倍。使法德两国人民互相亲爱，我敢说，像他们所值得的那样互相亲爱的，惟一法子是发明一种和火车完全相反的机器——一种机器使运输非常迟慢，使巴黎柏林相距得好像是各在地球的一面。设使一切运输的机器能够慢到像电影中用慢镜拍照的片子，那么再

the films, there would be no more world-wars. Men would have to look for nearer neighbours with whom to fight, and Mr. Chesterton would see his dream of the battle of the boroughs fulfilled and Notting Hill marching down the slope to make war on Kensington.

The truth is the easier it becomes to visit foreign nations, the less we seem to be intimate with them. The Englishman who went abroad in the days of sails and horses travelled as though[1] he were actually in a foreign country the language and customs of which it was necessary to understand. The Englishman who goes abroad today as a rule carries England abroad with him; and if he talks to anyone, it is nine times out of ten an inhabitant of the foreign country but a fellow-countryman. Steamboats and railway trains have simply established pieces of England and America all over France and Switzerland and Italy. In doing so, they have made the French and the Swiss and the Italians more distant than ever in everything but time and space. They have made men trippers instead of travellers.

Even so, I cannot help believing in the ultimate usefulness of railway trains, motor-cars and aeroplanes in bringing the nations nearer each other in understanding. In spite of the evidence on the other side, I hold the same theories about the future as did the early enthusiasts for railway trains. After all, railways are still in their in-

---

1 as though: as if 好似。

也不会有世界战争了。人们会去找更近的邻人来交战，哲斯脱敦先生各市镇互斗的梦相〔想〕也会实现，诺定山的住民会整队走下斜陂，来同垦星吞镇上的人们打仗。

实在说起来，我们愈容易到外国去，我们好像同他们愈不亲密。在帆船同骑马的时代，出外的英国人旅行起来，他们真可说是在外国，那里的文字同习俗，他们都是非懂不可。今日出外的英国人却照例带着英国同他一起走；若使他有对谁说话，十回有九回不是同外国人，却是同本国人谈天。汽船同火车简直是在法国、瑞士、意大利各地方上遍地建起小块的英国同美国。这么一来，他们同法国人，瑞士人，意大利人，在任一方面都是更疏远了，除开时空这两点。它们使人们由真正的旅行者变做远足旅行者了。

虽然是这样，我还是免不了相信，火车、汽车同飞机的最后用处是使各国在互相了解上更见接近。不管别方面有什么明显的事实，对于将来，我是和最初热烈地颂扬火车的人们抱有同样的意见。究竟火车还是在幼稚时期；它们才有一百多年的

fancy; they are only a hundred years old. When men grow tired of wars and of paying for wars, past, present and to come, good communications will at least make a Parliament of the World possible — not a Parliament of the World to write poetry about, but a Parliament that will be of some use in arranging a number of matters that concern all the Five Continents. It is an unpleasant prospect, but not quite so unpleasant as a continual series of wars carried on with poison-gas. The Stockton and Darlington Railway was an invention that in the end may help us to make the best of a bad business.

The Stockton and Darlington Railway, however, though it may ultimately turn out to be a useful thing for the world, has hardly yet justified itself as a useful thing for England. The railway train, unquestionably, enables the inhabitants of England to travel faster into the country, but it has also increased the towns to such an extent that, in order to get into the country, we have to travel further than we once needed to do, so that in the end[1] it takes just as much time to reach the country as before. In the days of horse-coaches, a Londoner in search of the country did not need to go beyond Hampstead. The railway has now made the country for twenty miles around a mere suburb of London, and Hemel Hempstead and Dorking are to-day less rural than Hampstead was a hundred years ago. All these quick means of transport hurry so many people into soli-

---

1 in the end: finally 最后。

过去。当人们以后厌倦于过去，现在和将来的战争的损失时候，良好的交通最少能够使"世界国会"变做可能的事情——不是个做诗料用的"世界国会"，却是个对于解决关于五大洲的许多事情有些用处的"世界国会"。这是个不妙的前途，但是也没有不断的采用毒气的战争那么不妙。斯拖克敦达林敦铁路是一种发明，最后可以帮助我们对于一个棘手的事情，找出个最佳的补救方法。

可是斯拖克敦达林敦铁路虽然最后可以变成有用于世界的东西，对于英国却几乎还没有证明出它是一个有用的东西。火车，无疑地，使英国住民能够更快地旅行到乡下去，但是同时也将城市扩大得许多，因此要想到乡下去，我们得比从前多走了许多路，结果是我们走到乡下去所花的时间还是和从前一样。在马车时代，一个寻求乡下的伦敦住民只要走到罕普斯忒就成了。火车现在却将周围二十哩的乡下化做只是伦敦的一个近郊，痕麦·痕普斯忒同多轻在今日还没有一百年前的罕普斯忒那样有乡下风味。一切这类迅速的交通工具很快地就能够送人们到

tude that it soon ceases to be solitude. St. Ives in August is no longer a fishing village but a congested area. Hay Tor is no longer a lonely height on a silent moor but a good pull-up for charabancs[1]. On the other hand, the destruction of solitude by railway trains and charabancs may easily be exaggerated. Railway trains and charabancs have certainly made an end of[2] many a haunt of ancient peace, but they have this virtue: they concentrate the crowds on a few famous places and have the rest of the country-side in almost as deep a silence as before. Luckily for those who prefer solitude, most human beings go where everybody else goes and are happiest in multitudes. The railway train enables us to indulge this passion of gregariousness and collects us in our thousands in Brighton and Worthing, leaving the hinterland of the downs to sheep and shepherds and the small minority of the wilfully solitary. As has been said already indeed, the houses have been far more effective than the railways in injuring the face of England and even the houses, innocent of[3] beauty as most of them are, are for the most part[4] lost in the green abundance of the countryside. Surrey is, according to the pessimists, built over till it is no longer Surrey, but a suburb; yet you can still stand on the top of a

---

    1 charabanc: long vehicle, with many seats looking forward, for holiday-makers 公共的大部车子。
    2 to make an end of: to finish; complete; kill 结果了。

孤寂的地方去，可是孤寂的地方不久也就不孤寂了。八月中的圣·壹夫斯已经不是渔村了，却是个拥挤的地方。嘿·托也不是静默的旷野里的孤峰了，却是停顿长形马车的好所在。然而，火车同长形马车的毁坏幽处也很容易言之过甚。火车同长形马车的确结果了不少古代静默的巢窟，但是它们有这个好处：它们把群众集中在几个名胜所在，让其余的乡下差不多和从前一样地沉酣在静默里面。爱幽居的人们真是有幸，因为其他的人们多半是去人人所去的地方，在群众里最感到快乐。火车帮助我们满足这种爱群的热情，集合有成千成万的我们在布来屯同卫定，让内地的高原给羊群，牧羊人同极小数孤僻的人们去享受。真像前面所说的，房屋的损害英国外观比火车是更有力得多，但是虽然多半房屋是毫无美观的，它们大多数是隐没在田野的青绿丛中。悲观主义者以为塞立遍地盖了房子，现在已经不是塞立了，只可说是个近郊；但是你还能够站在塞立高原的

---

3 innocent of：lacking 未曾有。
4 for the most part：mostly, in most cases 多半。

Surrey down and see little but trees and fields for many miles around. In the future, men will, I am sure, learn more and more the secret of concealing their houses so that they will do as little offence to the landscape as the birds' nests. Nothing can finally destroy the country so long as men love the country — not railways or houses or overpopulation. I have a notion that, a hundred years hence, England will look, not less rural, but more so than it does at the present moment.

If the railways must be indicted, indeed, it is not for destroying the countryside but for injuring the village. The village shop, I fancy, has decayed from what it used to be, now that it has been brought by the railways into competition with the great stores of the towns. There are people in villages who buy little or nothing from the small shops at their doors but do almost all their shopping in the cities. There is not the patriotism of place that there once was. Even this, however, may easily be exaggerated. There are thousands of women who prefer even a small shop at their doors to a great shops thirty miles away. Their very interest in their neighbours makes them happier in a village shop than in the soulless stores of a strange town, and the local shops put one of their chief pleasures within a few minutes' reach. So it is possible that railways have not done so

顶上，看出去周围好几哩内只是田树，没有什么别的东西。将来，我敢说，人们会渐渐学会隐存他们的房屋的秘诀，所以他们的房屋将同鸟巢一样，无损于天然的风景。没有一个东西能够将乡下毁灭得干干净净，只要人们心中还是恋着乡下——火车不会，房屋同太稠密的人口也不会。我想一百年后的英国比此刻的英国不至于减少，却是添加了田园的风味。

若使一定要讲铁路的坏话，真的，我们不能说它们毁坏了乡下，却只好指它们损害了村落的生活。村店，我想，是衰落下去，大非昔比了，因为现在火车弄得它要同城里的大公司竞争。村里有许多住民从他们门口的小店仅仅买一点儿东西，或者什么也不买，他们的购买几乎全是到城里去干的。这不是从前那种爱乡的情绪。可是，就是这点也容易说得太过。有整千整万的女人倒喜欢她们门前的小店，胜过于三十哩外的大铺子。她们对于她们邻居的关切使她们在店里比在异城的无灵魂的公司里快乐得多，并且她们只须走几分钟的路，就能从本地的店铺得到她们的主要快乐的一种（指闲谈）。所以也许铁路毕竟是

much harm after all. We may have little cause as yet for putting up a statue to George Stephenson¹, but neither is there any reason for execrating his memory. And, if it were put to the votes of children, he might even get his statue. We can forgive him the more easily when we remember that it was not only a machine he invented but a huge toy that has eased the lot of many a nursemaid with her unruly charge.

---

1 George Stephenson (1781—1848), 火车的发明者, Stockton and Darlington Railway 的工程师。

没有这么多的害处。我们还没有什么原因，要替乔治·斯蒂芬孙建个雕像，但是我们也没有什么理由，去咒骂他的遗名。若使请小孩子来投票，他或者居然可以得到他的雕像。我们能够更容易地赦宥了他，当我们记起，他所发明的不单是一种机器，却是许多保姆要宽松自己时，拿来哄她们所照顾的刁蛮小孩子的一件大玩具。

E. Temple Thurston

Ship's Logs

There is a yard by the riverside in London — opposite Lambeth or somewhere thereabouts, I think it must be — where you may come so close in touch with Romance as will set your fancy afire and transport you thousands of miles away upon the far-off seas of the Orient.

You may talk in disbelieving tones of wishing-rings[1], of seven-league boots[2] and magic carpets[3], counting them as fairy tales, food only for the minds of children; but they are after all only the poetic materialization of those same subtle things in life which give wings to our own imagination, or bring to eyes tired with reality the gentle

---

1 带〔戴〕上了那个指环，心中想要什么东西，立刻可以得到。
2 穿着那个靴子，一步可以走七十余里。league差不多等三英哩。

船　木

伦敦城里的河旁有一所围场——我想总是在兰伯斯的对面或者那里附近——在那地方你同"浪漫史"可以有很亲切的接触，使你的幻想燃着起来，神游到几千里外"东方"的远海里去。

你尽可以用不相信的口吻谈着如愿环，一步七十余里的长靴同有魔力的地毡，以为它们全是属于神话的，只有小孩子的心才能吸收的；然而究竟说起来，它们不过是用诗情将人生里微妙的东西拿来具体化，这些东西本来会加我们的想象以双翼，

---

3 坐在那里地毡上面，可以随意飞行。

sleep of a daydream.

Nearly every one must know the place I write of. It is where they break up into logs the timber of those ships which have had their days[1] — the ships that have ridden fearless and safe through a thousand storms, that have set forth so hopefully into the dim horizon of the unknown and evaded to the last the grim, grasping fingers of the hungry sea.

And there, you will see their death masks, those silent figure heads[2] which, for so many nights and so many days with untiring, ever-watchful eyes; have faced the mystery of the deep waters unafraid. There is something pathetic — there is something majestic, too, about those expressionless faces. They seem so wooden[3] and so foolish when first you look at them; but as your fancy sets its wings, as your ears become attuned to the inwardness that can be found in all things, however material[4] you will catch the sound of dim faint voices that have a thousand tales of the sea to tell, a thousand yarns to spin[5], a thousand adventures to relate.

Nothing is silent in this world. There is only deafness.

---

1 to have had its days: to be past, worn out or disused 用坏了。
2 figure head: the figure on the prow of a ship 船头的木像。
3 wooden: stupid 蠢。
4 material: unspiritual 物质的。
5 to spin a yarn: to relate a story 说故事。

或者替那倦于现实的眼睛带来白日梦的温柔好睡。

差不多个个人一定都知道我所说的这个地方。他们在那里将有了日子的海船的船骨打成碎木头——这些船曾经无畏地安全地走过成千的大风浪,曾经那么有希望地望着渺茫的模糊的地平线驶去,而始终能够逃避着饥饿的海的狞恶的,紧抓着的手指。

在那里,你会看到他们死时的脸孔,那班默默不言的船头像,它们在这么多深夜,这么多白日里,现着不倦的,老是注意的眼睛,毫不恐怕地同深海的神秘相抗。这些无表情的脸孔使人们觉到悲哀——又使人们感到凛然。它们好像是这么木然的,这么愚蠢的,当你起先看它们时候;但是你的幻想一鼓起翼来,你的耳朵一同东西内在的音乐调和好,那种音乐在一切东西里都可以找出,不管是多么物质的东西,你会听到模糊微弱的声音,里头说出成千个的海的故事,讲出成千句的大话,述出成千桩的冒险事情。

在这个世界里没有一件东西是缄默的。只是我们耳聋听不出。

It has always appealed to me as the most noble of human conceptions, that burial of the Viking[1] lord. The grandeur of it is its simplicity. There is a fine spectacular element in it, too, but never a trace of bombast. The modern polished oak coffin with its gaudy brass fittings, the super-ornate hearse, the prancing black stallions, the butchery of a thousand graceful flowers — all this is bombast if you wish. It no more speaks of death than speaks the fat figure of Britannia[2] on the top of the highest circus car of England. Funerals to-day have lost all the grandeur of simplicity. But that riding forth in a burning ship, stretched out with folded hands upon the deck his feet had paced so oft; riding forth towards that far horizon which his eyes had ever scanned, there is a generous nobility in that form of burial. You can imagine no haggling with an undertaker over the funeral about this. Here was no cutting down[3] of the prices, saving a little on the coffin here, there a little on the hearse.

No — this was the Viking's own ship — the most priceless possession that he had. Can you not see it plainly, with sails set, speeding forth upon its last voyage — the last voyage for both of them? And then, as the lapping, leaping flames catch hold upon the

---

1 Viking: Northern sea-robbor of 8th—10th century 八世纪到十世纪横霸在北海的海盗。

2 英国国神。

3 to cut down: to reduce 减价。

我老觉得八九及十世纪时横行欧洲北海岸的海贼大王的葬仪是人类最高贵的想头。庄严的地方是在于它的简朴。里面也带有壮观盛举的成分，但是绝没有夸张扬厉的痕迹。近代磨光的橡棺，同它华美的铜装饰，粉饰得再精美不过的柩车，腾跃的黑色雄马，糟塌〔蹋〕了成千娇艳的好花——这许多全是夸张扬厉，你很可以这样子说。它并不比英国最高的马戏车子顶上那个不烈颠里亚大神的胖像更能说出死的意义。今日的葬礼全失丢了简朴的一切庄严地方。但是乘着一艘火烧着了的大船出去，双手叉着，躺在他的脚那么常走来走去的舱面；出去向着他的眼睛老是注意的远处水平线，这种葬仪有种慷慨的清高。关于这种葬仪，你想象不出同司葬仪人的论价。这里不能有什么省钱，比如棺材的价钱省一点，柩车的租费又省一些。

不——这是海贼大王自己的船——他所有的最值钱的东西。你难道不能分明地看出这只大船，挂了帆，飞奔往前，做它最后的航行——大王同船本身的最后航行？然后，当舐食同跳跃的火焰抓着膨胀的布帆，我能够看她沉到波浪的摆动的摇篮里

bellied canvas, I can see her settling down in the swinging cradle of the waves. I can see the dense column of smoke mingling with and veiling the tongues of orange flame, until she becomes like a little Altar set out upon a vast sea, offering up its sacrifice of a human soul to the ever-implacable gods.

Now every time you burn a ship's log, you attend a Viking's burial. In those flames of green and gold, of orange, purple and blue, there is to be found, if you will use but the eyes for it, all the romance, all the spirit and colour of that majestic human sacrifice — the burial of a Viking lord. As you sit through the long evenings, while the rain is beating in sudden, whipping gusts, upon the streaming window-pane, and the drops fall spitting and hissing down the chimney into the fire below, then the burning of a ship's log is company enough for anyone. With every spurt of flame as the tar oozes out from the sodden wood, and the water, still clinging in the tenacious timber, bubbles and boils, you can distinguish, but faintly, the stirring voice of Romance telling of thrilling enterprise and of great adventure. There are few sailors can spin a yarn so much to your liking. Never was there a pirate ship so fleet or so bold; there were never escapes so miraculous, or battles so stern, as you can see when in those long-drawn[1] evenings you sit alone in the unlighted parlour

---

1 long-drawn: unduly prolonged 延长。

去。我能够看一阵阵的浓烟混着同遮住橘色的火舌,等到最后她变成放在大海中一座小"祭坛",献出它的牺牲,一个人的灵魂,给那永不息怒的神们。

现在每回你烧一块船木,是你参加一次海贼大王的葬礼。在那绿色,黄金色,橘色,紫色同蓝色的火焰里,你可以找出,只要你肯用你的眼睛去好好留神,一切浪漫史以及这种庄严的人的牺牲——一个海贼大王的安葬——的一切精神同色调。长夜里当你坐着,雨是乘着忽然的,鞭挞似地的疾风,打到倾泻着水的玻璃窗上,还有雨滴从烟囱里像唾吐一样,发出咝声降到下面的火里,那时的烧着一块船木由任何人看来都该说是个好伴侣。每个火舌的进出时,柏油从煮熟的木头里渗漏出,还依着黏韧的船骨的海水起泡沸腾着,你能够听出,确然只是微微地,"浪漫史"的颤动声音,说出惊人的壮举同伟大的冒险。没有几个水平能够说故事说得这么中你的意思。从来没有这么迅速或者勇敢的一艘盗船;从来没有这么神奇的出险或者这么持久的战斗,像你在这长夜里所能看见的,当你独自坐在没有

and watch a ship's log burning on the fire.

Pay no heed to them when they tell you the green flames come from copper, the blue from lead — the pale purple from potassium. The chemist's laboratory has its own romance, but it shares nothing in common with the high seas of imagination upon which you are riding now. Let the green flames come from copper! They are the emeralds, the treasure of the Orient to you. Let the blue flames come from lead, the pale purple from potassium! In your eyes as you sit there in that darkened room, with the flame-light flickering upon the ceiling and the shadows creeping near to listen to it all, they are the blue sash around the waist, the purple kerchief about the head of the bravest and the most bloodthirsty pirate that ever stepped.

At all times a fire is a companion. Yet set but a ship's log upon the flames and I warrant you will lose yourself and all about you; lose yourself until the last light flickers, the last red ember falls, and the good ship that has borne you so safely over a thousand seas sinks down into the grey ashes of majestic burial.

点灯的客厅里，注视一块船木在炉里燃烧。

别去理他们，当他们告诉你绿焰是从铜来的，蓝焰是从铅来的——浅灰〔紫〕色的焰是从钾来的。——化学家的试验室里有它自己的浪漫事，但是它同你现在所遨游的想象这个大海却满不相干。就说绿焰是从铜来罢！对于你，它们却是翡翠，"东方"的宝物。就说蓝焰是从铅来，浅紫焰是从钾来罢！当你坐在那黑暗的房里，火焰的光闪烁着照到天花板上，影子都爬到近旁去听它的声音时候，在你眼里，它们是来过世上最勇敢，最嗜杀的海贼的围腰蓝带同缚在头上的紫色头巾。

无论什么时候，一炉火总是一个伴侣。把一块船木放在火焰里，我敢包你会出神，忘记了自己同四围的一切；忘记了自己，一直等到最后的火焰摇动了，最后的红烬灭了，而这个曾经这么安稳地带你渡过成千个大海的好船最后陷下去，埋在庄严的安葬的残灰里去了。

A. A. Milne

The Chase

The fact, as revealed in a recent lawsuit, that there is a gentleman in this country who spends £10,000 a year upon his butterfly collection would have disturbed me more in the early nineties[1] than it does to-day. I can bear it calmly now, but twenty-five years ago the knowledge would have spoilt my pride in my own collection, upon which I was already spending the best part[2] of threepence a week pocket-money[3]. Perhaps, though, I should have consoled myself with the thought that I was the truer enthusiast of the two; for when my rival hears of a rare butterfly in Brazil, he sends a man out

---

1 nineties 是指一八九〇年与一九〇〇年之间，early nineties 是指这十年间的前几年。所以译作一八九二三年。
2 the best part: the largest part 最大部分。

追 蝴 蝶

最近一场官司泄露出一事实：我们国里有一位绅士，一年花一万金镑来收集蝴蝶，这件事在一八九二三年时会比今日更使我烦闷。我现在能够冷静地忍受着，但是二十五年以前这消息一定会伤害及我对于自己的收集的自负，为了那个收集我已经花去我一星期三辨士的零用钱的大部分了。然而，或者我会安慰自己，以为两人里我是更真实的热心人；因为当我这位仇敌听到巴西有一种罕见的蝴蝶，他就派一个人到巴西去捕拿，

---

3 pocket-money：child's weekly allowance 小孩子每星期所领到的零用钱。

to Brazil to capture it, whereas I, when I heard that there was a Clouded Yellow in the garden, took good care that nobody but myself encompassed¹ its death. Our aims also were different. I purposely left Brazil out of it.

Whether butterfly-hunting is good or bad for the character I cannot undertake to decide. No doubt it can be justified as clearly as fox-hunting. If the fox eats chickens, the butterfly's child eats vegetables; if fox-hunting improves the breed of horses, butterfly hunting improves the health of boys. But at least, we never told ourselves that butterflies liked being pursued, as (I understand) foxes like being hunted. We were moderately honest about it. And we comforted ourselves in the end² with the assurance of many eminent naturalists that "insects don't feel pain."

I have often wondered how naturalists dare to speak with such authority. Do they never have dreams at night of an after-life in some other world, wherein they are pursued by giant insects eager to increase their "naturalist collection" — insects who assure each other carelessly that "naturalists don't feel pain"? Perhaps they do so dream. But we, at any rate, slept well, for we had never dogmatized about a butterfly's feelings. We only quoted the wise men.

---

1 to encompass: to contrive 设法。
2 in the end: finally 最后。

可是当我听到园里有一个"暗澹黄"种的蝴蝶，我就留心除开自己外不让谁去图谋杀死它。并且我可说我们的目的是不同的。我本来存心把巴西放在我的收集范围之外。

到底追蝴蝶是有益或者有害于个人的性格，我不能去下个断言。无疑地，追蝴蝶也能够有很充分的理由同猎狐一样。若使狐吃有小鸡，蝴蝶蛹却吃有生菜；若使猎狐能够使马种进步，猎蝴蝶能够使小孩的身体强壮。但是最少，我们总未曾对自己说过蝴蝶喜欢被人们追捕，像（我听说）狐那样爱被人打猎。我们关于这点都还老实。最后我们安慰自己，相信许多有名的自然科学家所说的话："昆虫不会感觉到苦痛。"

我常常纳罕自然科举家怎么敢这样断然地说着。难道他们晚上绝没有梦着在别个世界里的一种来生，在那里他们被巨大的昆虫追赶着，它们也是热心想增加它们的"自然科学家的收集"——这班昆虫随随便便地互相安慰道"自然科学家不会感觉到苦痛"？也许他们有这样梦过。可是我们，无论如何，是睡得很好的，因为我们从来没有武断过一个蝴蝶的感觉。我们不过是引用聪明人的话。

But if there might be doubt about the sensitiveness of a butterfly; there could be no doubt about his distinguishing marks. It was amazing to us how many grown-up and (presumably) educated men and women did not know that a butterfly had knobs on the end of his antennae, and that the moth had none. Where had they been all these years to be so ignorant? Well-meaning but misguided aunts, with mysterious promises of a new butterfly for our collection, would produce some common Yellow Underwing from an envelope, innocent[1] (for which they may be forgiven) that only a personal capture had any value to us; but unforgivably ignorant that a Yellow Underwing was a moth. We did not collect moths; there were too many of them. And moths are nocturnal creatures. A hunter whose bedtime depends upon the whim of another is handicapped for the night-chase.

But butterflies come out when the sun comes out, which is just when little boys should be out; and there are not too many butterflies in England. I knew them all by name once, and could have recognized any that I saw — yes, even Hampstead's[2] Albion[3] Eye (or was it Albion's Hampstead Eye?), of which only one specimen had ever been caught in this country; presumably by Hampstead — or Albion.

---

1 innocent: ignorant 不懂。
2 Hampstead 是伦敦郊外的一个地方名字。
3 Albion 是 England 的古名。

但是若使对于一个蝴蝶的感觉性有怀疑的余地，对于它的特征却是绝无可疑的。由我们看来，这真是奇怪，有这么多成人的同（仿佛是）受过教育的男女不懂得一个蝴蝶的触角尖端有许多圆球，而蛾却没有。这许多年来他们到底是到那里去会弄得这么无知？好心肠但是走到错路了的姨娘们神秘地答应带一个新种的蝴蝶来增加我们的收集，却从一个信封里取出个普通的"黄翼里"，不懂得（这点还是可恕的）只有亲手的捕获对于我们才是有价值的，但是不可恕地不晓得一个"黄翼里"是一个蛾。我们并不收集蛾；它们的种类太多了。蛾又是晚上出现的动物。一个猎人，他睡觉的时间是随着别人的高兴，是不宜于夜间的狩猎的。

但是蝴蝶是当太阳出来的时候出现，那刚是小孩子该出来的时候；在英国蝴蝶的种类也没有太多。我曾经全能够说出它们的名字，随便碰到一个都能认清是属于那一种的——真的，甚至于晓得"罕普斯忒的阿尔比温眼睛"（或者是叫做阿尔比温的罕普斯忒眼睛吗？），关于这类蝴蝶在英国只采集有一个标本；

In my day-dreams the second specimen was caught by me. Yet he was an insignificant-looking fellow, and perhaps I should have been better pleased with a Camberwell Beauty, a Purple Emperor, or a Swallowtail. Unhappily the Purple Emperor (so the book told us) haunted the tops of trees, which was to take an unfair advantage of a boy small for his age, and the Swallowtail haunted Norfolk, which was equally inconsiderate of a family which kept holiday in the south. The Camberwell Beauty sounded more hopeful, but I suppose the trams disheartened him. I doubt if he ever haunted Camberwell in my time.

With threepence a week one has to be careful. It was necessary to buy killing-boxes and setting-boards, but butterfly-nets could be made at home. A stick, a piece of copper wire, and some muslin were all that were necessary. One liked the muslin to be green, for there was a feeling that this deceived the butterfly in some way; he thought that Birnam Wood was merely coming to Dunsinane[1] when he saw it approaching, and that the queer-looking thing behind was some local efflorescence. So he resumed his dalliance with the herbaceous border, and was never more surprised in his life than when

---

1 这是莎翁悲剧 Macbeth 里的一段故事。一个妖神告诉 Macbeth 一定要 Birnam 地方的森林自己走到 Dunsinane 来，他才会死。Macbeth 心里想这是绝不会有事的，因此十分放心。他的敌人却用树枝来缚在头上前进，守望的人就赶紧跑去报告 Macbeth，说 Birnam 的森林真是自己会向 Dunsinane 走来了，却不晓得已是兵临城下了。

当然是罕普斯忒所采集的——也许是阿尔比温采集的。在我们想里，那第二个标本是我所捕获的。但是他是无貌的家伙，也许若使我得到一个"坎柏卫尔的美人"，一个"紫皇帝"，或者一个"燕尾"，我会更喜欢些。不幸得很"紫皇帝"（书里这样告诉我们）只常在树顶上飞着，这真是太欺侮一个长得不到他的年纪所应有的高度的小孩了，"燕尾"常在诺福克那里出现，这也是同样地不顾到在南方渡〔度〕放暇〔假〕日子的家庭了。"坎柏卫尔的美人"听起来是更有希望的，但是我想煤车使他们灰心，不肯来临了。我怀疑当我在那里时候，他曾经飞到坎柏卫尔过。

每星期只有三辨士，自然是要小心点才行。杀蝶箱同保蝶板是非买不可的，但是扑蝶网可以用家制的。一条竿子，一串铜丝同一块洋纱，所需要就是这么多了。我们喜欢用绿色洋纱，因为我们觉得这大约总可以瞒得过蝴蝶；当他看网子走近时候，他会想这不过是柏喃森林自己走到丹息能来了，后面这个怪样子的东西不过是那地的一种花丛。因此他还在那里沾花惹草，他一生中最惊愕的时候是当这东西一变变做一个小孩同一个蝴

it turned out¹ to be a boy and a butterfly-net. Green muslin, then, but a plain piece of cane for the stick. None of your collapsible fishing-rode — "suitable for a Purple Emperor." Leave those to the millionaire's sons.

It comes backs² to me now that I am doing this afternoon what I did more than twenty-five years ago; I am writing an article upon the way to make a butterfly-net. For my first contribution to the press was upon this subject. I sent it to the editor of some boys' paper, and his failure to print it puzzled me a good deal, since every word in it (I was sure) was correctly spelt. Of course, I see³ now that you want more in an article than that. But besides being puzzled I was extremely disappointed, for I wanted badly⁴ the money that it should have brought in. I wanted it in order to buy a butterfly-net; the stick and the copper wire and the green muslin being (in my hands, at any rate⁵) more suited to an article.

---

1 to turn out: to prove in the result 结果是。
2 to come back: to return to memory 重新忆起。
3 to see: to comprehend; know 看出, 知道。
4 to want badly: to want urgently 很紧迫地需要着。
5 at any rate: certainly 一定。

蝶网的时候。那么，洋纱是要用绿色的，可是竿子只须一个通常的藤杖。绝不用你们那种可收缩的鱼竿——"宜于捕'紫皇帝'用的。"这些东西让大富豪的儿子去买罢。

我现在忽然记起，我今天下午是做二十五年前我所做的事情；我是写一篇文章说怎样去做一个蝴蝶网。因为我生平的第一次投稿是关于这个题目。我把稿送到一种小孩子看的刊物的编辑去，他没有把我登出来，使我很莫明其妙，因为里面每字（那时我很有把握）都是正确地拼着。自然，我现在看出你们对于一篇文章还要求其他的好处。但是在莫明其妙之外，我又是极端地失望，因为我非常需要这稿所应当有的代价。我要用那钱来买一个做好了的蝴蝶网；所谓竿子，铜丝同绿洋纱是（在我手里，无论如何）更宜于做一篇文章的材料。

Holbrook Jackson

The Spirit of the Dance

It is impossible to describe a great dancer or a great dance — I mean in words. It can be done in music, and Degas[1] and one or two others have done it in paint. More particularly is it beyond the art of letters to describe Pavlova[2]. There is nothing upon which words can hang themselves; she is intangible as air, as light and as wonderful. Genée, Polaire, and Isadora Duncan are also great dancers, but it is easier to capture some of their characteristics in a noose of words, because they have that something which we call individuality. They are dancers of a kind[3] individualists of dancing; personality domi-

---

1 Degas, Hilaire Germaim Edgar (1834—1917),法国名画家。
2 当时一个极出色的舞女。
3 of a kind: of some sort; not a typical or perfect specimen of the class 有几分,非模范的。

跳舞的精神

一位伟大的跳舞家或者一种伟大的跳舞不是能够形容出来的——我是指借着文字的能力。用音乐却能够做到,台加同两位其他画家曾经用图画来描状过。帕甫罗发的舞态尤其是超乎文学的描写能力之上。没有一处是呆的,可以让文字来抓住;她是同空气一样地不可捉摸的,轻飘的同奇妙的。真涅以,波勒尔同以锡多拉·当坎也都是大跳舞家,但是这还是比较容易些,用文字的活结去捉到些他们的特性,因为他们具有我们所谓个性。他们是不完全的跳舞家,跳舞中的个性主义者;个性

nates their art.

Pavlova is dancing incarnate; she is all the others in one; she is the very spirit of the dance, neither classical, traditional, nor modern, but all three — an ever-changing trinity of enraptured motion. She does not make you think of herself; she sets you dreaming of all the dancing that has ever been, of all the dancing that is. Whilst watching her I could not help thinking she was not merely following the rules of an art, but that she was following the rules of life. The leaves dance in the breeze, the flowers dance in the sun, the worlds dance in space, and Pavlova dancing is a part of this cosmic measure.

Everybody in the theatre must have felt some thing similar — especially when she and Michael Mordkin, her superb consort in the art, danced together the Bacchanale[1] of Glazunov. I imagine also those dim segments of faces in the darkened auditorium, many of them reflecting the frigid morality of English respectability, would be touched to strange emotions. Their staid owners would feel a new wakefulness, recalling as in a dream all that had ever happened to them of passion or beauty, all that might have happened to them had they followed their real desires, their sacred whims. You could indeed feel the heart of the audience in it; very happiness linking itself

---

1 Bacchus是古代的酒神，所以酒神舞叫做Bacchanale。

支配着他们的艺术。

帕甫罗发是跳舞的化身；她是混众人而为一的；她是跳舞的真正精神，既不是有古代风的，也不是传统的，也不是近代的，却是把三者全蕴在一身——令人狂喜的运动的一种常变不停的三位一体。她不使你想到她自己；她却叫你梦想到一切古往今来的跳舞。当看她跳舞时候，我免不了想起她不单是遵循一门艺术的定则，却是遵循着生命的定则。树叶在和风里跳舞着，花朵在太阳光里跳舞着，大千世界在空间跳舞着，帕甫罗发的跳舞是这个宇宙的节奏中的一部分。

戏院里的每位观客一定都有同这个相类的感觉——特别是当她和迈克尔·摩得金，她在艺术上的绝妙配偶，一起跳格拉尊洛夫的酒神舞。我又想在那黑暗的大厅里的脸孔——里面有许多脸孔反射出英国的尊严的，冷酷的道德——的微光部分一定染着奇怪的情感。这些脸孔的古板主人一定觉得一种新觉醒，好像在梦里一样回忆起他们所曾尝过的一切热情同美感，以及一切他会尝过的，若使他们一向是随着他们真实的情感，他们神圣的怪想做去。你当真能够觉得观众的心在这非常快乐时候

with memory and regret, for in the very temple of delight, as Keats[1] knew, veiled Melancholy hath her sovran shrine.

But for myself, regret was ever tinged with a fuller joy. I felt all the laughter of the world coursing through me; I was pulled back into a younger period when men and gods were on speaking terms[2] with one another:

"And as I sat, over the light blue hills

There came a noise of revellers: the rills

Into the wide stream came of purple hue —

　'Twas Bacchus and his crew!

The nearest trumpet spake, and silver thrills

From kissing cymbals[3] made a merry din —

　'Twas Bacchus and his kin!

Like to a moving vintage down they came,

Crowned with green leaves, and faces all on flame;

All madly dancing through the pleasant valley,

To scare thee, Melancholy!"

The swaying form of Pavlova rhymed and romped with life and

---

1 Keats, John (1795—1821), 英国三大浪漫诗人之一, 他在 *Ode on Melancholy* 里有二句: Ay, in the very temple of Delight/Veil'd Melancholy has her sovran shrine。

2 on speaking terms: knowing each other 彼此认识。

3 铙钹两片相碰作声好像是相互接吻一样, 所以用 kissing 这字。

钩连上了回忆同悔恨,因为在欣欢的神庙里面,像开茨所知道的,面蒙黑纱的"愁闷之神"有她的独立的神龛。

但是,关于我自己,悔恨老是染上了一种更圆满的快乐。我觉得世上一切的狂笑在我热血里奔驰;我被带到一个更幼稚的时期,当人们同神们是有交使的情谊时候:

"当我坐着的时候,从浅蓝的小山里

来了一阵闹酒的人们的声音:小河

也流到紫色的大江里去——

  这是酒神同他的全队同伴!

最近的喇叭响了,刺耳的银声

从两唇相触的铙钹做出一种欣欢的嘈声——

  这是酒神同他的亲戚!

像会动的葡萄一样他们来到下面,

顶上戴着绿叶,个个红得好似火烧;

大家颠狂地跳舞着经过这可爱的山谷,

  为着要把你赶去,'愁闷之神'!"

帕甫罗发摇动的身体同生命和快乐,同爱和美协调而乱跳。

joy, with love and beauty. O the wild flight across the stage, the hot pursuit, the sweet dalliance, and then the rich luxury of capture and supreme surrender! The very essence of life was there: life so full of joy that it overflowed with blissful abandonment until it sank from the only pardonable excess — excess of happiness.

She dances with soul as well as body; her beautiful slight form is but the instrument upon which she plays the psalm of life. And her face dances too, dances in joy and fear, in surrender, and in the rapture of accomplished passion. She is the first dancer I have seen whose face also dances. Rarely does one see such a vivid facial expression of absolute joy, never before in a dancer. Most other dancers' faces are too preoccupied with their steps. Pavlova looks as if she has no preoccupations — she just lives. For her there is neither future nor past, only the mad rhythmic present.

That really is what dancing should be. Dancing is rhythmic life. When life is most intense, when it is master of its own destiny, then it sways and rhymes and dances, it becomes lyrical. Dancing is the song of the body, the lyric of form. It bears the same relation to motion as the flower does to the plant: it is a phase of efflorescence, a sign of ripeness. William Blake[1] got very near the heart of this mys-

---

1 William Blake (1757—1827), 英国最伟大的神秘诗人。

呵，那种横过戏台的放恣的飞奔，那种热烈的追赶，那种甜蜜的调戏，然后那种擒获同极美的降服的深妙意味！生命的精髓就在这里；生命是这样充满了欣欢，简直是泛滥着极乐的放纵，一直等到它销沉下去，由于惟一可恕的过度——幸福的过度。

她不单是身体跳舞，她的灵魂同时也在跳舞；她美丽苗条的身体只是个工具，在上面她奏出生命的赞美歌。她的脸孔也在跳舞，为着欣欢，为着害怕，为着降服，为着得到了满足的热情的狂欢而跳舞。她是我所看到的第一个脸上也能跳舞的舞女。我们很少看见一种这么活泼的绝对快乐的脸上表情，从来没有在一个跳舞者脸上看见。别个跳舞者的脸孔多半是太关心到他们的脚步。帕甫罗发却是满不在乎的样子，好像她是什么也不关心的——她只一股活气。对于她，可说将来同过去全化为乌有了，只有个疯狂的，有节奏的现在。

跳舞真真应该是这样子。跳舞是有节奏的生命。当生命是在最紧张的时候，当生命是它自己的命运的主人时候，它就摇动着，协调着，跳舞着，它变成可歌的了。跳舞是身体唱出的歌，是风姿的抒情诗。它同运动的关系是像花同树木的关系：它是开花的一相，成熟的表征。威廉·勃来克差不多达到这个

terious thing when he said, "Exuberance is Beauty."

People only dance when they feel the exuberance of life coursing through their veins. And there is a very real link between the Danse Bacchanale[1] of Pavlova and Michael Mordkin and the circling scamper of the children on the village green to the delicious eternal nonsense of:

"Here we dance — Looby Loo![2]

And here we dance — Looby Light![3]

Here we dance — Looby Lum![4]

All on a Saturday night!"

But the conventional measures of the modern ballroom are not dancing: they are as far removed from the spirit of dance as an orgy in a modern ginpalace is from a festival of Dionysus[5]. The ballroom is a fashion, like rinking, and it will go the way of all fashions. It is a kill-time for those who are too weary to live, an amusement for those who have no life to spare, for people whose vitality is exhausted or atrophied. Now and then you do see a bit[6] of genuine dancing in a ballroom: two lovers are mysteriously moved by some strain in a

---

1 Danse Bacchanale: Bacchanale dance.
2、3、4 这几个字是没有意思的，只是拿来凑韵脚的。
5 Dionysus: 这是希腊酒神的名字，同拉丁文里的 Bacchus 是相等的。
6 a bit: little 一点儿。

神秘东西的内心,当他说,"充溢就是美"。

当人们感觉到生命的充溢在他们血管里奔流时候,他们才跳舞。帕甫罗发同迈克尔·摩德金的酒神舞同小孩子在乡村草地上拉着手打着圈圈的疾跑是有一个很真实的关系的,那时小孩子一面唱着那美妙的,永久是无意思的调子:

"我们在这儿跳舞——乐必乐!

我们是在这儿跳舞——乐必来!

我们在这儿跳舞——乐必蓝!

大家星期六晚上齐快乐!"

但是近代跳舞场里的通常跳舞不能算是跳舞:它们是同跳舞的精神离得很远了,好像近代一个酒馆里的痛饮是同酒神节的意义离得很远了。跳舞场是一个时尚,同滑冰场一样,它的结果也是跟一切别的时尚相同。这是那班太疲倦了不能去真真享受生活的人们的一种销磨岁月的办法,那班没有丰余的活力的人们同那班精力已经耗尽或者萎缩的人们的一种解闷的玩意儿。有时你在跳舞场里会看到一点儿真正的跳舞:两个爱人给普通二人旋转舞的调子里面的一些歌意神秘地感动着,他们真

common waltz tune, and they begin to dance. But a whisper immediately goes round[1] the room, starting from the dowagers' chairs, where elderliness is stamping on happiness, and the burst of exuberance is called improper.

Far otherwise is it, however, in the "sixpenny hops" of those who have no respectability to maintain. In the reeking atmosphere of the dancing-rooms of the East End[2] you will see dancing that has little art, but much life. It is gross and graceless, but it possesses what the ballroom lacks — passion, joy. I often think that our comfortable middle-class people should not attempt to dance. They no longer live: their ideals are money, appearance, prestige, and these things have nothing to do with[3] life. It is only those who have never had or who have long since abandoned such ideals that can dance: children, simple peasant folk, common East End Cockneys[4], and the elect — those who create, those who have the exuberance which is life and beauty. But the rest are still fortunate, for just as they live by proxy, so can they dance by proxy. Pavlova and the great dancers are very kind — they will dance before them, if not exactly for them.

---

1 to go round: to pass from one person to another in a company 辗转相传。
2 那是伦敦下等人聚集的地方。
3 to have nothing to do with: to have no connection with 毫不相关。
4 Cockney: native of London 伦敦本地人。

开始跳舞了。但是一种耳语立刻传遍全房,那是从富婆的椅子发起的,她们的老迈想践踏碎他人的幸福,就把充溢的发泄叫做不道德了。

但是那班没有体面来维持的人们的"六辨士跳舞"却大不同了。在伊斯特·恩得那里的跳舞场的烟雾腾腾的空气里,你会看到没有什么艺术,却有许多生气的跳舞。那是粗鄙无文的,但是它具有大跳舞场里所缺乏的东西——热情,欣欢。我常常想我们舒服的中等阶级的人民不应当去尝试跳舞。他们已经是行尸走肉了:他们的理想是钱,面子同威严,这些东西同生命是丝毫不相干的。只有那从来没有过或者已经弃丢了这类理想的人们才能跳舞:小孩子,脑筋简单的农人,伊斯特·恩得那里的普通伦敦住民,同特别的人们——会创造的人们,具有充溢生命同美的人们[1]。但是其余的人们还是有幸福的,他们的生活既是别人替他们活着,所以别人也可以替他们跳舞。帕甫罗发同其他大跳舞家是很仁爱的——他们肯在他们面前跳舞,虽然不一定刚刚是为他们而跳舞。

---

[1] 初版作"具有充溢,那就生命同美,的人们",此据1930年8月再版改。——编者注

"I will only believe in a God who can dance," said Nietzsche[1], and those who are alive to the real issues[2] of life will be with him. One should dance because the soul dances. Indeed, when one thinks of it what are any real things but dances? I mean the only realities — moments of joy, acts of pleasure, deeds of kindness. Even the long silences, the deep quietness of serene souls, are dances; that is why they seem so motionless. When the top dances most perfectly it seems most still; just as the apparently still earth is dancing round itself and round the sun; just as the stars dance in the night. All art is a dance; the painter is but a ballet-master marshalling the dance of light and colour; a poem is a dance of words; music a dance of tones. And why, therefore, should we not have gods that dance? Perhaps Pavlova and her sisters in the great art will teach them.

But maybe they dance already, only we cannot see them. Who knows? Let us not forget that religion and dance have often gone hand in hand[3]. There have been many guesses at the riddle of life, and there will be many more; for mystery still lies around us and about — it lies within us and above, it throws dust in our eyes, and lays in our path barricades that seem invincible. But we shall not

---

1 Nietzsche, Friedrich Wilhelm (1844—1900) 德国大哲学家，主张超人主义，反对基督教思想。

2 issue: outcome 结果。

3 to go hand in hand: to be closely united 不可须臾离。

"我只肯相信一个能够跳舞的神",尼采说着;凡是感动到生命的真正究竟的人们都会和他抱着同一的主张。我们应当跳舞,因为我们的灵魂是跳舞着。真的,我们追想到底,除开跳舞外,世上还有什么实在的东西?我是惟一的实在——喜欢的时候,快乐的动作,仁爱的举动。就是那长久的静默,清澈的心灵的深深的恬静,也是跳舞;所以它们才好像是这么不动样子。当陀螺跳舞得最完全时候,它好像是最静止的;正好像分明是静止的地球却是自转,又绕着太阳转;正好像星空在夜里的跳舞一样。一切艺术都是种跳舞;画家不过是一位舞队的领袖,指挥光同色的跳舞;一首诗是字的跳舞;音乐是声调的跳舞。所以,为什么我们不能有个会跳舞的神们?或者,帕甫罗发同她在这门伟大的艺术上的姊妹们会教导他们。

但是也许神们已经跳舞着了,只是我们不能看见。谁知道呢?让我们别忘记了宗教同跳舞一向是常携手在一块儿的。对于人生的谜已经有许多的臆测了,将来还会有许多;因为神秘还是躺在我们的四旁——它躺在我们心里同我们上面,它把尘土眯着我们的眼睛,在我们的路上放了好像是无法征服的障碍。

cease striving to peer through that veil of dust, to mount those barricades: to light the lamp of vision, after our own manner. I also shall guess. Indeed I have done so a thousand times, as which of us has not? Sometimes I fancy life is nothing after all but a glorious dance, a carnival of motion beginning in dance, continuing in dance; and when the end comes it is but a signal from the Mastor of the Ballet[1] that the dance shall begin again, for there is no end. Yes, there can be no further doubt, the gods are always dancing, and the great dancers are among the true prophets.

---

1 这是指万物的真宰。

但是我们不会停着不去努力从这层尘障里看去，越过这许多障碍；按着我们自己的态度来默燃幻想之灯。我也要来猜一下。真的，我已经猜有成千回了，我们里面谁没有这样猜过？有时我想究竟说起来，生命并不是别的，只是一个光荣的跳舞，一种运动的狂欢节，开头是跳舞，继续下去也是跳舞；当结局到了时候，这不过是"舞队的领袖"的一个记号，叫我们把这跳舞重新再来开始。因为世上实在是没有结局的。不错，这真是不能够再怀疑了，神们老是在跳舞着，伟大的跳舞家也可说是真正的预言者。

Some Best English Essays

小品文续选

（英汉对照）

梁遇春　译注

"自修英文丛刊"之一，上海北新书局，1935年1月付排，1935年6月初版

CONTENTS
目　次

序 ··· 327

Abraham Cowley
Of Solitude
孤居 ·· 330

David Hume
Of the Dignity or Meanness of Human Nature
人性的高尚或卑鄙 ··· 344

Charles Lamb
New Year's Eve
除夕 ·· 364

Dream-Children: A Reverie
梦里的小孩 ··· 392

William Makepeace Thackeray
On a Hundred Years Hence
百年之后 ································· 408

Alexander Smith
On Death and the Fear of Death
死同死的恐惧 ····························· 438

Richard Jefferies
Meadow Thoughts
草地上的默思 ····························· 486

Augustine Birrell
Actors
戏子 ······································ 518

Alfred George Gardiner
On Talking to One's Self
自言自语 ································· 562

Edward Verrall Lucus
The School for Sympathy
同情学校 ································· 574

序

　　小品文大概可以分做两种：一种是体物浏亮，一种是精微朗畅。前者偏于情调，多半是描写叙事的笔墨；后者偏于思想，多半是高谈阔论的文字。这两种当然不能截然分开，而且小品文之所以成为小品文就靠这二者混在一起。描状情调时必定含有默思的成分，才能蕴藉，才有回甘的好处，否则一览无余，岂不是伤之肤浅吗？刻划冥想时必得拿情绪来渲染，使思想带上作者性格的色彩，不单是普遍的抽象东西，这样子才能沁人心脾，才能有永久存在的理由。不过，因为作者的性格和他所爱写的题材的关系，每个小品文家多半总免不了偏于一方面，我们也就把他们拿来归儒归墨罢。二年前我所编的那部小品文选多半是偏于情调方面。现在这部续选却是思想成分居多。国人因为厌恶策论文章，做小品文时常是偏于情调，以为谈思想总免不了俨然；其实自 Montaigne 一直到当代思想在小品文里面一向是占很重要的位置，未可忽视的。能够把容易说得枯索的东西讲得津津有味，能够将我们所不可须臾离开的东西——思想——美化，因此使人生也盎然有趣，这岂不是个值得一干的盛举吗？话好像说得夸大了。就此打住罢！

这部续选的另一目的是里面所选的作家有一半不是专写小品文的。他们的技术有时不如那班常在杂志上写短文章的人们那么纯熟，可是他们有时却更来得天真，更来得浑脱，不像那班以此为业的先生们那样"修习之徒，缚于有得"。近代小品文的技术日精，花样日增，煞是有趣，可是天分低些的人们手写滑了就堕入所谓"新闻记者派头"（Journalistic），跟人生隔膜，失去纯朴之风，徒见淫巧而已，聪明如 A. A. Milne 者尚不能免此，其他更不用说了。

这九位作家里除 Lamb, Gardiner, Lucus 是熟人，不用介绍外，关于其他六位略谈几句。Cowley 是个诗人，他的诗光怪陆离，意思极多，所以有人把他称为"立学派"，他到晚年才开始写小品文，而且只写十一篇，可是这都是他不朽之作。这些小品很能传出他那素朴幽静的性格，文字单纯，开了近代散文的先河。Hume 是英国经验派哲学发展到极端的人，他走入惟心论同怀疑论了，同时他又是个历史家，他以怀疑主义者明澈的胸怀，历史家深沉的世故来写小品，读起来使人有清醒之感，仿佛清早洗脸到庭中散步一样。Thackeray 是十九世纪讽刺小说大家，他的心却极慈爱，他行文颇有十八世纪作家冲淡之风，写小品时故意胡说一阵，更见得秀雅生姿。Smith也是个诗人，也以诡奇瑰丽称于当世，所谓"痉挛派"诗人是也。他的小品文里思想如春潮怒涌，虽然形式上不如Hazlitt那么珠圆玉润，可是忧郁真挚，新意甚多，《梦村》（*Dreamthorp*）一书爱读者虽无多，这几个却是极喜欢他的人们。Jefferies是这几位里面惟一专写风景的散文作家，他以自己丰富的幻想灌注到他那易感心灵所看的自然美景里，结果是许多直迫咏景长诗的细腻文字，他真可说是在梦的国土里过活的人。Birrell是学法律出身的，他的小品文在英国小品文学里占有特殊的地位，他那大胆的诙谐口吻，打扮出的权威神气（一面又好像在那里告诉我们这只是打扮而已，这是〔使〕他胜过一班真以权威自豪的人们）以及胸罗万卷，吐属不凡的态度都是极可爱的，他现在已经八十多岁了，据说是个矮老头，终身不娶，对人极和蔼，恐怕念过他文章的人都想和他会一面。Lamb这里译有二篇，他是译者十年来朝夕聚首的惟一小品文家，从前写了一篇他的评传，后来自己越看越不喜欢，如今仿如家人，没有什么话可说了。去年曾立下译他那《伊里亚随笔》全集的宏原〔愿〕，岁月慢悠悠地过去，不知道何日能如愿，这是写这篇序时惟一的感慨。写序文似乎总该说些感慨，否则显得庸俗，所以就凑上这几句话。

于北平

Abraham Cowley

Of Solitude

"Nunquam minus solus, quam cum solus[1]" is now become a very vulgar saying. Every man, and almost every boy, for these seventeen hundred years has had it in his mouth. But it was at first spoken by the excellent Scipio[2], who was without question[3] a most eloquent and witty person, as well as the most wise, most worthy, most happy, and the greatest of all mankind. His meaning no doubt was this: that he found more satisfaction to his mind, and more improvement of it by solitude than by company; and to show that he spoke not this loosely or out of vanity, after he had made Rome mistress of almost

---

1 Nunquam minus solus, quam cum solus: Never less alone, than when alone 最不感到寂寞是当寂寞时候。

2 Scipio: Publius Cornelius Scipio Africanus Major (237—183? B. C.), 罗马将军，败汉尼拔于Zana。

3 without question: undoubtedly 无疑地。

孤　　居

"独居时最不感到孤独",现在变成为一句非常粗俗的老话了。一千七百年来,个个人,几乎个个小孩,都拿它做口头禅。但是最早说这句话的是那位优秀的西庇阿,他无疑地是一个最有辩才的,最有智慧的人,又是一切人类里最贤明,最有价值,最快乐,最伟大的人。他这句话的意思一定是这样:他觉得独处比群居更使自己心里愉快,于自己的心境也更有裨益;为着要显出他不是信口或者出于矜夸说了这句话,当他使罗马差不多成为全世界的主人之后,他自己下野,情愿流徙他方,在林

the whole world, he retired[1] himself from it by a voluntary exile and at a private house in the middle of a wood near Linternum passed the remainder of his glorious life no less gloriously. This house Seneca[2] went to see so long after with great veneration, and, among other things, describes his bath to have been of so mean a structure that now, says he, the basest of the people would despise them, and cry out, "Poor Scipio understood not how to live." What an authority is here for the credit of retreat! And happy had it been for Hannibal[3] if adversity could have taught him as much wisdom as was learnt by Scipio from the highest prosperites. This would be no wonder if it were as truly as it is colourably and wittily said by Monsieur de Montaigne[4], that ambition itself might teach us to love solitude: there is nothing does so much hate to have companions. It is true, it loves to have its elbows free[5], it detests to have company on either side, but it delights above all things in a train behind, ay, and ushers, too, before it. But the greater part of men are so far from the opinion of that noble Roman, that if they chance at any time to be without

---

1 retired: caused to retire 使退隐。

2 Seneca: Lucius Annaeus Seneca (4? B.C.—A.D. 65), 罗马克己学派的哲学家。

3 Hannibal (247—183 B.C.): 迦太基将军, 勇敢善战, 后以失望服毒自尽。

4 Montaigne: Michel Eyquem de Montaigne (1533—1592), 法国散文家, 居圆塔之中, 写下许多恬适深刻的小品文, 深有人生意味, 为小品文的鼻祖。

忒南姆邻近一座森林中间的私宅里同样光荣地渡〔度〕过他这个光荣生活的余年。这间屋子辛尼加许多年后还是怀着十分的虔敬去瞻仰,在其它东西之中,描状出他的浴室是盖得这么恶劣,他说,现在最下等的人也会瞧不起这些东西,喊道:"可怜的西庇阿不知道怎么过活。"这真是一个大权威,足以增加隐居的光荣!汉尼拔可以算做有福,假使厄运能够教他以西庇阿从不可一世的成功所学得到的这么多的智慧。这件事也不足为奇,若使蒙旦先生的话不单说得精彩新颖,而且是与事实相符的,他说野心会教我们喜欢独处:天下没有别的东西比它更厌恶伴侣。固然,它喜欢无人制〔掣〕肘,它厌恶两旁有人,但是它顶高兴有一大队人跟在后面,是的,而且还要有在前面喝道的人们。其实,一大半人们跟这位高尚的罗马人意见是差得这么

---

5 to have one's elbow free:to have plenty of room to move in 有行动自由、转肘如意的余地。

company, they are like a becalmed ship[1]; they never move but by the wind of other men's breath, and have no oars of their own to steer withal. It is very fantastical and contradictory in human nature that men should love themselves above all the rest of the world, and yet never endure to be with themselves. When they are in love with a mistress, all other persons are importunate[2] and burdensome to them. "Tecum vivere amem, tecum obeam lubens."[3] They would live and die with her alone.

"Sic ego secretis possum benè vivere silvis
　Quà nulla humano sit via trita pede,
Tu mihi curarum, requies, tu nocte vel atrâ
　Lumen, et in solis tu mihi turba locis."[4]

"With thee for ever I in woods could rest,
Where never human foot the ground has pressed,
Thou from all shades the darkness canst exclude,
And from a desert banish solitude."

And yet our dear self is so wearisome to us that we can scarcely support its conversation for an hour together. This is such

---

1 a becalmed ship: a ship kept from motion by lack of wind 因缺风而不能行动的船。

2 importunate: out of place; inappropriate 不相宜，非其时。

3 罗马诗人Horace的诗句，接着就是译文。

远,若使他们有时偶然没有伴侣,他们就好像一双因为风息而停行的帆船;他们全靠着别人气息的吹嘘才能转动,他们自己没有桨可以航行。这是人性中最古怪,最矛盾的地方,人们爱自己过于世上一切其它的人们,然而绝不能忍受独与自己为侣。当他们跟一个女人一往情深时候,在他们眼里一切别人都是烦琐同难堪的。他们要独自同她过活,他们要独自同她死去。

"我能够永远同你歇息于林中,

人们的脚所未践踏的地方,

你能使漆黑完全失掉阴影,

你能使旷野不现它的寂寞。"

可是我们亲爱的自己使我们觉得这么生厌,我们几乎不能跟这位亲爱的自己相处一小时。这是这么古怪的一个癖〔脾〕

---

4 罗马诗人 Tibullus 的诗句。

an odd temper of mind as Catullus[1] expresses towards one of his mistresses, whom we may suppose to have been of a very unsociable humour.

"Odi ct Amo, qua nam id faciam ratione requiris?

Nescio, sed fieri sentio, et excrucior."

"I hate, and yet I love thee too;
How can that be? I know not how;
Only that so it is I know,
And feel with torment that 'tis so."

It is a deplorable condition this, and drives a man sometimes to pitiful shifts in seeking how to avoid himself.

The truth of the matter is, that neither he who is a fop in the world is a fit man to be alone, nor he who has set his heart much upon[2] the world, though he has ever so much understanding; so that solitude can be well fitted and set right but upon a very few persons. They must have enough knowledge of the world to see the vanity of it, and enough virtue to despise all vanity; if the mind he possessed with any lust or passions, a man had better be in a fair than in a wood alone. They may, like petty thieves, cheat us perhaps, and pick

---

1 Catullus: Caius Valerius Catullus (87—54 B. C.), 也是罗马诗人。
2 to set one's heart upon: to fix the desires on 醉心于, 热衷。

气，正如卡塔拉斯对于他的一个情人所说的，我们可以猜想她大概是个性情非常冷慢的人。

"我厌恶，然而我又爱你；

怎么会这样呢？我不知道；

我只晓得情形是如此，

觉得万分难过事实会是这样。"

这是个可悲的情形，有时驱使一个人用惨憯的方策来设法躲避自己。

实在的情形是，世上愚人既不是宜于独居的人，太关心世事的人，虽然他非常通达人情，也不是合式的人；所以只有极少数的人宜于独居，安于独居。他们必得了解世界到能够看出它的空虚，修养到能够看轻这一切虚荣；若使心里被什么欲望或者烈情占住，一个人还是在市场比独居林中好些。这些欲情在大庭广众之中，像小窃一样，也许会欺骗我们，扒我们的袋

our pockets in the midst of company, but like robbers, they use[1] to strip and bind, or murder us when they catch us alone. This is but to retreat from men, and fall into the hands of devils. It is like the punishment of parricides[2] among the Romans, to be sewed into a bag with an ape, a dog and a serpent. The first work, therefore, that a man must do to make himself capable of the good of solitude is the very eradication of all lusts, for how is it possible for a man to enjoy himself while his affections are tied to things without himself? In the second place, he must learn the art and get the habit of thinking; for this too, no less than well speaking, depends upon much practice; and cogitation is the thing which distinguishes the solitude of a god from a wild beast. Now because the soul of man is not by its own nature or observation furnished with sufficient materials to work upon; it is necessary for it to have continual resource to learning[3] and books for fresh supplies, so that the solitary life will grow indigent[4], and be ready to starve without them; but if once we be thoroughly engaged in the love of letters[5], instead of being wearied with the length of any day, we shall only complain of the shortness of our whole life.

---

1 use: are accustomed to 常常。
2 parricides: murderers of any near relative 谋杀亲人的凶手。
3 continual resource to learning: continual recourse to learning 不断地求助于学问。
4 indigent: needy 困穷。
5 letters: literature 文学。

子，但是当他们抓到我们孤零零地一个人时候，像强盗一样，他们常常剥我们的衣服，把我们绑起，或者杀害了我们。这真可以说是从人群里退出，坠到魔鬼的手里去。这好像罗马谋杀亲族的犯人所受的责罚，跟一双猴子，一条狗，一条蛇同缝在一个布袋里。所以，一个人要享受独居的好处必要干的第一步工作是铲除一切欲情，因为一个人怎么能够自得其乐，当他的感情都是系于身外之物？第二下，他必得学会思想的艺术，造成思想的习惯；因为这正同善于言辞一样，是靠着时常的练习；冥想却是神的独处与野兽的独处所由分的地方。现在因为人的心灵本身未曾具有，就观察所得也没有得到，足够沉思默想的材料；所以它必得不断地求助于学问同书籍，去找新鲜的材料，因此没有它们，独居的生活会变成穷乏，大有精神上饥饿之概；但是若使我们曾经一度澈底地恋上了学问，那么不单不会厌于任一天的日长难遣，我们却将愁诉人生的短促了。

"O vita, stulto longa, sapienti brevis!"

"O life, long to the fool, short to the wise!"

The First Minister of State has not so much business in public as a wise man has in private; if the one have little leisure to be alone, the other has less leisure to be in company; the one has but part of the affairs of one nation, the other all the works of God and nature under his consideration. There is no saying shocks me so much as that which I hear very often, "that a man does not know how to pass his time." It would have been but ill-spoken by Methuselah[1] in the nine hundred and sixty-ninth year of his life, so far it is from us, who have not time enough to attain to the utmost perfection of any part of any science, to have cause to complain that we are forced to be idle for want of work. But this you will say is work only for the learned, others are not capable either of the employments or the divertisements that arise from letters. I know they are not, and therefore cannot much recommend solitude to a man totally illiterate. But if any man be so unlearned as to want entertainment of the little intervals of accidental solitude, which frequently occur in almost all conditions (except the very meanest of the people, who have business enough in the necessary provisions for life), it is truly a great shame

---

1 Methuselah: one of the patriarch, related to have lived 969 years 一位族长，据说活到九百六十九岁，见《圣经·创世记》中。

"啊,人的一生,傻子觉得悠长,智者却嫌短促!"

一国首相的公事还没有智者个人私事那么忙;若使首相没有独处的闲暇,智者更没有闲暇去群居;前一个不过有一国事情的一部分,后一个却得冥搜遍上帝同自然的全部创造品。天下最使我震骇的话是我常常听到的一句话:"一个人不知道怎样混过他的时间。"这句话还是讲得不好,若使马士撒拉在九百六十九岁时说了这话;我们既是在任一门科学的任一部分内都没有时间做到尽美尽美的地步,当然更不会有理由去埋怨因为缺乏工作,所以不得不懒惰过日。但是你将说,这只是学者的工作,别人既不能从事于研究学术,也不能拿它来做消遣的资料。我知道他们不能,所以不十分劝一个目不识丁的人去过独居的生活。但是若使一个人不学无术到连间或一些时候的独处,那常常发生于几乎任一种的生活状态里(除非最下等的人们,他们是谋生之不暇的),都无法排遣,这真是他父母同他自己的大

both to his parents and himself; for a very small portion of any ingenious art will stop up all those gaps of our time, either music, or painting, or designing, or chemistry, or history, or gardening, or twenty other things, will do it usefully and pleasantly; and if he happen to set his affections upon poetry (which I do not advise him too immoderately) that will overdo it; no wood will be thick enough to hide him from the importunities of company or business, which would abstract him from his beloved.

—O quis me gelidis sub montibus Hæmi

Sistat, et ingenti ramorum protegat umbrâ?

耻辱；因为任一门巧艺的极小部分就足以填满我们时间里这一切罅隙了，音乐，图书，设计，化学，历史，园艺，以及二十件其它的事情，个个都能有用地，愉快地干这种工作；若使他偶然钟情于诗歌（我不劝他太热烈地爱它），那么还会干得过分了；他将觉到没有森林深密得足以把他隐藏起来，不受伴侣同俗事的纷扰，那使他离开他的爱人。

——啊，谁能置我于巴尔干凉谷之中，

把我荫在树枝浓影的底下呢？

David Hume

Of the Dignity or Meanness of Human Nature

There are certain sects which secretly form themselves in the learned world, as well as factions in the political; and though sometimes they come not to an open rupture, they give a different turn to the ways of thinking of those who have taken part on either side. The most remarkable of this kind are the sects founded on the different sentiments with regard to the dignity of human nature; which is a point that seems to have divided philosophers and poets, as well as divines[1], from the beginning of the world to this day. Some exalt our species to the skies, and represent man as a kind of human demigod[2], who derives his origin from heaven, and retains evident marks of his lineage and descent. Others insist upon the blind sides of human

---

1 divines: theologians 神学家。

人性的高尚或卑鄙

学术界里面私自分下种种派别,正同政界的结党一样;虽然有时它们不至于公开地分裂,它们却使属于各派的人们思路各自不同。这类里面最显著的是关于"人性的高尚"这个问题纷岐〔歧〕的意见所生的派别;这一点好像是诗人,哲学家,以及神学家之所由分,自世界开始一直到今日始终是如此。有些人把人类恭维到天上去,说是世间里具有一半神性的动物,他的原始是来自天上,关于他的宗系和出身留有显著的痕迹。

---

2 demigod: being half divine and half human of bestial 半神半人或半神半兽的东西,据说中国才讲西学时候有一本字典把这字译作"半个上帝"。

nature, and can discover nothing, except vanity, in which man surpasses the other animals, whom he affects so much to despise. If an author possess the talent of rhetoric and declamation, he commonly takes part with[1] the former; if his turn lie towards irony and ridicule, he naturally throws himself into the other extreme.

 I am far from thinking that all those who have depreciated our species have been enemies to virtue, and have exposed the frailties of their fellow-creatures with any bad intention. On the contrary, I am sensible that a delicate sense of morals, especially when attended with a splenetic temper, is apt to give a man a disgust of the world, and to make him consider the common course of human affairs with too much indignation. I must, however, be of opinion, that the sentiments of those who are inclined to think favourably of mankind, are more advantageous to virtue than the contrary principles, which give us a mean opinion of our nature. When a man is prepossessed with a high notion of his rank and character in the creation, he will naturally endeavour to act up to it, and will scorn to do a base or vicious action which might sink him below that figure which he makes in his own imagination. Accordingly we find, that all our polite and fashionable moralists insist upon this topic, and endeavour to represent vice unworthy of man, as well as odious in itself.

---

 1 to take part with: to side in dispute with 辩论时援助。

另外有些人坚持人性盲目的那一方面，除开虚荣外，找不出人有那一点胜过禽兽，他们却是这么排架子瞧不起它们。若使一个作家有修辞同高谈的本领，他常是归于前一派；若使他的作风近于冷讽同热嘲，他自然投身到后一个极端了。

我绝不把凡是漫骂人类的人们都认为是道德的仇敌，怀有恶意来揭开他们同类的弱点。其实正相反，我知道对于道德的锐敏感觉，尤其是加上了郁郁的心情，容易使一个人厌恶世界，看到日常的世事愤怒难胜。然而，我将承认，偏于赞美人类的那一派的意见是比它的反对派于道德更有利，它的反对派使我们藐视人性。当一个人对于他在万物里的地位和性质有个崇高的观念，他自然会努力去做到那地步，不屑干一件卑鄙或坏恶的勾当，那也许使他沉沦，不是他自己所臆想的那么一个人了。所以我们看见一切流行的优美道德学家都坚持此点，极力主张罪恶不单本身是可憎的，而且不值得我们人类一干。

We find few disputes that are not founded on some ambiguity in the expression; and I am persuaded that the present dispute, concerning the dignity or meanness of human nature, is not more exempt from it than any other. It may therefore be worth while to consider what is real, and what is only verbal, in this controversy.

That there is a natural difference between merit and demerit, virtue and vice, wisdom and folly, no reasonable man will deny: yet it is evident that, in affixing the term, which denotes either our approbation or blame, we are commonly more influenced by comparison than by any fixed unalterable standard in the nature of things. [1] In like manner, quantity, and extension, and bulk, are by every one acknowledged to be real things: but when we call any animal great or little, we always form a secret comparison between that animal and others of the same species; and it is that comparison which regulates our judgment concerning its greatness. A dog and a horse may be of the very same size, while the one is admired for the greatness of its bulk, and the other for the smallness. When I am present, therefore, at any dispute, I always consider with myself whether it be a question of comparison or not that is the subject of controversy; and if it be, whether the disputants compare the same objects together, or

---

1 在伦理学里判断分为两种：事实判断与价值判断，两者性质截然不同。

我们看出不由于言辞的含糊而生的争辩是很少的；我相信这个关于人性的高尚或卑鄙的争辩正同其它一样未能免此。所以这是值得一考虑的，这个争论里意见真正的分歧在那里，只是文字上的纠纷在那里。

功绩与罪戾，善与恶，智与愚有个天然的分别，这是凡具有理性的人所无法否认的：可是，这也是很分明的，当安下一个指出我们的赞美或责备的字眼时候，我们常常更受比较的影响，不大注意事物性质上什么一成不变的标准。同样地，量，广阔，大小，个个人都承认为真的东西：但是当我们说一只动物"大"或"小"，我们常常暗地里拿它和它同类其它的动物相比；这个比较就规定了我们关于它的大小的判词。一条狗同一匹马可以正是同样大，一个却被人们赞美以为大得可观，一个却被人们赞美以为小得好玩。因此，每当我见到任何辩论时候，我总是先问自己一下，辩论的题目是不是一个关于比较的问题；若使是，辩论的人们是不是比较同一东西，或者彼此各自谈个

talk of things that are widely different.

In forming our notions of human nature, we are apt to make a comparison between men and animals, the only creatures endowed with thought that fall under our senses. Certainly this comparison is favourable to mankind. On the one hand, we see a creature whose thoughts are not limited by any narrow bounds, either of place or time; who carries his researches into the most distant regions of this globe, and beyond this globe, to the planets and heavenly bodies; looks backward to consider the first origin, at least the history of the human race; casts his eye forward to see the influence of his actions upon posterity, and the judgments which will be formed of his character a thousand years hence; a creature, who traces causes and effects to a great length and intricacy; extracts general principles from particular appearances; improves upon his discoveries; corrects his mistakes; and makes his very errors profitable[1]. On the other hand, we are presented with a creature the very reverse of this; limited in its observations and reasonings to a few sensible objects which surround it; without curiosity, without foresight; blindly conducted by instinct, and attaining, in a short time, its utmost perfection, beyond which it is never able to advance a single step. What a wide difference is there between these creatures! And how exalted a

---

1 所谓上当学乖是也。

绝不相同的题材。

当我们对于人性立下一定的意见时，我们易于拿人同禽兽来比较，它们是我们所知道的具有思想的惟一东西。这种比较当然是于人类有利。在这一方面，我们看见一个生物，他的思想不受时空狭窄的限制；他能够研究到地球上最远的地方，而且出地球之外，一直研究到行星和天体；他回过头来讨论最初的原始，最少人种的历史；向前瞻望他的行动会怎样影响后代，同千年后人们对于他的人格会下什么考语；一个生物，他能够追迹因果到很远同很纷杂的地方；从个体的现象上看出共通的原理；因发现而进步；知道更改错误；甚至于能使他的过失于他也有好处。在那一方面，我们见到一个与这个相反的生物：只能观察同推理关于它身旁几件可以感觉到的东西；没有好奇心，没有预知之明；盲目地顺从本能，在很短时间内达到极限的完善境界，它是绝不能再进一步了。这两种生物有多大的差异呀！跟后者相比，我们对于前面那个生物会具个多么崇高的

notion must we entertain of the former, in comparison of the latter.

There are two means commonly employed to destroy this conclusion: First, by making an unfair representation of the case, and insisting only upon the weakness of human nature. And secondly, by forming a new and secret comparison between man and beings of the most perfect wisdom. Among the other excellences of man, this is one, that he can form an idea of perfections much beyond what he has experience of in himself; and is not limited in his conception of wisdom and virtue. He can easily exalt his notions, and conceive a degree of knowledge, which, when compared to his own, will make the latter appear very contemptible, and will cause the difference between that and the sagacity of animals, in a manner[1], to disappear and vanish. Now this being a point in which all the world is agreed, that human understanding falls infinitely short of perfect wisdom, it is proper we should know when this comparison takes place, that we may not dispute where there is no real difference in our sentiments. Man falls much more short[2] of perfect wisdom, and even of his own ideas of perfect wisdom, than animals do of man: yet the latter difference is so considerable, that nothing but a comparison with the former can make it appear of little moment.

It is also usual to compare one man with another; and finding

---

1 in a manner: in some sense 在某种意义之下；也可说。
2 to fall short: not attain or come up to 不如；没有赶上。

意见呀。

有两种工具通常用来破坏这个结论：第一，不公正地陈述事实，专偏重人性的弱点；第二，偷偷里重新把人类同最睿智的人们相比。在人类的优点里，有一个是他能够臆想一个尽美尽善的境界，那是远超过他自己所经验的；他关于智慧同道德的观念是不受什么限制的。他能够很容易提高他的观念，臆想出一种特殊的智慧，拿它来同他自己的一比，他自己的简直是该受蔑视，而与禽兽智力的差异也可说消失得无影无踪了。人类智识跟完全的智慧相差得无限远，这一点既是世上人所公认的，所以我们应该知道何时人们提到这个比较，为的是免得无谓争辩，其实我们的意见并没有真正的冲突。人们跟完全智慧，甚至于跟他自己所臆测的完全智慧的相差，是远过禽兽跟人们智慧的相差；然而第二种的差别也就不小，只有拿它来同第一种差别比较时，才显得是无关重要的。

我们又常常拿一个人同其他一个人相比；看到很少人值得

very few whom we can call wise or virtuous, we are apt to entertain a contemptible notion of our species in general. That we may be sensible of the fallacy of this way of reasoning, we may observe, that the honourable appellations of wise and virtuous are not annexed to any particular degree of those qualities of wisdom and virtue, but arise altogether from the comparison we make between one man and another. When we find a man who arrives at such a pitch of wisdom, as is very uncommon, we pronounce him a wise man: so that to say there are few wise men in the world, is really to say nothing; since it is only by their scarcity that they merit that appellation. Were the lowest of our species as wise as Tully[1] or Lord Bacon[2], we should still have reason to say that there are few wise men. For in that case we should exalt our notions of wisdom, and should not pay a singular homage to any one who was not singularly distinguished by his talents. In like manner, I have heard it observed by thoughtless people, that there are few women possessed of beauty in comparison of those who want it; not considering that we bestow the epithet of beautiful only on such as possess a degree of beauty that is common to them with a few. The same degree of beauty in a woman is called deformity, which is treated as real beauty in one of our sex.

---

1 Tully：古代一个哲人。
2 Bacon：Francis Bacon（1561—1626），英国政治家，文人，他是英国最早写小品文，用Essay这个字的人。

我们称为"有智慧的"或"有道德的",我们很容易对于普通人类有个藐视的心情。为着要使我们晓得这种推理的错误,我们可以指出,有智慧的和有道德的这些光荣的称呼并不是附于某种程度的智慧同道德,却完全由于我们拿一个人同其他的人相比。当我们看见一个人达到很难得的智慧程度,我们叫他做智者:所以说世上智者甚少,是等于没有说;因为他们就是为着稀罕,才配得上这个尊称。假使最下等的人类都像屠累或者培根爵士那么聪明,我们还可以有理由说智者甚少。因为那么我们将提高我们智慧的概念,不是才力有特别过人之处的,我们绝不肯向他崇拜。同样地,我听见没有思想的人们说过,具有美貌的女人真少,若使同没有美貌的女人一比;他们却没有想到,"美丽的"这个形容字我们只加于那班具有少见的美貌的人们身上。同样的姿容在女人叫做丑容,在我们男性里却被认为真正的美貌了。

As it is usual, in forming a notion of our species, to compare it with the other species above or below it, or to compare the individuals of the species among themselves; so we often compare together the different motives or actuating principles of human nature, in order to regulate our judgment concerning it. And, indeed, this is the only kind of comparison which is worth our attention, or decides any thing in the present question. Were our selfish and vicious principles so much predominant above our social and virtuous, as is asserted by some philosophers, we ought undoubtedly to entertain a contemptible notion of human nature.

There is much of a dispute of words in all this controversy. When a man denies the sincerity of all public spirit or affection to a country and community, I am at a loss[1] what to think of him. Perhaps he never felt this passion in so clear and distinct a manner as to remove all his doubts concerning its force and reality. But when he proceeds afterwards to reject all private friendship, if no interest or self-love intermix itself; I am then confident that he abuses terms, and confounds the ideas of things; since it is impossible for any one to be so selfish, or rather so stupid, as to make no difference between one man and another, and give no preference to qualities which engage his approbation and esteem. Is he also, say I, as insensible

---

1 at a loss: puzzled 糊涂了；不知道怎么想好。

当我们对于人类定下一个批评时，我们常常拿他同比他高或比他低的种类相比，或者拿人类里个个人来比较；所以我们常常拿人性里各种动机或主意来比较，以定我们关于人性所下的判断。真的，这是惟一值得我们注意的比较，或者可说关于眼前问题惟一能下断语的比较。假使我们自私的同坏恶的主意是像有些哲学家所说的那样胜过我们合群的同善良的动机，那么我们应该无疑地对于人性怀个鄙视的观念。

这个争论里有一大部分是文字上的纠纷。当一个人否认一切公德心，爱国心，爱社会心的诚恳，我真不知道对他作何感想。也许他没有十分明白深切地感到这类情绪，所以不能扫除他对于它的力量同真实的怀疑。但是当他后来接着否认一切私人的友谊，以为总是有利益或自私混在一起；那时我敢说他乱用字眼，混淆事物的意义：因为那是不会有的事情，有人会自私或者可说愚蠢到这样地步，以至对于人们漠不关心，并不特别喜欢那些得到他称赞和钦重的性质。我说，他对于愤怒，也

to anger as he pretends to be to friendship? And does injury and wrong no more affect him than kindness or benefits? Impossible: he does not know himself: he has forgotten the movements of his heart; or rather, he makes use of a different language from the rest of his countrymen, and calls not things by their proper names. What say you of natural affection? (I subjoin), Is that also a species of self-love? Yes; all is self-love. Your children are loved only because they are yours: your friend for a like reason; and your country engages you only so far as it has a connection with yourself. Were the idea of self removed, nothing would affect you: you would be altogether unactive and insensible; or, if you ever give yourself any movement, it would only be from vanity, and a desire of fame and reputation to this same self. I am willing, reply I, to receive your interpretation of human actions, provided you admit the facts. That species of self-love which displays itself in kindness to others, you must allow to have great influence over human actions, and even greater, on many occasions, than that which remains in its original shape and form. For how few are there, having a family, children, and relations, who do not spend more on the maintenance and education of these than on their own pleasures? This, indeed, you justly observe, may proceed from their self-love, since the prosperity of their family and

像他所自命的对于友谊这么毫无感觉吗？伤害同冤枉也像殷勤同恩惠那样不能使他动心吗？这是绝不可能的！他不知道自己：他忘却他心里的动机了；或者可以说，他用一种与他本国其他人们不同的文字，不拿事物本有的名字喊它们。你以为天性怎么样呢？（我加上去），那也是一种自私吗？是的，一切都是为着利己。你爱"你"的孩子们，因为他们是你的；你爱"你"的朋友也是为着同样的理由："你"的祖国使你关心之处只在于跟"你自己"有关系的。假使"自己"这个观念取消了，没有一件东西能够感动你的心：你将变成完全不动同麻木了！或者，若使你动一下，那将是只出于虚荣，同想给这个同一的自己以荣誉和令名。我答道，我愿意接收你对于人们行动的解释，只要你肯承认下面这些事实。对他人表示殷勤的那种自私，你得承认是于人类行动上有大影响的，甚至于常有更大的影响，比起原原本本的自私。有了家庭，孩子同亲戚的人们，花在赡养同教育他们的比花在自己寻乐的钱还少的人们天下里有几个呢？不错，你很可以说，这是由于他们的自私，因为他们家庭同亲

friends is one, or the chief, of their pleasures, as well as their chief honour. Be you also one of these selfish men, and you are sure of every one's good opinion and good-will; or, not to shock your ears with their expressions, the self-love of every one, and mine among the rest, will then incline us to serve you, and speak well of you.

In my opinion, there are two things which have led astray those philosophers[1] that have insisted so much on the selfishness of man. In the first place, they found that every act of virtue or friendship was attended with a secret pleasure; whence they concluded, that friendship and virtue could not be disinterested. But the fallacy of this is obvious. The virtuous sentiment or passion produces the pleasure, and does not arise from it. I feel a pleasure in doing good to my friend, because I love him; but do not love him for the sake of that pleasure.

In the second place, it has always been found, that the virtuous are far from being indifferent to praise; and therefore they have been represented as a set of vainglorious men, who had nothing in view but the applauses of others. But this also is a fallacy. It is very unjust in the world, when they find any tincture of vanity in a laudable action, to depreciate it upon that account, or ascribe it entirely to that

---

1 those philosophers: 指 Hobbes 等，他主张人类一切行为都是以利己为出发点，然而他自己是个道德极高，深有修养的人。

戚的兴旺是他们快乐之一，或者可说是主要的快乐，而且是他们最大的光荣。请你也做这么一个自私的人罢，你必定会得到个个人的赞美同好意；或者，说得不使你耳朵听起难过罢，个个的自私，我的也在内，将使我们愿意为你服务，说你好话。

据我看来，有两件事把这班如是坚持人性的自私的哲学家弄入迷途。第一下，他们看见每个道德的或友谊的行动跟着都有一种内心的愉快；因此他们以为，友谊同道德不会是没有杂有私心的。但是这种推理的错误是显而易见的。善良的情绪或热情产生了这个愉快，并不是因为这个愉快而出来的。我对于我的朋友干一件好事，感到快乐，因为我爱他；但是并不是为着那快乐而去爱他。

第二下，人们总常发现，有道德的人对于人家的恭维绝不是毫不关心，所以人们把他们当做一群好虚荣的人，只望博得人们的称赞。可是这也是个推理上的错误。世人可说是很不公平，当他们看到一件值得颂扬的举动里含有一些虚荣的色彩，

motive. The case is not the same with vanity, as with other passions. Where avarice or revenge enters into any seemingly virtuous action, it is difficult for us to determine how far it enters, and it is natural to suppose it the sole actuating principle. But vanity is so closely allied to virtue, and to love the fame of landable actions approaches so near the love of laudable actions for their own sake, that these passions are more capable of mixture, than any other kinds of affection; and it is almost impossible to have the latter without some degree of the former. Accordingly we find, that this passion for glory is always warped and varied according to the particular taste or disposition of the mind on which it falls. Nero[1] had the same vanity in driving a chariot, that Trajan[2] had in governing the empire with justice and ability. To love the glory of virtuous deeds is a sure proof of the love of virtue.

---

1 Nero：（37—68），罗马暴王，非常喜欢同人比赛跑快车。
2 Trajan：（52 or 53—117），也是罗马皇帝，善理国家。

因此就毁谤它，或者认为完全出于那个动机。虚荣的情形是与其他情绪不同。当贪婪或报复做了一个似乎是道德的行动的成分，我们很难断定它居了多少成分，自然会以为它是惟一的动机。但是虚荣跟道德是有这么密切的关系，喜欢善举的令名跟为善举而爱善举是这么相近，这些情绪是比别的更能够和其他东西混在一起；有了爱善举之心几乎总免不了有些爱善举的令名。所以我们看见，这个爱好光荣的心情也随它所伴的趣味和心地而变质，而不同。尼罗对于赶马车所具的虚荣岂不是和国拉真对于公平地同能干地管理国家所具的一样哩。爱好善举的光荣却很可以证明一个人是具有好善之心了。

Charles Lamb

New Year's Eve

Every man hath two birthdays: two days, at least, in every year, which set him upon revolving the lapse of time, as it affects his mortal duration. The one is that which in an especial manner he termeth his. In the gradual desuetude[1] of old observances, this custom of solemnizing our proper birthday hath nearly passed away, or is left to children, who reflect nothing at all about the matter, nor understand anything in it beyond cake and orange. But the birth of a New Year is of an interest too wide to be pretermitted[2] by king or cobbler. No one ever regarded the First of January with indifference. It is that from which all date[3] their time, and count upon what is left. It is the

---

1 desuetude: discontinuance 废止。
2 pretermitted: neglected 忽略。

除　　夕

每人都有两个诞辰：一年里最少有两天使他想到光阴的消失对于他在世的有限时光的影响。一个诞辰，他特别叫做"他的"。古昔的礼节渐见废弛，在我们独有的诞辰举行隆重典礼这种习惯差不多也成为过去了，或者只让小孩们去干，他们对于这件事是毫无感想的，除开饼同橘子他们什么也不晓得。但是"新年"的诞生感动了一切人们，是不容皇帝或者补鞋匠的忽略。从来没有一个人把正月初一冷淡看过。大家都是以那天做根据来记他们的日期，算一算他们还剩有多少时光。那是我们

---

3 to date：to give the date of 算日子。

nativity of our common Adam[1].

Of all sound of all bells — (bells, the music nighest bordering upon heaven) — most solemn and touching is the peal which rings out the Old Year[2]. I never hear it without a gathering-up[3] of my mind to a concentration of all the images that have been diffused over the past twelvemonth[4]; all I have done or suffered, performed or neglected, in that regretted time. I begin to know its worth, as when a person dies. It takes a personal colour[5], nor was it a poetical flight in a contemporary, when he exclaimed —

I saw the skirts of the departing year.[6]

It is no more than what in sober sadness every one of us seems to be conscious of, in that awful leave-taking. I am sure I felt it, and all felt it with me, last night; though some of my companions affected rather to manifest an exhilaration at the birth of the coming year, than any very tender regrets for the decease of its predecessor. But I am none of those who.

---

1 Adam：我们都是亚当的子孙。
2 which rings out the Old Year：英俗于除夕十二时，教堂中钟声齐发，以表送旧迎新之意。
3 gathering-up：summoning up one's thought 聚精会神。
4 concentration of all the images...：a mental summary of my experiences 我种种经验汇集在心中。

公有的亚当的诞生日了。

一切钟的声音里——（钟是最近于天际的音乐）——最严肃的，最动人的是送旧岁时齐发的钟声。我每次听到总是聚精竭神把散在过去十二个月里的一切印象集到心头；一切我所曾做过的或者挨过的，履行的或者忽略的——在那深可惋惜的十二个月里。我才知道这些时光的价值，好像当一个人死去，我们才晓得他的好处。这些时光好像变成一个人了；这并不是当代一位作家做诗的胡想，当他说：

我看见将逝之年的裙边。

这仿佛是我们个个人在清愁里都感到的，当这可怕的告别时候。我敢说昨天晚上我感到这种情调，大家也同我一样的感到；虽然有几位朋友喜欢对于新年的诞生现出高兴，不愿意为着新年先辈的逝世现出什么非常深情的惋惜。但是我是不属于那一种人们，他们。

---

5 it takes a personal color: it becomes a real personage to my imagination 在我想像里他化成一个人了。

6 这是英浪漫派诗人 Samuel Taylor Coleridge 的句子。

Welcome the coming, speed the parting guest.[1]

I am naturally, beforehand, shy of novelties; new books, new faces, new years, — from some mental twist which makes it difficult in me to face the prospective. I have almost ceased to hope; and am sanguine only in the prospects of other (former) years. I plunge into foregone visions and conclusions. I encounter pell-mell with past disappointments. I am armour-proof[2] against old discouragements. I forgive, or overcome in fancy, old adversaries. I play over again for love[3], as the gamesters phrase it, games for which I once paid so dear. I would scarce now have any of those untoward accidents and events of my life reversed. I would no more alter them than the incidents of some well-contrived novel. Methinks, it is better that I should have pined away seven of my goldenest years, when I was thrall to the fair hair, and fairer eyes, of Alice W—n[4], than that so passionate a love adventure should be lost. It was better that our family should have missed that legacy, which old Dorrell cheated us of, than that I should have at this moment two thousand pounds in banco[5], and be without the idea of that specious old rogue.

---

1 这是英假古典主义诗人 Alexander Pope 的句子。
2 armour-proof: armed with impenetratable armour 穿有刀枪不能入的甲胄。
3 for love: with stakes 不下注的;赌趣的。
4 Alice W—n: 指他的初恋 Alice Winn。
5 in banco: banked; standing to your credit 放在银行里。

欢迎新来的，催促将去的客人赶快走开。

根本上，我生性对于新的东西总是害羞；新书，新脸孔，新年，——我心里一些乖僻癖〔脾〕气使我不敢去睇着将来。我几乎是不再有什么希望了；只是当着回忆到过去的希望时候，我才现出热诚。我跳到已往的好梦同结局里去。我跟过去的失望混战做一团。我对着早已过去的失意可说穿有刀枪不能入的盔甲。我在幻想里赦宥了或者打倒了我的冤家。我现在赌趣地（像赌钱的人们所说的）把这些玩意儿玩过，我曾经为这些玩意儿费了那么大的代价。我一生里种种不幸的事故，几乎没有一件我现在会愿意去望从前不是那样。我不肯改换它们，正好像我不肯改换一本结构极好的小说里面的情节。我想还是我将我最可贵的七年时光憔悴地消磨去好些，当我被亚俪斯·温——的美发同更美的眼睛迷了的时候，比起这么热情的一段情史没有发生。还是我们家庭没有得到老多尼所骗去的那笔遗产好些，比起我此刻有二千金镑存在银行里，却没有貌似君子的老滑头的影子留在心中。

In a degree beneath manhood[1], it is my infirmity to look back upon those early days. Do I advance a paradox when I say, that, skipping over the intervention of forty years, a man may have leave to love himself without the imputation of self-love?

If I know aught of myself, no one whose mind is introspective — and mine is painfully so — can have a less respect for his present identity, than I have for the man Elia[2]. I know him to be light, and vain, and humoursome; a notorious ...; addicted to ... averse from counsel, neither taking it, nor offering it; — ... besides; a stammering buffoon; what you will; lay it on[3], and spare not; I subscribe to it all, and much more, than thou canst be willing to lay at his door — but for the child Elia — that "other me," there, in the background — I must take leave to cherish the remembrance of that young master — with as little reference, I protest, to his stupid changeling of five and forty, as if it had been a child of some other house, and not of my parents. I can cry over its patient small-pox at five, and rougher medicaments. I can lay its poor fevered head upon the sick pillow at Christ's, and wake with it in surprise at the gentle posture of maternal tenderness hanging over it, that unknown had watched its sleep. I

---

1 in a degree beneath manhood: to a somewhat unmanly extent 有些不像男子汉的样子。
2 Elia: Elia是东印度公司兰姆一位同事的名字，他拿来做笔名。
3 lay it on: apply the lash freely 随便鞭挞罢。

真是有不像男子汉的样子，我老爱回想我的早年，这是我的毛病。当我说一个人可以有自由去爱四十年前的"他的自己"而不至于挨到爱自己这个罪名，我是不是发一句似是而非的话呢？

若使我具有自知之明，我可说知道没有一个生性爱内省的人——我自己是爱内省得使我苦痛——对他现在的自己会有我对伊里亚这人那样瞧不起。我晓得他（指自己）是轻浮，爱自夸同没有恒心；一个恶名昭彰的……；又是嗜……；不喜欢忠言，既没有听别人的，也没有给别人；而且是……；又是一个结巴的小丑；你爱怎么说都可以；把一切罪状加到他身上罢，别饶恕他；我全可以承认，还有你所不愿加到他身上的许多罪状，我也肯承认——但是对于小孩时代的伊里亚——站在远景里的（那个我）——我必定要去爱抚对于那个小孩子的追念——这对于这个四十五岁的傻家伙是满不相干的，我声明，好像那是别家的一个小孩，不是我父母的儿子。我现在还能够为他五岁时耐心出痘同蛮野的治疗而流泪。我能把他那可怜的发烧的头安放在基督学校的病枕上，同他一起醒来，对着俯在他上面的慈爱的和蔼姿势纳罕，她是暗暗地看护他的睡眠。我晓

know how it shrank from any the least colour[1] of falsehood. — God help thee, Elia, how art thou changed! — Thou art sophisticated. — I know how honest, how courageous (for a weakling) it was — how religious, how imaginative, how hopeful! From what have I not fallen, if the child I remember was indeed myself, — and not some dissembling guardian[2], presenting a false identity, to give the rule to my unpractised steps, and regulate the tone of my moral being!

That I am fond of indulging, beyond a hope of sympathy, in such retrospection, may be the symptom of some sickly idiosyncrasy. Or is it owing to another cause: simply, that being without wife or family, I have not learned to project myself enough out of myself; and having no offspring of my own to dally with, I turn back upon memory, and adopt my own early idea, as my heir and favourite? If these speculations seem fantastical to thee, reader — (a busy man, perchance), if I tread out of the way of thy sympathy, and am singularly conceited[3] only, I retire, impenetrable to ridicule, under the phantom cloud of Elia.

The elders, with whom I was brought up, were of a character not likely to let slip the sacred observance of any old institution; and

---

1 color: tinge; semblance 色彩；相像。
2 dissembling guardian: guardian angel assuming his personality 护身的天使来代替他自己。
3 singularly conceited: possessed of peculiar notions 具有奇怪的想头。

得他对于一点点的欺骗都也退缩着不肯干。——愿上帝助你，伊里亚，你是变得多么厉害，你现在变坏了。——我晓得你从前是多么诚实，多么勇敢（就柔弱的小孩而论）——多么虔敬，想像力多么丰富，怀有多大的希望！我是从多么善良坠落下来，若使我所记忆的那个小孩真是我自己——不是什么守护神攫住我的心，现出一个假人格来，使我这世路未惯的脚步有法则可依，而规定了那时我的精神生活的情调！

我喜欢自纵于这样的回顾（那是不能希望得到人们的同情的），这也许是什么病态的怪癖的征候罢。或者是出于别的缘故吗；只是因为无妻无家庭，没有学好把自己投射到自己身外；既没有我自己的后裔让我来玩弄，我回头来去找我的记忆，拿我自己早年的心境做我的嗣子，我所宠爱的人？若使这些空想在你眼里好像是荒诞的，读者——（或者是一位忙人）若使我走出你同情的范围之外，变成一个只是非常古怪的人，那么我退隐在伊里亚这个假名的迷雾之下，一切讥笑都无法侵入了。

那班前辈，我是在他们里面养大的，是不大肯让任何制度里的神圣风俗随便湮没的；鸣钟送旧岁这个古风他们保守着，

the ringing out of the Old Year was kept by them with circumstances of peculiar ceremony. — In those days the sound of those midnight chimes, though it seemed to raise hilarity in all around me, never failed to bring a train of pensive imagery into my fancy. Yet I then scarce conceived what it meant, or thought of it as a reckoning that concerned me. Not childhood alone, but the young man till thirty, never feels practically that he is mortal.[1] He knows it indeed, and, if need were, he could preach a homily on the fragility of life; but he brings it not home to himself, any more than in a hot June we can appropriate to our imagination the freezing days of December. But now, shall I confess a truth? — I feel these audits but too powerfully. I begin to count the probabilities of my duration, and to grudge at the expenditure of moments and shortest periods, like misers' farthings. In proportion as the years both lessen and shorten. I set more count[2] upon their periods, and would fain lay my ineffectual finger upon the spoke of the great wheel[3]. I am not content to pass away "like a weaver's shuttle." Those metaphors solace me not, nor sweeten the unpalatable draught of mortality. I care not to be carried with the tide, that smoothly bears human life to eternity; and reluct at the inevitable course of destiny. I am in love with this green earth;

---

1 Hazlitt 在 "The Sense of Immortality in Youth" 里面说他兄弟说过这么一句话，那篇文章就是讨论这一句话。

2 to set more count: to attach greater value 更看重。

还带有奇怪的仪式。——在那些日子里,这种午夜和鸣的钟声虽然对于我周围的人们都能引起欣欢,却总是带有一阵愁思到我心头。然而那时我几乎没有想到这含有什么意思同这是个同我有关系的纪数,不单稚年之时期,三十岁以前的青年实际上还是绝没有感到他是会死的。他真晓得这样事,若使有必要,还能演一篇劝世文,说生命的脆弱;但是他自己没有深切地感到,好似在炎热的六月里我们不能把十二月的冰冻日子放在我们的想像里。但是现在呢,我要说出真话吗?——我却是太强烈地感到这种年年的结算。我开始计算我大概还可以活多久,刻刻的光阴和最短的时间的销费我都是舍不得的,有如守财奴对着他的极小铜币。剩下的年数愈少了,过得愈快了,跟着我也愈看重一年一年的来去,真想把我这不会生效力的手指放在"时间大轮"的辐里,止住它的转动。我不甘心"像铁匠的梭子"那样一瞬即逝。那些比喻不能安慰我,我也没有把死亡这一口苦酒弄甜。我并不想任潮流去,平稳地从人生带到永生;我对于所谓运命里的必需过程是退缩不前。我爱上了这个青青

---

3 中国所谓羲和之轮也是这个意思。

the face of town and country; the unspeakable rural solitudes, and the sweet security of street. I would set up my tabernacle here. I am content to stand still at the age to which I am arrived; I, and my friends: to be no younger, no richer, no handsomer. I do not want to be weaned by age; or drop, like mellow fruit, as they say, into the grave. — Any alteration, on this earth of mine, in diet or in lodging, puzzles and discomposes me. My household gods plant a terrible fixed foot, and are not rooted up without blood. They do not willingly seek Lavinian shores[1]. A new state of being staggers me.

Sun, and sky, and breeze, and solitary walks, and summer holidays, and the greenness of fields, and the delicious juices of meats and fishes, and society, and the cheerful glass, and candlelight, and fireside conversations, and innocent vanities, and jests, and irony itself — do these things go out with life?

Can a ghost laugh, or shake his gaunt sides, when you are pleasant with him?

And you, my midnight darlings, my folios! Must I part with the intense delight of having you (huge armfuls) in my embraces? Must knowledge come to me, if it comes at all, by some awkward experi-

---

1 to seek Lavinian shores: to remove to strange countries 远徙到异乡去; 罗马诗人 Virgil 的长诗 *Aneid* 中 Aneas 听神的吩咐从 Troy 远徙到意大利的 Lavinium。

的大地，城市乡下的境况；那说不出的田园幽寂同街道上可喜的安全。我愿意在这里永居下去。我愿意老站在我现在所走到的年时；我同我的朋友：也不要更年青，更富，更漂亮。我不欲靠着老年的衰颓使我渐厌于生活；或者有如他们所说的，像熟果子落地那样掉到墓里去。——在我这大地上，任何的改变，饮食上或者居住上，都使我迷惑，使我不安。我的家神们的脚是生根地可怕地栽在地上，拔起来是会流血的。他们不愿到异地里去。一种新的方式使我站不稳双脚。

太阳，苍穹，和风，孤单的散步，暑假，田地的青青，鱼肉的美液，聚会，快乐的酒杯，烛光，炉边的闲话，无害的自夸，笑话，和冷风（就它本身的美处而言）——这些东西是随着生命一同消失吗？

一个鬼能够大笑吗，或者捧他的那瘦削的腹吗，当你对他说笑的时候？

还有你们，我午夜里的爱宠，我的书籍！我必定也要割舍把你拥在怀里（满抱的）这个无上的快乐吗？智识来到我心里，假使它还会来，一定要靠着直觉的钝拙尝试，而不再从阅读这

ment of intuition, and no longer by this familiar process of reading?

Shall I enjoy friendships there, wanting the smiling indications which point me to them here, — the recognizable face — the "sweet assurance of a look"?

In winter this intolerable disinclination to dying — to give it its mildest name — does more especially haunt and beset me. In a genial August noon, beneath a sweltering sky, death is almost problematic. At those times do such poor snakes as myself enjoy an immortality[1]. Then we expand and burgeon. Then we are as strong again, as valiant again, as wise again, and a great deal taller. The blast that nips and shrinks me, puts me in thoughts of death. All things allied to the insubstantial, wait upon that master feeling; cold, numbness, dreams, perplexity; moonlight itself, with its shadowy and spectral appearances, — that cold ghost of the sun, or Phoebus' sickly sister[2], like that innutritious one denounced in the *Canticles*[3]. — I am none of her minions — I hold with the Persian[4].

Whatsoever thwarts, or puts me out of my way, brings death

---

1 such poor snakes as myself enjoy an immortality: men like myself, who love to bask in the sunshine like snakes, forget our liability to death 像我这种喜欢曝日如蛇一样的人们此时忘却死的可能了。
2 Phoebus' sickly sister: 月神 Phoebe, 据说是日神的姊妹。
3 the *Canticles*: Song of Solomon《雅歌》。
4 Persian: 波斯人信拜火教。

条熟路来吗?

在那个国土里我也能享受友朋之乐吗,缺乏了笑脸的指示,在这里这些笑脸告诉我谁是我的朋友——缺乏了这可以认得的脸孔——缺乏了"脸上的表情所担保的他对于我的好意"?

在冬天里这种难堪的对于死的嫌厌——按下一个最温和的名字罢——特别更厉害地缠绕困窘着我。在一个温暖的八月中午,在一个酷热的青天之下,死差不多是个可怀疑的东西。在那时候,像我这样喜欢阳光的可怜人们(同蛇一样)享受到永生之乐。那时,我们心旷心怡,开出花来。那时,我们比从前加一倍力气,加一倍勇敢,加一倍聪明,也高了好多。而这个刺我,令我退缩的刮风使我又想到死。一切不实在的东西都做死的跟班;寒冷,僵冻,梦儿,烦恼,甚至于月光本身,那阴森森的神气——太阳的冷魂,或者太阳神的有病妹妹,真像《雅歌》里所骂的那个虚弱的人儿——我不是佞媚月亮的人——我和拜火教的波斯人抱有同一的主张。

一切逆意的事情都把死这观念勾在我心上。一切零碎的毒

unto my mind. All partial evils, like humours[1], run into that capital plague sore. — I have heard some profess an indifference to life. Such hail the end of their existence as a port of refuge; and speak of the grave as of some soft arms, in which they may slumber as on a pillow. Some have wooed death — but out upon thee[2], I say, thou foul, ugly phantom! I detest, abhor, execrate, and (with Friar John[3]) give thee to six score thousand devils, as in no instance to be excused or tolerated, but shunned as an universal viper; to be branded, proscribed, and spoken evil of! In no way can I be brought to digest thee, thou thin, melancholy Privation, or more frightful and confounding Positive!

　　Those antidotes, prescribed against the fear of thee, are altogether frigid and insulting, like thyself. For what satisfaction hath a man, that he shall "lie down with kings and emperors in death," who in his lifetime never greatly coveted the society of such bedfellows? — or, forsooth, that "so shall the fairest face appear?" — why, to comfort me, must Alice W—n be a goblin? More than all, I conceive disgust at those impertinent and misbecoming familiarities, inscribed upon your ordinary tombstones. Every dead man must take upon

---

　　1 humours: morbid fluids in the body, such as cause skin-eruptions 身中有毒的血液，以致皮肤破裂者。
　　2 out upon thee: shame upon thee! 你真该羞！
　　3 Friar John: 法国文豪 Rabelais 书中的人物。

恶,像身里的疮脓一样,都汇聚到那个大患里去。——我曾听过人们自认淡于死生。这班人把他们生命的终止称做安身处:说坟墓是个温柔的手臂,他们可以在里面睡眠,有如躺在枕头的上面。有人去追求死——但是你(指死)是多么可羞,我说,你这丑恶的,愚蠢的小鬼!我憎你(指死),恨你,咒你,(像托钵僧约翰那样)把你投给十二万个魔鬼去,因为你是没有一点能够得到我们的原谅的,可以忍受的;却该像大毒蛇一样,受天下人的弃避;该受烙面的刑,该宣告为法律所不保护的人,该挨前人的臭骂!我无法能够容忍你,你这瘦削的,愁闷的"不实在"或者更可怕的,更使人惊慌的"实在"!

那些定下来反抗对于你的恐惧的解毒力全是冷冰冰的,欺侮人的,正同你一样。一个人会得到什么安慰,当你说他"死时会同帝王躺在一起",他生时就从没有怎样地特别喜欢这种的同寝人?——或者当你说"最美的宠儿也是这么结局"?——怎么,为着要安慰我,亚俪斯·温——必定也变做恶鬼魔?我尤其讨厌你们通常墓石上面所刻的那些无礼的,不知本分的狎语。个个死人必得自居来教训我以他那可憎的真理吗,什么"他现

himself to be lecturing me with his odious truism, that "such as he now is, I must shortly be." Not so shortly, friend, perhaps, as thou imaginest. In the meantime I am alive. I move about. I am worth twenty of thee. Know thy betters! Thy New Year's days are past. I survive, a jolly candidate for 1821. Another cup of wine — and while that turncoat[1] bell, that just now mournfully chanted the obsequies of 1820 departed, with changed notes lustily rings in a successor, let us attune to its peal the song made on a like occasion, by hearty, cheerful Mr. Cotton[2].

The New Year

Hark, the cock crows, and you bright star

Tells us, the day himself's not far;

And see where, breaking from the night,

He gilds the western hills with light.

With him old Janus[3] doth appear,

Peeping into the future year,

With such a look as seems to say,

The prospect is not good that way.

Thus do we rise ill sights to see,

---

1 turncoat: traitor 奸贼；反戈者；讥其送旧迎新也。
2 Cotton: Charles Cotton (1630—1687), 英国诗人。
3 Janus: 罗马的神，有两面，前瞻后顾，两得其使。

在如是，我快也免不了那样"。或者并没有这么快哩，朋友，像你所想像的。在那时间未到之前，我却是活着。我到处行动。我值得二十个的你们。要懂得比你们高明的人！你的"新年元旦"是已过去了。我却还活在人间，做一八二一年里一个快乐分子。再来一杯酒——当这倒戈的钟，他现在正悲哀地唱已去的一八二〇的葬钟，换过调来，大声地迎来他的承继者，让我们和着他的调子以热诚欣欢的考通在同一时节所做的短歌罢。

新年

听呀！鸡啼了，那边的明星

告诉我们白天已是快来了；

你看从黑夜里冲出，

他把西面小山照成金黄。

年老的"两面神"同他一起出现，

向着来年偷望，

现在这样的脸孔，好像说，

那边的前程不佳，

如是地我们起来就看到不祥的东西，

And, 'gainst ourselves to prophesy;

When the prophetic fear of things,

A more tormenting mischief brings,

More full of soul tormenting gall,

Than direst mischiefs can befall.

But stay! but stay! methinks my sight,

Better informed by clearer light,

Discerns sereneness in that brow,

That all contracted seem'd but now.

His revers'd face may show distaste,

And frown upon the ills are past;

But that which this way looks is clear,

And smiles upon the New-born Year.

He looks too from a place so high,

The year lies open to his eye;

And all the moments open are

To the exact discoverer[1].

---

1 exact discover: the sun which reveals everything clearly 朗照万物的太阳。

预言自己来年的否运,

当这对于自己的担心,

带来个更苦痛的烦恼,

更满了困恼灵魂的苦味,

比起当前的麻烦。

但是停口!停口!我想我的眼睛,

现在看得更清楚些,因为光线也明亮得许多,

在那眉梢上看出了恬静气概,

那里刚才好像满是皱纹。

他那个反面也许现出不欢,

对着已过的祸患而皱眉;

但向这边望的那个脸孔是蔼然的,

朝着"新生的年"微笑。

他又是从这么高的地方下望,

这年头分明地躺在他的眼前;

一年里的一切时刻

给那精密的探寻者全看见了。

Yet more and more he smiles upon

The happy revolution.

Why should we then suspect or fear

The influences of a year,

So smiles upon us the first morn,

And speaks us good so soon as born?

Plague on't! the last was ill enough,

This cannot but make better proof[1];

Or, at the worst, as we brush'd through

The last, why so we may this too;

And then the next in reason shou'd

Be superexcellently good:

For the worst ills (we daily see)

Have no more perpetuity

Than the best fortunes that do fall;

Which also bring us wherewithal

Longer their being to support,

---

1 to make better proof: to turn out better when it is tested 试起来却比所预期的好。

他却更欣欢地笑着

对这快乐时日的来临。

我们还用怀疑还用怕

这个年头的命运吗？

它第一早就这么样向我们笑，

一生下地就说我们的好话。

该死的去年！去年是够坏了，

今年总是会好些；

或者就最坏的着想罢，我们既然挨过了

去年，今年怎会不能挨过呢；

那么照道理说明年

必是绝妙的年头：

因为极坏的厄运（我们天天都能看出）

也是不能长久下去的，

正同那会变的极好幸运一样，

好运留下的影响

又是较长久的，

Than those do of the other sort:

And who has one good year in three,

And yet repines at destiny,

Appears ungrateful in the case,

And merits not the good he has.

Then let us welcome the New Guest

With lusty brimmers of the best[1];

Mirth always should Good Fortune meet,

And renders e'en Disaster sweet:

And though the Princess turn her back,

Let us but line ourselves with sack[2],

We better shall by far hold out.

Till the next Year she face about.

How say you, Reader — do not these verses smack of the rough magnanimity of the old English vein? Do they not fortify like a cordial; enlarging the heart, and productive of sweet blood, and generous spirits, in the concoction? Where be those puling fears of death, just

---

1 brimmers of the best: overflowing glasses of the best liquor 美酒盈杯。
2 to line ourselves with sack: to fill ourselves with wine 肚里排着一行一行的酒。

比着厄运所留下的:

三年里有个好年的人

还去埋怨运命,

真可算是个忘恩的人,

不值得享受他所有的幸运。

那么让我们欢迎这新客,

用快乐的美酒盈杯;

我们该用欣欢去接"好运",

甚至能把灾患化做甜蜜:

虽然"好运娘娘"转过面去不睬我们,

让我们肚里排满葡萄酒罢,

我们能够更有力气得多支持下去,

等明年她回过脸来。

你怎么说,读者——这首小歌不是带点古英国人粗野的豪爽气味吗?那不是像兴奋剂保守着我们的勇气吗;涨大我们的胸怀,吟味起来会生出甜蜜的热血同慷慨的精神吗?那些小孩

now expressed or affected?— Passed like a cloud — absorbed in the purging sunlight of clear poetry — clean washed away by a wave of genuine Helicon[1], your only Spa[2] for these hypochondries. And now another cup of the generous! And a merry New Year, and many of them, to you all, my masters!

---

1 genuine Helicon: real poetry 真诗；Helicon 是文艺之神所居之山。
2 Spa: tonic 补剂；本来是比国镇名，以出矿水著名。

般对于死的恐惧,刚才所说的,所感到的,到那里去了?——消灭得有如一朵乌云——溶在清澈的诗歌的净化万物的阳光里——被文艺之神所居的山岭的清泉所发的微波漂去得无影无踪了,那清泉是医这忧郁病的惟一补身剂。——现在再饮一杯这鼓舞精神的美酒罢!对诸君,我的先生们,敬祝一声"新年快乐"同将来还有许许多多的新年。[1]

(原载于《北新》1930年第4卷第1、2期合刊)

---

[1] 该文发表于《北新》时文末还有一段文字:"Janus是司百物之初(如人生之初,年月之初),及天门之神,有二个脸孔,January这字就是从这位神的名字来的。"——编者注

Dream-Children: A Reverie

Children love to listen to stories about their elders, when they were children; to stretch their imagination to the conception of a traditionary great-uncle or grandame, whom they never saw. It was in this spirit that my little ones crept about me the other evening to hear about their great-grandmother Field, who lived in a great house in Norfolk (a hundred times bigger than that in which they and papa lived) which had been the scene — so at least it was generally believed in that part of the country — of the tragic incidents which they had lately become familiar with from the ballad of the *Children in the Wood*[1]. Certain it is that the whole story of the children and

---

1 the ballad of the *Children in the Wood*: 这是英国一首古歌谣，里面述一对夫妇临终时把不到三岁的两个小孩子托他们的叔父养大，他们所应得的遗产也由这位叔父去保管，他贪得这笔款，就叫两个流氓把他们带到林中害

梦里的小孩

小孩子喜欢听关于他们长辈的故事,当"他们"也是小孩子时候;喜欢逞他们的想像力,想到家里传说的,而是他们自己从来没有见过的一位叔祖父,或者祖母。那天晚上,我的小孩子就是以这种心情爬到我身旁,来听我谈他们的曾祖母飞尔德。她住在诺福克地方一所大屋里(比他们和爸爸住的屋子要大一百倍)。他们最近从《森林中两个小孩》这首歌谣里所晓得的那件悲惨事情就是发生于那个地方——最少那里人们是这么相信的。的确,这两个小孩同他们残忍叔叔的全部故事可以看

死,他们的尸首还亏知更雀用树叶来掩埋,那个坏人后来当然家破人亡了。

their cruel uncle was to be seen fairly carved out in wood upon the chimney-piece of the great hall, the whole story down to the Robin Redbreasts, till a foolish rich person pulled it down to set up a marble one of modern invention in its stead, with no story upon it. Here Alice put out[1] one of her dear mother's looks, too tender to be called upbraiding. Then I went on to say, how religious and how good their great-grandmother Field was, how beloved and respected by everybody, though she was not indeed the mistress of this great house, but had only the charge of it (and yet in some respects she might be said to be the mistress of it too), committed to her by the owner, who preferred living in a newer and more fashionable mansion which he had purchased somewhere in the adjoining county; but still she lived in it in a manner as if it had been her own, and kept up the dignity of the great house in a sort[2] while she lived, which afterwards came to decay, and was nearly pulled down, and all its old ornaments stripped and carried away to the owner's other house, where they were set up, and looked as awkward as if some one were to carry away the old tombs they had seen lately at the Abbey[3], and stick them up in Lady C.'s tawdry gilt drawing-room. Here John smiled, as much as to say, "that would be foolish indeed."

---

1 put out: put forth; displayed 拿出；现出。
2 in a sort: to some extent; in certain fashion 也可以说。
3 the Abbey: 指 Westminster Abbey, 英国名人都葬在那里。

见十分精致地刻在大厅的火炉架木头上面，全部故事一直到知更雀用树叶掩埋他们为止。后来一个愚蠢的富人把这块木头折毁下来，安上新发明的大理石火炉架，上面是一点故事也没有的。说到这个，亚丽司现出她亲爱母亲特有的一种微愠神情，那是太仁慈了，不能说含有责备的意思。然后我接着说到他们的曾祖母菲尔德是多么虔敬，多么善良，怎样子受人人的敬爱，虽然她实在并不是这大屋子的主妇，却只是照管这大屋子的（然而在有些方面她也可以说是里面的主妇），受了屋主人的付托，那位主人却高兴去住他在邻郡某处带有一所比较新些同时时髦些的屋子；但是她住在里面好似这是她自己的屋子。当她活着时候那屋子还保存些高贵门第的尊严，后来颓废了，差不多拆毁了。里面一切古老的装饰品也扯下，运到主人别所屋子里去，就安在那里，现出不相称的神气，好似有人把他们最近在违斯敏斯德礼拜堂看见的古墓移去栽在丝太太俗气的，涂上泥金的客厅里面一样。说到这里，约翰微笑起来，等于说"这

And then I told how, when she came to die, her funeral was attended by a concourse of all the poor, and some of the gentry too, of the neighbourhood for many miles round, to show their respect for her memory, because she had been such a good and religious woman; so good indeed that she knew all the psaltery[1] by heart, ay, and a great part of the *Testament* besides. Here little Alice spread her hands. Then I told what a tall, upright, graceful person their great-grandmother Field once was; and how in her youth she was esteemed the best dancer — here Alice's little right foot played an involuntary movement, till upon my looking grave, it desisted — the best dancer. I was saying, in the county, till a cruel disease, called a cancer, came, and bowed her down with pain; but it could never bend her good spirits, or make them stoop, but they were still upright, because she was so good and religious. Then I told how she was used to sleep by herself in a long chamber of the great lone house; and how she believed that an apparition of two infants was to be seen at midnight gliding up and down the great staircase near where she slept, but she said "those innocents would do her no harm;" and how frightened I used to be, though in those days I had my maid to sleep with me, because I was never half so good or religious as she — and yet I

---

1 psaltery: psalter; the book of the psalms as printed in the *Book of Common Prayer*,《祈祷书》中的诗篇。

真傻"。然后我说当她死去,安葬时好几哩内的一切穷人都聚集一起,以及几位绅士,来参加葬礼,表示他们对于她遗念的敬意,因为她是一个这么善良虔敬的妇人;她真善良,能够背出全部赞美诗同《圣经》的大部分。说到这里,小亚俪司惊讶地伸直她的手指。然后我说他们曾祖母飞尔德曾经是一个如何苗条,正直同多姿的人儿!在她年青时候,她是怎样被人们认为最善于跳舞的姑娘——说到这里,亚俪司右边小脚发出一种不自觉的跳动,等到我现出严肃的脸孔,她才停止了——我说,她是一区里最善于跳舞的姑娘,等到一种苛酷的毛病,叫做癌肿,降临她身上,苦痛使她变成驼背;但是绝不能压下她乐天的精神,或者使变为郁闷,她的精神却还是屹然不屈,因为她是这么虔敬善良。然后我说她怎样常常独自在那寂寥大屋子里面一间寂寥的房子里睡觉;同她怎样相信可以看见两个小孩的幽灵午夜里沿着她睡觉地方近旁的大楼梯溜上溜下,但是她说"这班天真孩子们不会害她;"同我常是多么吓住了,虽然那时候我有我的女仆伴着我睡,因为我从来没有她的一半善良或者

never saw the infants. Here John expanded all his eyebrows and tried to look courageous. Then I told how good she was to all her grand-children, having us to the great house in the holydays, where I in particular used to spend many hours by myself, in gazing upon the old busts of the Twelve Caesars[1], that had been Emperors of Rome, till the old marble heads would seem to live again, or I to be turned into marble with them; how I never could be tired with roaming about that huge mansion, with its vast empty rooms, with their worn-out hangings, fluttering tapestry, and carved oaken panels, with the gilding almost rubbed out — sometimes in the spacious old-fashioned gardens, which I had almost to myself, unless when now and then a solitary gardening man would cross me — and how the nectarines and peaches hung upon the walls, without my ever offering[2] to pluck them, because they were forbidden fruit[3], unless now and then, — and because I had more pleasure in strolling about among the old melancholy-looking yew trees, or the firs, and picking up the red berries, and the fir apples, which were good for nothing but to look at — or in lying about upon the fresh grass, with all the fine garden smells around me — or basking in the orangery[4], till

---

1 the Twelve Caesars：罗马皇帝从 Julius Caesar 到 Domitian。
2 offering：attempting 试；打算。
3 forbidden fruit：《圣经》中亚当夏娃吞禁果，被除出伊甸园。

虔敬——可是我绝对没有见到这两个小孩。说到这里，约翰把他的眉毛全张开了，设法现出勇敢的气概。然后我说她待所有的孙子是多么好，叫我们在放假日子到那大屋子里去住，我尤其常独自在那里花许多时光直着眼睛望那十二古老该撒的半身石像，他们是罗马皇帝，等到古老的大理石人头好像复活起来了，或者我随着他们变做大理石了；我怎样子绝不会厌倦于在那大屋子里漫游，里面有许多宽大的空房子，房里有用旧了挂帘，振摇不定的绣花帷幕，同雕刻的橄木镶板，上面的泥金几乎擦掉了——有时在广大旧式的花园里，那是我差不多独占了，除非偶然有一个孤单的园丁碰到我——以及油桃和桃子怎样挂在墙上，我却从没有试去攀摘，因为它们是禁果，除开偶然一两次摘吃——还因为我更喜欢在愁然的松柏丛林里蹓跶，检〔捡〕些红浆同松子，那除开了看看之外是没有别的用处的——或者躺在新鲜的青草上面，四围是园中美妙的香味——或者在

---

4 orangery: a glass-roofed conservatory, artificially heated, in which oranges are grow一间玻璃屋，用人工使它温暖，以便橘子的生长。

I could almost fancy myself ripening too along with the oranges and the limes in that grateful warmth — or in watching the dace that darted to and fro in the fish-pond, at the bottom of the garden, with here and there a great sulky pike hanging midway down the water in silent state, as if it mocked at their impertinent friskings, — I had more pleasure in these busy-idle[1] diversions than in all the sweet flavours of peaches, nectarines, oranges, and such-like common baits of children. Here John slily deposited back upon the plate a bunch of grapes, which, not unobserved by Alice, he had meditated dividing with her, and both seemed willing to relinquish them for the present as irrelevant. Then in somewhat a more heightened tone, I told how, though their great-grandmother Field loved all her grandchildren, yet in an especial manner she might be said to love their uncle, John L—, because he was so handsome and spirited a youth, and a king[2] to the rest of us; and, instead of moping about in solitary corners, like some of us, he would mount the most mettlesome horse he could get, when but an imp no bigger than themselves, and make it carry him half over the country in a morning, and join the hunters when there were any out — and yet he loved the old great house and

---

1 busy-idle: frivolous, yet engrossing 虽然是零星琐事, 却极有意思, 弄得一个人非常忙。

2 a king: a person likened to a king as being supreme 因为一个人优越过其他人们, 我们就把他比做"王"。

橘树的暖房里晒太阳，等到我差不多能够想自己在这值得感谢的暖气之下，也和橘子菩提树同时渐渐成熟了——或者注视园的深处鱼池里往来飞驰的鲦鱼，一两处有一条含怒的大梭鱼静静地倒挂在水之中层，好像讥笑它们无谓的跳跃——我更喜欢这些闲里带忙的游戏，比起桃子，油桃，橘子的一切甜味，同小孩子这类通常的饵。说到这里，约翰偷偷把一束葡萄归还到盘子里去，这葡萄既然也被亚俪司看到了，他起先想跟她平分，现在两个人却好像都愿意放弃它们，当做是和他们不相干的。然后用一种有点更热烈的声调，我说虽然他们的曾祖母飞尔德爱她所有的孙子，她可以说特别喜欢他们的伯父，约翰·兰——，因为他是一个这么漂亮同这么英俊的少年；是在我们兄弟里可以称王的；他不爱滞在孤寂的隐僻处发傻，像我们里面有些人那样，他当只有他们这么大的一个小鬼时候，就乘他所能得到的最有火气的马，使它带他一个早晨跑过半区的地方，还和猎人打伙，当他们有人出去打猎时候——然而他也爱古老

gardens too, but had too much spirit to be always pent up within their boundaries — and how their uncle grew up to man's estate as brave as he was handsome, to the admiration of everybody, but of their great-grandmother Field most especially; and how he used to carry me upon his back when I was a lame-footed boy — for he was a good bit older than me — many a mile when I could not walk for pain; — and how in after life he became lame-footed too, and I did not always (I fear) make allowances enough for him when he was impatient, and in pain, nor remember sufficiently how considerate he had been to me when I was lame-footed; and how when he died, though he had not been dead an hour, it seemed as if he had died a great while ago, such a distance there is betwixt life and death; and how I bore his death as I thought pretty well at first, but afterwards it haunted and haunted me; and though I did not cry or take it to heart[1] as some do, and as I think he would have done if I had died, yet I missed him all day long, and knew not till then how much I had loved him. I missed his kindness, and I missed his crossness, and wished him to be alive again, to be quarrelling with him (for we quarrelled sometimes), rather than not have him again, and was as uneasy without him, as he their poor uncle must have been when the doctor took off his limb. Here the children fell a crying, and asked if

---

1 to take to heart: to be much affected by 深为感动。

的大屋子同花园，但是血气太旺了，不能老被关在它们周围里面——以及他们的伯父成年后怎样勇敢得不下于他的漂亮，受人人的赞美，尤其是最受他们曾祖母的激赏；他怎样常载我在他背上，当我是个跛脚的小孩时候——因为他的年岁比我大得很多——走了许多哩的路，当我因为脚痛不能行动；——以及后来他怎样也变跛脚了，当他耐不住同感到苦痛时我没有老是（我恐怕）十分原谅他，没有充分地记到他对于我是多么体贴，当我跛脚时候；以及怎样当他死了，虽然他还没有死去一个钟头，就好像已在好久以前死去了，生和死是相隔得这么远呀；我起先怎样以为我还能勉强忍受他的去世，但是后来这事常常萦扰我的心，虽然我没有哭着或者非常哀痛，像有些人那样，我想他也会那样，若使我先死了，但是我忆念着他，那时我才晓得我其实是多么爱他。我忆念他的仁慈，我也忆念他的使气，希望他能够复活，再和他吵嘴（因为我们有时也吵嘴过），总胜过不能再得他，我没有了他觉得不安，好像他，你们可怜的伯父，从前必定感觉过的，当医生拿去他的一只腿。说到这里，

their little mourning which they had on was not for uncle John, and they looked up, and prayed me not to go on about their uncle, but to tell them some stories about their pretty dead mother. Then I told how for seven long years, in hope sometimes, sometimes in despair, yet persisting ever, I courted the fair Alice W — n[1]; and, as much as children could understand, I explained to them what coyness, and difficulty[2], and denial, meant in maidens — when suddenly, turning to Alice, the soul of the first Alice looked out at her eyes with such a reality of re-presentment, that I became in doubt which of them stood there before me, or whose that bright hair was; and while I stood gazing, both the children gradually grew fainter to my view, receding, and still receding, till nothing at last but two mournful features were seen in the uttermost distance, which, without speech, strangely impressed upon me the effects of speech; "We are not of Alice, nor of thee, nor are we children at all. The children of Alice call Bartrum father.[3] We are nothing; less than nothing, and dreams.

---

1 Alice W—n：兰姆隐指他的初恋 Alice Winn。

2 difficulty：an attitude of aloofness；an unwillingness to respond to a lover's advances，backwardness 超然的态度，不愿意接受恋人的爱情；退缩不前。

3 The children of Alice call Bartrum father：这位妞妮姑娘后来嫁给一位开当铺的有钱人 Bartrum，他们的女婿 William Coulson，是英国有名的外科医生。

小孩子都哭起来，问我他们所穿的小丧服是不是为着约翰伯父，他们望着我，求我不再往下谈他们的伯父，却要我告诉他们一些关于他们已死的美丽母亲的故事。然后我说怎样子七个长年里，有时满着热望，有时失望，然而总是没有馁志，我向标致的亚俪思·温——求婚；尽小孩子所能懂的，我向他们解说闺女的害羞，超然态度同不允是多么不容易对付的——我转过来一望着亚俪司，她的母亲的神情忽然现在她的眼里，相像得这么逼真，我怀疑起来了是她们的那一个站在那里，现于我的面前，那光亮的头发是属于那一个的呢；当我站着细瞧时候，两个小孩在我眼界里渐渐地变模糊了，向后面退去，老向着后面退去，等到最后什么也没有了，只剩下两个悲哀的面貌可以看得见在最远的地方，不说话，却很奇怪地使我感到他们对我露出底下这些意思；"我们不是亚俪司的小孩子，我们也不是你的，我们简直不是小孩子。亚俪司的小孩子认巴杜兰做父亲。我们是虚空；虚空之不如，只是梦儿而已。我们只是也许可以

We are only what might have been, and must wait upon the tedious shores of Lethe¹ millions of ages before we have existence, and a name"— and immediately awaking, I found myself quietly seated in my bachelor armchair, where I had fallen asleep, with the faithful Bridget² unchanged by my side — but John L. (or James Elia) was gone for ever.

---

1 Lethe: the river of Hades, of the waters of which whosoever drank, straightway all his past became to him a blank 地狱里一条河，喝了那水人们就把过去完全忘却了。

2 the faithful Bridget：兰姆指他的姊姊 Mary Lamb，他俩相依为命，他因为她早年发狂误杀母亲，就终身不娶陪她，她对于他也是体贴备至，堪称良姊。

发生的事情，必定要在忘川的无聊河岸等了万万世，我们才有实体，才有一个名字"——我立刻醒来了，看到我自己安详地坐在我的单身汉的圈手椅上，我起先在那里睡着了，忠实的布立泽特仍然不变地在我身旁——但是约翰·兰——是已永逝了。

（原载于《新月》1929年第2卷第8号）

William Makepeace Thackeray

On a Hundred Years Hence

Where have I just read of a game played at a country house? The party assembles round a table with pens, ink, and paper. Some one narrates a tale containing more or less incidents and personages. Each person of the company then writes down, to the best of his memory and ability, the anecdote just narrated, and finally the papers are to be read out. I do not say I should like to play often at this game, which might possibly be a tedious and lengthy pastime, not by any means[1] so amusing as smoking a cigar in the conservatory; or even listening to the young ladies playing their piano-pieces; or to Hobbs and Nobbs[2] lingering round the bottle and talking over the

---

1 not by any means: certainly not 绝不。

百年之后

我刚才在那里念到一家别墅里所玩的一种游戏呢?大家聚集围着一张放有笔,墨水,纸的桌子。某一位叙述一件多少含些事变同人物的故事。然后在座各人就尽他记忆同能力之所及,写下刚才叙述的故事,末了这些笔记都念出来。我并不说我很想常常玩这种游戏,那也许是一种沉闷的,费时间的娱乐,绝不会有趣得像在花房里抽雪茄;或者简直不如听年青姑娘们奏她们的钢琴调子;或者听无话不说的酒友们留连酒瓶旁边,谈

---

2 Hobbs and Nobbs:to hobnob 是 to drink together; to hold familiar intercourse 共饮,昵谈,所以 Hobbs and Nobbs 作畅谈的酒友解。

morning's run with the hounds; but surely it is a moral and ingenious sport. They say the variety of narraties is often very odd and amusing. The original story becomes so changed and distorted that at the end of all the statements you are puzzled to know where the truth is at all. As time is of small importance to the cheerful persons engaged in this sport, perhaps a good way of playing it would be to spread it over a couple of years. Let the people who played the game in '60[1] all meet and play it once more in '61, and each write his story over again. Then bring out your original and compare notes[2]. Not only will the stories differ from each other, but the writers will probably differ from themselves. In the course of the year the incidents will grow or will dwindle strangely. The least authentic of the statements will be so lively or so malicious, or so neatly put[3], that it will appear most like the truth. I like these tales and sportive exercises. I had begun a little print collection once. I had Addison[4] in his nightgown in bed at Holland House, requesting young Lord Warwick to remark how a Christian should die. I had Cambronne[5] clutching his cocked-

---

1　'60：作者是十九世纪的人，所以这指1860。

2　to compare notes：to compare brief records of facts 拿彼此简单的报告来相比，也有当作"交换意见"解。

3　so neatly put：so neatly worded 说得这么清楚。

4　Addison：Joseph Addison（1672—1719），英国小品文家，为人拘谨，行文亦如是，蕴藉可亲。

早上带着猎狗出去打猎的经过；但是这的确是个有益的，巧妙的游戏。他们说笔述的参差不同常是非常古怪的，非常好笑的。原来的故事变成这么换个样子，这么误传附会，弄到听完这许多笔记，你莫明其妙，不晓得那个是对的。时光对于干这个玩意儿的快乐人们既是无关紧要的，也许玩这把戏的一个好法子是将它延长到两年。让在一八六〇年玩这游戏的人们于一八六一年再重会重玩一下，每人重新写下他的故事。然后把你们原来写的拿出，比较一下。那么不单个个人的故事不同，笔记者也许跟他们前次自己写的就不一样了。在一年里那些事变将奇怪地增加枝节或者变为简单。最不近实的笔记也许是这么生动的或者这么刻毒的，或者说得这么伶俐，它将好像是最近于真实。我喜欢这些故事，这类嬉戏。我曾经收集过印刷画。我有一张画阿迭生穿着睡衣，躺在荷兰屋里的床上，请年青的窝立克爵士说一个基督教徒应该怎样死去。我有一张画空布纶紧握

---

5 Cambronne：这些惊心动魄、古怪有趣的事情是大家都知道的传说，但是有些恐怕只见历代相传的谎话。

hat, and uttering the immortal "la Garde meurt et ne se rend pas." I had the "Vengeur" going down, and all the crew hurraying like madmen. I had Alfred toasting the muffin; Curtius (Haydon) jumping into the gulf; with extracts from Napoleon's bulletins, and a fine authentic portrait of Baron Munchausen[1].

What man who has been before the public at all has not heard similar wonderful anecdotes regarding himself and his own history? In these humble essaykins[2] I have taken leave[3] to egotize. I cry out about the shoes which pinch me.[4] And, as I fancy, more naturally and pathetically than if my neighbour's corns were trodden under foot. I prattle about the dish which I love, the wine which I like, the talk I heard yesterday — about Brown's absurd airs — Jones's ridiculous elation when he thinks he has caught me in a blunder (a part of the fun, you see, is that Jones will read this, and will perfectly well know that I mean him, and that we shall meat and grin at each other with entire politeness). This is not the highest kind of speculation, I

---

1 Baron Munchausen（1720—1797），德国探险家，说出许多奇怪的故事。

2 essaykins：little essays 短篇的小品文字，kin 本来是一个字尾，表示"小"的意思，如 lambkin（小羊）等。

3 to take leave：to ask permission 请允许。

4 I cry out about the shoes which pinch me：Plutarch 在 Aemilius Paulus 传里述一段故事，"有一个人同他妻子离婚，他的朋友们都责备他，说她不是很贞洁吗，她不是很美丽吗；他就脱下鞋子，问朋友们，这不是很新吗，样子也很好吗，然而你们那位晓得它什么地方太紧，把我的脚挤痛了"。

着他的制帽,说出那句不朽的话:"等候着死,不能活了。"我有一张画《复仇》沉下去,船上所有的水手慌张地乱跑有如疯人。我有一张画亚勒弗烈烘油煎松饼;一张画库耳齐乌斯(嘿敦)跳到深渊里去;还有拿破仑告示的选录,同一幅泼喜豪赠男爵精美的真像。

有那个在社会里面的人没有听到同样古怪的故事关于他自己和他过去的历史?在这些素朴的小品里,我请人们让我自私一番。我高喊我的鞋把我的脚挤痛,我想,会更自然地,更动情地,比起假使我邻人的鸡眼被我践踏。我细谈我所爱的碟子,我所喜欢的酒,我昨天听到的话——关于勃朗荒谬的装腔作势——关于琼斯可笑的得意洋洋,当他以为抓到我的一个错处了(这事有趣的一部分,你们看,是在于琼斯会念到这篇文章,将完全晓得我指的是他,我们将来相会时将十分有礼地相视狞笑)。我也承认这并不是最高尚的冥想,然而这是人家听着会觉

confess, but it is a gossip which amuses some folks. A brisk and honest small-beer will refresh those who do not care for the frothy outpourings of heavier taps[1]. A two of clubs may be a good, handy little card somtimes, and able to tackle a king of diamonds, if it is a little trump. Some philosophers get their wisdom with deep thought and out of ponderous libraries; I pick up my small crumbs of cogitation at a dinnertable; or from Mrs. Mary and Miss Louisa, as they are prattling over their five-o'clock tea.

Well, yesterday at dinner Jucundus was good enough to tell me a story about myself, which he had heard from a lady of his acquaintance, to whom I send my best compliments. The tale is this. At nine o'clock on the evening of the 31st of November[2] last, just before sunset, I was seen leaving No. 96, Abbey Road, St. John's Wood, leading two little children by the hand, one of them in a nankeen pelisse, and the other having a mole on the third finger of his left hand (she thinks it was the third finger, but is quite sure it was the left hand). Thence I walked with them to Charles Borough-bridge's, pork and sausage man, No. 29, Upper Theresa Road. Here, whilst I left the little girl innocently eating a polony in the front shop, I and Borough-bridge retired with the boy into the back parlour, where Mrs.

---

1 heavier taps: pipes from which strong liquor is drawn 倾出强烈的酒的注管。

2 此日期原文有误。——编者注

得有趣味的一种闲谈。一些老老实实的起泡淡麦酒也足以使不喜欢口味强烈的酒管所泻出冒着白沫的浓酒的人们神爽。两点棍棒有时也许是一张良好方便的小牌，能够拉拢一张金钢〔刚〕钻式的王，假使这是一张小胜牌。有些哲学家靠着深思默虑，得到他们的智慧，并且来自庞大的图书馆；我捡起我这些小块的杂感，却是从餐桌上；或者从玛丽太太同路易萨小姐用他们五点钟茶点时的喋喋闲谈。

好罢，昨天大餐时候，犹卡答斯居然肯告诉我一件关于我自己的故事，他是从他认得的一位女太太那里听到的，我谨向这位太太致敬意。那故事是这样。去年十一月三十一日晚上九点钟时候，太阳快下山了，人家看见我离开圣·约翰森林僧院路九十六号，拉着两个小孩子，一个穿有紫花布外衣，一个左手第三指上有一粒痣（她以为是第三指，但是很有把握是左手）。然后我同他们走到上德利撒路二十九号查理斯·巴洛布立治商店，一家买〔卖〕猪肉同腊肠的铺子。在那里，我留小女孩在铺子前面天真地吃一条香肠，我同巴洛布立治就跟男孩退到后

Borough-bridge was playing cribbage. She put up[1] the cards and boxes, took out a chopper and a napkin, and we cut the little boy's little throat (which he bore with great pluck and resolution), and made him into sausage-meat by the aid of Purkis's excellent sausage-machine. The little girl at first could not understand her brother's absence, but, under the pretence of taking her to see Mr. Fechter in *Hamlet*[2], I led her down to the New River at Sadler's Wells, where a body of a child in a nankeen pelisse was subsequently found, and has never been recognized to the present day. And this Mrs. Lynx can aver, because she saw the whole transaction with her own eyes, as she told Mr. Jucundus.

I have altered the little details of the anecdote somewhat. But this story is, I vow and declare, as true as Mrs. Lynx's. Gracious goodness! how do lies begin? What are the averages of lying? Is the same amount of lies told about every man, and do we pretty much all tell the same amount of lies? Is the average greater in Ireland than in Scotland, or vice versa — among women than among men? Is this a lie I am telling now? If I am talking about you, the odds[3] are, perhaps, that it is. I look back at some which have been told about me, and speculate on them with thanks and wonder. Dear friends

---

1 to put up: to put in its proper place 归还原处。
2 *Hamlet*: 莎翁悲剧杰作之一。
3 the odds: the balance of advantage 优势；上风。

面客厅，巴洛布立治太太正在那儿打纸牌。她把牌同盒子反起来，拿出一把屠刀同一条布巾，我们就割小孩子的小颈（他却很勇敢地，很有决心地忍受），靠着浦极斯号巧妙的腊肠制造机把他造成腊肠肉。小女孩起先不知道她兄弟为什么不见了，但是，借口带她去看斐喜忒先生演《哈姆雷特》，我引她到马鞍匠井旁的新河，后来人家在那里发现一具穿紫花布外衣的女孩尸首，一直到现在还没有人认去。这些事林克司太太能够有把握地说出，因为她亲眼看见全部的经过，她对犹卡答斯先生是这样说的。

我把这个轶事的细节稍微变更一些。但是我肯立誓向大众宣布，我刚才所说的故事正同林克司太太的故事一样地真实。仁爱的女神呀！谎言是怎样开始呢？每人所推的诬言在数量上是相等的吗，我们所铸的谎话在数量上大概都差不多吗？爱尔兰谎言的平均量会比苏格兰大吗，或者是正相反吗——男人扯谎的平均量比女人大吗？我现在说的是一句谎言吗？假使我正谈着你，那么这句话大概是。我回想起关于我的一些诬言，细思一下真是又感谢，又惊奇。亲爱的朋友们曾经关于我说了许

have told them of me, have told them to me of myself. Have they not to and of you,¹ dear friend? A friend of mine was dining at a large dinner of clergymen, and a story, as true as the sausage story above given, was told regarding me, by one of those reverend divines, in whose frocks sit some anile chatterboxes², as any man who knows this world knows. They take the privilege of their gown. They cabal, and tattle, and hiss, and cackle comminations under their breath. I say the old women of the other sex are not more talkative or more mischievous than some of these. "Such a man ought not to be spoken to," says Gobemouche, narrating the story — and such a story! "And I am surprised he is admitted into society at all." Yes, dear Gobemouche, but the story wasn't true; and I had no more done the wicked deed in question than I had run away with the Queen of Sheba³.

I have always longed to know what that story was (or what collection of histories), which a lady had in her mind to whom a servant of mine applied for a place, when I was breaking up my establishment once, and going abroad. Brown went with a very good character⁴ from us, which, indeed, she fully deserved after several years'

---

1 Have they not told them to you and have they not told them of you?
2 in whose frocks sit some anile chatterboxes：牧师们老而不死，饱食终日，专说闲话，喋喋不休，所以作者调侃他们。
3 the Queen of Sheba：古时波斯一位美后。
4 character：written account of person's qualities 品格证明书。

多无稽之谈,而且曾经对我说出关于我的这许多无稽之谈。他们不是也对你说过,而且是关于你的吗,亲爱的朋友?我的一个朋友赴一位牧师的大宴会,正在用餐,听到人们说起一件跟前面所讲的腊肠故事同一真实的关于我的故事,那是一位可敬的牧师说出的,他的僧服里坐有老弱的话匣子,这一点凡有些世故的人们都晓得。他们利用他们地位的特权。他们阴谋,谈人私事,表示不满,喋喋不休地低声说出遣责的话。我说真正老太婆还没有像这种男性老太婆那么多话,那么捣乱。"这么一个人我们不应该向他说话,"哥布穆鼠说,一面叙述那故事——这么胡说八道的一个故事!"我真纳罕人们居然肯让他混到社会里去。"不错,亲爱的哥布穆鼠,然而那故事不是真的;我之没有干你所怀疑的那件恶事正如我未曾跟示巴女王一同跑掉。

我一向想知道那个故事(或者那一大堆历史)是怎么样,那是一位太太心里明白的,我的一个女仆曾向她寻位置,当我有一次解散我的仆人,到外国去的时候。勃朗走时带了我们给她的非常良好品行的证明书,她真是十分值得受这个称赞,她

faithful service. But when Mrs. Jones read the name of the person out of whose employment Brown came, "That is quite sufficient," says Mrs. Jones, "You may go. I will never take a servant out of that house." Ah, Mrs. Jones, how I should like to know what that crime was, or what that series of villanies, which made you determine never to take a servant out of my house. Do you believe in the story of the little boy and the sausages? Have you swallowed that little minced infant? Have you devoured that young Polonius[1]. Upon my word you have maw enough. We somehow greedily gobble down all stories in which the characters of our friends are chopped up[2], and believe wrong of them without inquiry. In a late serial work written by this hand, I remember making some patheic remarks about our propensity to believe ill of our neighbours — and I remember the remarks, not because they were valuable, or novel, or ingenious, but because, within three days after they had appeared in print, the moralist who wrote them, walking home with a friend, heard a story about another friend, which story he straightway believed, and which story was scarcely more true than that sausage

---

1 Polonius：*Hamlet*剧中一个奸臣的名字，他被哈姆雷特杀死，这里拿他来作"被杀之人"解。

2 in which the characters of our friends are chopped up：把我们的朋友骂得体无完肤可以说将他们的品格研成粉碎。

忠实地伏伺我们好几年了。但是当琼斯太太念到勃朗所从来的那个主人的名字,"这已很够了,"琼斯太太说,"你可以去。我绝不肯用从'那'家出来的仆人。"唉,琼斯太太,我多么想知道那是什么罪,或者是什么一套下流的行为,使你决定绝不雇一个从我家里出来的仆人。你相信小孩子同腊肠那个故事吗?你大口吃进去那个切碎的小孩子吗?你把年青的坡罗尼阿斯吞下去了吗?我敢说你的胃口真不差。我们总是饕餮地狼吞虎咽下我们朋友性格切成粉碎的一切故事,毫不查询,就相信他们错了。在我手下最近写出的一串文字里,我记得说过几句沉痛的话,关于我们偏向相信我们邻人的坏处——我记起这几句话,并不是因为它们是有价值的,或者新鲜的,或者巧妙的,却是因为这些话出版三天之内,说这些话的那位道学先生跟一位朋友同走回家,听到关于另一位朋友的一个故事,他就立刻相信,那故事却几乎不比这里所载的腊肠传说更见真实。啊,我的错

fable which is here set down. O mea culpa, mea maxima culpa![1] But though the preacher trips, shall not the doctrine be good? Yea, brethren! Here be the rods. Look you, here are the scourges. Choose me a nice long, swishing, buddy[2] one, light and well-poised in the handle, thick and bushy at the tail. Pick me out a whip-cord thong with some dainty knots in it — and now — we all deserve it — whish, whish, whish! Let us cut into each other all round.

A favourite liar and servant of mine was a man I once had to drive a brougham. He never came to my house, except for orders, and once when he helped to wait at dinner so clumsily that it was agreed we would dispense with his further efforts. The (job) brougham horse used to look dreadfully lean and tired, and the livery-stable keeper complained that we worked him too hard. Now, it turned out that there was a neighbouring butcher's lady who liked to ride in a brougham; and Tomkins lent her ours, drove her cheerfully to Richmond and Putney, and, I suppose, took out a payment in mutton-chops. We gave this good Tomkins wine and medicine for his family when sick — we supplied him with little comforts and extras which need not now be remembered — and the grateful creature rewarded us by informing some of our tradesmen whom he hon-

---

1 O mea culpa, mea maxima culpa!: O, my fault, my greatest fault!
2 buddy: bushy.

误,我最大的错误!但是布道者虽然失节,主义难道因此也是坏的吗?好罢,兄弟们!答鞭就在这儿。你们看,夏楚是在这儿了。替我拣出一条精细的,便于挞打的,蓬松的长鞭子,柄要轻的,平衡适中的,尾要厚的,蓬松的。替我选择一条皮鞭,上面打有巧妙的结子的——现在——我们都该挨打——呼呼,呼呼,呼呼!让我们彼此到处乱打一番罢。

我所喜欢的一个扯谎仆人是我曾经雇来赶轿式马车的一个马夫。他绝不到我家里来,除非我去召他,有一次他帮忙伺候用大餐,却干得这么笨拙,大家同意我们此后不要他再费力了。(租来的)赶轿式马车的马常是这么可怕地瘦削同疲倦的样子,租马处看马的人总是埋怨我们太把它累了。现在才知道有一位邻近的屠户太太喜欢坐轿式马车出游;汤姆金斯却把我们的借给她,快乐地送她到里士满同帕特尼,我想,拿羊排骨来做报酬。我们赠送这个良好汤姆金斯的家庭以酒同药,当他们病了时候——我们供给他零星好东西同额外的财物,那些现在也用不着回忆了——这位感恩图报的家伙却报答我们以告诉他所照

oured with his custom, "Mr. Roundabout[1]? Lor'[2] bless you! I carry him up to bed drunk every night in the week." He, Tomkins, being a man of seven stone weight and five feet high; whereas his employer was — but here modesty interferes, and I decline to enter into the avoirdupois question.

Now, what was Tomkins' motive for the utterance and dissemination of these lies? They could further no conceivable end or interest of his own. Had they been true stories. Tomkins' master would still, and reasonably, have been more angry than at the fables[3]. It was but suicidal slander on the part of Tomkins — must come to a discovery — must end in a punishment. The poor wretch had got his place under, as it turned out[4], a fictitious character. He might have stayed in it, for of course Tomkins had a wife and poor innocent children.[5] He might have had bread, beer, bed, character, coats, coals. He might have nestled in our little island, comfortably sheltered from the storms of life; but we were compelled to cast him out, and send him driving, lonely, perishing, tossing, starving, to sea — to drown.

---

1 Mr. Roundabout: Thackeray 的笔名。
2 Lor': Lord.
3 the fables: the lies 谎话。
4 as it turned out: as it was ultimately proved 后来泄露出来。
5 he might have stayed in it, for of course Tomkins had a wife and poor innocent children: 这是说，若使他主人发现他的品行证明书是假造的，他一定拿他的妻子儿女来做乞情的理由，就可以滞下去了。

拂的一些卖东西给我们的商人,"迂远先生?愿上帝保佑你们!一星期里夜夜我背他沉醉着上床去。"他,汤姆金斯,一个只有九十八磅重,五呎高的人;而他的雇主却是——但是谦逊来干涉了,我就不细谈衡量问题了。

汤姆金斯说出同传布这些假话到底有什么动机呢?这些话我们想不出会给他什么好处或者怎样与他有利。若使真有这些事,汤姆金斯的主人会比这是荒谬的胡说时更生气,而且也更有生气的理由。在汤姆金斯方面,这简直是等于自杀的造谣——必定会被发觉——必定终于受罚。后来我们知道这个可怜的东西是借一张假造的品行证明书得到他的位置。他很可以老干这件差事,因为汤姆金斯当然有个妻子同可怜的无辜小孩。他很可以有面包,麦酒,床铺,品行证明书,衣服,煤炭。他很可以安居于我们这小岛里,十分舒服地免受人海的风波;但是我们逼得不能不把他赶走,叫他到外面去飘零,孤单单的,毁灭,颠簸,挨饿,到海里去——泅死。泅死?流氓还有别的

To drown? There be other modes of death whereby rogues die. Goodby, Tomkins. And so the nightcap is put on, and the bolt is drawn for poor T.

Suppose we were to invite volunteers amongst our respected readers to send in little statements of the lies which they know have been told about themselves; what a heap of correspondence, what an exaggeration of malignities, what a crackling bonfire of incendiary falsehoods, might we not gather together! And a lie once set going, having the breath of life breathed into it by the father of lying, and ordered to run its diabolical little course, lives with a prodigious vitality. You say, "Magna est veritas et prævalebit." [1] Psha! Great lies are as great as great truths, and prevail constantly, and day after day. Take an instance or two out of my own little budget. I sit near a gentleman at dinner, and the conversation turns upon a certain anonymous literary performance which at the time is amusing the town. "Oh," says the gentleman, "everybody knows who wrote that paper: it is Momus's." I was a young author at the time, perhaps proud of my bantling: "I beg your pardon," I say, "it was written by your humble servant." "Indeed!" was all that the man replied, and he shrugged his shoulders, turned his back, and talked to his other

---

1 Magna est veritas et prævalebit: truth is mighty and will prevails.

死法哩！再见，汤姆金斯。于是乎，我戴上睡帽，把门闩上不让可怜的汤进来了。

假使我们请可敬的读者自愿送来他们知道所挨的诬言的简短报告；我们准会收到多么一大堆的通信呀，恶意将被人们多么铺张扬历〔厉〕地说出来呀，含有煽动性质的谎话其势兴旺真像轧轧作响的烟火哩！而且一句谎话既已发动了，带有首先说这句谎话人所吹进去的生命力量，注定了走完他那恶魔般的短途，是具有可惊的生命力活着的。你们说，"真理无敌，终能操胜"。咄！伟大的谎话是跟伟大的真理一样地伟大，常常操胜，而且天天操胜。从我自己有限的经验里举一两个例子罢。用餐时我坐在一位先生邻近，大家谈话说到当时社会所喜欢的某一篇匿名著作。"啊，"这位先生说，"个个人都知道谁写那篇文章：那是摩马斯的东西。"我那时是个年青的作家，也许对于自己的小作品觉得骄傲！"我请你原谅，"我说，"那是鄙人写的。""真的吗！"他就只答这么一句话，耸一下肩膀，转过背，

neighbour. I never heard sarcastic incredulity more finely conveyed than by that "indeed." "Impudent liar," the gentleman's face said, as clear as face could speak. Where was Magna Veritas, and how did she prevail then? She lifted up her voice, she made her appeal, and she was kicked out of court. In New York I read a newspaper criticism one day (by an exile from our shores who has taken up his abode in the Western Republic[1]), commenting upon a letter of mine which had appeared in a contemporary volume, and wherein it was stated that the writer was a lad in such and such a year, and, in point of fact, I was, at the period spoken of, nineteen years of age. "Falsehood, Mr. Roundabout," says the noble critic: "you were then not a lad; you were then six-and-twenty years of age." You see he knew better than papa and mamma and parish register. It was easier for him to think and say I lied, on a twopenny matter[2] connected with my own affairs, than to imagine he was mistaken. Years ago, in a time when we were very mad wags, Arcturus[3] and myself met a gentleman from China who knew the lauguage. We began to speak Chinese against him. We said we were born in China. We were two

---

1 the Western Republic: The United States of America 因为居于西半球，所以称之为"西方共和国"。

2 on a twopenny matter: on an insignificant matter 关于一件不重要的事情。

3 Arcturus: 作者在这篇文字里故意用罗马姓名来代替近代通常名字，以增诡奇滑稽之趣。

跟其他坐在邻近的人去谈天了。我从没有听到带有冷讽的怀疑传达得比这句"真的吗"更漂亮。"不要脸的扯谎人",这位先生的脸孔好像这样说,脸孔的表情也只能够这么明白了。所谓无敌的真理跑到那里去呢,她又怎么能够操胜呢?她扬声上诉,却被踢到法院之外了。在纽约时候,有一天我读新闻报纸上一篇批评文字(作者是远离英伦三岛,寄寓西方共和国的一个天涯游子),提到当时出版一本书里所印的我一封信,那本书说写这封信的人在某某年还不过是个小孩子,事实上,我在所说的那个年头的确才十九岁。"假话,迂远先生,"高贵的批评家说,"那时你不是个小孩子;那时你已经有二十六岁了。"你们看他比爸爸妈妈同教区里登记员更懂得清楚。一件纯粹关于我自己的极小事体,他宁其认为,而且说出,我扯谎,与其相信他错了。好多年以前,当阿克忒剌斯同我是非常胡闹的捣乱小孩子,我们碰到一位从中国回来的先生,他懂得那里的语言。我们却反向他说起中国话。我们说我们是生在中国的。我们对于他是

to one. We spoke the mandarin dialect with perfect fluency. We had the company with us¹; as in the old, old days, the squeak of the real pig was voted not to be so natural as the squeak of the sham pig. O Arcturus, the sham pig squeaks in our streets now to the applause of multitudes, and the real porker grunts unheeded in his sty!

I once talked for some little time with an amiable lady: it was for the first time; and I saw an expression of surprise on her kind face, which said as plainly as face could say, "Sir, do you know that up to this moment² I have had a certain opinion of you, and that I begin to think I have been mistaken or misled?" I not only know that she had heard evil reports of me, but I know who told her — one of those acute fellows, my dear brethern, of whom we spoke in a previous sermon³, who has found me out — found out actions which I never did, found out thoughts and sayings which I never spoke, and judged me accordingly. Ah, my lad! Have I found you out? O risum teneatis⁴. Perhaps the person I am accusing is no more guilty than I.

How comes it that the evil which men say spreads go widely

---

1 we had the company with us: the company agreed with us 大家都以我们为然。

2 up to this moment: until this moment 一直到这个时候。

3 in a previous sermon: Thackeray 在杂志上写有一串小品文，叫做 Roundabout Papers，这就是里面一篇，前一篇见《被人发觉》（"On Being Found Out"）。

4 O risum teneatis. : O, hold your laugh.

二与一之比。我们仿佛非常流利地说官话。大家也都相信我们；正像古昔的时候，大家觉得真猪的叫声没有假猪的叫声那么来得自然。啊，阿克忒剌斯呀，假猪此刻在我们街上叫着，得到大众的喝彩，真正的小猪却在他的圈里发嗯嗯声，没有人去理他！

我有一次同一位和蔼的太太谈了一些时候：那是第一次的谈话；我看见她温和脸上有个惊奇的神情，那分明说，脸上表情也只能如此明白了，"先生，你知道吗，一直到此刻，我对于你有某一种品评，现在我才想起我恐怕错了或者被人们蒙蔽了？"我不单知道她听到人们说我的坏话，而且知道是谁说的——所谓精明人们里面的一个，我亲爱的同胞呀，我们在前一章劝言里不是提到了吗，他发现了我种种的事情——发觉我素来没有干过的行为，发觉我素来没有说出的思想同意见，就靠这些来判定我。吓，我的孩子！我不是发现你的坏处了吗？呵，不要乱笑。也许我现在所归罪的人正同我一样地无辜。

为什么人们所说的坏话传布得这么广，存留得这么久，而

and lasts so long, whilst our good, kind words don't seem somehow to take root and bear blossom? Is it that in the stony hearts of mankind these pretty flowers can't find a place to grow? Certain it is that scandal is good, brisk talk, whereas praise of one's neighbour is by no means lively hearing. An acquaintance grilled, scored, devilled, and served with mustard and cayenne pepper, excites the appetite;[1] whereas a slice of cold friend with currant jelly is but a sickly, unrelishing meat.

Now, such being the case, my dear worthy Mrs. Candour, in whom I know there are a hundred good and generous qualities: it being perfectly clear that the good things which we say of our neighbours don't fructify, but somehow perish in the ground where they are dropped, whilst the evil words are wafted by all the winds of scandal, take root in all soils, and flourish amazingly — seeing, I say, that this conversation does not give us a fair chance, suppose we give up censoriousness altogether, and decline uttering our opinions about Brown, Jones, and Robinson (and Mesdames B., J., and R.) at all. We may be mistaken about every one of them, as, please goodness, those anecdote-mongers[2] against whom I have uttered my meek protest have been mistaken about me. We need not go to the

---

1 这就是说拿一个朋友来乱骂，参看P420注2。
2 anecdote-mongers: dealers of anecdote 专会传布无根故事的人们。

我们善良仁爱的话好像总不能够生根开花呢？是不是因为在人们的铁石心肠里这些美丽花卉不能找到一个生长的地方吗？那是的确的情形，谣言是兴致勃勃谈话的材料，赞美邻人却绝不是动听之言。把一位认识的人拿来烘，烧，加上热烈调味品煎炙，和胡椒芥辣一起捧上来，是会激起食欲的；而一片冷清清的友谊，旁边排些葡萄干果膏，是令人起厌恶的，不可口的食物。

情形既已如此，我亲爱的，可敬的公平太太，我知道这位太太是有一百个善良慷慨的美德：事实既然很分明地是，我们所说关于我们邻人的好话不会开花结果，它们掉到地面，就灭亡了，而坏话却被谣言的风吹得到处飘游，在各种土上生根，繁殖得真是惊人——看到，我说，这种谈话没有给我们一个公平的机会，我们为什么绝不臧否人物，完全不说出我们对于勃朗，琼斯，鲁滨逊（以及三位太太）的品评。也许对于他们个个人我们都误解了，正如，上帝安排的，我刚才所轻轻指斥的这些轶事制造家对于我的误解。我们也用不着去说孟宁太太是

extent of saying that Mrs. Manning was an amiable creature, much misunderstood; and Jack Thurtell a gallant, unfortunate fellow, not near so black as he was painted; but we will try and avoid personalities altogether in talk, won't we? We will range[1] the fields of science, dear madam, and communicate to each other the pleasing results of our studies. We will, if you please, examine the infinitesimal wonders of nature through the microscope. We will cultivate entomology. We will sit with our arms round each other's waists on the pons asinorum[2], and see the stream of mathematics flow beneath. We will take refuge in cards, and play at "beggar my neighbour[3]," not abuse my neighbour. We will go to the Zoological Gardens and talk freely about the gorilla and his kindred, but not talk about people who can talk in their turn. Suppose we praise the High Church[4]? We offend the Low Church[5]. The Broad Church[6]? High and Low are both offended. What do you think of Lord Derby as a politician? And what is your opinion of Lord Palmerston? If you please, will you

---

1 range: rove; wander 漫游。

2 pons asinorum: bridge of asses of donkeys bridge i. e. anything difficult or puzzling to a learner e. g. the 5th proposition in the first book of Euclid is so-called 骡子桥；就是指不易学会的东西，这句话本来是《欧几里几何》第一卷第五命题的题名。

3 beggar my neighbour: 打牌时用的一句术语。

4 High Church: party giving high place to authority of priesthood, saving grace, etc. 看重牧师，仪式等的教派。

个可亲的人儿，人家太把她误解了；杰克·忒题鲁是个豪侠的，不幸的汉子，并没有人们所说的那么黑暗；可是我们谈话时绝对避免评判人们，行不行？我们决定从事于科学的探讨，把我们研究的有趣味结果彼此相告。我们决定，若使你们愿意，用显微镜来窥自然界中无限小的奇观。我们决心研究昆虫学。我们决定彼此手臂圈着腰肢坐在骡子桥上面，看数学之川在底下流过。我们决定躲到门牌里面去，要"求我邻人"，而不去毁谤我的邻人。我们决定到动物园去，信口谈论大猩猩同它的血属，却不去谈也能够谈论起来的人们。假使我们赞美高派教会？我们得罪低派教会了。恭维广派教会？高低两派教会都生气了。你看德贝爵士是不是一个有本领的政治家？你对于判麦斯敦爵士有什么批评？不谈这些话罢，若使你愿意，可否弹给我听

---

5 Low Church：the less ritualistic party in Church of England 英国教会没有那么注重仪式的那一派。

6 Broad Church：party favoring comprehension and not pressing doctrines 偏重了解宗教的神髓，不拘于教义的教派。

435

play me those lovely variations of "In my cottage near a wood?" It is a charming air (you know it in French, I suppose? Ah! te dirai-je, maman![1]) and was a favourite with poor Marie Antoinette[2]. I say "poor," because I have a right to speak with pity of a sovereign who was renowned for so much beauty and so much misfortune. But as for giving any opinion on her conduct, saying that she was good or bad, or indifferent, goodness forbid![3] We have agreed we will not be censorious. Let us have a game at cards — at écarté[4], if you please. You deal. I ask for cards. I lead the deuce of clubs...

What? There is no deuce! Deuce take it![5] What? People will go on talking about their neighbours, and won't have their mouths stopped by cards, or ever so much microscopes and aquariums? Ah, my poor dear Mrs. Candour, I agree with you. By the way, did you ever see anything like Lady Godiva Trotter's dress last night? People will go on chattering, although we hold our tongues; and, after all, my good soul, what will their scandal matter a hundred years hence?

---

1 Ah! te dirai-je, maman!: Ah! please tell me, mamma!

2 Marie Antoinette（1755—1793），路易十六的皇后，后来被人们杀死。

3 goodness forbid!：god forbid! 上帝所不允许的。

4 écarté：a cardgame for two 两人打的一种牌戏。

5 Deuce take it!：是一种怒骂之词，Deuce 本来有 the two at card 和 devil 二义，作者就利用这两个含义，说出双关的话，所谓 pun 是也。

"森林邻近我的茅屋里面"那些可喜的变调？这是个动情的小调（我想你知道它的法文原文？啊，告诉我罢，妈妈！）又是可怜的马利·安他涅特所爱听的。我说"可怜"，因为对于以如此美貌，如此不幸出名的皇后我有带着怜悯说话的权利。可是，至于对她的行为加上什么批评，说她是好，或者是坏，或者不好不坏，这是上帝所不容的！我们已经约好不再说人是非了。让我们打一下牌罢——玩二人纸牌戏罢，若使你愿意。请你分牌。我来要牌。我要棍棒二点……

怎么？没有二点！坏了！怎么？人们总是继续谈论他们的邻人，绝不肯住口，就说有牌打，或者甚至于有这么多显微镜同养鱼器？唉，我可怜的，亲爱的公平太太；我同你意见一致。我却记得一件事了。你曾看见过像哥带发·特鲁忒太太昨夜所穿的衣服那样东西吗？人们总是饶舌下去，虽然我们缄口无言了；而且，究竟说起来，我的好人儿呀，这些谣言百年之后还会有什么效力吗？

Alexander Smith

On Death and the Fear of Death[1]

Let me curiously analyse eternal farewells and the last pressures of loving hands. Let me smile at faces bewept, and the nodding plumes and slow paces of funerals. Let me write down brave heroical sentences — sentences that defy death, as brazen Goliath[2] the hosts of Israel.

"When death waits for us is uncertain; let us everywhere look for[3] him. The premeditation of death is the premeditation of liberty; who has learnt to die, has forgot to serve.[4] There is nothing of evil in

---

1 该篇原文标题为 On Death and the Fear of Dying，此据目录改。——编者注

2 Goliath：系菲利士军队里一员大将，当他们同以色列军队打仗时候，他严装骂阵，目空一切，却被以色列的大辟用一块石子就打死了。

3 to look for：to seek 寻找。

死同死的恐惧

让我们好奇地来分析永诀和亲爱的手最后的一握。让我对着哭丧的脸孔，点首的羽毛同出丧的慢步微笑。让我写下勇敢的，英雄的句子——向死挑战的句子，正如厚颜的歌利亚向着以色列的军队一样。

"死会在什么时候等待我们是不定的；让我们到处寻找它罢。死的预料就是自由的预料；学会了死之术的人忘记了什么叫做苦役了。庖卢斯·伊密力阿斯对可怜的马其顿王，他的囚

---

4 who has learnt to die, has forgot to serve：这段所从来的那篇小品文题目是 To Philosophize is to Learn to Die。

life for him who rightly comprehends that death is no evil; to know how to die delivers us from all subjection and constraint.[1] Paulus Aemilius answered him whom the miserable king of Macedon, his prisoner, sent to entreat him that he would not lead him in his triumph[2], 'Let him make that request to himself.' In truth, in all things, if nature do not help a little, it is very hard for art and industry to perform anything to purpose. I am, in my own nature, not melancholy, but thoughtful; and there is nothing I have more continually entertained myself withal than the imaginations of death, even in the gayest and most wanton time of my age. In the company of ladies, and in the height of mirth, some have perhaps thought me possessed of some jealousy, or meditating upon the uncertainty of some imagined hope, whilst I was entertaining myself with the remembrance of some one surprised[3] a few days before with a burning fever, of which he died, returning from an entertainment like this, with his head full of idle fancies of love and jollity, as mine was then; and for aught I knew[4], the same destiny was attending me. Yet did not this thought wrinkle my forehead any more than any other."... "Why dost thou fear this last day? In contributes no more to thy destruction than every one of the rest. The last step is not the cause of lassitude,

---

1 此句原文缺译。——编者注
2 lead him in his triumph: 古代凯旋时俘虏缚车旁带到城里去。

犯，派来求他不要在凯旋时把他带回的使者答道：'让他去向自己请求罢。'真的，无论任何事情，若使没有一点儿天然的底子，专靠人工同勤勉是很难有什么成就的。我本质上并不忧愁，却耽于冥想；我总是老把死的默想来消遣自己，比任何别的想头都常，甚至于在我最快乐的，最恣情的年纪里。跟姑娘们在一起，最兴高彩〔采〕烈的时候，有些人也许以为我一心一意在妒忌着，或却暗想着一些臆造的希望能否实现，其实我却正在替自己解闷，想起某人前几天忽然感到灼热的发烧，就死去了，他那一次正从像这样的一个盛会回去，起先脑子里满是爱情同寻欢这些无聊幻想，正同我那时一样；据我所知，也许有同样的命运等候着我。然而，这种思想并不比别种更使我额上生皱纹。"……"你为什么怕这个末日呢？它并不比别的日子更促成你的灭绝。最后的一步绝不是衰弱的原因，它只是拿衰弱

---

3 surprised: attacked.
4 for aught I knew：in spite of anything one knew 虽照其所知者。

it does but confer it. Every day travels toward death; the last only arrives at it. These are the good lessons our mother nature teaches. I have often considered with myself whence it should proceed, that in war the image of death — whether we look upon it as to our own particular danger, or that of another — should, without comparison[1], appear less dreadful than at home in our own houses (for if it were not so, it would be an army of whining milksops), and that being still in all places the same, there should be, notwithstanding, much more assurance in peasants and the meaner sort of people, than others of better quality[2] and education; and I do verily believe, that it is those terrible ceremonies and preparations wherewith we set it out[3], that more terrify us than the thing itself; a new, quite contrary way of living, the cries of mothers, wives, and children, the visits of astonished and affected friends, the attendance of pale and blubbered servants, a dark room set round with burning tapers, our beds environed with physicians and divines; in fine[4], nothing but ghostliness and horror round about us, render it so formidable, that a man almost fancies himself dead and buried already. Children are afraid even of those they love best, and are best acquainted with, when disguised in a vizor, and so are we; the vizor must be removed as well from

---

1 without comparison: incomparally 不能相比地；远超过。
2 quality: social standing 社会地位。

加到我们身上。每天都是向死走去；最后的一天不过抵达那里了。这是我们的母亲'大自然'给我们的好教训。我常常自己暗自忖度为什么在战争时候死的影子——无论我们想到自己的危险或者别人的危险——是远不如我们舒服地滞在家里时那么可怕（因为假使不如此，那将成为一队哀啼的懦夫了），还有死虽然到处是一样的，可是农夫同下等人比上流社会，受过教育的人却更有把握，我真相信，我们拿来放在死的四旁的那些可怕的礼节同设备比死更令人畏惧；一种与日常完全相反的，新的，生活法，母亲，妻子同儿女的啼哭，深为惊骇同感动的朋友的慰问，脸孔苍白，面目哭肿的仆役的服事，四围点着蜡烛的一间黑暗房子，医生同牧师围绕着的我们的床铺；总之，没有别的，只是我们周围的鬼气同恐怖使它变成这么可怕，一个人几乎以为他自己已经死去了，安埋了。小孩子甚至于怕他们最亲爱的，最熟识的人们，当这班人戴上鬼脸壳时候，我们也

---

3 to set out：to spread for display 铺张。
4 in fine：in short 总之。

things as persons; which being taken away, we shall find nothing underneath but the very same death that a mean servant, or a poor chambermaid, died a day or two ago, without any manner of apprehension or concern."[1]

"Men feare[2] death as children feare to goe[3] in the darke[4], and as that natural feare in children is increased with tales, so in the other. Certainly the contemplation of death as the wages of sinne[5], and passage to another world, is holy and religious; but the feare of it as a tribute due unto nature, is weake[6]. Yet in religious meditations there is sometimes mixture of vanitie[7] and of superstition. You shal[8] reade[9] in some of the friar' books of mortification[10], that a man should thinke unto himself what the paine[11] is if he have but his fingerend pressed or tortured; and thereby imagine what the paines of death are when the whole body is corrupted and dissolved; when many times death passeth[12] with lesse[13] paine than the torture of a lemme[14].

---

1 上面这些话是Montaigne小品文里的一段，关于Montaigne，可参看《孤居》注。

2 feare: fear这段是伊利沙伯时代文字，所以拼法与现代不同。

3 goe: go.

4 darke: dark.

5 sinne: sin.

6 weake: weak.

7 vanitie: vanity.

8 shal: shall.

9 reade: read.

是如此；不单人不该戴鬼脸壳，事物也不该戴，把它取下，我们将看出底下没有别的，只是个普通的死，正如一两日前一个底下人或者一个可怜的丫头毫无恐惧地死去那样。"

"人怕死，好像小孩子怕到黑暗的地方去；小孩子天然的恐惧会因听到胡说而增加，大人天然的恐惧也是这样。把死认为是罪恶的代价同到另一世界的道路，这的确是个神圣的，宗教的想头；但是认为是对于大自然的纳贡，这个恐惧是弱者的。然而，在宗教的冥想里常杂有无聊同迷信的成分。你将在一些僧徒著的清苦修行书里读到他们说，一个人应该自己想一下那是多么苦痛，假使他有一只指端被压或者受苦刑；从这里可以推想死的苦痛是怎么样，那时整个身体是腐烂同溃烂了；其实死很常还不如一只肢体的受磨折那么苦痛。因为身体上最紧要

---

10 books of mortification: works intending to lead to the subduing of earthly appetites 劝人们压制欲望的著作。

11 paine: pain.

12 passeth: passes.

13 lesse: less.

14 lemme: limb.

For the most vitall[1] parts are not the quickest[2] of sense. Groanes and convulsions, and a discoloured face, and friends weeping, and blacks[3], and obsequies, and the like, shew death terrible. It is worthy the observing, that there is no passion in the minde of man so weake but it mates[4] and masters the feare of death; and therefore death is no such terrible enemy when a man hath so many attendants about him that can winne[5] the combat of him. Revenge triumphs over death, love sujects it, honour aspireth to it, griefe[6] fleeth[7] to it, feare pre-occupieth[8] it; nay, we read, after Otho the emperor had slaine him-selfe[9], pitty[10], (which is the tenderest of affections,) provoked many to die, out of meer[11] compassion to their soveraigne[12], and as the tru-est sort of followers... It is as naturall[13] to die as to be borne; and to a little infant, perhaps, the one is as painfull as the other. He that dies in an earnest pursuit is like one that is wounded in hot blood, who for the time scarce feels the hurt; and, therefore, a minde[14] fixt[15] and

---

1 vitall: vital.
2 quickest: most sensitive 感觉最锐敏的。
3 blacks: mourning 丧服。
4 to mate: to overpower 压倒；战胜。
5 winne: win.
6 griefe: grief.
7 fleeth: flees.
8 pre-occupieth: anticipates, viz by suicide 提前，就是指自杀。
9 himselfe: himself.

的部分不一定是感觉最灵敏的。呻吟，骚动，失色的脸孔，呜咽的朋友，丧礼，葬礼，以及其他这类的东西使死变成可怕。这是值得我们注意的，人们心里一切的情感没有一个是弱得不能制胜同管理死的恐惧，当一个人身边有这么多守卫都能打倒他，死真不是个这么可怕的敌人了。复仇战胜死，爱情以死为奴隶，义心希望死，悲哀躲到死那里去，恐惧把死拉来；而且，我们读过，当鄂国王自杀后，怜悯（那是最柔弱的情感），鼓舞许多人去寻死，完全出于对他们主子的同情，做个最忠实的部下……死同生是一样自然的事；对于婴孩，也许这两件事的苦楚是相等的。专心致志于某事工作时死去的人是像在热血中受伤一样，当时几乎不觉得痛苦；所以一心专注于，倾向于某种

10 pitty: pity.
11 meer: mere.
12 soveraigne: soveraign.
13 naturall: natural.
14 minde: mind.
15 fixt: fixed.

bent upon somewhat that is good, doth avert the sadness of death. But above all, believe it, the sweetest canticle is, Nune Dimittis[1], when a man hath obtained worthy ends and expectations. Death hath this also; that it openeth the gate to good fame, and extinguisheth envie[2]."

These sentences of the great essayists are brave and ineffectual as Leonidas[3] and his Greeks. Death cares very little for sarcasm or trope[4], hurl at him a javelin or a rose, it is all one. We build around ourselves ramparts of stoical maxims, edifying to witness, but when the terror comes these yield as the knots of river flags to the shoulder of Behemoth[5].

Death is terrible only in presence. When distant, or supposed to be distant, we can call him hard or tender names, nay, even poke our poor fun at him. Mr. Punch[6], on one occasion, when he wished to ridicule the useful-information leanings of a certain periodical publication, quoted from its pages the sentence, "Man is mortal," and people were found to grin broadly over the exquisite stroke of humour. Certainly the words, and the fact they contain, are trite enough. Utter the sentence gravely in any company, and you are cer-

---

1 Nune Dimittis: "Lord, now lettest thou thy servant depart in peace."

2 envie: envy.

3 Leonidas（491—480 B. C.）斯巴达王，曾以三百人死抗波斯人于Thermopylae，勇敢称于世；然终以众寡不敌而全军覆没。

4 trope：figurative use of a word 隐喻；比拟。

5 河马是一种庞大的动物，铜筋铁骨，每饮辄尽一河。

善良事情的人可以避免死的忧愁。但是，请相信，在乎一切之上最甜蜜的小歌是，'主呀，让你的仆人安详地离开这世界罢'，当一个人做到值得有结果同希望的时候。死还有这个好处；它打开到令誉之门，把妒忌毁灭了。"

这两位小品文家的名言是跟李奥倪大和他的希腊兵同样地勇敢，同样地无用。死不大理我们的冷讽同隐议；向他扔一把标枪或者一朵玫瑰，于他都是一样的。我们在身边筑起克情箴言的璧〔壁〕垒，看起来足以启导人心，但是当恐怖来时，这些却顺服了，好像河里菖蒲打的结子，挡不住河马的肩膀。

死只当现在眼前时我们才觉得可怕。当在这处，或者我们以为是在远处，我们能够漫骂他或者低声喊他，而且，甚至于跟他开玩笑。丑角先生有一次想讥笑某一种定期刊物爱载有用的知识，就从它里面引这句话，"人皆有死"，有些人对这下微妙的滑稽露齿大笑。这句话同它所包含的事实的确是再常见不过的。可是无论在任何人们里你假使严重地说出这句话，一定

---

6 Mr. Punch：英国最有名的滑稽报的名字是 *Punch*。

tain to provoke laughter. And yet some subtle recognition of the fact of death runs constantly through the warp and woof¹ of the most ordinary human existence. And this recognition does not always terrify. The spectre has the most cunning disguises, and often when near us we are unaware of the fact of proximity. Unsuspected, this idea of death lurks in the sweetness of music; it has something to do with the pleasure with which we behold the vapours of morning; it comes between the passionate lips of lovers; it lives in the thrill of kisses. "An inch deeper, and you will find the emperor." Probe joy to its last fibre, and you will find death. And it is the most merciful of all the merciful provisions of nature, that a haunting sense of insecurity should deepen the enjoyment of what we have secured; that the pleasure of our warm human day and its activities should to some extent arise from a vague consciousness of the waste night which environs it, in which no arm is raised, in which no voice is ever heard. Death is the ugly fact which nature has to hide, and she hides it well. Human life were otherwise an impossibility. The pantomime runs on merrily enough; but when once Harlequin² lifts his vizor, Columbine³ disappears, the jest is frozen on the

---

1 warp and woof: constitution 经验；组织。

2 Harlequin: a sprite in the British pantomime, supposed to be unseen by all except colum bine. He prevents the knaveries of the Clown, who is in love with Columbine, and who is aided by Pantaloon, an old dotard, 他是英国哑剧里一个精灵，除开 Columbine 外，别人都看不见他，他阻止 Clown

会引起大笑。然而死这件事一些隐约的承认却常杂在人们最通常的生活经纬里。这个承认并不叫我们害怕。那双幽灵有最狡猾的假装，当他在我们身旁时候，我们常常还不知道他是近在咫尺。我们毫没有料到，死的观念却躲在音乐的悦耳柔声里；我们看见朝雾时所得的欣欢与它也有些相关，它夹在情人热情的嘴唇中，它活在接吻的震动里。"再掘深一吋，你将发现帝王的骨头了。"细察欣欢到它最后的纤微，你将遇见死的成分了。这真是自然一切仁慈的安排里最仁爱的一个，一个缠绕心中的不安感觉会使我们更深切感到我们所获得的快乐；我们在世暖和日子的和它各种活动的欣欢一部分却来自茫然地感到它四围的凄凉长夜，在那夜里没有手臂举起来拥抱，也听不到人声了。死是自然该遮住的一件丑恶事实，她真遮得不错。否则，人生是不可能的事了。哑剧演得很起劲；但是当丑角一翻开他的面具，丑夫人就不见了，另一丑角嘴上的笑话冻结了，另一丑角

的捣乱，Clown是爱上了Columbine，还有一个老丑角Pantaloon帮助他。

3 参看注2，她是Harlequin的女人。

Clown's[1] lips, and the hand of the filching Pantaloon[2] is arrested in the act. Wherever death looks, there is silence and trembling. But although on every man he will one day or another look, he is coy of revealing himself till the appointed time. He makes his approaches like an Indian warrior, under covers and ambushes. We have our parts to play, and he remains hooded till they are played out. We are agitated by our passions, we busily pursue our ambitions, we are acquiring money or reputation, and all at once, in the centre of our desires, we discover the "shadow feared of man[3]." And so nature fools the poor human mortal evermore. When she means to be deadly, she dresses her face in smiles; when she selects a victim, she sends him a poisoned rose. There is no pleasure, no shape of good fortune, no form of glory in which death has not hid himself, and waited silently for his prey.

And death is the most ordinary thing in the world. It is as common as births; it is of more frequent occurrence than marriages and the attainment of majorities. But the difference between death and other forms of human experience lies in this, that we can gain no information about it. The dead man is wise, but he is silent. We cannot wring his secret from him. We cannot interpret the ineffable calm

---

1 参看注P450注2,他非常滑稽。
2 参看注P450注2,他非常笨傻,刚好跟Clown相反。
3 shadow feared of man: death, 死神,见Tennyson诗中。

正在偷东西的手也就在偷窃之中停住了。死所凝视的地方，就是静默同战栗。但是虽然他迟早总得向个个人瞧一下，他却不轻容易现出色相，必得等到那定好的时候。他步步走近，好像一队印度兵，隐身于遮掩同埋伏之后。我们各有各的事要干，他总是遮盖着，一直等这些事干完了。我们被我们的热情所激动；我们忙碌地追逐我们的野心，我们正在求名或求利，忽然间，于我们种种希望的当中，我们发现"人们所畏的影子"。自然这样子老把可怜的凡人骗了。当她打算致人死命的时候，她却装出笑脸来；当她拣中一个牺牲品，她送它一朵有毒的玫瑰。任何种快乐，任何样幸运，任何形式的光荣都有死伏在里面，静静地等待它的食物。

死是世界里最普通的东西。它同生一样地平常；比结婚和成丁更常发生。但是死与其他人生经验不同的点是这个，我们不能得到它的消息。死人是明白死的情形了，可是他默然。我们不能从死人强夺来他的秘密。我们不能解释硬化了的脸孔上

which gathers on the rigid face. As a consequence, when our thought rests on death we are smitten with isolation and loneliness. We are without company on the dark road; and we have advanced so far upon it that we cannot hear the voices of our friends. It is in this sense of loneliness, this consciousness of identity and nothing more, that the terror of dying consists. And yet, compared to that road, the most populous thoroughfare of London or Pekin[1] is a desert. What enumerator will take for us the census of the dead? And this matter of death and dying, like most things else in the world, may be exaggerated by our own fears and hopes. Death, terrible to look forward to, may be pleasant even to look back at. Could we be admitted to the happy fields, and hear the conversations which blessed spirits hold, one might discover that to conquer death a man has but to die; that by that act terror is softened into familiarity, and that the remembrance of death becomes but as the remembrance of yesterday. To these fortunate ones death may be but a date, and dying a subject fruitful in comparisons; a matter on which experiences may be serenely compared. Meantime, however, we have not yet reached that measureless content[2], and death scares, piques[3], tantalises, as mind

---

1 Pekin: 十八世纪人们写北京都没有 g 这个字，大概因为由法国传入，尚未完全具英国字的形式罢。

2 the measureless content: 指"死之国土"，见莎翁悲剧 *Macbeth* 中。

3 to pique: to arouse curiosity 引起好奇心。

一片口舌难尽的安详神情。因此当我们想到死这件事,我们被孤单同寂寞之感所打击。在那黑暗的途上我们是没有伴侣的;我们却已走得这么远了,我们听不见我们朋友的声音。死的恐惧就在于这个寂寞之感,这样只觉得自己,此外别无所觉。然而,跟这条路一比,伦敦或北京最热闹的市街也好像是一片沙漠了。那个计数员能够替我们统计死人的总数目。而且,死同弥留这件事,像世上其他许多的事情一样,也许给我们自己的恐惧同希望形容得过度了。死,在前瞻里是这么可怕,也许回顾起来却很有意思。若使我们能够走进那快乐的田地,听见有福的幽灵谈话,我们或者会发现要战胜死,一个人只要死去就行;死了之后,恐怖化成一件熟识的事情了,死的回忆宛如昨日陈事的回忆。对于这班幸运的人们,死将只是一个日期,弥留变成个很可以拿来比较的题目,各人可以恬静地比较彼此的经验。然而,此刻我们还未达到这么含有无限大的内容的地步时候,我们既是这么一个血肉之躯,死是使我们害怕,激怒我

and nerve are built. Situated as we are, knowing that it is inevitable, we cannot keep our thoughts from resting on it curiously, at times. Nothing interests us so much. The Highland[1] seer pretended that he could see the windingsheet high upon the breast of the man for whom death was waiting. Could we behold any such visible sign, the man who bore it, no matter where he stood — even if he were a slave watching Caesar[2] pass — would usurp every eye. At the coronation of a king, the wearing of that order would dim royal robe, quench the sparkle of the diadem, and turn to vanity the herald's cry. Death makes the meanest beggar august, and that augustness would assert itself in the presence of a king. And it is this curiosity with regard to everything related to death and dying which makes us treasure up the last sayings of great men, and attempt to wring out of them tangible meanings. Was Goethe's[3] "Light — light, more light!" a prayer, or a statement of spiritual experience, or simply an utterance of the fact that the room in which he lay was filling with the last twilight? In consonance with our own natures, we intepret it the one way or the other — he is beyond our questioning. For the same

---

1 Highland: Northern part of Scotland 苏格兰北部，其地多山，所以叫做高地。

2 Caesar: Roman emporer 罗马皇帝。

3 Goethe: 歌德（1749—1832），德国大文豪，《浮士德》的作者。

们，逗着我们。我们的地位既然如此，知道那是不能避免的，我们的思想有时不能不好奇地专注于上面。没有一件其他事情如是感动我们。高地的圣者自命他能够看见死神等候的人胸前有尸衣高挂着。若使我们能够看见一个这么显著的标记，带了这个标记的人无论站在什么地方——甚至于他是个奴隶，看该撒过去——总会吸引个个眼睛的注意。在一个皇帝加冕时候，带上"这个勋章"会使皇帝的衣服减色，扑灭了王冠的辉煌，传令官的喝道也变成没有意义了。死使最可鄙的叫化子显得尊严，那种尊严就是在王者之前也会露出头角。就是这种对于一切关于死和弥留事情的好奇心叫我们珍存起来伟人临终的话，该从它们榨出一些明白的意义。歌德弥留时所喊的，"光明——光明，更光明！"是一句祈祷呢，是精神经验的报告呢，或者只是说出事实，以为他所躺的房子满是薄暮的微光了？随我们各人的性情，我们这样或者那样解释它——我们已经无法追问他了。人们对于正法的趣味也出于同样的理由——从槐特和尔的

reason it is that men take interest in executions — from Charles I[1] on the scaffold at Whitehall, to Porteous[2] in the Grassmaket execrated by the mob. These men are not dulled by disease, they are not delirious with fever; they look death in the face, and what in these circumstances they say and do has the strangest fascination for us.

What does the murderer think when his eyes are forever blinded by the accursed nightcap[3]? In what form did thought condense itself between the gleam of the lifted axe and the rolling of King Charles's head in the sawdust? This kind of speculation may be morbid, but it is not necessarily so. All extremes of human experience touch us; and we have all the deepest personal interest in the experience of death. Out of all we know about dying we strive to clutch something which may break its solitariness, and relieve us by a touch of companionship.

To denude death of its terrible associations were a vain attempt. The atmosphere is always cold around an iceberg. In the contemplation of dying the spirit may not flinch, but pulse and heart, colour and articulation, are always cowards. No philosophy will teach them

---

1 Charles I (1600—1649),英国皇帝,清教徒之乱被杀。

2 Porteous: John Porteous,他是爱丁堡城里的警卫长,有一次举行正法,群众围观甚拥挤,他向群众开枪,引起众怒,于是他老先生自己也被人们拿去正法,缢死于这班群众之前。

3 the accursed nightcap: 绞死的罪犯总是戴一顶白睡帽,所以说那该咒的睡帽。

绞架上的查理斯第一到格剌斯马刻地方被群众咒骂的普洛条斯。这班被处决的人没有病得昏迷,他们也没有发烧到精神错乱了;他们睬着死,在这种情形之下他们所说的同所干的对于我们具有非常奇特的魔力。

凶手心里想什么呢,当他的眼睛被那该咒的睡帽永远遮住了?在举起的斧头的一闪同查理斯王的头颅打滚于锯屑之上中间这一刹那,被杀人的思想凝聚成什么样子呢?这种空想也许是病态的,但是不一定是如此。人类一切尖端的经验都能感动我们;尤其死这个经验于我们有极深切的个人利益关系。从我们所知道弥留的情形,我们极力想抓到一些东西,以破死的幽寂,俾有一点同伴之感,因此可以减轻我们的忧愁。

将死一切可怕的运想完全剥夺去是个徒然的试验。冰山周围的空气总是冷的。默想死的时候,我们的精神也许能够不退缩,但是脉搏同心脏,脸色同口音总显得出我们是懦夫。没有什么哲学能够教它们当这个严肃幽灵的前面显出勇敢。然而有

bravery in the stern presence. And yet there are considerations which rob death of its ghastliness, and help to reconcile us to it. The thoughtful happiness of a human being is complex, and in certain moved moments, which, after they have gone, we can recognise to have been our happiest, some subtle thought of death has been curiously intermixed. And this subtle intermixture it is which gives the happy moment its character — which makes the difference between the gladness of a child, resident in mere animal health[1] and impulse, and too volatile to be remembered, and the serious joy of a man, which looks before and after, and takes in both this world and the next. Speaking broadly, it may be said that it is from some obscure recognition of the fact of death that life draws its final sweetness. An obscure, haunting recognition, of course; for it more than that, if the thought becomes palpable, defined, and present, it swallows up everything. The howling of the winter wind outside increases the warm satisfaction of a man in bed; but this satisfaction is succeeded by quite another feeling when the wind grows into a tempest, and threatens to blow the house down. And this remote recognition of death may exist almost constantly in a man's mind, and give to his life keener zest and relish. His lights may burn the brighter for it, and his wines taste sweeter. For it is on the tapestry of a dim ground that the

---

1 animal health: natural health 天然的健康。

些考究可以使死失掉它的可憎形状,帮助我们安于死的观念了。一个人沉静的愉快是很复杂的,在某种感动时候,那种时候过去后我们才认出是我们最愉快的时光,一些关于死的微妙观念总是杂在里头。这个愉快时光的特性就从这个混合得来——这个混合分别出一个小孩子的欣欢,那是完全靠着生活力的丰满和一时的冲动,太轻飘了不能记住,同一个大人真实的愉快,那是瞻前顾后,将现在同未来两世界都打量一下。大概说起来,我们可以说,人生最甜蜜的时光是来自隐约地承认死这件事实。当然,只是个隐约的,回绕心际的承认;因为若使更进一步,若使那观念变成明显的,确定的,现在眼前的,它把一切其他的东西都吞没了。冬天外面大风的怒号会增加一个躺在床上的人的暖和快感;但是这快感变成完全不同的情绪了,若使大风刮成暴风雨,屋子有吹倒的危险。这个隐约的死的认识可以几乎老在一个人心里,给他的生活以更深切的兴味和风趣。他的灯将因此而更见光明,他的酒将因此而更见可口。因为在暗色

figures come out in the boldest relief and the brightest colour.

If we were to live here always, with no other care than how to feed, clothe, and house ourselves, life would be a very sorry business. It is immeasurably heightened by the solemnity of death. The brutes die even as we; but it is our knowledge that we have to die which makes us human. If nature cunningly hides death, and so permits us to play out our little games, it is easily seen that our knowing it to be inevitable, that to every one of us it will come one day or another, is a wonderful spur to action. We really do work while it is called to-day, because the night cometh when no man can work. We may not expect it soon — it may not have sent us a single avant-courier[1] — yet we all know that every day brings it nearer. On the supposition that we were to live here always, there would be little inducement to exertion. But, having some work at heart, the knowledge that we may be, any day, finally interrupted, is an incentive to diligence. We naturally desire to have it completed, or at least far advanced toward completion, before that final interruption takes place. And knowing that his existence here is limited, a man's workings have reference to others rather than to himself, and thereby into his nature comes a new influx of nobility. If a man plants a tree, he

---

1 avant-courier: forerunner 前驱。

的帷帐之前，人物才显得轮廓非常分明，彩色非常夺目。

若使我们永远在世上活下去，除开衣食住外没有别的忧愁，那么生活将变成一件非常无聊的勾当了。那是因为有死的尊严而高尚得无限倍了。禽兽同我们一样地死去；但是我们知道我们会死，我们所以别于禽兽就在这点。假使自然狡猾地将死这件事掩盖起来，让我们弄完我们的小把戏，那么我们将看出我们知道它是不可避免的，个个人尽早总有一天遇到它，这是我们动作一个极有力的刺激。我们的确于所谓今天里干事情，因为夜一到没有人能够工作了。我们也许还用不着期待它——它也许还没有派来一个先锋——然而我们知道一天一夜它更接近我们了。设使我们永远活在世上，我们也绝不想努力了。但是心里打算有所为，知道了我们任一天都有断然地被阻止的可能，因此就有勤勉的动机了。我们自然希望在这断然的阻止发生以前把那件事办好，最少也要做得快成功了。晓得他在世之日有限，一个人的工作跟别人比跟自己更有关系了，借此一股高贵的新潮流来到他的生活里面。若使一个人种一棵树，他知道别

knows that other hands than his will gather the fruit; and when he plants it, he thinks quite as much of those other hands as of his own. Thus to the poet there is the dearer life after life; and posterity's single laurel leaf is valued more than a multitude of contemporary bays. Even the man immersed in money-making does not make money so much for himself as for those who may come after him. Riches in noble natures have a double sweetness. The possessor enjoys his wealth, and he heightens that enjoyment by an imaginative entrance into the pleasure which his son or his nephew may derive from it when he is away, or the high uses to which he may turn it. Seeing that we have no perpetual lease[1] of life and its adjuncts, we do not live for ourselves. And thus it is that death, which we are accustomed to consider an evil, really acts for us the friendliest part, and takes away the commonplace of existence. My life, and your life, flowing on thus day by day, is a vapid enough piece of business; but when we think that it must close, a multitude of considerations, not connected with ourselves, but with others, rush in, and vapidity vanishes at once. Life, if it were to flow on forever and thus, would stagnate and rot. The hopes, and fears, and regrets, which move and trouble it, keep it fresh and healthy, as the sea is kept alive by the

---

1 lease：本来是指土地租借期限，这里移来指我们对于这个血肉躯能够寄身多少年。

人的手将采到这果实；他种的时候，想别人的手不下于想他自己的了，这样子，由一个诗人看来，身后的生活比在世的更可爱；后代一声的称赞比当时众人的喝彩更来得可贵，就是说那惟钱是务的人，为他自己挣钱还不如为将来的人的成分多。财富落到禀性高尚的人身上可以生出双倍的快乐。他有了钱自己觉得愉快，他的愉快更加多了，当他臆想到他儿子或者他侄儿从这上面所得的快乐，当他已经去世了；或者他可以拿这笔款所做的善良事业。看到我们对于人生同它的附属物不能永远占住，我们就不完全为着自己而生活了。所以我们一向承认为一个缺陷的这个死却的确大帮我们的忙，去掉人世的无聊了。你我的生活这样一天一天地过去是件够无聊的事情；但是我们一想起它必得结束，一群的考虑，不是关于自己的，却是关于别人的，都奔到心头，乏味之感登时消灭了。生活假使"如是"永远过下去将停滞而腐烂了。激动生活同打扰生活的种种希望，忧愁同追悔使生活保留他的新鲜同健康，正如海是因潮流的骚

trouble of its tides. In a tolerably comfortable world, where death is not, it is difficult to see from what quarter these healthful fears, regrets, and hopes could come. As it is, there are agitations and sufferings in our lots enough; but we must remember that it is on account of these sufferings and agitations that we become creatures breathing thoughtful breath. As has already been said, death takes away the commonplace of life. And positively, when one looks on the thousand and one[1] poor, foolish, ignoble faces of this world, and listens to the chatter as poor and foolish as the faces, one, in order to have any proper respect for them, is forced to remember that solemnity of death, which is silently waiting. The foolishest person will look grand enough one day. The features are poor now, but the hottest tears and the most passionate embraces will not seem out of place[2] then. If you wish to make a man look noble, your best course is to kill him. What superiority he may have inherited from his race, what superiority nature may have personally gifted him with, comes out in death. The passions which agitate, distort, and change, are gone away for ever, and the features settle back into a marble calm, which is the man's truest image. Then the most affected look sincere, the most volatile, serious — all noble, more or less. And nature will not be

---

1 thousand and one：无非很多的意思，也许因为"天方夜谭"叫做"千零一夜"，所以有这种用法。

2 out of place：in appropriate 不相宜。

乱而有生气。在一个都还舒服的世界上,没有死这件事,我们真不容易看出这些健全的忧愁,追悔同希望会从何方来。照眼前的情形,我们命运里的震动和挨苦是够多的,但是我们必得记住就是因为有这些震动和挨苦,我们才是呼吸有思想的气息的动物。我们既已说过,死去掉人生的无聊了。在积极方面,当我们看见世上成千累百可怜的,愚蠢的,下流的脸孔,听到同那脸孔一样可怜同愚蠢的胡谈,我们若使对他们要有相当的敬意,就不得不记起死的严肃,那是在静默地等候他们。最傻的人有一天会显得够尊严的。这些容貌此刻是难看的,但是最热烈的眼泪同最深情的拥抱到那时也不觉得过分了。你想叫一个人显得高贵,你最好的法子是把他杀死。他从他的种族遗传下来的上等性质,自然亲自给他的上等性质,到死时候都呈现出来了。那些激动人们的,扭歪人们的,变化人们的烈情永远消失了,相貌回到大理石一样的沉静了,那是人们真正的本来面目。到那时最虚伪的也现出诚恳的脸孔了,最轻浮也现出严重的脸孔了——大家多少都有些高尚的气分〔氛〕。而且自然绝

surprised into disclosures. The man stretched out there may have been voluble as a swallow, but now — when he could speak to some purpose[1] — neither pyramid[2] nor sphinx[3] holds a secret more tenaciously.

Consider, then, how the sense of impermanence brightens beauty and elevates happiness. Melancholy is always attendant on beauty, and that melancholy brings out its keenness as the darkgreen corrugated leaf brings out the wan loveliness of the primrose. The spectator enjoys the beauty, but his knowledge that it is fleeting, and that he is fleeting, adds a pathetic something to it; and by that something the beautiful object and the gazer are alike raised.

Everything is sweetened by risk. The pleasant emotion is mixed and deepened by a sense of mortality. Those lovers who have never encountered the possibility of last embraces and farewells are novices in the passion. Sunset affects us more powerfully than sunrise, simply because it is a setting sun, and suggests a thousand analogies. A mother is never happier than when her eyes fill over her sleeping child, never does she kiss it more fondly, never does she pray for it more fervently; and yet there is more in her heart than visible red cheek and yellow curl; possession and bereavement are

---

1 to some purpose: with considerable effect 有相当的效果。
2 pyramid: 埃及金字塔包含无限神秘, 庞然位于大地之上, 默默不语。
3 sphinx: 狮身人面兽曾以谜问过路之人, 不能猜出者则杀之。他才不肯说出这个谜的意思。

不至于慌张失检,泄露秘密。正寝在那里的人也许从前多活得像一只燕子,但是现在——当他能够说出一些值得听的话了——金字塔同人首狮身怪都不能比他更坚执地保守一个秘密。

然后,请想一下,无常之感多么增加美丽的光辉,提高快乐的内容。愁总是随着美,这种愁使我们的美感更见锐敏,正如深绿色的皱叶更显出蔷薇的惨淡容光。观者的美感油然而生,但是他知道这是消逝的,他自己也是消逝的,因此添了一种凄然的酸辛;这酸辛同是提高了美的对象和凝眸者的精神。

一切事情都因有危险而加甜了,快感与毁灭之感相杂,就越来深刻了。没有遇过最后拥抱同最后诀别的可能的爱人还是柔情的门外汉。夕阳感动我们过于朝暾,无非因为它是落日,会引起成千的连〔联〕想。一个母亲最欣欢的时候是当她双眼溢着泪珠,看她睡着的孩子;她在别的时候绝没有这么痴心地吻他,她也没有这么热烈地为他祈祷;然而,她心里所想的不单是红的脸颊和黄的卷发;在这样至妙的慈母心情中占有和失

strangely mingled in the exquisite maternal mood, the one heightening the other. All great joys are serious; and emotion must be measured by its complexity and the deepness of its reach. A musician may draw pretty notes enough from a single key, but the richest music is that in which the whole force of the instrument is employed, in the production of which every key is vibrating; and, although full of solemn touches[1] and majestic tones, the final effect may be exuberant and gay. Pleasures which rise beyond the mere gratification of the senses are dependent for their exquisiteness on the number and variety of the thoughts which they evoke. And that joy is the greatest which, while felt to be joy, can include the thought of death and clothe itself with that crowning pathos. And in the minds of thoughtful persons every joy does, more or less, with that crowning pathos clothe itself.

In life there is nothing more unexpected and surprising than the arrivals and departures of pleasure. If we find it in one place to-day, it is vain to seek it there to-morrow. You cannot lay a trap for it. It will fall into no ambuscade, concert it ever so cunningly. Pleasure has no logic; it never treads in its own footsteps. Into our commonplace existence it comes with a surprise, like a pure white swan from the airy void into the ordinary village lake; and just as the swan, for

---

1 touches: notes or strains of music 音乐的调子。

却两种情绪奇怪地混在一起，互相刺激。一切大欢悦都是严重的；情调是要用它的复杂程度同它的深刻影响来量的。一个音乐家从一个主音也可以奏出妙乐，但是最富丽的音乐是整个乐器的全部力量都用到的，奏的时候个个主音都得颤动；虽然满是严肃的情调同堂皇的音韵，最后的印象也许是生气勃勃的，称心喜悦的。超过感官满足之上的高尚快乐，它们的锐敏程度是靠着它们所启发的思想的数目和种类。最大的快乐是那种当我们觉得是快乐时候，还能包含死的观念，就以这种奇绝的凄其情绪来装饰自己。在心境沉静的人们心里每个快乐多少都是用这种奇绝的凄其情绪来妆饰自己。

人生里没有一件别的东西像快乐的来去这么飘忽，这么惊人。若使我们今天在某一地方找到它，明天再到那儿寻觅就是徒然了。你们不能给它安下一个陷阱。它总不至于遇到埋伏，无论你们多么狡猾地万方设计。快乐是没有遵守什么规例的；它绝不依着前次的足迹走路。它令人惊喜地来到我们日常的生活里，像一只白天鹅从空中投到乡村普通的湖里；正同天鹅一

no reason that can be discovered, lifts itself on its wings and betakes itself to the void again, it leaves us, and our sole possession is its memory[1]. And it is characteristic of pleasure that we can never recognise it to be pleasure till after it is gone. Happiness never lays its finger on its pulse. [2] If we attempt to steal a glimpse of its features it disappears. It is a gleam of unreckoned gold. From the nature of the case, our happiness, such as in its degree it has been, lives in memory. We have not the voice itself; we have only its echo. We are never happy; we can only remember that we were so once. And while in the very heart and structure of the happy moment there lurked an obscure consciousness of death, the memory in which past happiness dwells is always a regretful memory. This is why the tritest utterance about the past, youth, early love, and the like, has always about it an indefinable flavour of poetry, which pleases and affects. In the wake of a ship there is always a melancholy splendour. The finest set of verses of our modern time[3] describes how the poet gazed on the "happy autumn fields," and remembered the "days that were no more." After all, a man's real possession is his

---

1 memory：小品文家都喜欢谈"记忆"，那可说是他们的宝库，Hazlitt有几篇论memory的文字尤妙。

2 happiness never lays its finger on its pulse：happiness never sounds its own feeling，快乐绝没有去测量自己的感觉。

3 the finest set of verses of our modern time：指Tennyson长诗 *Princess* 第四章开头是"Tears, idle tears, I know not what they mean"那一段。

样，绝不能找到一个理由，它又举翼飞回空中了，它离开我们，我们惟一所得的是它的回忆，这是快乐的一个特征，我们绝不能晓得它是快乐，必得等到它已过去了。快乐绝不用手指量一量自己的脉搏。若使我们想偷觑一下它的形相〔象〕，它登时消失得毫无踪迹了。那是一堆没有数过的黄金的一瞥。因为它本质是这样，我们的快乐原来到了什么程度，也就那样程度只在我们的记忆里活着。我们没有听到原来的声音，我们只听到回响。我们当下不觉得快乐；我们只能记起我们曾经快乐过。在快乐时光的核心同组织里既然埋伏了隐约的死的观念，过去快乐所寄身的记忆又总是一种惘然的回忆。所以最俗套的关于过去，青春，少年恋史，以及这类事情的感慨总带有一股难于形容的诗的气味，那使我们喜欢，使我们感动。船走过去了所留的痕迹总有一阵愁惨的光荣。近代最美妙的一串诗开头描写诗人怎样瞩目于"快乐的秋之田野"，想到"不可再得的日子"。其实说起来，个人真正占有的东西是他的回忆。别的东西不能

memory. In nothing else is he rich, in nothing else is he poor.

In our warm imaginative youth, death is far removed from us, and attains thereby a certain picturesqueness. The grim thought stands in the ideal world as a ruin stands in a blooming landscape. The thought of death sheds a pathetic charm over everything then. The young man cools himself with a thought of the winding-sheet and the charnel, as the heated dancer cools himself on the balcony with the night-air. The young imagination plays with the idea of death, makes a toy of it, just as a child plays with edge-tools[1] till once it cuts its fingers. The most lugubrious poetry is written by very young and tolerably comfortable persons. When a man's mood becomes really serious he has little taste for such foolery. The man who has a grave or two in his heart[2], does not need to haunt church-yards. The young poet uses death as an antithesis; and when he shocks his reader by some flippant use of it in that way, he considers he has written something mightily fine. In his gloomiest mood he is most insincere, most egotistical, most pretentious. The older and wiser poet avoids the subject as he does the memory of pain; or when he does refer to it, he does so in a reverential manner, and with some sense of its solemnity and of the magnitude of its issues. It was

---

1 edge-tools: cutting tools 切东西的工具。
2 who has a grave or two in his heart: 就是说他有一两个亲爱的人过去了。

使他富,别的东西也不能叫他穷。

在我们热血奔腾,幻想丰富的年少时候,死跟我们还隔得很远,因此有如远景之可以入画。这个狰狞的念头站在思想里正如一座废墟站在各花盛开的美景里。年青人用殓衣同埋尸所这些观念来做清凉剂,正如热烈地跳舞的人到露台去吸收夜的空气凉爽一下。青年的想像玩弄死的观念,拿来当一件玩意儿,正如小孩子耍有刃的东西,要等到它打〔把〕手指割伤了,才知道厉害。最阴气森森的诗歌是非常年青,都还舒服的人们写下的。当一个人心境变成真真严肃了,他是不喜欢干这样无意识的举动。心头有了一两座墓的人用不着徘徊于教堂坟地之旁。年青的诗人用死来做对照;当他巧言滑舌地用死来做反面文章震动读者的时候,他认为他写了非常俏皮的东西。在他最忧郁的心境里他是最不诚恳,最自私,最妄自尊大。年纪老些,智慧多些的诗人躲避这个题目,正如他躲避苦痛的回忆;或者当他提起它时候,他也是用一种凛然的态度,感到它的尊严和它

in that year of revelry, 1814, and while undressing from balls, that Lord Byron[1] wrote his *Lara*[2], as he informs us. Disrobing, and haunted, in all probability, by eyes in whose light he was happy enough, the spoiled young man, who then affected death-pallors, and wished the world to believe that he felt his richest wines powdered with the dust of graves — of which wine, notwithstanding, he frequently took more than was good for him — wrote.

"That sleep the loveliest, since it dreams the least."

The sleep referred to being death. This was meant to take away the reader's breath; and after performing the feat, Byron betook himself to his pillow with a sense of supreme cleverness. Contrast with this Shakspeare's far out-looking and thought-heavy[3] lines — lines which, under the same image, represent death —

"To die — to sleep; —

To sleep: perchance to dream; — ay, there's the rub;

For in that sleep of death what dreams may come!"[4]

And you see at once how a man's notions of death and dying are

---

1 Lord Byron (1788—1824), 英国浪漫派诗人，少年英俊，生平韵事甚多，好作悲哀语，有时难免矫情。

2 *Lara*：一首长诗，述一个海盗和他的爱人（假装为他的跟人）的冒险故事。

3 thought-heavy：lader with thought 满是思想的。

4 莎翁悲剧《哈姆雷特》中有名的独语。

所含的重大意义。拜伦爵士是当那纵饮之年,一八一四,从跳舞会回来脱下衣服时候写出他的《拉刺》,他是这样告诉我们。一面宽衣,一面大概萦心于喜欢他这个人的那班女子的美目。这位当时爱着死人的惨白脸色,要世人相信他觉得最芬郁的酒是沾有坟墓的灰尘——然而这种酒他常常喝得太多了——的被人们太容纵了的年青人写出这么一行诗。

"那个睡眠是最可留恋的,因为他的梦最少。"

这里所说的睡眠是指死。这里要使读者出不了气;干了这个壮举,拜仑就枕而眠,觉得自己聪明过人。试将这个和沙士比亚所见远大的,思想堆得很厚重的名句——那是用同样象征来代表死的名句——

"死去——睡去;——

睡去:也许会做梦;——吓,这是个麻烦;

因为在死的睡眠里来的是那一种的梦呢!"

你们立刻可以看出一个人更宽阔的经验如何会使他关于死和弥

deepened by a wider experience. Middle age may fear death quite as little as youth fears it; but it has learned seriousness, and it has no heart to poke fun at the lean ribs, or to call it fond names like a lover, or to stick a primrose in its grinning chaps, and draw a strange pleasure from the irrelevancy.

The man who has reached thirty, feels at times as if he had come out of a great battle. Comrade after comrade has fallen; his own life seems to have been charmed[1]. And knowing how it fared with his friends — perfect health one day, a catarrh the next, blinds drawn down[2], silence in the house, blubbered faces of widow and orphans, intimation of the event in the newspapers, with a request that friends will accept of it, the day after — a man, as he draws near middle age, begins to suspect every transient indisposition; to be careful of being caught in a shower, to shudder at sitting in wet shoes; he feels his pulse, he anxiously peruses his face in a mirror, he becomes critical as to the colour of his tongue. In early life illness is a luxury, and draws out toward the sufferer curious and delicious tendernesses, which are felt to be a full overpayment of pain and weakness; then there is the pleasant period of convalescence[3], when

---

1 to have been charmed: to have been protected by magic 受魔术的保护。
2 blinds drawn down: 英俗死人之家百叶窗紧闭。
3 the pleasant period of convalescence: Lamb 有一篇小品文叫 The Convalescent 在 *The Lest Essay of Elia* 集中，极能道出此中的妙味。

留的观念更见深刻。中年可以不怕死不下于青年；但是他懂得严重，无心去向瘦削的肋骨开玩笑，或者用亲昵的名字喊它像一个爱人那样，或者插一朵莲馨花在它狞笑的面颊，从这两者的绝不调和得到乐趣。

年纪到了三十的人有时觉得他仿佛从一场大战走出来。同伴一个一个地倒了；他自己的生命好像有什么特别魔力保护着。知道了他朋友们所遭遇的是怎么样——今天十分健康，明天伤风感冒，于是屋里的百叶窗拉下，家中到处是静寂，寡妇孤儿哭肿了脸孔，第二天报纸上提起这件事，还附带个朋友们肯接收的请求——一个人当他走近中年时候，开始担心于个个暂时的微恙；怕碰到骤雨，穿湿的鞋子坐着就吓得打寒噤；他按自己的脉搏，他焦心地对镜看自己的脸孔，他对于他舌头颜色很加考究。早年里病是一种享乐，使挨苦的人得到奇怪的，可口的温存，那可认为苦痛同衰弱的完全赔偿了；此后又有复元这

one tastes a core and marrow of delight in meats, drinks, sleep, silence; the bunch of newly-plucked flowers on the table, the sedulous attentions and patient forbearance of nurses and friends. Later in life, when one occupies a post, and is in discharge of duties which are accumulating against recovery, illness and convalescence cease to be luxuries. Illness is felt to be a cruel interruption of the ordinary course of things, and the sick person is harassed by a sense of the loss of time and the loss of strength. He is placed hors de combat[1], all the while he is conscious that the battle is going on around him, and he feels his temporary withdrawal a misfortune. Of course, unless a man is very unhappily circumstanced, he has in his later illnesses all the love, patience, and attention which sweetened his earlier ones; but then he cannot rest in them, and accept them as before as compensation in full[2]. The world is ever with him[3], through his interests and his affections he has meshed himself in an intricate network of relationships and other dependences, and a fatal issue — which in such cases is ever on the cards[4] — would destroy all these, and bring about more serious matters than the shedding of tears. In a

---

  1 hors de combat: disabled 无能。
  2 in full: without reduction 全额，不折不扣。
  3 the world is ever with him: Wordsworth 有两句诗，可做这句话注脚——"The world is too much with us; late and soon, getting and spending, we lay waste our powers."

个快乐时期,那是对于肉,饮料,睡眠,静默都感到无上的欣欢;桌上新采来的一束鲜花,看护妇同朋友们的殷勤照呼同耐心忍受。后来,当一个人居一个位置,要执行职务,那是一天天一堆积起来等候他的恢复健康,病同复元都不是乐事了。病被认为是日常事情一个残酷的阻碍,病人总是不安,有个失掉时间和失掉力气的感觉。他真得失却战斗力了;他老是觉得战争还是在他四面进行着,而他暂时的撤退是件不幸。当然,除非一个人处于非常不幸的环境里,他在中年害病的时候也可以有那些使他早年的害病变为乐事的一切爱情,耐心同注意;可是他不能安于这些上面了,不能像从前把这些看来十足的赔偿了。世界总是同他有关系;因为他的利益同感情的缘故,他已经投身于非常纷乱的关系和其他依靠的密网里去了,一个致命的结果——中年时候这是随时会发现的——要毁坏这一切关系和依靠,带来比淌眼泪更严重的事情。在一个人早年的疾病里,

---

4 which is ever on the cards:which is quite possible 那是很可能的。

man's earlier illnesses, too, he had not only no such definite future to work out[1], he had a stronger spring of life and hope; he was rich in time, and could wait; and lying in his chamber now, he cannot help remembering that, as Mr. Thackeray expresses it, there comes at last an illness to which there may be no convalescence. What if that illness be already come? And so there is nothing left for him, but to bear the rod with patience, and to exercise a humble faith in the Ruler of all[2]. If he recovers, some half-dozen people will be made happy; if he does not recover, the same number of people will be made miserable for a little while, and during the next two or three days, acquaintances will meet in the street — "You've heard of poor So-and-so? Very sudden! Who would have thought it? Expect to meet you at —'s on Thursday. Good-bye." And so the end. Your death and my death are mainly of importance to ourselves. The black plumes will be stripped off our hearses within the hour; tears will dry, hurt hearts close again, our graves grow level with the churchyard, and although we are away, the world wags on. It does not miss us; and those who are near us, when the first strangeness of vacancy wears off, will not miss us much either.

---

1 to work out: to accomplish by effort; to plan all details of 努力造成; 仔细计划。

2 the Ruler of all: God 上帝。

他不但用不着解决这么具体的将来问题,而且他更有强的生活力同希望;他有的是时候,能够等待着;现在躺在室中,他就免不了想起,像塔刻立先生所说的,那种没有复元期的病此刻也许来临了。假使那样病已经来了,怎么样呢?他真是毫无办法了,只好耐心忍受这鞭笞,低首相信全能的主宰。若使他病好了,半打左右的人们会高兴;若使他的病不好,同样数目的人们暂时会受苦;在最近二三天之内,认识他的人们在街上相遇会说道——"你听可怜的某某的消息吗?真来的突然!谁会料到?星期四在——处再会罢。再见。"就这么结束了。你的逝世和我的逝世无非对于我们自己算是很重要的。黑羽毛在一小时之内将从我们的棺车摘下;泪也干了,伤损的心儿又将伤痕补满了,我们的坟墓将变成和礼拜堂的墓地地面一样平,虽然我们不在了,世界还是摇摇摆摆望〔往〕前行。它并不怀念我们,我们亲近的人们,当起先空虚的奇感消失了,也不会很感到我们的去世。

We are curious as to death-beds and death-bed sayings; we wish to know how the matter stands; how the whole thing looks to the dying. Unhappily — perhaps, on the whole, happily — we can gather no information from these. The dying are nearly as reticent as the dead. The inferences we draw from the circumstances of death, the pallor, the sob, the glazing eye, are just as likely to mislead us as not. Manfred[1] exclaims, "Old man, 'tis not so difficult to die!" Sterling[2] wrote Carlyle[3] that it was all very strange, yet not so strange as it seemed to the lookers on. And so, perhaps, on the whole it is. The world has lasted six thousand years now, and, with the exception of those at present alive, the millions who have breathed upon it — splendid emperors, horny-fisted clowns, little children in whom thought has never stirred — have died, and what they have done, we also shall be able to do. It may not be so difficult, may not be so terrible, as our fears whisper. The dead keep their secrets, and in a little while we shall be as wise as they — and as taciturn.

---

1 Manfred：拜仑长诗里一个英雄。

2 Sterling：John Sterling（1806—1844），文学家，Carlyle 为他作一部传记。

3 Carlyle：Thomas Carlyle（1795—1881），英国大思想家，著有《英雄崇拜论》《衣服哲学》等。

我们对于临终和临终的话具有好奇心；我们想知道事情到底是怎么样；从将死的人看来，全部的情形是如何。不幸得很——也行，就全局说起来是侥幸得很——我们不能从这些采到消息。将死的人几乎是同死人一样的缄默。从死的环境，颜色惨白，呜咽，板滞的眼神，这些情形所得的推论错与不错的可能性相等。曼夫勒德喊道，"老头子，死去并不是这么一件难事！"司特令写信告诉喀莱尔"死的确是非常奇怪的一件事，但是不如旁观者所以为的那么奇怪"。也许大概的情形是如此罢。世界到如今已经有六千年了，除开现在活着的人们外，在那上面呼吸过的无数的亿万人们——堂皇的君王，手拳坚硬的乡下人，以及思想绝没有活动过的小孩子——都死了，他们所干过了，我们当然也能够干，它也许没有那么难，也许没有那么可怕，像我们的恐惧对我们所耳语的。死人保守他们的秘密，过一会儿，我们也将像他们那么明白——也像他们那么默然了。

Richard Jefferies

Meadow Thoughts

The old house stood by the silent country road, secluded by many a long, long mile, and yet again secluded within the great walls of the garden. Often and often I rambled up to the milestone which stood under an oak, to look at the chipped inscription low down — "To London, 79 miles." So far away, you see, that the very inscription was cut at the foot of the stone, since no one would be likely to want that information. It was half hidden by docks and nettles, dispised and unnoticed. A broad land this seventy-nine miles — how many meadows and corn-fields, hedges and woods, in that distance? — wide enough to seclude any house, to hide it like an acorn in the grass. Those who have lived all their lives in remote places do not feel the remoteness. No one else seemed to be conscious of the breadth that separated the place from the great centre,

草地上的默思

老屋站在乡下里寂寞的路旁,有许多哩路把它同城市隔离,又有花园的大墙把它围着隔离起来。我常常信步走到站在一棵橡树底下的一块哩数标石,去瞧刻在低处的铭字——"离伦敦七十九哩"。跟大城是离这么远,你们看,连铭字都凿在石头的脚上,因为大概不会有人想知道这个情形。它一半是被酸模同苎麻遮住,受人蔑视,没有人去注意它。这七十九哩一片大平原——这里面有多少草场同谷田,篱笆同森林?——广阔到足以使任何屋子幽独,把它藏起来像蔓草中的一粒橡实。一生都在幽静辽远的地方过活的人们不觉得它的幽静辽远。其他别人没有一个感到这地方同大城市相距漫漫长途,但是也许正是这

but it was, perhaps. that consciousness which deepened the solitude to me. It made the silence more still; the shadows of the oaks yet slower in their movement; everything more earnest[1]. To convey a full impression of the intense concentration of Nature[2] in the meadows in very difficult — everything is so utterly oblivious of man's thought and man's heart. The oaks stand — quiet, still — so still that the lichen loves them. At their feet the grass grows, and heeds nothing. Among it the squirrels leap, and their little hearts are as far away from you or me as the very wood of the oaks. The sunshine settles itself in the valley by the brook, and abides there whether we come or not. Glance through the gap in the hedge by the oak, and see how concentrated it is — all of it, every blade of grass, and leaf, and flower, and living creature, finch or squirrel. It is mesmerized upon itself.[3] Then I used to feel that it really was seventy-nine miles to London, and not an hour or two only by rail, really all those miles. A great, broad province of green furrow and ploughed furrow between the old house and the city of the world. Such solace and solitude seventy-nine miles thick cannot be painted; the trees cannot be placed far enough away in perspective. It is necessary to stay in it like the oaks to know it.

---

1 earnest: serious; zealous 严肃，热心。
2 the intense concentration of Nature: "大自然"是这么恬静，好像她正凝神。

样意识使我更深切地觉得它的寂寞。那使静默更深沉了；使橡树的影子移动得更慢了；使一切东西更显得严肃了。要完全传出草场上"自然"潜心凝聚的神情是很不容易办到的——一切东西是这么浑然与人们的思想同人们的心儿毫不相关。橡树站着——安详宁静——是这么宁静，薛苔也爱上它们了。它们脚旁生有荒草，什么事也不留意。草里有松鼠跳跃，他们小心儿的不睬你我正同橡树的木头不睬我们一样。阳光安身于谷里的溪旁，滞在那儿，不管我们来或不来。请从橡树旁篱笆上的罅隙看去，你看那是多么恬然凝神——那一切，每片草，叶子，花朵，以及个个生物，黄雀或松鼠。那是把自己催眠了。当时我常觉得这跟伦敦真是相距七十九哩，并不是无非一两点钟火车上的旅行，的确有许多哩在中间。一片广大的青畦沟同犁沟把老屋同俗世的大城隔开。七十九哩深这样的安慰同孤寂是不能描状的；透视法也无从把树林放在够远的地方。必得滞在里面像那棵橡树才能领略它。

---

3 It is mesmerized upon itself.：使自己沉醉于自己了，还是前往的意思。

Lime-tree branches overhung the corner of the garden-wall, whence a view was easy of the silent and dusty road, till overarching oaks concealed it. The white dust heated by the sunshine, the green hedges, and the heavily massed trees, white clouds rolled together in the sky, a footpath opposite lost in the fields, as you might thrust a stick into the grass, tender line leaves caressing the cheek, and silence. That is, the silence of the fields. If a breeze rustled the boughs, if a greenfinch called, if the cart-mare in the meadow shook herself, making the earth and air tremble by her with the convulsion of her mighty muscles, these were not sounds, they were the silence itself. So sensitive to it as I was, in its turn[1] it held me firmly, like the fabled spells of the old time[2]. The mere touch of a leaf was a talisman to bring me under the enchantment, so that I seemed to feel and know all that was proceeding among the grass-blades and in the bushes. Among the lime-trees along the wall the birds never built, though so close and sheltered. They built everywhere but there. To the broad coping-stones[3] of the wall under the lime boughs speckled thrushes came almost hourly, sometimes to peer out and reconnoitre if it was safe to visit the garden, sometimes

---

1 in its turn: in its part in a rotation 转流到它身上时候。
2 the fabled spells of the old time: 古时故事里常说有些妖怪有魔力，能把人迷住，变成糊涂了。

菩提树的树枝挂在花园围墙的基角上，从那里可以望见那条满布尘土的静寂道路，等到悬着如弓形的橡树把它遮住。阳光晒热的白色尘埃，绿色的篱笆，满载着果实的树，天上卷在一起的白云，对面没于田地里的一条小路，正如你掷一根手杖到草丛里，柔嫩的菩提树叶抚弄面颊，以外还有静默。那是田地的静默。若使有一阵和风吹动树枝，若使有一只黄鹂歌唱，若使草场上拖车的牝马振身一下，以她坚硬筋肉的抽动使地面同空气都震颤起来，这些不是声音，它们就是静默的化身。我对于它是具有这么敏锐的感觉，它转过来也决然地把我抓住，像古时神话里所说的魔力。一叶的触手等于一道符咒使我魂迷，所以我好似感到同懂得青草里同丛莽里一切进行的事情。墙边菩提树里绝没有鸟儿来做窝，虽然是这么紧密同可避风雨。它们到处筑巢，却总不在这儿。菩提树枝底下宽阔的墙顶石差不多每点钟都有花斑的画眉飞来，有时从此下望，窥探到花园去有

---

3 coping-stone：the stone of the highest course of a wall, often with a sloping top 墙顶的石头，常作斜坡状。

to see if a snail had climbed up the ivy. Then they dropped quietly down into the long strawberry patch immediately under. The cover of strawberries is the constant resource of all creeping things; the thrushes looked round every plant and under every leaf and runner. One toad always resided there, often two, and as you gathered a ripe strawberry you might catch sight of his black eye watching you take the fruit he had saved for you.

Down the road skims an eave-swallow[1], swift as an arrow, his white back making the sun-dried dust dull and dingy; he is seeking a pool for mortar, and will waver to and fro[2] by the brook below till he finds a convenient place to alight. Thence back to the eave here, where for forty years he and his ancestors built in safety. Two white butterflies fluttering round each other rise over the limes, once more up[3] over the house, and soar on till their white shows no longer against the illumined air. A grasshopper calls on the sward by the strawberries, and immediately fillips himself over seven leagues[4] of grass blades. Yonder a line of men and women file across the field, seen for a moment as they pass a gateway, and the hay changes from hay-colour to green behind them as they turn the under but still

---

1 eave-swallow: swallow who builds under eaves 筑巢于檐下的燕子。
2 to and fro: backwards and forwards; up and down 前后；上下。
3 up: rise up.

无危险,有时看一看有没有一只蜗牛爬到长〔常〕春藤上。然后他们悄悄地投到底下一长块莓树丛中。莓树丛薮是一切爬虫的汇聚所;画眉向每株树四旁,每片叶同每根纤匋枝底下探看。一只虾蟆总是蹲在那儿,常常有两只,当你捡起一粒已熟的梅莓时候,你也许会瞧见他的黑眼睛看你把他替你留下的果子拿去。

一只檐燕顺着路掠飞而来,猛得像一条箭,他的白背使太阳晒干的尘埃相形减色;他是在找个池沼取灰泥,在下面小溪之上,来往飞翔等到他寻出一个便于停足的地方。从那儿又回到这里的檐上,四十年来他同他的祖宗都是安然筑巢于此。两只白蝴蝶互相围着飘荡,飞过菩提树顶,又超过一回屋顶,一直往前飞,等到他们的白色不再衬着光天显在眼前了。一只蟋蟀在莓树旁草地上细吟,立刻一下子跳过二十一哩的草片。那处一阵男女列队穿着田地走,我们瞧见一会儿,当他们正行过一道门;他们后面的干草从干草色变成绿色,因他们的脚步把

---

4 seven leagues:从前有个传说,有一双鞋穿上了一步可走七leagues,合二十一哩,不知道跟戴宗的甲马比起来如何?

sappy side upwards. They are working hard, but it looks easy, slow, and sunny. Finches fly out from the hedgerow to the overturned hay. Another butterfly, a brown one, floats along the dusty road — the only traveller yet. The white clouds are slowly passing behind the oaks, large puffed clouds, like deliberate loads of hay, leaving little wisps and flecks behind them caught in the sky. How pleasant it would be to read in the shadow! There is a broad shadow on the sward by the strawberries cast by a tall and fine-grown American crab-tree[1]. The very place for a book; and although I know it is useless, yet I go and fetch one and dispose myself on the grass.

I can never read in summer out of doors. Though in shadow the bright light fills it, summer shadows are broadest daylight. The page is so white and hard the letters so very black, the meaning and drift[2] not quite intelligible, because neither eye nor mind will dwell upon it. Human thoughts and imaginings written down are pale and feeble in bright summer light. The eye wanders away, and rests more lovingly on greensward and green lime leaves. The mind wanders yet deeper and farther into the dreamy mystery of the azure sky. Once now and then[3], determined to write down that mystery and delicious sense while actually in it. I have brought out table and ink and paper,

---

1 American crab-tree: crab-apple tree.
2 drift: purpose; meaning 意义。
3 now and then: occasionally 偶然。

向底的，可是还有汁液的那一面翻转过来。他们勤苦工作着，但是看起来好像从容不迫同和煦快乐。黄雀从篱笆飞到翻过来的干草上去。又有一只蝴蝶，棕色的，顺着尘埃弥漫的道路漂游——算作惟一的旅行者。白云慢悠悠地在橡树丛后移动，大块的，涨着的云团，好似一堆一堆细心捆好的干草，留下小束同斑点，拘于天际。在阴影里读书是多么快乐呀！草场上莓树旁一大块影子，那是一株高高的，长得很美观的野苹果树射下的。这的是读书的所在；虽然我晓得是徒然的，我却去拿一本书来，自己安身于草地上。

夏天里我绝不能在户外读书。虽说是阴影，明亮的阳光却满照着，夏天的阴影其实是最耀目的日光。书页是这么雪白同难堪，字母是墨黑得这么厉害，意思同大旨不十分明了了，因为眼睛同心儿都不能专注到上面。写下来的人类思想和幻想在夏天明亮光线之下变成灰白无力了。眼睛走到别处了，更痴心地落到青青草场同菩提树片树叶上面。心儿更深刻地，更辽远地走到蓝蔚天空梦一般的神秘里去。有时，决定写下这种神秘同甜蜜的感觉，当我正沉浸于里面时候，我搬出桌子，墨水，

and sat there in the midst of the summer day. Three words, and where is the thought? Gone. The paper is so obviously paper, the ink so evidently ink, the pen so stiff; all so inadequate. You want colour, flexibility, light, sweet low sound — all these to paint it and play it in music, at the same time you want something that will answer to and record in one touch[1] the strong throb of life and the thought or feeling, or whatever it is that goes out into the earth and sky and space, endless as a beam of light. The very shade of the pen on the paper tells you how utterly hopeless it is to express these things. There is the shade and the brilliant gleaming whiteness; now tell me in plain written words the simple contrast of the two. Not in twenty pages, for the bright light shows the paper in its common fibre-ground, coarse aspect, in its reality, not as a mind-tablet[2].

The delicacy and beauty of thought or feeling is so extreme that it cannot be inked in[3], it is like the green and blue of field and sky, of veronica flower and grass blade, which in their own existence throw light and beauty on each other, but in artificial colours repel. Take the table indoors again, and the book; the thoughts and imaginings

---

1 touch: stroke 一笔；描写。
2 mind-tablet: 英国经验派哲学家认为人类一切知识都是来自经验，没有什么先天的观念（innate ideas），所以把人心比成一块白板（tablet），知识是后来刻上去的。
3 to be inked in: to be written down 写下来。

纸，夏日艳丽中坐在那儿。写下三个字，思想到那儿去了呢？消失了。纸是这么分明地一张纸，墨水这么显然地是墨水，笔是这么生硬；一切都是这么不合式。你需要色彩，柔性，光，甜蜜的低音——要这些东西来画出那情调。要这些东西来构成音乐传出那情调，同时你要某一个东西能响应同一下子记下生命力强烈的跳动同冲入天地空间的，不绝如一线光明的思想，或者情感，或者其他任何东西。纸上笔的影子就告诉你想传出这些情调是多么完全绝望的事情。这里有阴影同明朗发亮的白色；现在请你用明白的字句来说出这二者简单的相反。二十页也说不完，因为明亮的阳光照出纸的本身，它通常纤维的质地，粗糙的表面，它的真实，不是雕上思想的板子。

思想或情感的精致同美丽是这么趋于极端，简直不能用墨水勾来；它是像田地同天空，水苦荬花同草片那种青色同蓝色：它们天然彼此互相增光同美，但是一变成人工的彩色就令人厌恶了。再把桌子同书搬进去罢；别人的思想同幻想是看不进去

of others are vain, and of your own too deep to be written. For the mind is filled with the exceeding beauty of these things, and their great wondrousness and marvel. Never yet have I been able to write what I felt about the sunlight only. Colour and form and light are as magic to me. It is a trance. It requires a language of ideas to convey it. It is ten years since I last reclined on that grass plot, and yet I have been writing of it as if it was yesterday, and every blade of grass is as visible and as real to me now as then. They were greener towards the house, and more brown tinted on the margin of the strawberry bed, because towards the house the shadow rested longest. By the strawberries the fierce sunlight burned them.

The sunlight put out the books I brought into it just as it put out the fire on the hearth indoors. The tawny flames floating upwards could not bite[1] the crackling sticks when the full beams came pouring on them. Such extravagance of light overcame the little fire till it was screened from the power of the heavens. So here in the shadow of the American crab tree the light of the sky put out the written pages. For this beautiful and wonderful light excited a sense of some likewise beautiful and wonderful truth, some unknown but grand thought hovering as a swallow above. The swallows hovered and did not alight, but they were there. An inexpressible thought quivered in

---

1 to bite: to burn 燃烧。

的，你自己的思想同幻想又深沉得无法描状出来。因为心儿是充满了这些东西非常的美妙同它们的瑰奇伟丽。单是我对于阳光的感觉，我一向就无法传之于墨笔。色，形，光对于我简直是含有魔力。这是一阵的消魂。必定要全是观念，不落言诠的文字才能传出内中的感觉。我前次躺在这块草地上于今已十年了，然而我描摹时恍如是昨日的事，每片叶此时正同那时一样显明，一样地真实。这些草近屋子那方更青些，莓树丛旁更带棕色些，因为近屋子的地方阴影滞得最久。莓树旁边猛烈的日光把它们烧焦。

阳光把我带到它里面去的书弄得黯淡无光，正如它把户内火炉处的火弄得黯淡无光。黄褐色的上升火焰不能燃烧那发出嘎嘎声的木头，当充满的日光泻水一般向它们射来。这种光线的挥霍把小火压倒了，等到有帘幕把它同天空的威力隔开。同样地，在这里野苹果树下，天光使写着字的书页显出惨淡。因为这个美丽奇怪的光叫我们感到一种同样美丽奇怪的真理，一些我们所不知的，但是很伟大的思想徘徊空中，有如燕子。燕子徘徊于上，并不栖止，但是它们的确在那儿。一些说不出的

the azure overhead; it could not be fully grasped, but there was a sense and feeling of its presence. Before that mere sense of its presence the weak and feeble pages, the small fires of human knowledge, dwindled and lost meaning. There was something here that was not in the books. In all the philosophies and searches of mind there was nothing that could be brought to face it, to say. This is what it intends, this is the explanation of the dream. The very grass-blades confounded the wisest, the tender lime leaf put them to shame[1], the grasshopper derided them, the sparrow on the wall chirped his scorn. The books were put out, unless a screen were placed between them and the light of the sky — that is, an assumption, so as to make an artificial mental darkness. Grant some assumptions — that is, screen off the light — and in that darkness everything was easily arranged, this thing here and that yonder. But Nature grants no assumptions, and the books were put out. There is something beyond the philosophies in the light, in the grass-blades, the leaf, the grasshopper, the sparrow on the wall. Some day the great and beautiful thought which hovers on the confines of the mind will at last alight. In that is hope, the whole sky is full of abounding hope. Something beyond the books, that is consolation.

---

1 to put to shame: to disgrace by excelling 羞辱之。

思想在上头蓝蔚里颤动；它不让我们一手抓到，却叫我们晓得同感到它在那儿。只要一觉得它的出现，微弱的文字，人类知识的小火，就渐见衰落，以至于失却意义了。从这里就可以见天下有些东西是书里找不到的。在一切哲学同心灵的追求里，没有一件东西值得拿出来跟它相对，说，"这是它的意义，这是这一场梦的解释"。草片就把最有智慧的人弄迷惑了，柔嫩的菩提树叶叫他们惭愧，蟋蟀讥笑他们，墙上的黄雀歌唱出他的藐视。书籍是变成黯淡无光了，除非它同天光用一个帘幕隔开——那是说，立一个假定，以做成人造的心灵黑暗。肯立下一些假定——那是说，把亮光遮住——在黑暗里一切东西都易于安排，这个东西放这里，那个东西放那里。但是"自然"不许有这种假定，书籍于是就黯淡无光了。光，草片，叶子，蟋蟀，墙上的黄雀含有一种神秘，那是哲学力所不能及的。有一天，这些徘徊心中境界旁边的伟大美丽思想会终于栖止人间了。这里面含有一个希望，整个天空全是默默地含着这个希望。一些跳出书籍范围以外的东西，这是个安慰。

The little lawn beside the strawberry bed, burned brown there, and green towards the house shadow, holds how many myriad grass-blade? Here they are all matted together, long and dragging each other down. Part them, and beneath them are still more, overhung and hidden. The fibres are intertangled, woven in an endless basket-work and chaos of green and dried threads. A blamable profusion this; a fifth as many would be enough; altogether a wilful waste here. As for these insects that spring out of it as I press the grass, a hundredth part of them would suffice. The American crab tree is a snowy mount in spring; the flakes of bloom[1], when they fall, cover the grass with a film — a bushel of bloom, which the wind takes and scatters afar. The extravagance is sublime. The two little cherry trees are as wasteful; they throw away handfuls of flower; but in the meadows the careless, spendthrift ways of grass and flower and all things are not to be expressed. Seeds by the hundred million float with absolute indifference on the air. The oak has a hundred thousand more leaves than necessary, and never hides a single acorn. Nothing utilitarian — everything on a scale of splendid waste. Such noble, broadcast, open-armed waste is delicious to behold. Never was there such a lying proverb as "Enough is as good as a feast." Give me the feast; give me squandered millions of seeds, luxurious

---

1 the flakes of bloom: 这里以雪片来比盛开的白花。

莓丛邻近的小草地，那方面烧焦了，近屋影的地方却是绿色，含有多少亿万的草片呢？这儿它们都纠缠一起，长的，互相望〔往〕下拉扯的。将它们劈开，它们底下却更多，被盖着的，瞧不见的。它的纤维是头绪纷繁的，织成个无限复杂，像篮子一样的组织，和绿色的，干燥的一团混淆的线条。这就是个该骂的奢靡；只要五分之一就已够了；这里全是一场故意的浪费。至于我手一压到草上，跳出来的小虫，它们的一百分之一就足够了。野苹果树春天里是一座雪山；雪片一般的繁花，当它们下落，把草地铺上一层薄膜——整篓的花，风儿来抓住，散之四方。那种奢靡真是壮丽。两株小樱桃树是同样的浪费；它们扔开盈握的鲜花；但是草地上花草同其他东西浪子般，不在乎的态度是无法形容了。无数亿兆的种子极端随便地在空中浮游。橡树有十万片多余的叶子，而且一粒橡实也不隐藏。毫无唯用主义的精神———一切都是大规模的阔绰虚费。这样高贵的，撒种似的，两臂张开的浪费看起来真有意思。"足够等于过多"这是个再错不过的一句俗话。给我过多罢；给我以乱花掉

carpets of petals, green mountains of oak leaves. The greater the waste, the greater the enjoyment — the nearer the approach to real life. Casuistry is of no avail; the fact is obvious; Nature flings treasures abroad, puffs them with open lips alone on every breeze, piles up lavish layers of them in the free open air , packs countless numbers together in the needles of a fir tree. Prodigality and superfluity are stamped on everything she does. The ear of wheat returns a hundredfold the grain from which it grew. The surface of the earth offers to us far more than we can consume — the grains, the seeds, the fruits, the animals, the abounding products are beyond the power of all the human race to devour. They can, too, be multiplied a thousandfold. There is no natural lack. Whenever there is lack among us it is from artificial causes, which intelligence should remove.

From the littleness, and meanness, and niggardliness forced upon us by circumstances, what a relief to turn aside to the exceeding plenty of Nature! There are no bounds to it, there is no comparison to parallel it, so great is this generousity. No physical reason[1] exists why every human being should not have sufficient, at least, of necessities. For any human being to starve, or even to be in trouble about the procuring of simple food, appears, indeed, a strange and

---

1 physical reason: 就是指 natural lack。

的百万种子，柔软如地毡的落下花瓣，青山似的橡树叶子罢。越是过多，越是快乐——也更近于真实的生活了。诡辩曲解是无用的；事实非常分明；"自然"四散宝贝，用张开的嘴唇顺着每阵和风把它们吹飞，滥堆起无数层于自由的大气之中，捆起数不尽的宝贝于一棵松树的松针里面。她所干的一切都载有奢侈和多余的色彩。麦穗还它所从生的一粒种子以百倍的谷粒。地面所供给的远超过我们所能消耗的——谷物，种子，鲜果，走兽，丰富的产物是人类绝不能吃光的。而且，它们还可以增加千倍。并没有天然缺乏这么一回事。无论何时我们感到缺乏，那是由于人造的原因，是智力所该想法消灭的。

看见了环境迫到我们身上的小气，卑鄙同吝惜，再掉过头来一瞧"自然"十分的丰饶，是多么觉得神爽呀！它没有界限，没有一个别的东西能够跟它比得上，它的慷慨是这么伟大呀。从自然界里找不出一个理由为什么个个人不能都得到，最少，生活的必需品。有人挨饿，甚至于有人会为谋得粗食而焦虑，真是件没有道理的奇怪事情，完全颠倒的，与常识相违的，假

unaccountable thing, quite upside down[1], and contrary to sense, if you do but consider a moment the enormous profusion the earth throws at our feet. In the slow process of time, as the human heart grows larger, such provision, I sincerely trust, will be made that no one need ever feel anxiety about mere subsistence. Then, too, let there be some imitation of this open-handed generosity and divine waste. Let the generations to come feast free of care, like my finches on the seeds of the mowing-grass, from which no voice drives them. If I could but give away as freely as the earth does!

The white-backed eave-swallow has returned many, many times from the shallow drinking-place by the brook to his half-built nest. Sometimes the pair of them cling to the mortar they have fixed under the eave, and twitter to each other about the progress of the work. They dive downwards with such velocity when they quit hold that it seems as if they must strike the ground, but they shoot up again, over the wall and the lime trees. A thrush has been to the arbour yonder twenty times; it is made of crossed laths, and overgrown with "tea-plant"[2], and the nest is inside the lath-work. A sparrow has visited the rose tree by the wall — the buds are covered with aphides. A brown tree-creeper has been to the limes, then to the cherries, and even to a stout lilac stem. No matter how small the

---

1 upside down: inverted 相反的。

使你只想一下地面扔到我们脚旁的这巨大的丰饶产物。时间慢慢地过去，人心渐渐能并包兼容，我诚心相信能够有这样设备，没有个人用得着为糊口问题而操心。到那时，让我们也以这种放开手的慷慨同神圣的浪费罢。让将来的时代无忧无虑地大吃特吃，像我的黄雀吃割下的草的种子一样，没有声音把它们从那里赶走。若使我能够像地面那样随意给与，那是多么好呀！

白背的檐燕从溪旁的浅水回到他筑成一半的巢窝已经有许多回了。有时，他们一对抓着他们黏在檐下的泥土，彼此呢喃，漫话他们工作的进行。当他们松脚时侯，他们这么猛烈地望〔往〕下冲去，好像他们一定会触地，但是他们又一直飞起，飞过墙头同菩提树。一只画眉到那边的亭子有二十次了；那是父互的条板做成的，外面长上茶树，巢是在编织的条板的里面。一只黄雀来访问墙旁的玫瑰树——花蕾上满是蚜虫。一只棕色的旋木雀到菩提树去，然后到樱桃树，甚至于栖止在丁香花的

---

2 tea-plant：a climbing shrub with small lilac flowers 一种爬树，有淡紫色小花。

tree, he tries all that are in his way. The bright colours of a bullfinch were visible a moment just now, as he passed across the shadows farther down the garden under the damson trees and into the bushes. The grasshopper has gone past and along the garden-path, his voice is not heard now; but there is another coming. While I have been dreaming[1], all these and hundreds out it the meadow have been intensely happy. So concentrated on their little work in the sunshine, so intent on the tiny egg, on the insect captured, on the grass-tip to be carried to the eager fledglings[2], so joyful in listening to the song poured out for them or in pouring it forth, quite oblivious of all else. It is in this intense concentration that they are so happy. If they could only live longer! — but a few such seasons for them — I wish they could live a hundred years just to feast on the seeds and sing and be utterly happy and oblivious of everything but the moment they are passing. A black line has rushed up from the espalier apple yonder to the housetop thirty times at least. The starlings fly so swiftly and so straight that they seem to leave a black line along the air. They have a nest in the roof, they are to and fro it and the meadow the entire day, from dawn till eve. The espalier apple, like a screen, hides the meadow from me, so that the descending starlings appear to dive

---

1 dreaming: day-dreaming 白天做梦。
2 fledgling: young bird 小鸟。

粗干上。不管是株多么细弱的树,是他路之所经的他总得试一试。刚才看见大为鲜明的彩色一瞥眼过去,当他路过花园那边小梅树阴影之下,穿过灌木丛中。蟋蟀走过花园里的小路,他的声音现在听不见了;但是另有一个来。当我这样沉醉于梦的情调时候,这许多以及草地里成千成万的东西都在兴高采烈。是这样专心于他们太阳光下的小工作,这样注意于他们的小蛋,攫得的小虫同将带给渴望着的小鸟的草尖,这样快乐倾听为他们而唱的歌声或者自己振喉高唱,完全忘却其他一切的东西了。因为是这样热心地精神专注,他们才得如是欣欢。若使他们能够命活得长些!——只要能过几季这样的生活也是好的——我希望他们能够活一百岁,只是尽量大吃种子,歌唱,极端怡然,忘却了一切,只晓得当下的良好时光。一条黑线从那边苹果棚突然射到屋顶最少有三十回了。椋鸟飞得这么疾,这么直,他们仿佛留下一条黑线在空中。他们有个窝在屋顶,终日自破晓到黄昏就来往于屋顶与草地之间。苹果棚像个帘幕将草地遮住,使我看不见,所以下降的椋鸟好似突入它后面的一个空间。向

into a space behind it. Sloping downwards the meadow makes a valley; I cannot see it, but know that it is golden with buttercups, and that a brook runs in the groove of it.

Afar yonder I can see a summit beyond where the grass swells upwards to a higher level than this spot. There are bushes and elms whose height is decreased by distance on the summit, horses in the shadow of the trees, and a small flock of sheep crowded, as is their wont, in the hot and sunny gateway. By the side of the summit is a deep green trench, so it looks from here, in the hill-side: it is really the course of a streamlet worn deep in the earth. I can see nothing between the top of the espalier screen and the horses under the elms on the hill. But the starlings go up and down into the hollow space, which is aglow with golden buttercups, and, indeed, I am looking over a hundred finches eagerly searching, sweetly calling, happy as the summer day. A thousand thousand grasshoppers are leaping, thrushes are labouring, filled with love and tenderness, doves cooing — there is as much joy as there are leaves on the hedges. Faster than the starling's flight my mind runs up[1] to the streamlet in the deep green trench beside the hill.

Pleasant it was to trace it upwards, narrowing at every ascending step, till the thin stream, thinner than fragile glass, did but

---

1 my mind runs up: my fancy hurries to 我的幻想跑到。

下倾斜去，草地变成一个谷；我不能瞧见它，但是知道那是丛生了毛茛，显出金黄色，有一条溪水流过谷里的细沟。

那边远处，我能望见一个高原，高原之后草向上长，比此地高一层。高原上生有灌木同榆树，它们的高度因为距离远而减低了，树影里有几匹马，一小群羊聚在太阳晒得很热的门口，它们总是喜欢这样。高原旁边，从这儿看去，有一个绿色的深沟；其实是条河道深陷入地中。在树棚的顶同山上榆树下的马匹中间，我瞧不出什么。但是椋鸟飞进飞出这个空间，那是丛生了毛茛，显出金黄色，真的，我看见许多黄雀热烈地觅食，甜蜜地叫唤，快乐得有如夏天。整千整万的蟋蟀跳动着，画眉工作着，满心是爱同柔情，鸽子作鸪鸪声——乐事真是有如篱上绿叶那么多。比椋鸟飞得更快，我神驰到山旁绿色深沟里的溪水。

这真快乐，望上追踪这个溪水，它是一步一步窄上去的，等到末了这条细流，比纤草还细，只是在石头上滑过。再小一

merely slip over the stones. A little less and it could not have run at all, water could not stretch out to greater tenuity. It smoothed the brown growth on the stones, stroking it softly. It filled up tiny basins of sand and ran out at the edges between minute rocks of flint. Beneath it went under thickest brooklime, blue flowered, and serrated waterparsnips, lost like many a mighty river for awhile among a forest of leaves. Higher up masses of bramble and projecting thorn stopped the explorer, who must wind[1] round the grassy mound. Pausing to look back a moment there were meads under the hill with the shortest and greenest herbage, perpetually watered, and without one single buttercup, a strip, of pure green among yellow flowers and yellowing[2] corn. A few hollow oaks on whose boughs the cuckoos stayed to call, two or three peewits coursing up and down, larks singing, and for all else silence. Between the wheat and the grassy mound the path was almost closed, burdocks and brambles thrust the adventurer outward to brush against the wheat-ears. Upwards till suddenly it turned, and led by steep notches in the bank, as it seemed, down to the roots of the elm trees. The clump of elms grew right over[3] a deep and rugged hollow; their branches reached out across it, roofing[4] in the cave.

  Here was the spring, at the foot of a perpendicular rock, moss-

---

  1 to wind: to go in curved course 绕过去。

点儿,就不能流动了,水是无法弄得更细的。它洗滑石上长的棕色东西,轻轻地抚摩着。它灌满沙砾砌成的小凹处,从小燧石的两旁流出。下边,它从极密的开着绿花的婆婆纳同锯齿形的防风草底下走过,像许多大河那样暂时隐藏于群叶之中。再高些,一堆一堆的覆盆子同伸出来的荆棘把探幽者挡住了,他必得绕着这块草丘走。停步回头一看,山下有小草地,长有极短极绿的草,永远有水灌溉着,没有一根毛茛,是黄花同转黄的谷粒中的一条纯绿。几棵空心的橡树,鸽子就栖息枝上发出鸪鸪声音,两三只田凫上下飞翔,天鹨歌唱着,此外就是静寂了。麦田同草丘之间路差不多塞满了,牛蒡同覆盆子将探险者推出来去拂麦田的麦穗。一直上升,等到忽然转个方向,顺着两岸的陡谷,好像一直引到榆树的根旁。榆丛的正底下有个崎岖的深坑;它们的树枝斜横于上面,将这个洞盖住。

  泉水就出这里,在壁直岩石的脚旁,岩石下部满生了藓苔,

---

 2 yellowing:turning yellow 正在转黄色。

 3 right over:directly over 刚在上面。

 4 roofing:covering with roof 盖着;遮着。

grown low down, and overrun with creeping ivy higher. Green thorn bushes filled the chinks and made a wall to the well, and the long narrow hart's-tongue streaked the face of the cliff. Behind the thick thorns hid the course of the streamlet, in front rose the solid rock, upon the right hand the sward came to the edge — it shook every now and then as the horses in the shade of the elms stamped their feet — on the left hand the ears of wheat peered over the verge. A rocky cell in concentrated silence of green things. Now and again a finch, a starling, or a sparrow would come meaning to drink — athirst from the meadow or the cornfield — and start and almost entangle their wings in the bushes, so completely astonished that any one should be there. The spring rises in a hollow under the rock imperceptibly, and without bubble or sound. The fine sand of the shallow basin is undisturbed — no tiny water-volcano pushes up a dome of particles. Nor is there any crevice in the stone, but the basin is always full and always running over. As it slips from the brim a gleam of sunshine falls through the boughs and meets it. To this cell I used to come once now and then on a summer's day, tempted, perhaps, like the finches, by the sweet cool water, but drawn also by a feeling that could not be analysed. Stooping, I lifted the water in the hollow of my hand — carefully, lest the sand might be disturbed — and the sunlight gleamed on it as it slipped through my fingers. Alone in the green-roofed cave, alone with the sunlight and the pure water, there

高一些都是爬藤。绿色的茨丛塞着裂罅，做成了这口井的一面围墙，长而窄的凤尾草一条一条附于峭壁之上。泉水的来路隐匿于浓密的茨丛之后，坚固的岩石立在前面，右边草地直到边际——泉水时时颤动，当榆树影里的马儿在那儿顿足——左边麦穗从边际俯视着。绿物的十分静寂之中一所岩石的小穴。有时一只黄雀，一只椋鸟或者一只麻雀来这儿打莫〔尖〕饮水——从草地或谷田口渴飞来——惊愕一下，几乎将它们的翅膀缠在茨丛里，他们是这么奇怪会有人来到这儿。泉水不知不觉地从岩石下一空处涌出，没有潺潺的声音，真是一点儿也不响。浅凹处里面的细砂是丝毫不动的——并没有向上爆发的水散出一圈一圈的水泡。当它滑出凹处的边沿时候，一线日光从树枝射来，与它相遇。夏天里我常到这个小穴，也许像黄雀一样，给甜蜜的冷水所引诱，但是还有一种不能分析的感觉把我拉来。弯下腰来，我用掌心盛水——小心地，怕的是沙会被扰动了——当它顺我手指滑去时候，阳光照着它。独自在这绿色盖着的小穴，独自跟阳光同净水一起，我所感觉到的不止这些东西。

was a sense of something more than these. The water was more to me than water, and the sun than sun. The gleaming rays on the water in my palm held me for a moment, the touch of the water gave me something from itself. A moment, and the gleam was gone, the water flowing away, but I had had them. Beside the physical water and physical light I had received from them their beauty; they had communicated to me this silent mystery. The pure and beautiful water, the pure, clear, and beautiful light, each had given me something of their truth.

So many times I came to it, toiling up the long and shadowless hill in the burning sunshine, often carrying a vessel to take some of it home with me. There was brook, indeed; but this was different, it was the spring; it was taken home as a beautiful flower might be brought. It is not the physical water, it is the sense of feeling that it conveys. Nor is it the physical sunshine; it is the sense of inexpressible beauty which it brings with it. Of such I still drink, and hope to do so still deeper.

对于我水不是普通的水，太阳也不是普通的太阳了。我手掌里的水反映的阳光使我凝神一会儿，水的接触给我以它特有的感觉。一会儿，光散了，水流了，但是我已获得它们的神髓了。在物质上的水同物质上的光之外，我还从它们得到它们的美；它们与我以这个默然的神秘。洁净美丽的水，洁净美丽而明澈的光，各给我以它们真实的一部分。

有许多次我到这里来，在灼热的阳光之下勉力走上这长的、没有阴影的小山，常常带一只瓶去取一些水回家。邻近有一条小河，不错；但是这个却不同，它是泉水；把它带回正如采一朵美丽的花回家。重要的不在物质上的水，而在它所含的那种情调，不在物质上的日光，而在它所带来的无法形容的甜美感觉。我现在还是喝这种饮料，希望能够更深切地喝着。

Augustine Birrell

Actors

Most people, I suppose, at one time or another in their lives, have felt the charm of an actor's life, as they were free to fancy it, well-nigh irresistible.

What is it to be a great actor? I say a great actor, because (I am sure) no amateur ever fancied himself a small one. Is it not always to have the best parts[1] in the best plays; to be the central figure of every group; to feel that attention is arrested the moment you come on the stage; and (more exquisite satisfaction still) to be aware that it is relaxed when you go off; to have silence secured for your smallest utterances; to know that the highest dramatic talent has been exercised to invent situations for the very purpose of giving effect to your

---

1 parts: particular characters acted in a drama 戏中的脚色。

戏　　子

许多人，我想，一生里总有一个时期觉得戏子生活，他们自己所臆测的，具有几乎不能抵抗的魔力。

当一个名角是怎么样呢？我说一个名角，因为（我敢说）没有一个喜欢唱戏的人曾经承认自己是个小戏子。那岂不是常常演最好剧本里那些最好的脚色；做每一群脚色里的中心人物；觉得你一上台，大家注意都被吸到你身上来；而且（那是更甜蜜的满意）知道空气不会那么紧张了，当你下台时候；就是你最细微的一句话，大家也得肃静倾听，知道最高的编剧天才一向从事于创造局面，他们惟一的目的是使"你"的话动人，

words and dignity to your actions; to quell all opposition by the majesty of your bearing or the brilliancy of your wit; and finally, either to triumph over disaster, or if you be cast in tragedy, happier still, to die upon the stage, supremely pitied and honestly mourned for at least a minute? And then, from first to last[1], applause loud and long — not postponed, not even delayed, but following immediately after. For a piece of diseased egotism[2] — that is, for a man[3] — what a lot is this!

  How pointed, how poignant the contrast between a hero on the boards[4] and a hero in the streets! In the world's theatre[5] the man who is really playing the leading part — did we but know it — is too often, in the general estimate, accounted but one of the supernumeraries, a figure in dingy attire, who might well be spared, and who may consider himself well paid with a pound a week. His utterances procure no silence. He has to pronounce them as best he may, whilst the gallery sucks its orange, the pit pares its nails, the boxes babble, and the stalls yawn. Amidst these pleasant distractions he is lucky if

---

  1 from first to last: from beginning to end 从始至终。
  2 diseased egotism: abnormal egotism 病态的利己主义。
  3 for a man: 这里讥笑人们都是病态的利己主义者。
  4 the boards: the stage.
  5 the world's theatre: the world is a theatre, the earth a stage, 这是十七世纪英国诗人 Thomas Heywood 的名句。

"你"的行动庄严；利用你态度的堂皇或者你才智的灿烂来压下一切反对的势力；最后，也许是打倒不幸，得胜而回，或者，若使你演悲剧，那么更幸福了，就在舞台上死去，受人们深刻地怜悯，诚实地哀悼，最少有一分钟？而且，从始至终，响亮的，长久的喝彩——不是延期的，甚至于不是犹豫的，却是立刻跟着的。由一个病态的惟我主义者看来——这就是说由一个凡人看来——这是个多么可羡的命运呀！

舞台上的英雄同大街上的英雄的显著差异是多么分明，多么痛切！在世界舞台上，真真主要的脚色——假使我们看得出——常常被一般人们认为不过是个冗物，一个色彩暗淡的人，十分用不着的，他假使每星期挣到一镑钱，就得自满，以为得到很好的报酬了。"他"说的话没有人静默去听。他得尽他的本领把那些话好好地说出，而楼座人们却在那儿吮啜橘子，后厅人们却在那儿修指甲，包厢人们却在喋喋胡谈，正厅人们却在打呵欠。在这些乐意的纷扰之中，他总算运气好，若使有人肯

he is heard at all; and perhaps the best thing that can befall him is for somebody to think him worth the trouble of a hiss. As for applause, it may chance with such men, if they live long enough, as it has to the great ones who have preceded them, in their old age.

"When they are frozen up within, and quite
The phantom of themselves,
To hear the world applaud the hollow ghost,
Which blamed the living man."

The great actor may sink to sleep, soothed by the memory of the tears or laughter he has evoked, and wake to find the day far advanced, whose close is to witness the repetition of his triumph, but the great man will lie tossing and turning as he reflects on the seemingly unequal war be is waging with stupidity and prejudice, and be tempted to exclaim, as Milton[1] tells us he was, with the sad prophet Jeremy: "Woe is me, my mother, that thou hast borne me, a man of strife and contention!"

The upshot[2] of all this is, that it is a pleasanter thing to represent greatness than to be great.

But the actor's calling is not only pleasant in itself — it gives pleasure to others. In this respect, how favourably it contrasts with

---

1 John Milton (1608—1674),英国大诗人,《失乐园》的作者。
2 upshot: conclusion 结论。

去听他说的话；也许，他所能遇到的最好事情是有人会以为他还值得一哑。至于喝彩，这班人也许会碰到，假使他们的命活得够长，正如生于他们之前那些大人物所遭遇的，在他们老年时候——

"当他们心里冻得冷冰冰了，

外面也只剩有从前他们的影子，

听到世界向这空心的幽灵喝彩，

从前却漫骂他，当他是个活人时候。"

伟大的戏子可以记起他所激发的泪或笑，觉得安慰而入睡，醒时看见早晨已经去一大半了，黄昏时他的胜利又将重现出来；但是伟人却将辗转反侧躺着，当他想到他跟愚蠢同偏见所打的这个好像战斗力不平均的仗，他将像米尔敦告诉我们的那样，学起悲哀预言者泽里米的口吻，呐喊道："悲哉，我的母亲呀，你生下了我，一个竞争奋斗的人！"

这些话的结论是：扮一个伟人比当一个伟人是可乐得多。

戏子的职业不单本身是可乐的——它而且使别人快乐。在

the three learned professions[1]!

Few pleasures are greater than to witness some favourite character, which hitherto has been but vaguely bodied forth by our sluggish imaginations, invested with all the graces of living man or woman. A distinguished man of letters, who years ago was wisely selfish enough to rob the stage of a jewel and set it in his own crown, has addressed to his wife some radiant lines which are often on my lips:

"Beloved, whose life is with mine own entwined,

In whom, whilst yet thou wert my dream, I viewed,

Warm with the life of breathing womanhood,

What Shakespeare's visionary eye divined—

Pure Imogen[2]; high-hearted Rosalind[3],

Kindling with sunshine all the dusk greenwood;

Or changing with the poet's changing mood,

Juliet[4], or Constance[5] of the queenly mind."

But a truce to these compliments.

"I come to bury Caesar, not to praise him."[6]

---

1 the three learned profession：指牧师，律师，医生这三种职业。

2 Imogen：莎翁悲剧 *Cymbeline* 中一个被冤枉的贤妻。

3 Rosalind：莎翁喜剧 *As You Like It* 中一个快乐的姑娘。

4 Juliet：莎翁悲剧 *Romes & Juliet* 中殉情的少女。

5 Constance：莎翁历史剧 *King John* 中一个良母。

6 这是莎翁悲剧 *Julius Caesar* 中的名句。

这方面，它同三种学者职业比较起来是好得多了！

世上没有几件乐事能够超过看到所爱好的戏中人物，一向只靠我们这迟钝的想像模糊地把它虚拟出来，现在却加上活人一切优美的仪容态度了。一个有名的文人许多年前自私自利得很聪明，把舞台上一朵明星抢去，安在自己冠冕上面，他献给他妻子几行漂亮的诗，是常在我的嘴上：

"亲爱的人儿，她的生命跟我自己的连在一起了，

当你还只是我的梦中人时候，

在你身上我看到沙士比亚的灵眼所预先瞧见的，

却加上了生机活泼的女性生命——

你是洁净的易摩真；心地高尚的洛扎林德，

用精神阳光照耀了蒙眬的绿林；

或者随诗人变换的心境而变换，

是个朱丽叶，或者端庄有如皇后的昆丝坦司。"

但是不再说这些赞美戏子的话题。

"我是来安埋该撒，不是来赞美该撒。"

It is idle to shirk disagreeable questions, and the one I have to ask is this, "Has the world been wrong in regarding with disfavour and lack of esteem the great profession of the stage?"

That the world, ancient and modern, has despised the actor's profession cannot be denied. An affecting story I read many years ago — in that elegant and entertaining work. Lemprière's *Classical Dictionary* — well illustrates the feeling of the Roman world. Julius Decimus Laberius was a Roman knight and dramatic author, famous for his mimes, who had the misfortune to irritate a greater Julius[1], the author of the *Commentaries*, when the latter was at the height of his power. Caesar, casting about[2] how best he might humble his adversary, could think of nothing better than to condenm him to take a leading part in one of his own plays. Laberius entreated in vain. Caesar was obdurate, and had his way[3]. Laberius played his part— how, Lemprière sayeth not; but he also took his revenge, after the most effectual of all fashions, the literary. He composed and delivered a prologue of considerable power, in which he records the act of spiteful tyranny, and which, oddly enough, is the only specimen of his dramatic art that has come down to us. It contains lines which, though they do not seem to have made Caesar, who sat smirking in

---

1 Julius：指 Julius Caesar。
2 casting about：trying to discover 试去找。
3 to have one's way：to carry out one's purpose 达到目的。

躲避不快意的问题是没有用的，我所要发的问题是这个，"世人到底有没有错，那样嫌恶同瞧不起舞台这个大职业？"

古往今来世上的人们对于优伶职业加以藐视，这是个无法否认的事实。许多年前我念过的一篇动人的故事——见于那部秀丽有趣的著作，楞普里耳的《古典辞林》——很可以描摹罗马时代人们的意见。朱理亚·狄西马斯·拉俾立阿斯是罗马一个骑士同编剧家，以哑剧有名于当世，不幸触怒了一个比他更伟大的朱理亚，《纪事》的作者，而且当这第二个朱理亚威权极盛的时候。该撒细思怎样最能使他的敌人丢脸，觉得最好的法子是罚他演他自己编的一本剧里的主角。拉俾立阿斯恳求无效。该撒绝不通融，一定要为所欲为。拉俾立阿斯演他所扮的角色了——怎样演呢，楞普里耳却没有说；但是他也报复一下，而且是各种样子里最可怕的那一个，文字上的报复。他编好背出一段颇有力气的序词，记载这可鄙的专制行为，真是奇怪，他所编的戏剧只有这一小段流传下来，做个样子。里面有些文字确然好像没有使坐在正厅上强装笑容的该撒赧颜，却使一千九

the stalls, blush for himself, make us, 1,900 years afterwards, blush for Caesar. The only lines, however, now relevant are, being interpreted, as follows:

"After having lived sixty years with honour, I left my home this morning a Roman knight, but I shall return to it this evening an infamous stage-player. Alas! I have lived a day too long."

Turning to the modern world, and to England, we find it here the popular belief that actors are by statute rogues, vagabonds, and sturdy beggars. This, it is true, is founded on a misapprehension of the effect of 39 Eliz. chap. 4, which only provides that common players wandering abroad without authority to play, shall be taken to be "rogues and vagabonds;" a distinction which one would have thought was capable of being perceived even by the blunted faculties of the lay mind.

But the fact that the popular belief rests upon a misreading of an Act of Parliament three hundred years old does not affect the belief, but only makes it exquisitely English[1], and as a consequence entirely irrational.

Is there anything to be said in support of this once popular prejudice?

It may, I think, be supported by two kinds of arguments. One

---

1 exquisitely English：这是嘲笑英国人是多半不懂道理专重成见的。

百年后的我们替该撒赧颜。可是同我们现在所说有关的文句解释起来是如下：

"光荣地活了六十年了，今早离家时我是一个罗马骑士，今晚回去时我却是个声名狼藉的戏子。唉呀！我多活这一天了。"

转过来看一看近代世界同英国，我们瞧见在这儿大家都相信按法律戏子是真做无赖，浪子同顽梗的乞丐。不错，这是由于误解伊利沙伯朝三十九年所颁的法令第四章的意思，那只指定没有得到演剧权利，到处漫游的普通戏子当被认做"无赖同浪子"；这么一种分别人们会以为就是外行人的迟钝感觉也可以看出。

但是这个事实，一种普遍的意见由于误解三百年前议会所通过的一个法令，并不变更那个意见，只使它更显得带有英国习气，因此是完全没有道理的。

关于这个曾经风行一时的偏见到底有什么话可以替它辩护呢？

我想可以用两种理由来辩护。一个是根据这种职业的本质，

derived from the nature of the case, the other from the testimony of actors themselves.

A serious objection to an actor's calling is that from its nature it admits of no other test of failure or success than the contemporary opinion of the town. This in itself must go far[1] to rob life of dignity. A Milton may remain majestically indifferent to the "barbarous noise" of "owls and cuckoos, asses, apes, and dogs," but the actor can steel himself to no such fortitude. He ran lodge no appeal to posterity. The owls must hoot, the cuckoos cry, the apes yell, and the dogs bark on his side, or he is undone. This is of course inevitable, but it is an unfortunate condition of an artist's life.

Again, no record of his art survives to tell his tale or account for his fame. When old gentlemen wax garrulous over actors dead and gone, young gentlemen grow somnolent. Chippendale the cabinet-maker is more potent than Garrick[2] the actor. The vivacity of the latter no longer charms (save in Boswell[3]); the chairs of the former still render rest impossible in a hundred homes.

This, perhaps, is why no man of lofty genius or character has ever condescended to remain an actor. His lot pressed heavily even on so mercurial a trifler as David Garrick, who has given utterance

---

1 to go far: to achieve much 很成功。
2 David Garrick (1717—1779), 英国十八世纪名角。
3 James Boswell (1740—1795), 约翰生传记的作者。

一个是根据戏子们自己的证据。

戏子职业一个严重的毛病是由于它的本质。它除开当时城市里人们的意见外不能有其他成败的标准。这一点就大可以使生活失去尊严。像米尔敦那么一个大诗人可以俨然地不理"猫头鹰,杜鹃,驴子,猴子,狗","野蛮的叫声",但是一个戏子不能这么刚愎冷然。他不能留下什么诉诸后世。猫头鹰,杜鹃,猴子,狗必得叫喊啼吠来喝他的采,否则他就毁了。这当然是无法避免的事情,但是这是一个艺术家生活的一个不幸条件。

而且,他的艺术没有留下什么记载来说出他的艺术或者解释他的所以成名。当老年人津津有味细谈起已死的过去戏子,年青人就昏昏思睡了。细工木匠契盆对尔是比戏子加立克更有势力。后者的轻快活泼不再感动我们了(除开在波兹卫尔的书里);前者做的椅子还使一百个家庭不能安坐。

也许因此所以没有一个才力或者性格崇高的人肯屈身甘于永远当一个戏子。戏子的命运甚至于使像大辟·加立克这么一个生性乐天,随随便便的人也觉得有沉重的担压着,他用其他

to the feeling in lines as good perhaps as any ever written by a successful player:

> "The painter's dead, yet still he charms the eye,
> While England lives his fame shall never die;
> But he who struts his hour upon the stage,
> Can scarce protract his fame thro' half an age;
> Nor pen nor pencil can the actor save —
> Both art and artist have one common grave."

But the case must be carried farther than this, for the mere fact that a particular pursuit does not hold out any peculiar attractions for soaring spirits will not justify us in calling that pursuit bad names[1]. I therefore proceed to say that the very act of acting, i.e., the art of mimicry, or the representation of feigned emotions called up by sham situations, is, in itself, an occupation an educated man should be slow to adopt as the profession of a life.

I believe — for we should give the world as well as the devil its due — that it is to a feeling, a settled persuasion of this sort, lying deeper than the surface brutalities and snobbishnesses visible to all, that we must attribute the contempt, seemingly so cruel and so ungrateful, the world has visited upon actors.

---

1 calling bad names: appling disparaging terms 骂。

成功戏子所未曾写下的那么精美文字来发泄这种牢骚：

"画家死了，然而他还能使人们看着喜悦，

英国存在于世上时候，他的令誉绝不会灭亡；

可是在戏台上大踏步走来走去的人，

他的令誉几乎不能够延长到下半代；

文字同图画都不能救起戏子——

艺术家死了，艺术也就随之俱亡。"

但是话还得讲深一层，因为单单这么一个事实，某一种事业在志趣高尚人们看来没有什么特别好处，还不足贻我们以口实来漫骂这种事业。因此我接着要说做戏这个举动——摹拟的艺术，或者可以叫做虚设情境所引起的假情感的表现——本身就是受过教育的人所不愿采为终身职业的一种工作。

我相信——我们不要冤枉世人，正如我们不要冤枉魔鬼——这种感觉，这种深信，比大家都看得见的表面上的凶横同趋炎更深一层，我们当认为是世人对于戏子的蔑视，好像是这么残忍同忘恩的，之所由来。

I am no great admirer of beards, be they never so luxuriant or glossy, yet I own I cannot regard off the stage the closely shaven face of an actor without a feeling of pity, not akin to love. Here, so I cannot help saying to myself, is a man who has adopted as his profession one which makes upon him at the very outset the demand that he should destroy his own identity. It is not what you are, or what by study you may become, but how few obstacles you present to the getting of yourself up as somebody else[1], that settles the question of your fitness for the stage. Smoothness of face, mobility of feature, compass of voice — these things, but the toys of other trades, are the tools of this one.

Boswellians[2] will remember the name of Tom Davies as one of frequent occurrence in the great biography. Tom was an actor of some repute, and (so it was said) read *Paradise Lost*[3] better than any man in England. One evening, when Johnson was lounging behind the scenes at Drury (it was, I hope, before his pious resolution to go there no more).[4] Davies made his appearance on his way to the stage in all the majesty and millinery of his part. The situation is pic-

---

  1 the getting of yourself up as somebody else：把自己打扮成别人。
  2 Boswellians：admirers of Bowell's writings 喜欢阅读 Boswell 著作（《约翰生传》）的人们。
  3 *Paradise Lost*：英国最伟大的史诗，记亚当被摈出乐园事。
  4 约翰生从前喜欢到后台去，后来觉得与自己不好，就下个决心不再到那儿去。

我不是个非常热烈地赞美胡子的人，不管它们是多么华美或者明亮，然而我自认看到下台戏子刮得非常光的脸孔，我不能不感到一种怜悯，不是近于爱的那么一种怜悯。我免不了向自己说道：这里有一个人他所采的职业一开头就要他破坏他的自我。不是靠你这人本身是怎么样，或者经过揣摩后你会变成怎么样，而是靠着从你到你所打扮的他人中间阻碍是多么少，来解决你宜不宜于舞台生活这个问题。脸孔的平滑，面貌的易变，音调的范围——这些东西在别种职业里不过是好玩的成分，在这个职业里却变成工具了。

熟读波兹卫尔的《约翰生传》的人们会记得汤姆·苔微士这个名字常见于这本伟大传记里。汤姆是个颇有声望的戏子，（据说）念《失乐园》比英国任何人都好。一天晚上，当约翰生在德鲁立剧院后台闲逛时候（我希望这是在他立下不再到那儿去的那个虔敬决心之前），苔微士走出来到前台去，穿了他所扮的角色的华丽衣服同装饰。情境是堪入画的。十八世纪伟大的，

turesque. The great and dingy Reality of the eighteenth century, the Immortal[1], and the bedizened little player. "Well, Tom," said the great man (and this is the whole story), "well, Tom, and what art thou to-night?" "What art thou to-night?" It may sound rather like a tract, but it will. I think, be found difficult to find an answer to the question consistent with any true view of human dignity.

Our last argument derived from the nature of the case is, that deliberately to set yourself as the occupation of your life to amuse the adult and to astonish, or even to terrify, the infant population of your native land, is to degrade yourself.

Three-fourths of the acted drama is, and always must be, comedy, farce, and burlesque. We are bored to death by the huge inanities of life. We observe with horror that our interest in our dinner becomes languid. We consult out doctor, who simulates an interest in our stale symptoms, and after a little talk about Dr. Diet, Dr. Quiet, and Dr. Merriman, prescribes Toole[2]. If we are very innocent we may inquire what night we are to go, but if we do we are at once told that it doesn't in the least matter when we go, for it is always equally funny. Poor Toole! To be made up every night as a safe prescription

---

1 the Immortal：指约翰生。
2 Toole：英国有名的丑角，据说有一次他患病，医生劝他去看 Toole 演戏，一开心病就会好了。

黯淡的"现实",不朽的大人物,同这华装的小戏子。"喂,汤姆,"这位伟人说道(这是全部的故事),"喂,汤姆,今晚你是谁?""今晚你是谁?"听起来这好像是宗教论文的话,但是我想很不容易找一句答话跟人们真正的尊严不相冲突。

根据这种职业的本质我们用来辩护的最末一个理由是,故意拿替你祖国的大人们解闷同使你祖国的孩子们惊讶,甚至于恐慌,来做你终身的职业,是贬黜你自己的身价。

排演的戏剧的四分之三是,不得不是,喜剧,趣剧,杂剧。我们给人生的大空虚厌烦得要死了。我们不胜惶恐地看到我们的吃饭趣味变冷淡了。我们就诊于我们的医生,他假装出关心我们衰弱现象的样子,稍稍谈一下慎饮食,安逸,同快乐三者都可以治病,就叫我们去看丑角图鲁。若使我们很不知世故,我们也许会问那一晚去好哩,但是假使我们问了,他会立刻答道,我们那一晚去,这是毫无关系的,因为总是同样的可笑。可怜的图鲁呀!夜夜化装起来做人们忧郁病的对症药方!使人

for the blues[1]! To make people laugh is not necessarily a crime, but to adopt as your trade the making people laugh by delivering for a hundred nights together another man's jokes, in a costume the anthor of the jokes would blush to be seen in, seems to me a somewhat unworthy proceeding on the part of a man of character and talent.

To amuse the British public is a task of herculean[2] difficulty and danger, for the blatant monster is, at times, as whimsical and coy as a maiden, and if it once makes up its mind not to be amused, nothing will shake it. The labour is enormous, the sacrifice beyond what is demanded of saints. And if you succeed, what is your reward? Read the lives of comedians, and closing them, you will see what good reason an actor has for exclaiming with the old-world poet:

"Odi profanum vulgus!"[3]

We now turn to the testimony of actors themselves.

Shakespeare is, of course, my first witness. There is surely significance in this. "Others abide our question," begins Arnold's[4] fine sonnet on Shakespeare — "others abide our question; thou art free." The little we know about our greatest poet has become a commonplace. It is a striking tribute to the endless loquacity of man, and a

---

1 the blues: low spirits 忧郁。
2 herculean: requiring the strength of Hercules 需巨大力的。
3 Odi profanum vulgus!: I hate the vulgar public.
4 Matthew Arnold（1822—1888），英国诗人同大批评家。

们发笑并不一定是罪恶，但是以此为职业，一百晚接连着背诵另一个人所编的笑话，披上这些笑话的作者穿起来会赧颜的衣服，由我看起来，这好像是有品格，有本领的人不值得一干的勾当。

使英国大众开心是个极难，极危险的工作，因为这个吵闹的怪物有时却奇异同害羞得有如处女，假使它曾下个决心不受娱乐，那么没有一个东西能够撼动它。所费的力气非常大，牺牲有甚于被尊为圣者的人们。假使你成功了，你的报酬是什么呢？请念演喜剧的戏子的传记，掩卷之后，你将看出一个戏子会很有理由去跟古代的诗人喊道："啊，我厌恶这庸俗的观众！"

我们现在转过来看一看戏子自己的证据。

莎士比亚当然是我第一个的见证。"别人让我们细问，"安诺德歌颂莎士比亚的那首美妙的十四行诗是这样开头——"别人让我们细问；你却是逍遥自在的。"关于我们最伟大的诗人我们所知道的一些已变成老生常谈了。这真是人类无限度饶舌的一个显著的成绩，同时也可以证明这个大动物是不肯被剥夺去

proof how that great creature is not to be deprived of his talk, that he has managed to write quite as much about there being nothing to write about as he could have written about Shakespeare if the author of *Hamlet*[1] had been as great an egoist as Rousseau[2]. The fact, however, remains that he who has told us most about ourselves, whose genius has made the whole civilized world kin[3], has told us nothing about himself, except that he hated and despised the stage. To say that he has told us this is not, I think, any exaggeration. I have, of course, in mind the often quoted lines to be found in that sweet treasury of melodious verse and deep feeling, the *Sonnets of Shakespeare*[4]. The 110th begins thus:

"Alas! 'tis true I have gone here and there,

And made myself a motley to the view,

Gor'd[5] my own thoughts, sold cheap what is most dear.

Made old offences of affections new."

And the 111th:

"O for my sake do thou with Fortune chide,

---

1 *Hamlet*：莎翁的悲剧杰作。

2 Rousseau：Jean Jacques Rousseau（1712—1778），法国大文学家，《民约论》的作者。

3 whose genius has made the whole civilized world kin：莎翁有一名句，one touch of nature makes the whole world kin。

4 *Sonnets of Shakespeare*：莎翁十四行诗一百六十四首真情流露，恳挚动人，为莎翁集中惟一自白的诗。

说话的权利,他居然能够设法写下许多说关于莎士比亚是没有什么可说的;假使这位《哈姆雷特》的作者像卢骚那样喜欢谈自己,这班人所能说的话也不过这么多了。然而事实仍然是:这位作者向我们说出许多关于我们的话,他的天才使整个文明世界感到亲密,关于他自己是丝毫没有提到的,除开说他厌恶同蔑视舞台这一点。说他告诉我们了这些,我想并不是过实之言。我当然心里记着那常常引用的句子,见于那本音调甜美,情感深刻的可喜诗库,《莎士比亚十四行诗集》里。第一百十首开头是这样子:

"唉呀!不错,我四处漫游,

把我自己打扮成五颜六色让人们瞧,

扯碎我自己的思想,将顶宝贵的贱卖出去,

在新情感上加了旧的陵辱。"

一百十一首开头是这样子:

"为我的缘故,你毁骂'运命之神'罢,

---

5 gor'd: rent assender 扯破。

> The guilty goddess[1] of my harmful deeds,
> That did not better for my life provide
> Than public means, which public manners breeds.
> Thence comes it that my name receives a brand,
> And almost thence my nature is subdued
> To what it works on, like the dyer's hand:
> Pity me, then, and wish I were renewed."

It is not much short of three centuries since those lines were written, but they seem still to bubble with a scorn which may be indeed called immortal.

"Sold cheap what is most dear."

There, compressed in half a line, is the whole case against an actor's calling.

But it may be said Shakespeare was but a poor actor. He could write *Hamlet* and *As You Like It*; but when it came to casting the parts, the Ghost in the one and old Adam in the other[2] were the best he could aspire to. Verbose biographers of Shakespeare, in their dire extremity, and naturally desirous of writing a big book about a big man, have remarked at length that it was highly creditable to Shake-

---

1 the guilty goddess: 指"命运"之女神。
2 the Ghost in the one and old Adam in the other: 都是剧中最不重要的脚色。

这个有罪的女神迫我干下有害的事情,

她没有好好地安顿我的生活,

只使我靠大众为生,因此生了下流的习气,

因此我的名字受了一个玷污,

我的性情几乎因此也变得像,

它所作的工作,正如染师的手:

那么,可怜我罢,希望我能够更新。"

这几行诗写下已经快有三百年了,但是它们好像还吐出一种真可以说是不朽的怨声。

"将顶宝贵的贱卖出去。"

这里,在半句诗里,说尽戏子生涯的毛病。

但是也可以说莎士比亚只是个歹角。他能够写出《哈姆雷特》同《如愿》;但是说明扮剧中的人物,前一出戏的"鬼"同后一出戏的"老亚当"恐怕是他所能演的最高角色了。莎士比亚传记的累赘作者已经无话可说,觉得很窘迫了,又天然地想关于一个大人物该写一本大书,就拉拉扯扯说一大阵莎士比亚

speare that he was not, or at all events that it does not appear that he was, jealous, after the true theatrical tradition, of his more successful brethren of the buskin.

It surely might have occurred, even to a verbose biographer in his direst need, that to have had the wit to write and actually to have written the soliloquies in *Hamlet*, might console a man under heavier afflictions than the knowledge that in the popular estimate somebody else spouted those soliloquies better than he did himself. I can as easily fancy Milton jealous of Tom Davies as Shakespeare of Richard Burbage[1]. But — good, bad, or indifferent — Shakespeare was an actor, and as such I tender his testimony.

I now — for really this matter must be cut short — summon pell-mell all the actors and actresses who have ever strutted their little hour on the stage, and put to them the following comprehensive question: is there in your midst one who had an honest, hearty, downright pride and pleasure in your calling, or do not you all (tell the truth) mournfully echo the lines of your great master (whom nevertheless you never really cared for), and with him

"Your fortunes chide,

That did not better for your lives provide

---

1 Richard Burbage（1567—1619），专演莎翁剧的一个名角。

真值得钦佩，他没有，最少他并未见得有，妒忌那班更成功的优孟衣冠同志，像普通戏子一向那样子。

这是很分明的，就是觉得非常窘迫的传记家也会想到，有了写出，而且的确写出了，《哈姆雷特》里那段独语的本领，也足以安慰一个人了，就说他所蒙的不幸更有甚于知道在一般人们的评价里某一个人大声背诵这段比他来得高明。我不相信莎士比亚妒忌理查·柏贝治，正如我不能相信米尔敦会妒忌汤姆·苔微士。但是——不管好坏，或者是不好不坏——莎士比亚总是个戏子，因此我拉他来做一个证见。

我现在——这种讨论真该截短了——乱七八糟瞎召一切曾在舞台上踱〔度〕过他们的时间的男戏子同女戏子，向他们提出底下这个概括的问题：你们中间有没有一个人对于你们的职业是个老实的，出乎衷心的，十分的矜夸同喜欢，或者你们是不是（说句实话）都悲哀地附和你们大师（然而你们绝没有真真关心他）的诗句，同他一气〔起〕来——

"毁骂运气之神，

他没有好好地安顿我的生活，

Than public means, which public manners breeds."

They all assent: with wonderful unanimity.

But, seriously, I know of no recorded exception, unless it be Thomas Betterton, who held the stage for half a century — from 1661 to 1708 — and who still lives, as much as an actor can, in the pages of Colley Cibber's[1] *Apology*. He was a man apparently of simple character, for he had only one benefit-night all his life.

Who else is there? Read Macready's[2] *Memoirs* — the King Arthur of the stage[3]. You will find there, I am sorry to say, all the actor's faults — if faults they can be called which seem rather hard necessities, the discolouring of the dyer's hand; greedy hungering after applause, endless egotism, grudging praise — all are there; not perhaps in the tropical luxuriance[4] they have attained elsewhere, but plain enough. But do we not also find, deeply engrained and constant, a sense of degradation, a longing to escape from the stage for ever?

He did not like his children to come and see him act, and was always regretting — Heaven help him![5] — that he was not a barrister-

---

1 Colley Cibber (1671—1757),英国编剧家同戏子。

2 William Charles Macready (1793—1873),英国演悲剧的名角。

3 the King Arthur of the stage：King Arthur是古代名王,这里拿来比他是剧界大王。

4 the tropical luxuriance：热带植物特别茂盛,故云。

5 此句原文缺译。——编者注

只使我靠大众为生，因此生了下流的习气。"

他们全承认了，而且一致得出奇。

但是，严重说起来，我不知道有一个例外留于记载里，除非是汤马斯·柏忒吞，他执舞台的牛耳有半世纪——从一六六一年到一七〇八年——在科勒·息柏的《自传》里他可以说是不朽了，戏子也只能够这样不朽。他分明是个性格简单的人，因为他一生里只演一次慈善剧。

此外还有谁呢？请念马克里狄的《回忆录》——他可算做舞台上的亚塔尔王。你们将看到，说起来我觉得难过，戏子所有的恶习——若使那些可以叫做恶习，其实好像是残酷环境使其不得不然，正如染师的手，贪得观众的喝彩，无穷的自私自利，吝于赞美他人——这些恶习他全是有了；也许不像别地方那样茂盛得有如热带植物，可是也够显明了。但是我们不是也看到深深染上的，常在心头的一种受辱之感，一种永远跟舞台脱离关系的希冀？

他不喜欢他子女去看他演戏，总是惋惜——他不是个律师。

at-law. Look upon this picture and on that. Here we have Macbeth¹, that mighty thane; Hamlet, the intellectual symbol of the whole world of modern thought; Strafford², in Robert Browning's fine play; splendid dresses, crowded theatres, beautiful women, royal audiences; and on the other side, a rusty gown, a musty wig, a fusty court, a deaf judge, an indifferent jury, a dispute about a bill of lading, and ten guineas on your brief — which you have not been paid, and which you can't recover — why, "'tis Hyperion³ to a satyr!"

Again, we find Mrs. Siddons⁴ writing of her sister's marriage:

"I have lost one of the sweetest companions in the world. She has married a respectable man, though of small fortune. I thank God she is off the stage." What is this but to say, "Better the most humdrum of existences with the most 'respectable of men,' than to be upon the stage"?

The volunteered testimony of actors is both large in bulk and valuable in quality, and it is all on my side.

Their involuntary testimony I pass over lightly. Far be from me the disgusting and ungenerous task of raking up a heap of the weak-

---

1 Macbeth：莎翁悲剧杰作。
2 Strafford：Robert Browning（1812—1889），英国大诗人所编的戏中间的脚色。
3 Hyperion：A Titan 天神之一。
4 Mrs. Siddons（1755—1831），英国演悲剧的有名女伶。

请看这种生活同那种生活的写真。在这方面我们有马克白，这位伟大的贵族；哈姆雷特，整个近代思想界理智的象征；罗伯·勃浪宁美妙剧本中的斯得拉得福；华丽的服装，拥挤的戏院，美女，娇客；在那方面却只有一件变色的长衫，一顶发霉的假发，一所酸臭的法庭，一位耳聋的法官，一班冷淡的陪审，关于一纸提单的辩论，你的诉状代价十个金币——这笔款你还没有收到，而且你也无法追讨——嗳吓，"这真是天神与魑魅之分！"

此外，我们又有息顿斯太太的信做证据，信里提到她妹妹的结婚：

"我失掉了世上最可亲的一个伴侣。她嫁给一个有身分的人，虽然没有多少财产。我谢谢上帝，她现在离开舞台了。"这岂不是等于说，"还是跟最'有身分'的人度最无聊的生活好些，比起献身舞台上"？

戏子自愿说出的证据其量甚多，其质甚可贵，而且都是可以证实我的意见的。

戏子无意中呈现出的证据我将轻轻地忽略过去。我绝不肯干那惹人厌恶的刻薄勾当，去遍搜过去已死的男戏子女戏子一

nesses, vanities, and miserableness of actor and actresses dead and gone. After life's fitful fever they sleep (I trust) well[1]; and in common candour, it ought never to be forgotten that whilst it has always been the fashion — until one memorable day Mr. Froude[2] ran amuck of it — for biographers to shroud their biographees (the late Mr. Russell Lowell[3] must bear the brunt of this word on his broad shoulders) in a crape veil of respectability, the records of the stage have been written in another spirit. We always know the worst of an actor, seldom his best. David Garrick was a better man than Lord Eldon, and Macready was at least as good as Dickens[4].

There is, however, one portion of this body of involuntary testimony on which I must be allowed to rely, for it may be referred to without offence.

Our dramatic literature is our greatest literature. It is the best thing we have done. Dante may overtop Milton, but Shakespeare surpasses both. He is our finest achievement; his plays our noblest possession; the things in the world most worth thinking about. To live daily in his company, to study his works with minute and loving care — in no spirit of pedantry searching for double endings, but in order

---

1 莎翁的名句：After life's fitful fever, he sleeps well. — Macbeth。
2 Mr. Froude：James Anthony Froude（1818—1894），英国历史家。
3 Russell Lowell（1819—1891），美国诗人，那个字是他创出来的。
4 Charles Dickens（1812—1870），英国大小说家。

大堆的弱点，虚荣同卑贱。度了一生像旋作旋辍的热病的生活，他们将睡得（我相信）很熟；而且说句公平话，我们千万不要忘却素来——等到值得纪念的那一天夫鲁德先生横冲直撞乱闹一阵——传记作家总是拿一层体面的薄纱遮住被传记的人们（这个字的锐气罗素•罗厄尔得拿他的宽肩来承当），舞台生活的记载一向却是用另一种精神来描写。我们总是知道一个戏子最大的坏处，很少晓得他最大的好处。大辟•加立克是比厄尔顿爵士具有更好的性格，马克里狄最少总同迭更司一样的善良。

可是有一部分无意中现出的证据我却要利用，因为那说出来是不会开罪于任何人的。

我们的戏剧文学是我们最伟大的文学。那是我们最大的成就。但丁也许高过米尔敦，但是莎士比亚都在他们两人之上。他是我们最美妙的成绩；他的剧本是我们最高贵的财产；是世上最值得沉思默索的东西。天天与他为伍，仔细地，缱绻地攻读他的作品——绝不是带了寻找押韵的学究精神，却是为着要

to discover their secret, and to make the spoken word tell upon[1] the hearts of man and woman — this might have been expected to produce great intellectual if not moral results.

The most magnificent compliment ever paid by man to woman is undoubtedly Steele's[2] to the Lady Elizabeth Hastings. "To love her," wrote he, "is a liberal education." As much might surely be said of Shakespeare.

But what are the facts — the ugly, hateful facts? Despite this great advantage — this close familiarity with the noblest and best in our literature — the taste of actors, their critical judgment, always has been and still is, if not beneath contempt, at all events far below the average intelligence of their day. By taste, I do not mean taste in flounces and in furbelows, tunics and stockings; but in the weightier matters of the truly sublime and the essentially ridiculous. Salvini's[3] Macbeth is undoubtedly a fine performance; and yet that great actor, as the result of his study, has placed it on record that he thinks the sleep-walking scene ought to be assigned to Macbeth instead of to his wife. Shades of Shakespeare and Siddons, what think you of that?

It is a strange fatality, but a proof of the inherent pettiness of

---

1 to tell upon: to affect 感动。
2 Richard Steele (1672—1729), 英国初期小品文作家。
3 Tommaso Salvini (1829—1916), 意大利名角。

发现它们的秘密，使背出的话能够感动男女的心——我们总是预料这会产生理智上，若使不是道德上良好的结果。

男人向女人所说过的最伟丽的恭维话无疑地是斯提尔向伊利莎伯·哈斯丁斯所说的那句名言。"爱她，"他说，"等于受一遍高等普通教育。"关于莎士比亚的确也很可以这样说。

但是事实怎么样呢——丑恶的，讨厌的事实？虽然有这个大便宜——跟我们文学里最高尚，最伟大的作家亲切的接近——戏子的趣味，他们的批评能力。一向是，而且此刻还是，假使没有到不值得藐视的程度，也远不如当时一般人们的智力了。我说趣味，我不是指关于裙襞，缘饰，紧身衣，袜子的趣味；却是关于更重要的事情，真正壮伟的情调同精粹纯正的诙谐。萨尔微尼扮的马克白无疑地是个巧妙的串演；然而这位伟大的戏子经过一番研究之后，写下来告诉人们说他认为梦中步行那一幕应当属马克白，不该属于他的妻子。莎士比亚同息顿斯太太的幽灵呀，你们觉得这句话怎么样呢？

这真是个奇怪的厄运，但是也可以证明戏子艺术本身的下

the actor's art, that though it places its votary in the very midst of literary and artistic influences, and of necessity informs him of the best and worthiest, he is yet, so far as his own culture is concerned, left out in the cold — art's slave, not her child.

What have the devotees of the drama taught us? Nothing! It is we who have taught them. We go first, and they come lumbering after. It was not from the stage the voice arose bidding us recognise the supremacy of Shakespeare's genius. Actors first ignored him, then hideously mutilated[1] him; and though now occasionally compelled, out of deference to the taste of the day, to forego their greenroom traditions, to forswear their Tate and Brady[2] emendations, in their heart of hearts they love him not; and it is with a light step and a smiling face that our great living tragedian flings aside Hamlet's tunic or Shylock's gaberdine to revel in the melodramatic glories of *The Bells* and *The Corsican Brothers*.

Our gratitude is due in this great matter to men of letters, not to actors. If it be asked, "What have actors to do with literature and criticism?" I answer, "Nothing;" and add, "That is my case."

But the notorious bad taste of actors is not entirely due to their living outside Literature, with its words for ever upon their lips, but

---

1 then hideously mutilated him：英国从前演员对于剧本常随意更改字句，莎翁作品亦蒙此难。

2 Tate and Brady：改窜莎翁戏剧辞句的人。

劣，虽然它把它的信徒放在文学同艺术各种影响的当中，而且不得不告诉他以世上最佳美，最可贵的杰作，他在自己修养方面还是有向隅之感——他是艺术的奴才，不是她的娇儿。

戏剧的信徒教了我们什么呢？一点也没有！我们却教了他们。我们打头走，他们笨拙地追随着。舞台并没有叫我们承认莎士比亚天才的高超。戏子们起先不理他，后来可恶地残害他的著作；现在虽然有时逼于尊重目下大家的意见，舍弃他们戏房的传统，断然誓绝像他们前辈退特同布累狄那种修改剧文的习惯，可是在他们心的深处他们并不爱他；我们现在演悲剧的伟大戏子是脚步轻快，脸上微笑地把哈姆雷特的束腰紧身衣或晒罗克的宽阔上身衣扔在一边，去纵姿于《钟》或者《科西嘉兄弟》这类戏杂剧般的热闹。

在赏识莎氏天才这件大事情上，我们该感谢文人，不是该感谢戏子。若使有人问，"戏子与文学同批评有何关系？"我将答道："毫无关系；"而且加一句，"这足以证明我的主张。"

但是戏子有名的趣味恶劣也不完全因为他们心灵与文学没

none of its truths engraven on their hearts. It may partly be accounted for by the fact that for the purposes of an ambitious actor bad plays are the best.

In reading actors' lives, nothing strikes you more than their delight in making a hit[1] in some part nobody ever thought anything of before. Garrick was proud past all endurauce of his Beverley in the *Gamester,* and one can easily see why. Until people saw Garrick's Beverley, they didn't think there was anything in the *Gamester*; nor was there, except what Garrick put there. This is called creating a part, and he is the greatest actor who creates most parts.

But genius in the author of the play is a terrible obstacle in the way of an actor who aspires to identify himself once and for all with the leading part in it. Mr. Irving[2] may act Hamlet well or ill — and, for my part, I think he acts it exceedingly well — but behind Mr. Irving's Hamlet, as behind everybody else's Hamlet, there looms a greater Hamlet than them all — Shakespeare's Hamlet, the real Hamlet.

But Mr. lrving's Mathias is quite another kettle of fish[3], all of Mr. Irving's own catching. Who ever, on leaving the Lyceum, after seeing *The Bells*, was heard to exclaim, "It is all mighty fine; but

---

1 making a hit: making a success 成功。
2 Henry Irving (1838—1905), 英国名角。
3 quite another kettle of fishes: quite different affairs.

有融化在一起，它的字老是在他嘴上，它的深意却丝毫没有印到心上。还有一个事实也可以解释一部分，那就是由一个具有野心的戏子看来，坏剧本是最易串演很成功的。

阅读戏子的传记，最叫你惊奇的是他们喜欢把人们一向没有注意到的某一个剧中人物演得很出色。加立克扮《赌棍》中的柏味力得意到叫人难堪，我们很容易看出这里面的理由。在人们看见加立克所扮的柏味力之前，他们以为《赌棍》这本戏没有什么意思；的确是没有什么，除开加立克所加进去的表演。这叫做创造一个脚色，脚色创造得最多的就是最伟大的戏子。

但是编剧者的天才是戏子想一下子完全代表剧中主要脚色的一个可怕的障碍。伊文先生演哈姆雷特不管是好是坏——据我所知，他演得非常好——但是在伊文先生所扮的哈姆雷特，正如在个个其他人所扮的哈姆雷特之后，隐隐地有个比它们都更伟大的哈姆雷特——莎士比亚的哈姆雷特，真正的哈姆雷特。

可是伊文先生的马地亚斯却是完全另一回事了，那是伊文先生一手造成的。谁看完了《钟》，将走出来栖安戏院时候，会

that is not my idea of Mathias?" Do not we all feel that without Mr. Irving there could be no Mathias?

We best like doing what we do best; and an actor is not to be blamed for preferring the task of making much of a very little to that of making little of a great deal.

As for actresses, it surely would be the height of ungenerosity to blame a woman for following the only regular profession commanding fame and fortune the kind consideration of man has left open to her. For two centuries women have been free to follow this profession, onerous and exacting though it be, and by doing so have won the rapturous applause of generations of men, who are all ready enough to believe that where their pleasure is involved, no risks of life or honour are too great for a woman to run. It is only when the latter, tired of the shams of life, would pursue the realities, that we become alive to the fact — hitherto. I suppose, studiously concealed from us — how frail and feeble a creature she is.

Lastly, it must not be forgotton that we are discussing a question of casuistry, one which is "stuff o" the conscience, and where consequently words are all important.

Is an actor's calling an eminently worthy one? — that is the question. It may be lawful, useful, delightful, but is it worthy?

说,"演得很不错,但是我心中的马地亚斯不是这样子?"我们不是都觉得没有伊文先生就无从有马地亚斯吗?

我们最喜欢干我们能够干得最好的事情;戏子更喜欢在小事上有大成就,比起在大事上只有小成就,也是可以原谅的。

至于女戏子,那是再鄙贱不过的举动,去毁骂一个女人,因为她从事于男人仁爱为怀所让她干的惟一正当的名誉与钱财两得的职业。两世纪以来女人可以随意以此为业,虽然这是很麻烦同费劲的,她们这样干博得了历代男人的喝彩,他们肯相信凡是与他们快乐有关的事,女人生命同名誉的牺牲都是无妨。只是当她们厌倦于假装的人生,想去追求现实时候,我们才深切地觉得——我想一向是故意不去理这事实——她是个多么微弱无力的动物。

末了,我们千万别要忘却我们是讨论一个难下断语的问题,那是与内心有关系的,所以我们所用的字眼非常重要。

戏子的职业是个很值得干的吗?——这是我的问题。那也许是合法的,有用的,快乐的,但是值得干吗?

An actor's life is an artist's life. No artist, however eminent, has more than one life, or does anything worth doing in that life, unless he is prepared to spend it royally in the service of his art, caring for nought else. Is an actor's art worth the price? I answer, No!

戏子的生活是个艺术家的生活。一个艺术家，不管他多么有名，只能有此一生，在那一生里也不配说干了值得干的事情，除非他打算好好地将此生供献于他所从事的艺术，别的事全不在意。戏子的艺术值得这样牺牲吗？我答道，不！

Alfred George Gardiner

On Talking to One's Self

I was at dinner at a well-known restaurant the other evening when I became aware that someone sitting alone at a table near by[1] was engaged in an exciting conversation with himself. As he bent over his plate his face was contorted with emotion, apparently intense anger, and he talked with furious energy, only pausing briefly in the intervals of actual mastication. Many glances were turned covertly upon him, but he seemed wholly unconscious of them, and, so far as I could judge, he was unaware that he was doing anything abnormal. In repose his face was that of an ordinary business man, sane and self-controlled, and when he rose to go his agitation was over, and he looked like a man who had won his point.

---

1 near by: adjacent 邻近。

自 言 自 语

有一天晚上我在一家有名的馆子里用晚餐，那时我看出独自坐在我邻近桌子旁边的某一位先生正在热烈地跟自己说话。他对着盘子弯下身子，他的脸孔是被情感激动得变形了，分明是在盛怒之中；他愤然地用劲说话，只在真真咀嚼时候才暂停一会儿。许多人的眼睛都偷偷地射到他身上，他好像完全不觉得这些，据我所能推测的，他自己简直不知道他有一个变态的行动。沉静时候，他的脸孔是通常一个经纪人的脸孔，清醒的，能够自制的；当他站起来要走时候，他的兴奋已过去了，看起来他像一个辩论胜利了的人。

It is probable that this habit of talking to one's self has a less sinister meaning than it superficially suggests. It may be due simply to the energy of one's thought and to a concentration of mind that completely shuts out the external world. In the case I have mentioned it was clear that the man was temporarily detached from all his surroundings, that he was so absorbed by his subject that his eyes had ceased to see and his ears to hear. He was alone with himself, or perhaps with his adversary, and he only came back to the present with the end of his dinner and the paying of his bill. He was like a man who had emerged from another state of consciousness, from a waking sleep filled with tumultuous dreams. Obviously he was unaware that he had been haranguing the room in quite an audible voice for half an hour, and I daresay that if he were told that he had the habit of talking to himself he would deny it as passionately as you (or I) would deny that you (or I) snore in our sleep. And he would deny it for precisely the same reason. He doesn't know.

And here a dreadful thought assails me. What if I talk to myself, too? What if, like this man, I get so absorbed in the drama of my own mind that I cannot hear my own tongue going nineteen to the dozen[1]? It is a disquieting idea. A strong conviction to the contrary, I see, amounts to nothing. This man, doubtless, had a strong

---

1 nineteen to the dozen: pace of busy tongue.

也许这种自言自语的习惯不像外表上所暗示的那样含有不吉利的意思。也许只是因为一个人思想力的强壮，同他注意的集中，以致把外界完全忽略不管了。在我所提的这个例子里，那是很明显的，这个人暂时跟他的环境脱离关系了，他是如是被他所考虑的题材吸引住，他的眼睛停止看，他的耳朵停止听了。他独自跟自己，也许是跟他的对敌，一起等到食完付帐时候，他才回到眼前的世界来。他像一个从另一种意识状况里，从白天睁着眼睛做了许多狂梦里出来的人。他分明不晓得有半个钟头他很可以听得见的声音向房里人讲演，我敢说若使人们告诉他有自言自语的习惯，他将热烈地否认，不下于你（或者我）的否认你（或者我）当我们睡着时发鼾声。他的否认也刚是出于同样的理由。他自己是不晓得的。

这时候一个可怕的意思向我来袭。我有没有自言自语的习惯呢？那怎么好呢？我是不是也像这个人，如是沉迷于我自己心里的把戏，以致不能听到我的舌头在那儿胡说一阵？这是个使我不安的观念。我知道，坚决地相信自己没有这习惯，是毫无用处的。这个人无疑地坚决相信自己没有这习惯——也许对

conviction to the contrary — probably expressed an amused interest in anyone talking to himself as he passed him in the street. And the fact that my friends have never told me of the failing goes for nothing also. They may think I like to talk to myself. More probably, they may know that I do not like to hear of my failings. I must watch myself. But, no, that won't do[1]. I might as well say I would watch my dreams and keep them in check. How can the conscious state keep an eye on the unconscious? If I do not know that I am talking how can I stop myself talking?

Ah, happy thought. I recall occasions when I have talked to myself, and have been quite conscious of the sound of my voice. They have been remarks I have made on the golf links — brief, emphatic remarks dealing with the perversity of golf clubs and the sullen intractability of golf balls. Those remarks I have heard distinctly, and at the sound of them I have come to myself[2] with a shock, and have even looked round to see whether the lady in the red jacket playing at the next hole was likely to have heard me or (still worse) to have seen me.

I think this is evidence conclusive, for the man who talks to himself habitually never hears himself. His words are only the echo of his thoughts, and they correspond so perfectly that, like a chord in

---

1 to do: to answer the purpose; to serve 使得；足；行跟目的相合。
2 to come to oneself: to return to one's senses 清醒起来。

于其他自言自语的人还现出开心的注意,当他在街上从他身旁走过时候。我的朋友们从来没有说我有这个毛病,这也是无济于事的。他们也许以为我喜欢自言自语。他们也许知道我不喜欢听人们说我的缺点,这是更可能的。我必得自己留神。不,这也不行。我正可以说我要留神我的梦,不让它们做下去。意识状态怎么能够注目到无意识状态呢?若使我不知道我正在自言自语,我怎么能够挡住自己呢?

吓,一个快乐的意思。我记起来有时我自言自语,我就十分觉得自己的音调。那是我在高尔夫球场中所说的话——简短的,有力的话,关于高尔夫球棍的故意捣乱和高尔夫球的冥顽倔强。这些话我听得很清楚,听到那声音我吓了一跳清醒起来,甚至于转过身来看一看在邻近球孔打球的那位穿红短衣的姑娘大概听到了没有,或者(那是更坏了)看见了没有。

我想这是个确凿的证据,因为有自言自语习惯的人是绝不会自己听到的。他的话只是他思想的回声,它们是这么凑巧地相合,有如音乐上的和弦,是没有杂音的。我所看见的一位在

music, there is no dissonance. It was thus with the art student I saw copying a picture at the Tate Gallery. "Ah, a little more blue," he said, as he turned from the original to his own canvas, and a little later: "Yes, that line wants better drawing." Several people stood by watching his work and smiling at his uttered thoughts. He alone was unconscious that he had spoken.

There are, it is true cases in which the conscious and unconscious states seem to mingle — in which the intentional word and the unintentional come out almost in the same breath. It was so with Thomas Landseer, the father of Sir Edwin. He was one day visiting an artist, and inspecting his work. "Ah, very nice, indeed!" He said to his friend. "Excellent colour, excellent!" Then, as if all around him had vanished, and he was alone with himself, he added: "Poor chap, he thinks he can paint!"

And this instance shows that whether the habit is a mental weakness or only a physical defect, it is capable of extremely awkward consequences, as in the case of the banker who was ruined by unwittingly revealing his secrets while walking in the street. How is it possible to keep a secret or conduct a bargain if your tongue is uncontrollable? What is the use of Jones explaining to his wife that he has been kept late at the office if his tongue goes on to say, entirely without his knowledge or consent, that had he declared "no trumps"

忒特美术陈列所里摹画一张名画的艺术学生就是这样子。"吓,还是再加些蓝色,"他说,当他从原画抽过头来看他的幕布,过了一会儿又说:"是的,那条线应该好一点才是。"有几个人站在一旁,看他工作,对他这说出的思想微笑。只有他一个人不觉得他说话了。

不错,在一些情形里,意识的同无意识的状态好像混在一起——在这种时候,有意的和无意的话差不多一口气出来。托马斯·莲德丝儿,哀得音爵士的父亲,就是如此。一天他访问一位艺术家,看到他的作品,"吓,非常妙,真的!"他对他朋友说,"颜色配得极好,极好!"然后,仿佛他四旁的人们都消失了,他是独在一室之中的样子,他又说道:"可怜的孩子,他以为他会画图画!"

这个例子指出给我们看,无论这个习惯是心理的弱点或者只是生理的毛病,它是能够弄出极不好的结果,一位银行家就是如此,他当在街上闲步时胡里胡涂把他自己的秘密泄露了。怎么能够守个秘密,或者做生意,若使你的舌头不肯听你调度?琼斯向他妻子解释他在办公室有事情所以迟回来了,这有什么用呢,若使他自己毫不知道或者许可,他的舌头就自然而然说

in that last hand he would have been in pocket by his evening at the club? I see horrible visions of domestic complications and public disaster arising from this not uncommon habit.

And yet might there not be gain also from a universal practice of uttering our thoughts aloud? Imagine a world in which nobody had any secrets from anybody — could have no secrets from anybody. I see the Kaiser, after consciously declaring that his only purpose is peace, unconsciously blurting out to the British Ambassador that the ultimatum to Serbia is a "plant"[1] that what Germany means is war, that she proposes to attack Belgium, and so on. And I see the British Ambassador, having explained that England is entirely free from commitments, adding dreamily, "But if there's a war we shall be in it." In the same way Jones, after making Smith a firm offer of £30 for his horse, would say, absentmindedly, "of course it would be cheap at £50, and I might spring £55 if he is stiff about it."

It would be a world in which lies would have no value and deception would be a waste of time — a world in which truth would no longer be at the bottom of the well, but on the tip of every man's tongue. We should have all the rascals in prison and all the dishonest traders in the bankruptcy court. Secret diplomacy would no longer play with the lives of men, for there would be no secrets. Those little

---

1 plant: pre-arranged swindle 骗局。

道，假使最后一手说出了"不要胜牌"，那么他这晚上在俱乐部里会赢钱了？我臆测出可怕的景象，那是这个并不罕见的习惯引起的家庭纠纷同社会灾祸。

然而假使大家都大声说出他的思想，不是也有个好处吗？试想一个世界，里面没有一个人对于任何人守了什么秘密——不能够对于任何人有什么秘密。我看见德皇自觉地宣布他惟一的目的是和平，后来不自觉地对英国大使泄露出对于塞国的哀的米敦书是一种"骗局"——德国所要的是战争，她打算攻比利时，如此等等。我又看见英国大使声明了英国是完全没有参加了这个纠纷，做梦一般地说出，"但是若使打起仗来，我们将在内。"同样地，琼斯向斯密士坚决提出三十镑做他马的价钱，将心不在焉说道："就说五十镑还是便宜，我也许会增到五十五镑，若使他老不肯让价。"

那将是一种世界，在里面谎话是没有价值的，欺骗无非白费时候——一种世界，在里面真理不再躲在井底，而在个个人的口头上了。我们将把一切坏人都抓到监狱里去，一切不老实的商人都传到破产法庭来。秘密外交不再拿人命来做儿戏了，

perverse concealments that wreck so many lives would vanish. You, sir, who find it so easy to nag at home and so difficult to say the kind thing that you know to be true, would be discovered to your great advantage and to the peace of your household.

Yes, I think the world would go very well if we all had tongues that told our true thoughts in spite of us. But what a lot of us would be found out. My own face crimsons at the thought. So, perhaps, does yours.

因为不会有秘密了。那些牺牲这么多生命的乖戾的小隐蔽将消散了。你，先生，觉得在家发脾气是这么容易，说出你知道是真的那种殷勤话是那么困难，将被家人看破，与你大有利，你家庭也得到和平了。

是的，我想世界将弄得非常好，若使我们都有自己禁止不住的，说出我们实在思想的舌头。但是我们里面有多少人会被人们看破了。想到这里我自己的脸绯红了。你的也许也是这样罢。

Edward Verrall Lucus

The School for Sympathy

I had heard a great deal about Miss Beam's school, but not till last week did the chance come to visit it.

The cabman drew up at a gate in an old wall, about a mile out of the town. I noticed as I was waiting for him to give me change[1] that the Cathedral spire was visible down the road. I rang the bell, the gate automatically opened, and I found myself in a pleasant garden facing a square red ample Georgian[2] house, with the thick white window-frames that to my eyes always suggest warmth and welcome and stability. There was no one in sight but a girl of about twelve, with her eyes covered with a bandage, who was being led

---

1 change: money returned as balance of that tendered for payment 付钱后找还的零头钱。

同 情 学 校

我听过许多关于俾谟斯小姐办的学校的消息,可是一直到前星期才有机会去参观。

车夫停在古墙中的大门前,离城有一哩多远。当我等着车夫找零头钱给我的时候,我看到大礼拜堂的尖塔浮露在路的极端。我按了门铃,门自己开了,我面前就现有一个可爱的花园,对面有座红色的乔治时代的方正大屋,那种密密地布着的雪白窗格子我每看到时心中总起暖和,欢迎,稳固这些感觉。我只看见一个大约十二岁大的小姑娘,双眼都用绷带缚着,有一个

---

2 Georgian: of the time of Kings George I-IV,乔治第一至第四时代的。

carefully between the flower-beds by a little boy of some four years her junior. She stopped, and evidently asked who it was that had come in, and he seemed to be describing me to her. Then they passed on, and I entered the door which a smiling parlourmaid — that pretty sight! — was holding open for me.

Miss Beam was all that I had expected — middle-aged, authoritative, kindly, and understanding[1]. Her hair was beginning to turn grey, and her figure had a fulness likely to be comforting for a homesick child to look upon.

We talked idly for a little white, and then I asked her some questions as to her scholastic methods, which I had heard were simple.

"Well," she said, "we don't as a matter of fact[2] do much teaching here. The children that come to me — small girls and smaller boys— have very few formal lessons: no more than is needful to get application into them, and those only of the simplest — spelling, adding, subtracting, multiplying, writing. The rest is done by reading to them and by illustrated discourses, during which they have to sit still and keep their hands quiet. Practically there are no other lessons at all."

"But I have heard so much," I said, "about the originality of your system."

---

1 understanding: intelligent 有才干，有智力。

2 as a matter of fact: in point of fact, used expecially to introduce correction, 事实是如此，多半用做改正错误的引子。

差不多比她小四岁的男孩小心地带她缘着花床走。她停着不前，明明是问他进来的人是谁，他好像在那里描状我的样子给她听。一会儿他们走过去了，我也走进厅门，一个含笑的客厅女仆——那种使人看到会高兴的女仆！——开门请我进来。

俾谟斯小姐果然是像我所预料的——中年的岁数，很有权力的神气，可是又很和蔼可亲，聪明能干样子。她的头发已经有些转成灰色了，她的体态很丰满，那能够叫思家的小孩看着得到安慰。

我们闲谈一会儿，我就询问她所用的教育方法，我听说她的办法是很简单的。

她说："我们这里实在并没有教多少书。来我这里的小孩子——小小的女孩和更小的男孩——念规规矩矩的课本时间很少，都是那最浅易的入门功课：拼字，作文，加，减，乘，除。其余都是教员讲给他们听，拿些图书给他们看，那时候只要他们两只手不动，好好地坐着就是了。实际上我们除开这些以外并没有别的功课。"

"但是我听过许多人，"我说，"谈到你用的制度的新奇地方。"

Miss Beam smiled. "Ah, yes," she said, "I am coming to that. The real aim of this school is not so much to instil thought as thoughtfulness — humanity, citizenship. That is the ideal I have always had, and happily there are parents good enough to trust me to try and put it into execution. Look out of the window a minute, will you?"

I went to the window, which commanded a large garden and playground at the back.

"What do you see?" Miss Beam asked.

"I see some very beautiful grounds," I said, "and a lot of jolly children; but what perplexes me, and pains me too, is to notice that they are not all as healthy and active as I should wish. As I came in I saw one poor little thing being led about owing to some trouble with her eyes, and now I can see two more in the same plight; while there is a girl with a crutch just under the window watching the others at play. She seems to be a hopeless cripple."

Miss Beam laughed. "Oh, no," she said; "she's not lame, really; this is only her lame day. Nor are those others blind; it is only their blind day." I must have looked very much astonished, for she laughed again. "There you have an essential part of our system in a nutshell[1]. In order to get a real appreciation and understanding of misfortune into these young minds we make them participants in

---

1 in a nutshell: in few words 包含在几个字里。

俾谟斯小姐微微一笑。"呵，是的，"她说道，"我就要说到这点了。这个学校的真真目的不在于灌输思想，而在养成沉思默想的心境——仁爱，良好公民的态度。这是我始终不忘的理想，可喜的是有许多父母很好，肯相信我，让我把这理想拿来实行，试一试。请你望〔往〕窗外看一下。"

我走到窗前，看见一片大花园，后面是个游戏场。

"你看到什么没有？"俾谟斯小姐问我。

"我看见非常美丽的草地，"我说，"和一群快乐的小孩；但是使我莫名其妙的，又叫我心痛的是，我观察出他们都不像我所希望地那么健康活泼。我走进来时候，我瞧到一个可怜的小东西别人带着走，因为她的眼睛有毛病，现在我看见有两个也受同种的苦痛；窗户面前有一个倚着拐杖的女孩站着看旁人游戏。她好似是不可以救药的跛子。"

俾谟斯小姐大笑起来。"呵，不，"她说，"她的确不是个跛子；这不过是她当跛子的日子。旁的那几位也没有瞎了眼睛；这不过是他们当瞎子的日子。"我听了这话，脸上一定现出十分惊讶的神情，因为她又大笑了。"这点是我们制度的神髓所在。为的是要叫这些年青小孩心中对于人世的不幸有真切的同情和了解，我们使他们也受一下这些不幸的苦痛。每学期中每个小

misfortune too. In the course of the term every child has one blind day, one lame day, one deaf day, one maimed day, one dumb day. During the blind day their eyes are bandaged absolutely, and it is a point of honour not to peep. The bandage is put on overnight; they wake blind. This means that they need assistance in everything, and other children are told off to help them and lead them about. It is educative to both of them — the blind and the helpers."

"There is no privation[1] about it," Miss Beam continued. "Everyone is very kind, and it is really something of a joke, although, of course, before the day is over the reality of the affliction must be apparent even to the least thoughtful. The blind day is of course really the worst," she went on, "but some of the children tell me that the dumb day is the most dreaded. There, of course, the child must exercise will-power only, for the mouth is not bandaged... But come down into the garden and see for yourself how the children like it."

Miss Beam led me to one of the bandaged girls, a little merry thing, whose eyes under the folds were, I felt sure, as black as ash-buds. "Here's a gentleman come to talk to you," said Miss Beam, and left us.

"Don't you ever peep?" I asked, by way of an opening.

"Oh no," she exclaimed, "that would be cheating. But I'd no idea it was so awful to be blind. You can't see a thing. One feels one

---

1 privation: hardship 痛苦。

孩有瞎子日，跛子日，聋子日，残废日，哑巴日各一日。轮到他们当瞎子那天，他们的眼睛绝对是用绷带包着，若使跑去窥视那就算有损于人格。那绷带是在前一晚上缚好，第二天他一醒来就是个瞎子了。因此他的一切行动都得有人来帮忙，我们也告诉别个小孩去看护他，带着他走路。这样子他们两面——瞎子同那帮助他的人们——都学懂新道理。"

"对于装盲这个人并没有苦痛，"俾谟斯小姐继续着说，"个个人对他都是很仁慈的，实在有些开玩笑样子，虽然在那一日完了以前，就是最不用思想的小孩也会明白瞎子苦痛的真相。瞎子日当然真是最糟的，可是有些小孩告诉我哑巴日是最可怕的。那天小孩子当然要用他的毅力，嘴是没有绷带缚住的……还是走去园里，你自己看小孩子们怎么干罢。"

俾谟斯小姐带我到一个蒙着眼睛的女孩面前，一个快乐的小东西，我敢说带子后面的眼睛是槐花蕊一般黑的。"这里有位先生来同你说话，"俾谟斯小姐说着就走开了。

"你有偷看没有？"我用这句话来开头。

"没有，"她大声说道，"那变做骗人了。可是我起先不晓得瞎了眼睛是这么可怕的事。一些东西也瞧不到。时时刻刻总怕

is going to be hit by something every moment. Sitting down's such a relief."

"Are your guides kind to you?" I asked.

"Pretty good. Not so careful as I shall be when it's my turn. Those that have been blind already are the best. It's perfectly ghastly not to see. I wish you'd try!"

"Shall I lead you anywhere?" I asked.

"Oh, yes, " she said, "let's go for a little walk. Only you must tell me about things. I shall be so glad when today's over. The other bad days can't be half as bad as this. Having a leg tied up and hopping about on a crutch is almost fun, I guess. Having an arm tied up is a little more troublesome, because you have to get your food cut up for you, and so on; but it doesn't really matter. And as for being deaf for a day, I shan't mind that — at least, not much. But being blind is so frightening. My head aches all the time, just from dodging things that probably aren't there. Where are we now?"

"In the playground," I said, "going towards the house. Miss Beam is walking up and down the terrace with a tall girl."

"What has the girl got on?" my companion asked.

"A blue serge skirt and pink blouse."

"I think it's Millie," she said. "What colour's hair?"

"Very light," I said.

碰到什么东西。坐下来却减轻了不少的恐惧。"

"带你走路的人对于你很仁爱吗?"我问她。

"都还好。当轮到我来干他这种事,我会比他更小心些。已经有过瞎子日的人对我最好。看不见东西叫人会疑神疑鬼。我希望你也试一下。"

"我现在要带你到什么地方去呢?"我问道。

"呵,是的,"她说,"让我们散一会儿步。你却要告诉我许多东西。今天过了,我会喜欢得了不得。别个坏日子不会有这个日子一半的坏。把一只腿绑起来,倚着拐杖步步跳着走,我想差不多是玩笑。将一只手臂缚住了的确是比较麻烦些,因为你的菜要别人替你切,以及一切别的不便;但是实在也不什么碍事。至于整天装聋子,我是满不在乎的——最少,没有这么难过。变成个瞎子却是吓人的事。我的头不停地痛,有许多东西并不在那里,我却恐怕相撞,费力去避它。我们现在到那里了?"

我说:"在一个朝着屋子的游戏场。俾谟斯小姐同一个高高的女孩在草地上溜达。"

"那女孩穿着的是什么?"我的伴侣问我。

"毛绒蓝裙子,红色的斗篷。"

"我想是美利,"她说,"她头发是什么颜色?"

"很鲜明的。"我说。

"Yes, that's Millie. She's the head girl. She's awfully decent."

"There's an old man tying up roses," I said.

"Yes, that's Peter. He's the gardener. He's hundreds of yours old!"

"And here comes a dark girl in red, on crutches."

"Yes," she said, "that's Beryl."

And so we walked on, and in steering this little thing about I discovered that I was ten times more thoughtful already than I had any notion of, and also that the necessity of describing the surroundings to another makes them more interesting.

When Miss Beam came to release me I was quite sorry to go, and said so.

I returned to the town murmuring (inaccurately as ever) the lines:

Can I see another's woe

And not share their sorrow too?

O no, never can it be,

Never, never, can it be.

"不错,那是美利。她是班长。她非常规矩。"

"那儿有个老头扎玫瑰树。"我说。

"对的,是彼得。他是园丁。他的年纪有一百岁!"

"来了一个棕黑色脸孔穿红衣的女孩,靠着拐杖。"

"不错,"她说,"这是贝里鲁。"

我们这样子散步下去,那〔带〕着这小东西到处走,我觉得我现在心里沉思默想的程度是十倍于我所能料到的,而且因为不得不把周围的东西说给别人听,那些东西也变为更有趣味了。

当俾谟斯小姐来替我的职务,我舍不得走开,也就同她说我真舍不得走。

我回城的途中一路喃喃地唱底下这几行诗(和从前一样的,总是唱得有些错):

我能够看到别人的苦痛,

不会去同情于他的悲哀吗?

不,这是绝对不会的,

绝对,绝对不会的![1]

(原载于1929年第2卷第2期《奔流》)

---

[1] 该文发表于《奔流》时文末有一段说明:"这篇小品是由 E. V. Lucas 自己选的他的小品文集《什么东西都有一点》(*A Little of Everything*)里译出,原名系 'The School for Sympathy'。Lucas 是英国现在第一流的小品文作家,他和 Hilaire Belloc 几乎可以说〈是〉当代小品文界的南北高峰。"——编者注